P9-DFW-835

Francine Pascal's

SWEET VALLEY HIGH

Academic All-Star?

Katy Rex • Devaki Neogi • Pippa Mather • Cardinal Rae

DYNAMITE.

CREATED BY
Francine Pascal

WRITTEN BY
Katy Rex

ART BY
Devaki Neogi

COLORS BY
Pippa Mather

LETTERS BY
Cardinal Rae

EDITED BY
Joseph Rybandt

COLLECTION DESIGN BY
Cathleen Heard

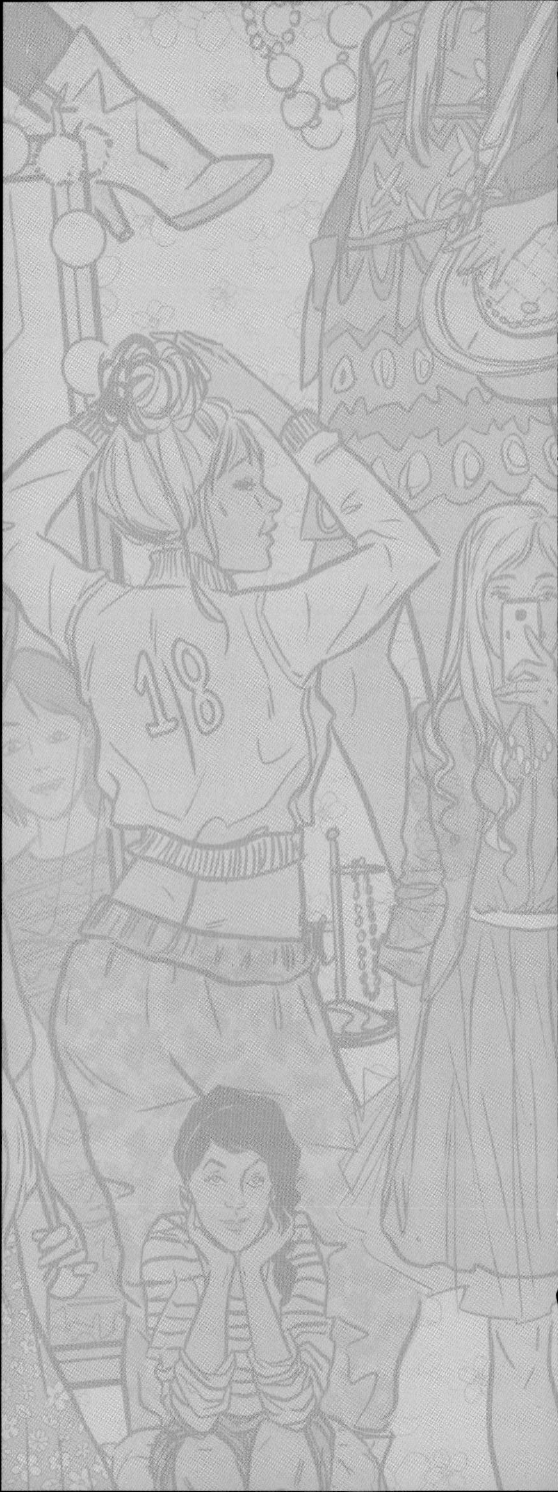

Online at www.DYNAMITE.com
On Facebook /Dynamitecomics
On Instagram /Dynamitecomics
On Twitter @dynamitecomics

Nick Barrucci, CEO / Publisher
Juan Collado, President / COO
Brandon Dante Primavera, V.P. of IT and Operations

Joe Rybandt, Executive Editor
Matt Idelson, Senior Editor
Kevin Ketner, Associate Editor

Cathleen Heard, Senior Graphic Designer
Rachel Kilbury, Digital Multimedia Associate
Alexis Persson, Graphic Designer
Katie Hidalgo, Graphic Designer

Alan Payne, V.P. of Sales and Marketing
Jay Spence, Director of Product Development
Rex Wang, Director of Consumer Sales
Pat O'Connell, Sales Manager
Mariano Nicieza, Marketing Manager
Vincent Faust, Marketing Coordinator

Amy Jackson, Administrative Coordinator

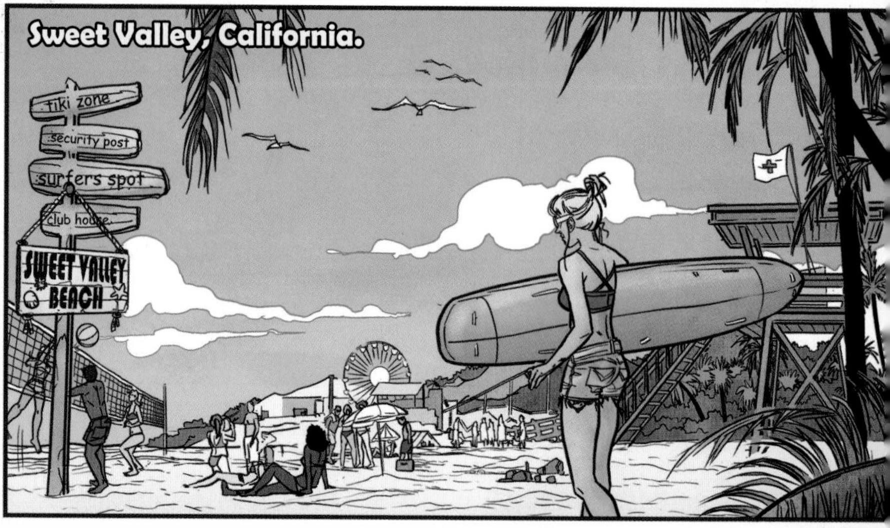
Sweet Valley, California.
tiki zone
security post
surfers spot
club house
SWEET VALLEY BEACH

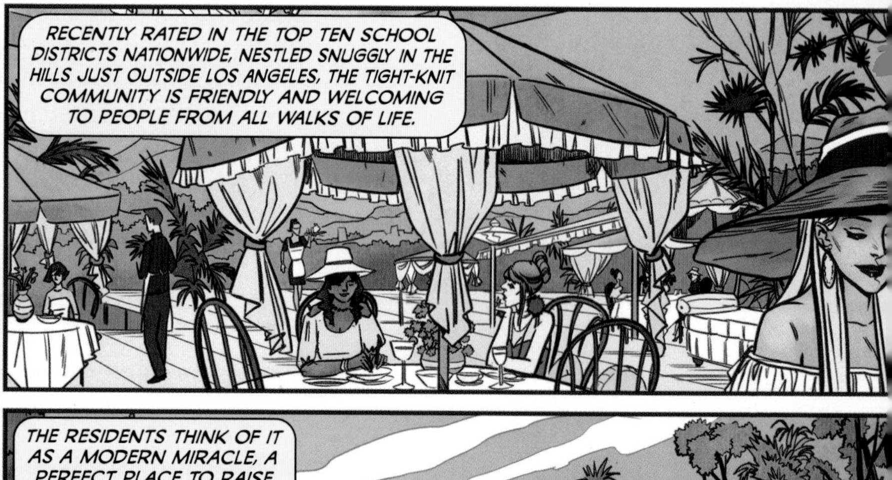
RECENTLY RATED IN THE TOP TEN SCHOOL DISTRICTS NATIONWIDE, NESTLED SNUGGLY IN THE HILLS JUST OUTSIDE LOS ANGELES, THE TIGHT-KNIT COMMUNITY IS FRIENDLY AND WELCOMING TO PEOPLE FROM ALL WALKS OF LIFE.

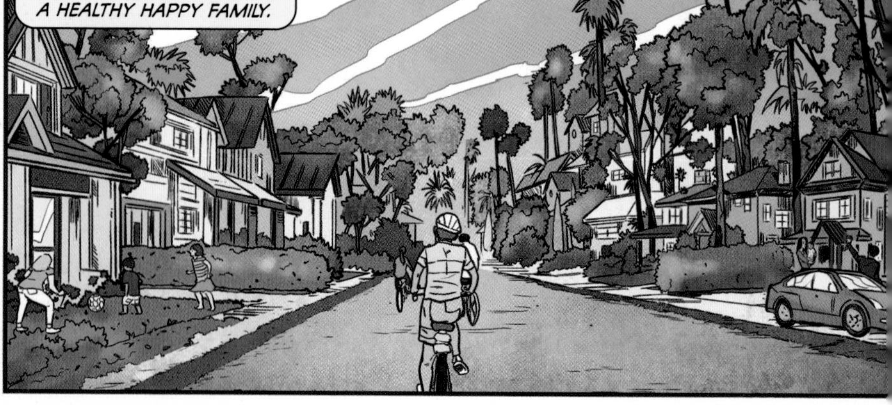
THE RESIDENTS THINK OF IT AS A MODERN MIRACLE, A PERFECT PLACE TO RAISE A HEALTHY HAPPY FAMILY.

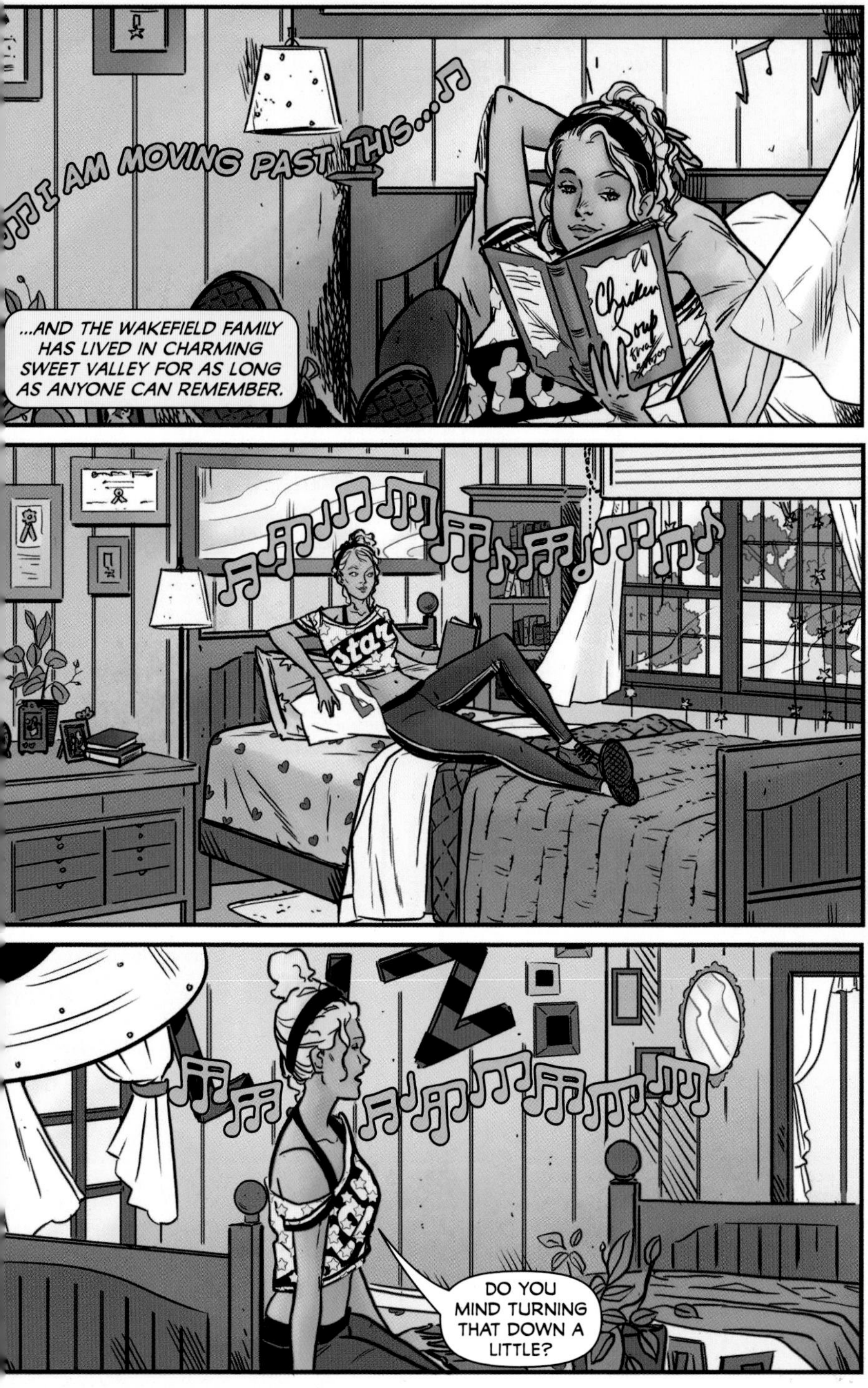

I AM MOVING PAST THIS...
...AND THE WAKEFIELD FAMILY HAS LIVED IN CHARMING SWEET VALLEY FOR AS LONG AS ANYONE CAN REMEMBER.
Chicken Soup
DO YOU MIND TURNING THAT DOWN A LITTLE?

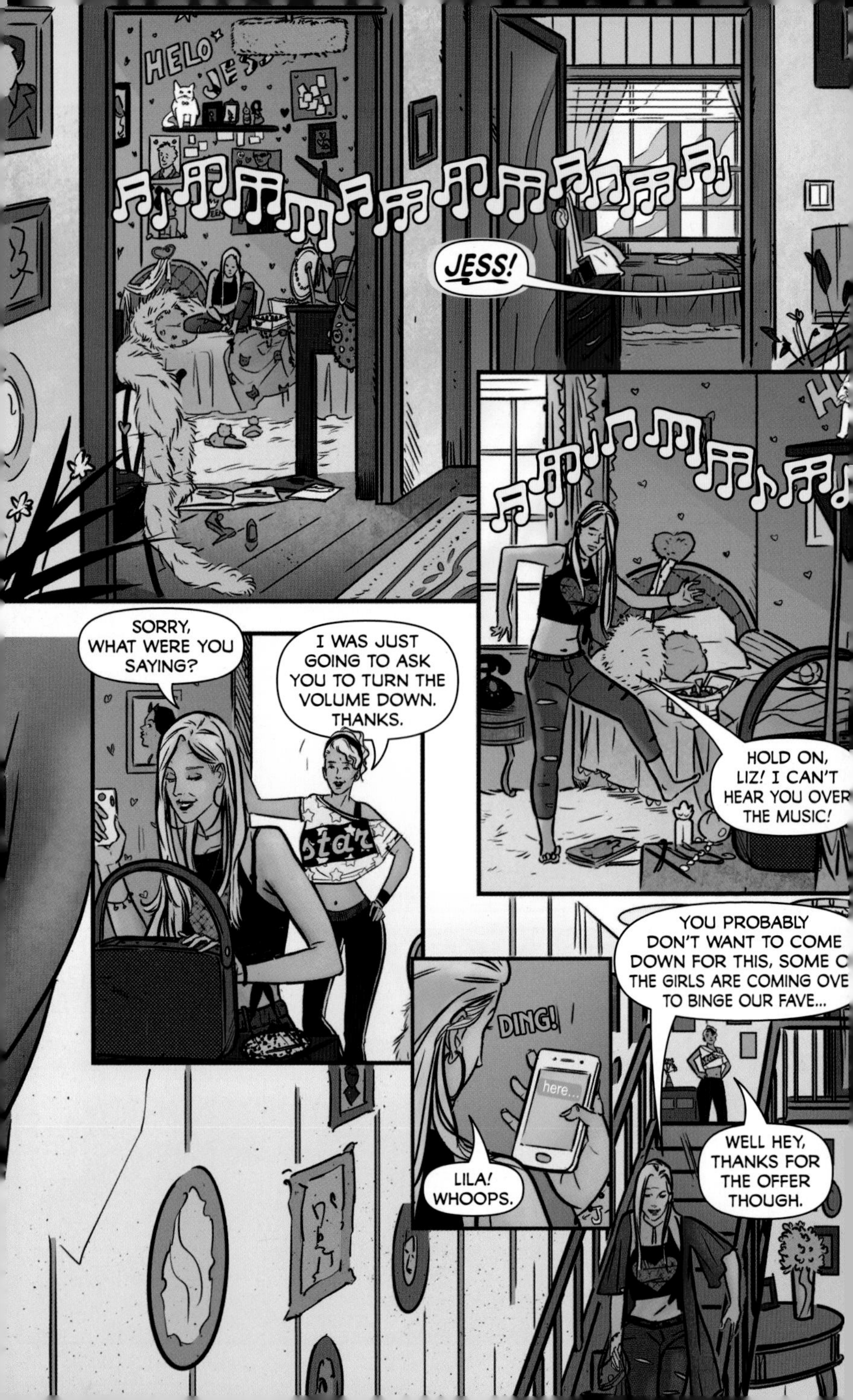
HELO
JESS!
HOLD ON, LIZ! I CAN'T HEAR YOU OVER THE MUSIC!
SORRY, WHAT WERE YOU SAYING?
I WAS JUST GOING TO ASK YOU TO TURN THE VOLUME DOWN. THANKS.
star
YOU PROBABLY DON'T WANT TO COME DOWN FOR THIS, SOME OF THE GIRLS ARE COMING OVER TO BINGE OUR FAVE...
DING!
here...
LILA! WHOOPS.
WELL HEY, THANKS FOR THE OFFER THOUGH.

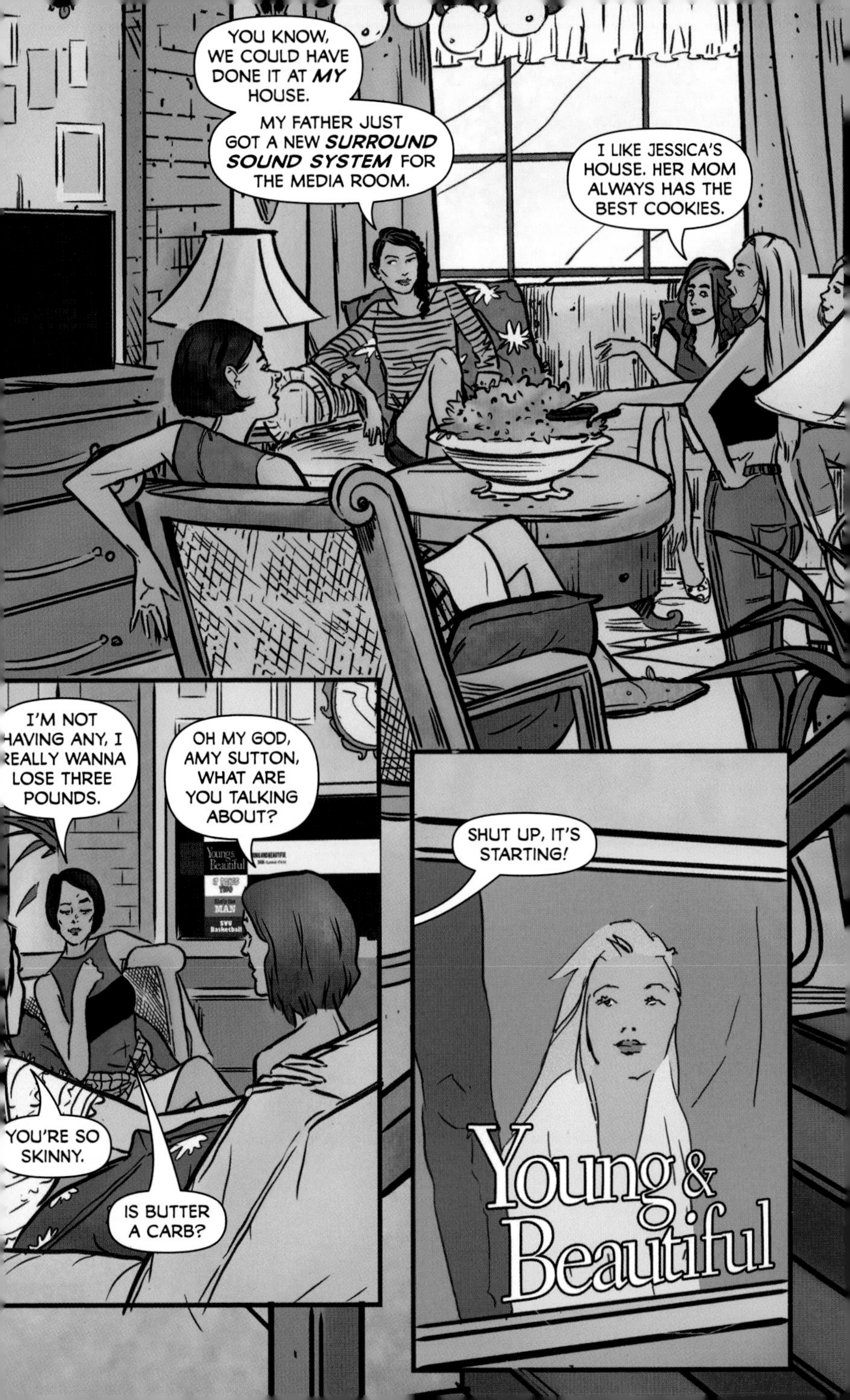
YOU KNOW, WE COULD HAVE DONE IT AT *MY* HOUSE.
MY FATHER JUST GOT A NEW ***SURROUND SOUND SYSTEM*** FOR THE MEDIA ROOM.
I LIKE JESSICA'S HOUSE. HER MOM ALWAYS HAS THE BEST COOKIES.
I'M NOT HAVING ANY, I REALLY WANNA LOSE THREE POUNDS.
OH MY GOD, AMY SUTTON, WHAT ARE YOU TALKING ABOUT?
YOU'RE SO SKINNY.
IS BUTTER A CARB?
SHUT UP, IT'S STARTING!
Young & Beautiful

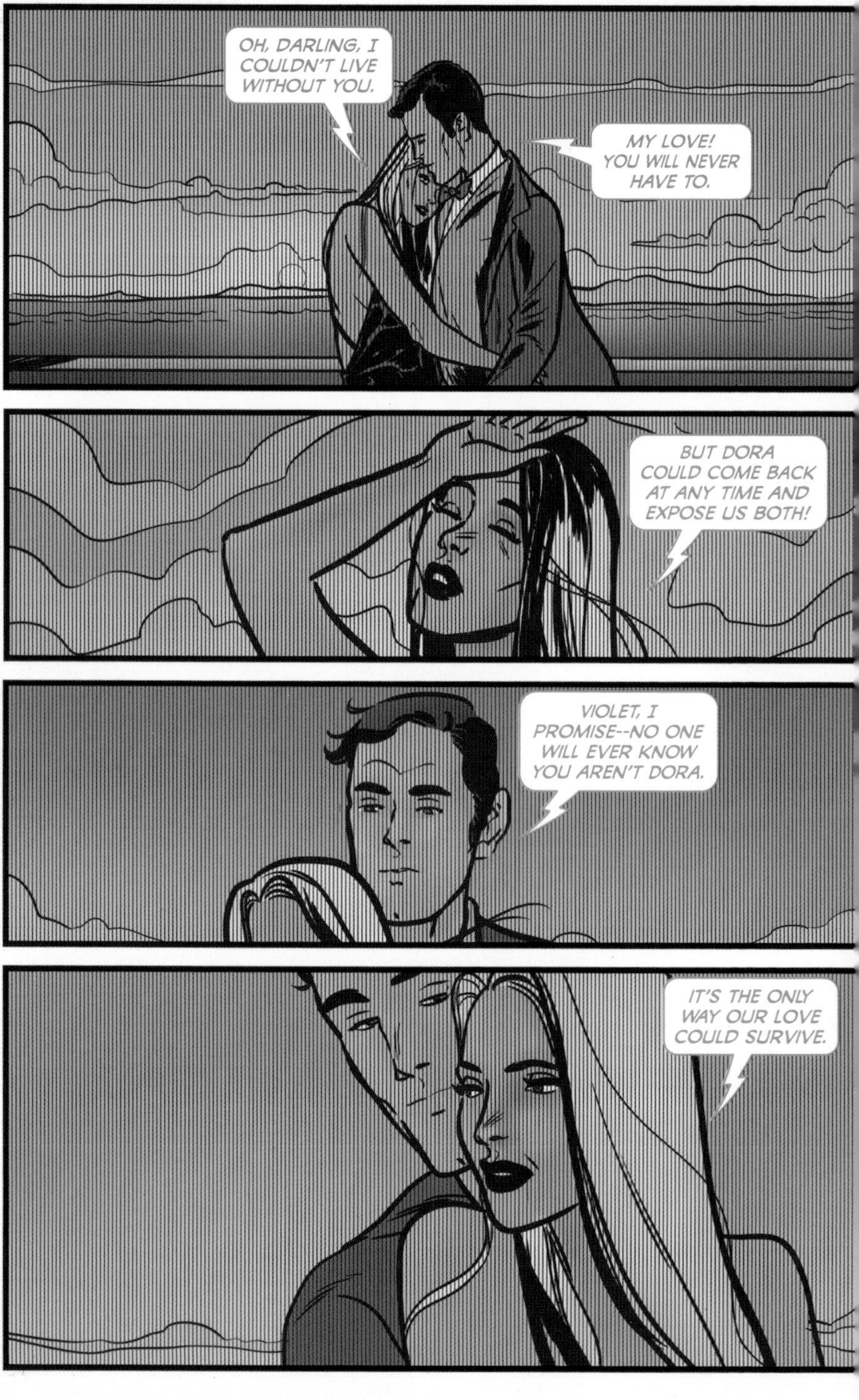
OH, DARLING, I COULDN'T LIVE WITHOUT YOU.
MY LOVE! YOU WILL NEVER HAVE TO.
BUT DORA COULD COME BACK AT ANY TIME AND EXPOSE US BOTH!
VIOLET, I PROMISE--NO ONE WILL EVER KNOW YOU AREN'T DORA.
IT'S THE ONLY WAY OUR LOVE COULD SURVIVE.

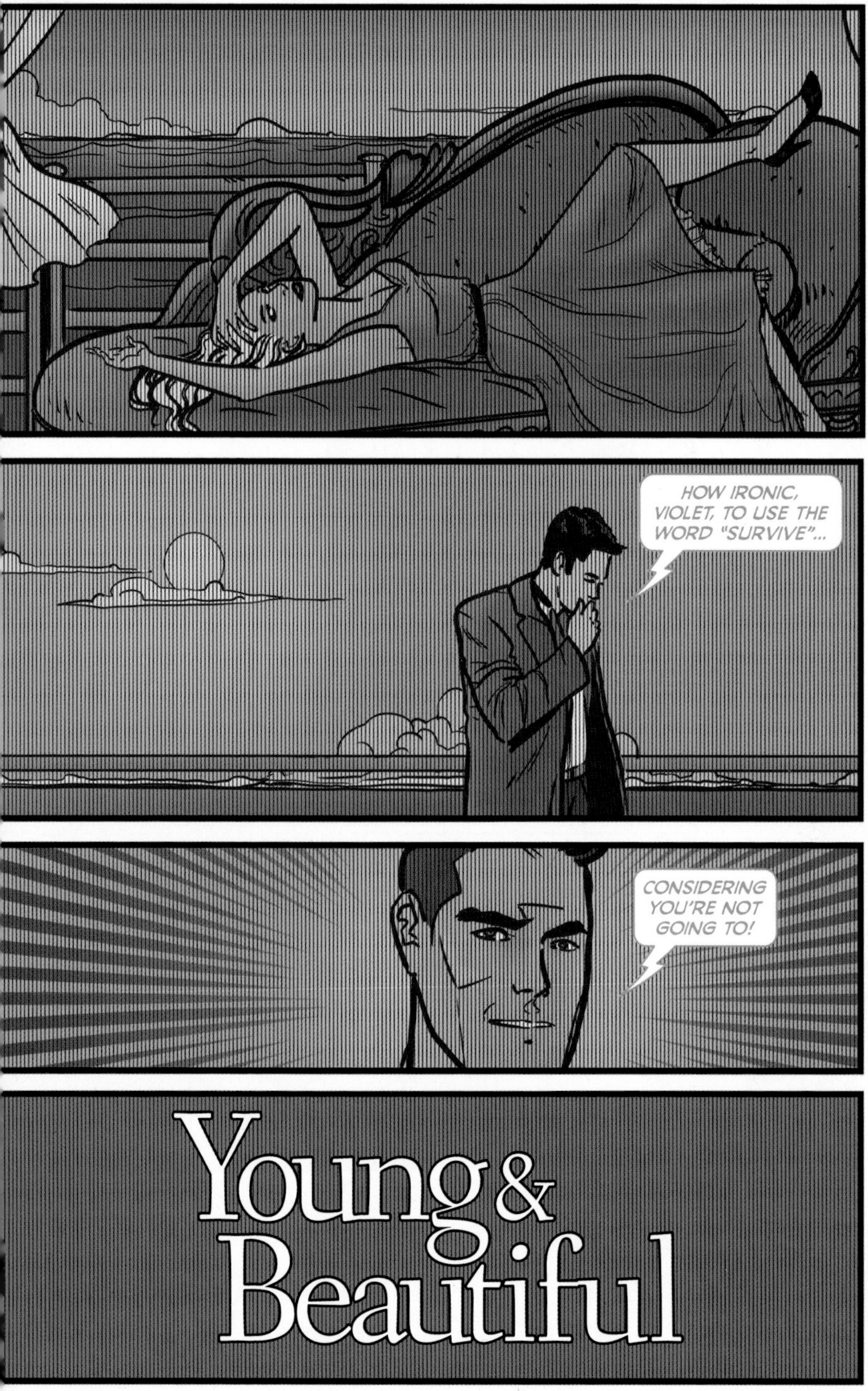
HOW IRONIC, VIOLET, TO USE THE WORD "SURVIVE"...
CONSIDERING YOU'RE NOT GOING TO!
Young & Beautiful

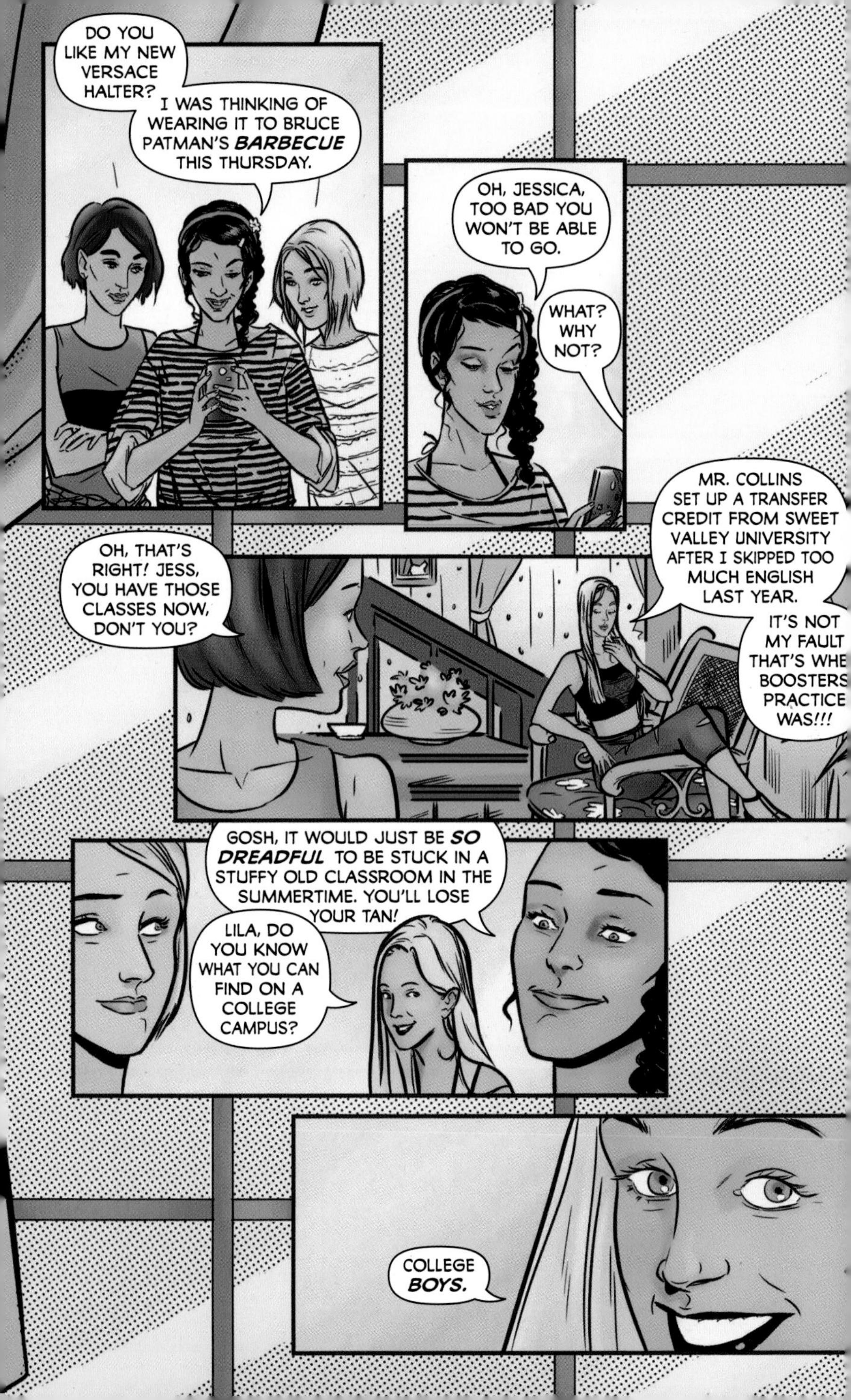
DO YOU LIKE MY NEW VERSACE HALTER?
I WAS THINKING OF WEARING IT TO BRUCE PATMAN'S **BARBECUE** THIS THURSDAY.
OH, JESSICA, TOO BAD YOU WON'T BE ABLE TO GO.
WHAT? WHY NOT?
OH, THAT'S RIGHT! JESS, YOU HAVE THOSE CLASSES NOW, DON'T YOU?
MR. COLLINS SET UP A TRANSFER CREDIT FROM SWEET VALLEY UNIVERSITY AFTER I SKIPPED TOO MUCH ENGLISH LAST YEAR.
IT'S NOT MY FAULT THAT'S WHE BOOSTERS PRACTICE WAS!!!
GOSH, IT WOULD JUST BE **SO DREADFUL** TO BE STUCK IN A STUFFY OLD CLASSROOM IN THE SUMMERTIME. YOU'LL LOSE YOUR TAN!
LILA, DO YOU KNOW WHAT YOU CAN FIND ON A COLLEGE CAMPUS?
COLLEGE **BOYS.**

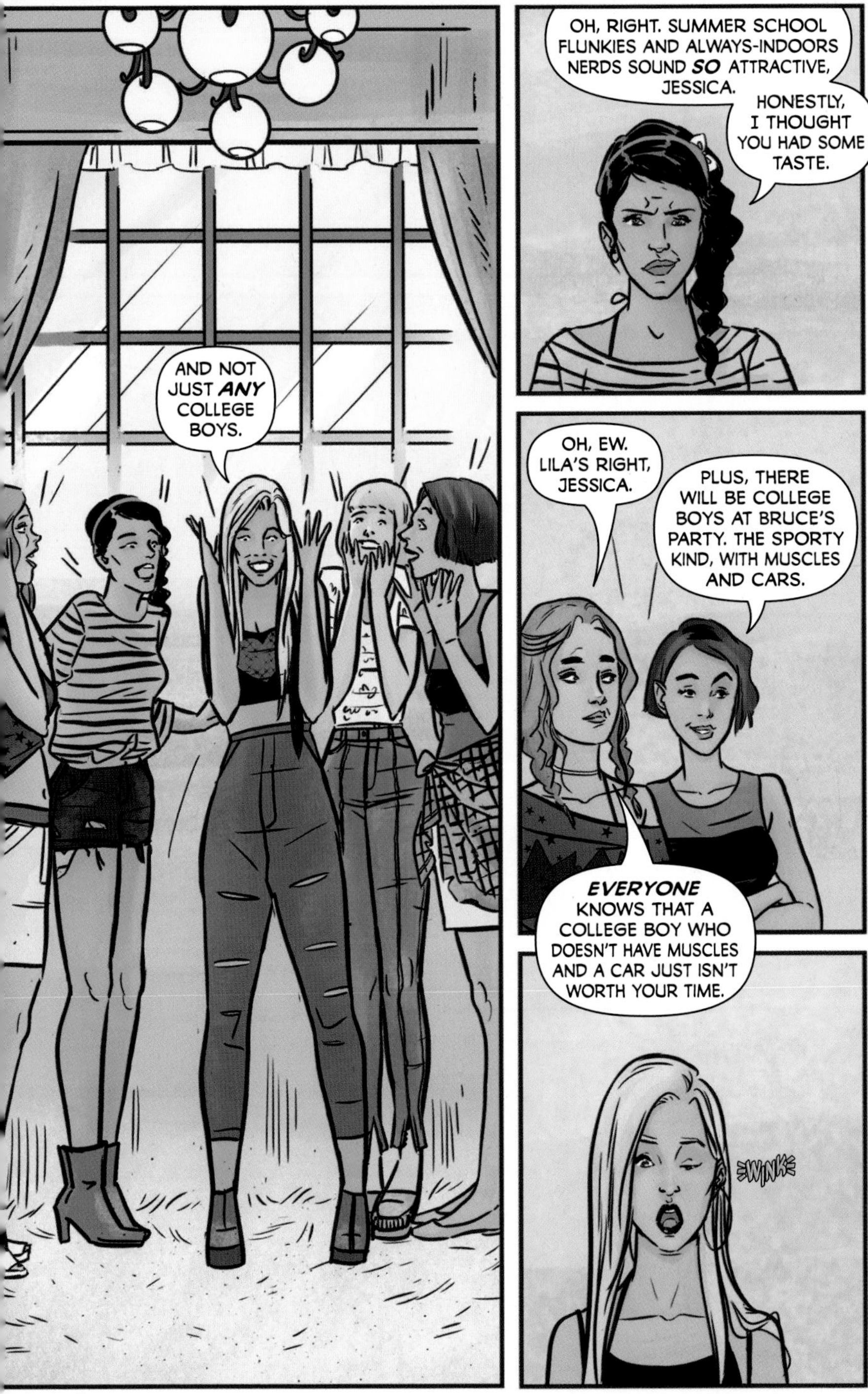
AND NOT JUST *ANY* COLLEGE BOYS.
OH, RIGHT. SUMMER SCHOOL FLUNKIES AND ALWAYS-INDOORS NERDS SOUND *SO* ATTRACTIVE, JESSICA.
HONESTLY, I THOUGHT YOU HAD SOME TASTE.
OH, EW. LILA'S RIGHT, JESSICA.
PLUS, THERE WILL BE COLLEGE BOYS AT BRUCE'S PARTY. THE SPORTY KIND, WITH MUSCLES AND CARS.
EVERYONE KNOWS THAT A COLLEGE BOY WHO DOESN'T HAVE MUSCLES AND A CAR JUST ISN'T WORTH YOUR TIME.
WINK

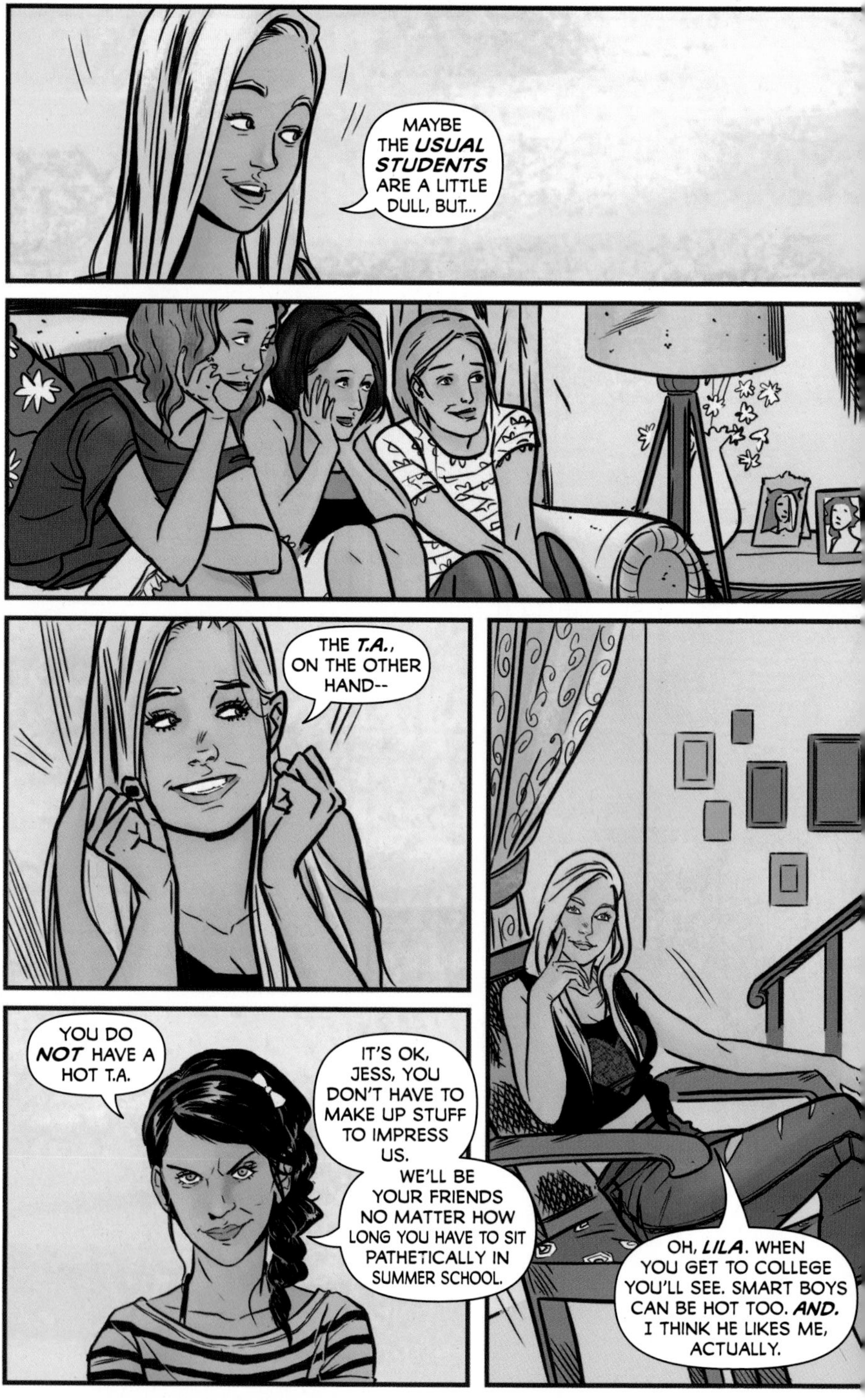
MAYBE THE *USUAL STUDENTS* ARE A LITTLE DULL, BUT...
THE *T.A.*, ON THE OTHER HAND--
OH, *LILA*. WHEN YOU GET TO COLLEGE YOU'LL SEE. SMART BOYS CAN BE HOT TOO. *AND.* I THINK HE LIKES ME, ACTUALLY.
YOU DO *NOT* HAVE A HOT T.A.
IT'S OK, JESS, YOU DON'T HAVE TO MAKE UP STUFF TO IMPRESS US.
WE'LL BE YOUR FRIENDS NO MATTER HOW LONG YOU HAVE TO SIT PATHETICALLY IN SUMMER SCHOOL.

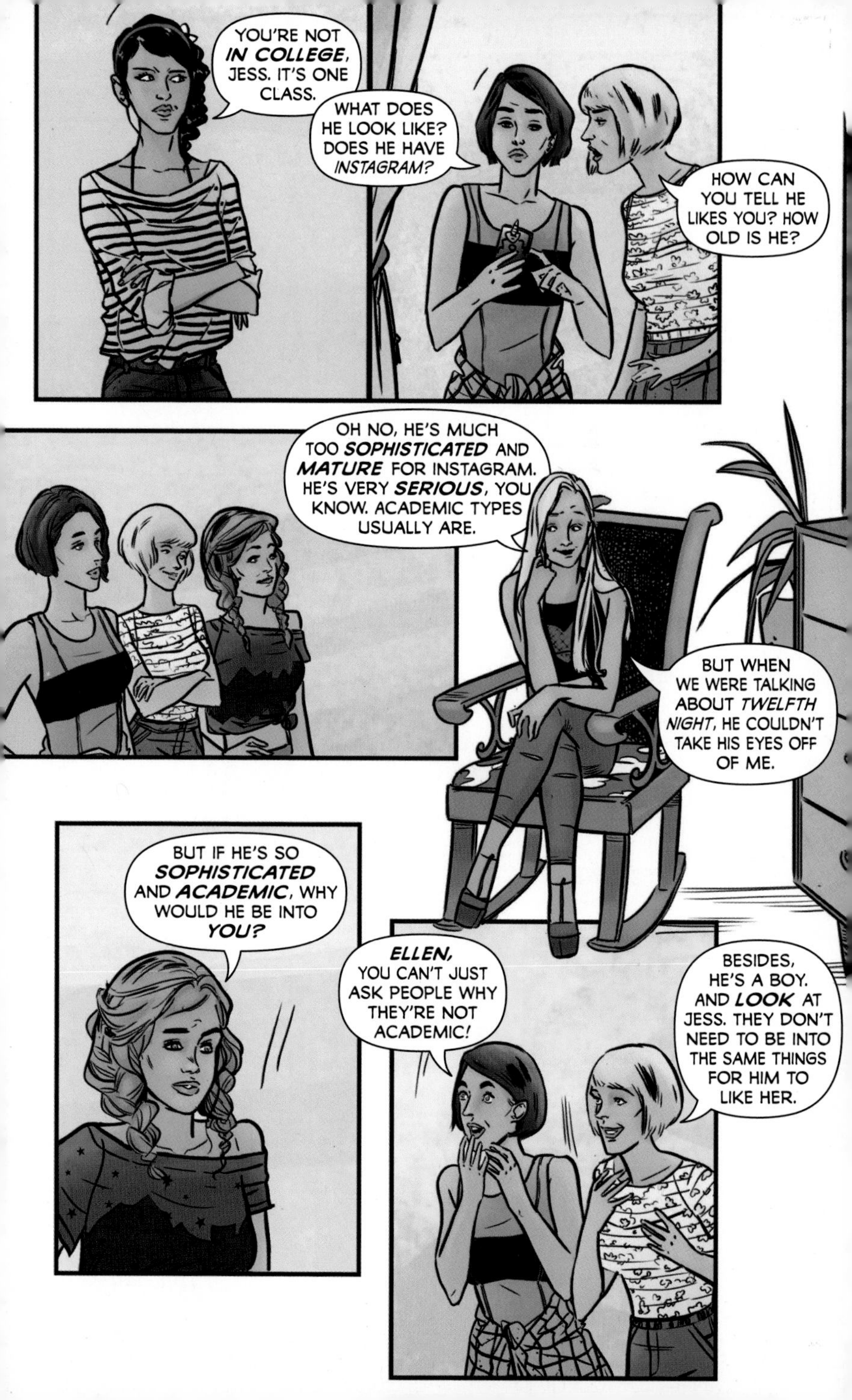
YOU'RE NOT *IN COLLEGE*, JESS. IT'S ONE CLASS.
WHAT DOES HE LOOK LIKE? DOES HE HAVE *INSTAGRAM?*
HOW CAN YOU TELL HE LIKES YOU? HOW OLD IS HE?
OH NO, HE'S MUCH TOO ***SOPHISTICATED*** AND ***MATURE*** FOR INSTAGRAM. HE'S VERY ***SERIOUS***, YOU KNOW. ACADEMIC TYPES USUALLY ARE.
BUT WHEN WE WERE TALKING ABOUT *TWELFTH NIGHT*, HE COULDN'T TAKE HIS EYES OFF OF ME.
BUT IF HE'S SO ***SOPHISTICATED*** AND ***ACADEMIC***, WHY WOULD HE BE INTO ***YOU?***
ELLEN, YOU CAN'T JUST ASK PEOPLE WHY THEY'RE NOT ACADEMIC!
BESIDES, HE'S A BOY. AND ***LOOK*** AT JESS. THEY DON'T NEED TO BE INTO THE SAME THINGS FOR HIM TO LIKE HER.

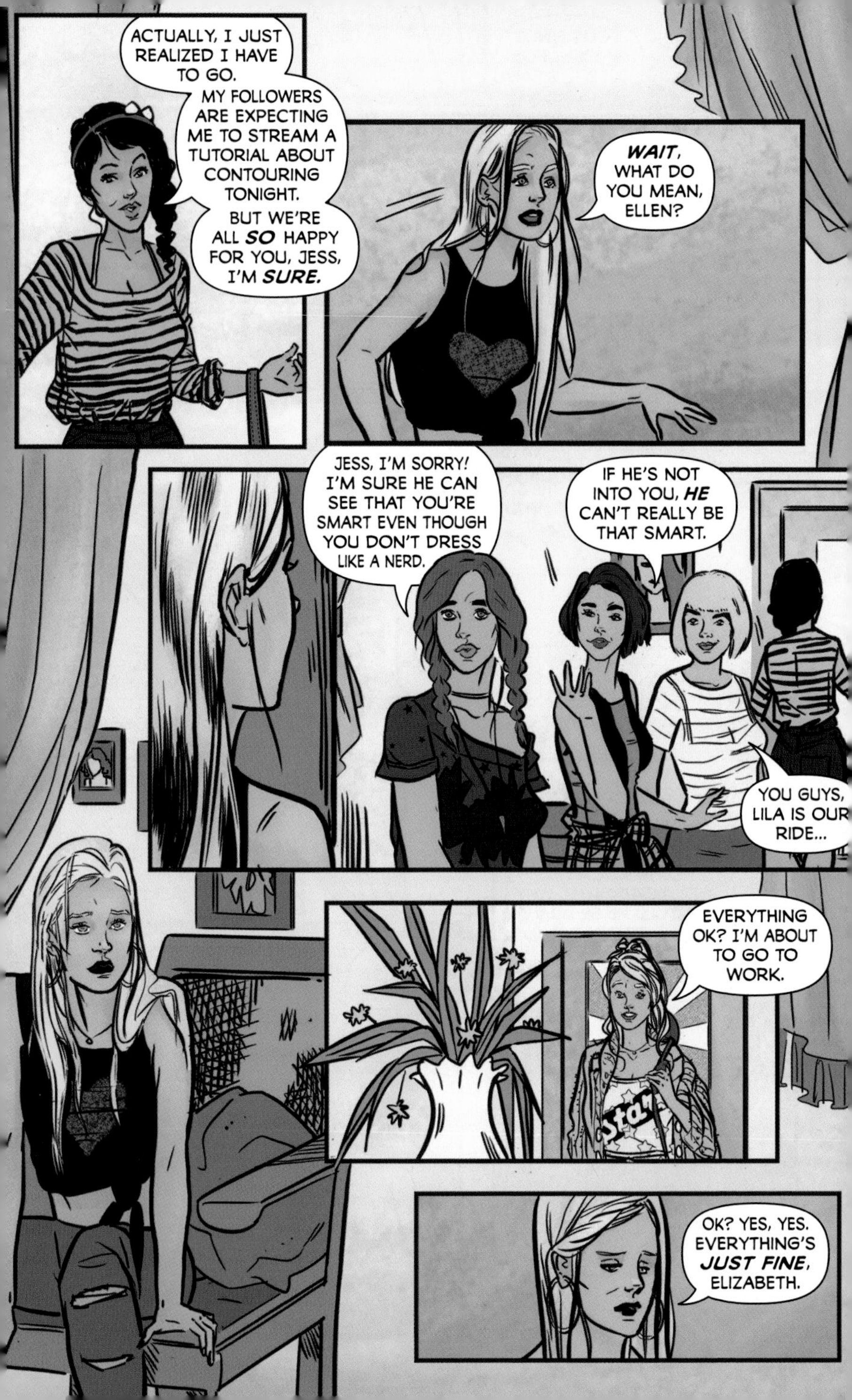
ACTUALLY, I JUST REALIZED I HAVE TO GO.
MY FOLLOWERS ARE EXPECTING ME TO STREAM A TUTORIAL ABOUT CONTOURING TONIGHT.
BUT WE'RE ALL ***SO*** HAPPY FOR YOU, JESS, I'M ***SURE.***
WAIT, WHAT DO YOU MEAN, ELLEN?
JESS, I'M SORRY! I'M SURE HE CAN SEE THAT YOU'RE SMART EVEN THOUGH YOU DON'T DRESS LIKE A NERD.
IF HE'S NOT INTO YOU, ***HE*** CAN'T REALLY BE THAT SMART.
YOU GUYS, LILA IS OUR RIDE...
EVERYTHING OK? I'M ABOUT TO GO TO WORK.
OK? YES, YES. EVERYTHING'S ***JUST FINE***, ELIZABETH.

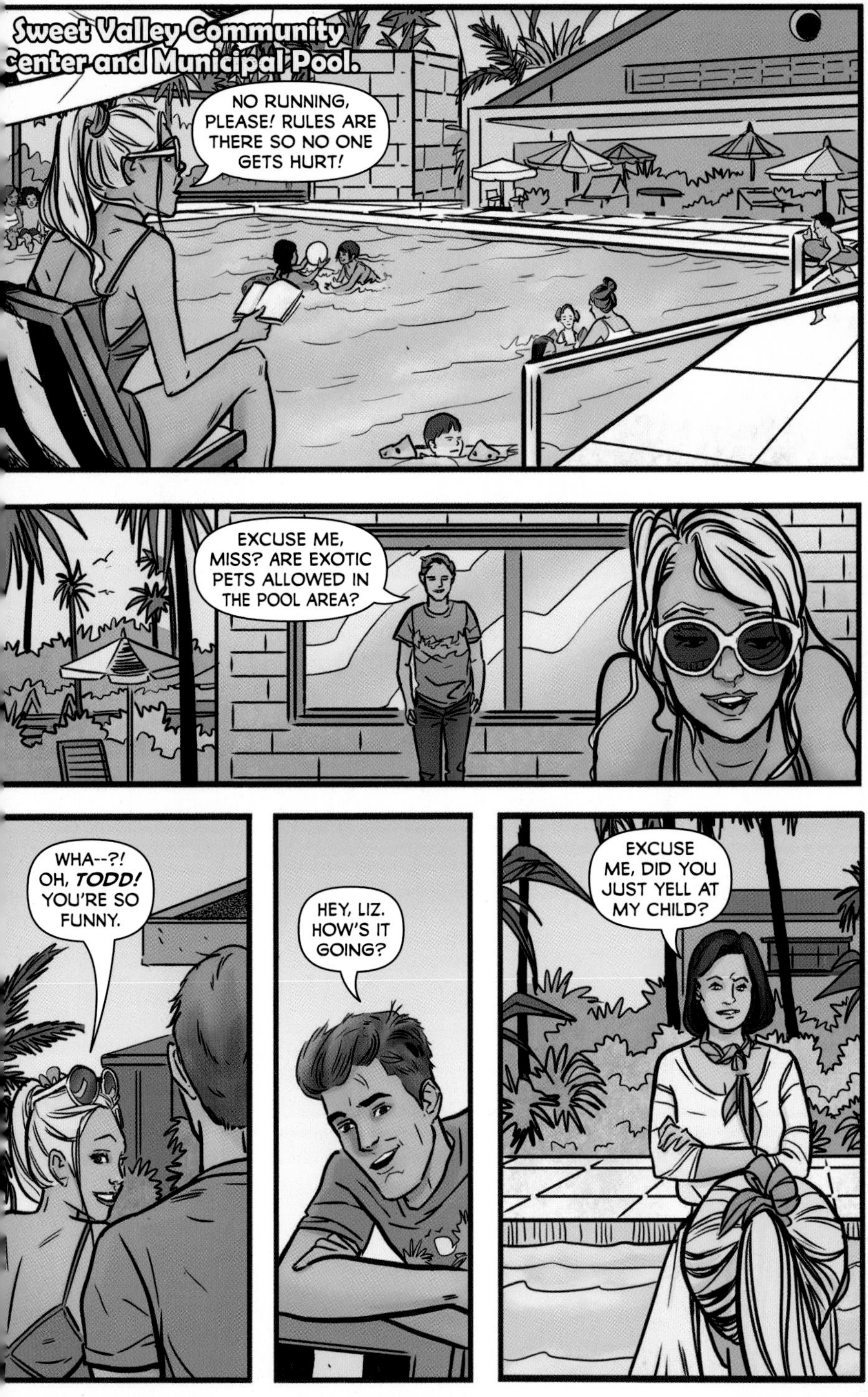
Sweet Valley Community Center and Municipal Pool.
NO RUNNING, PLEASE! RULES ARE THERE SO NO ONE GETS HURT!
EXCUSE ME, MISS? ARE EXOTIC PETS ALLOWED IN THE POOL AREA?
WHA--?! OH, *TODD!* YOU'RE SO FUNNY.
HEY, LIZ. HOW'S IT GOING?
EXCUSE ME, DID YOU JUST YELL AT MY CHILD?

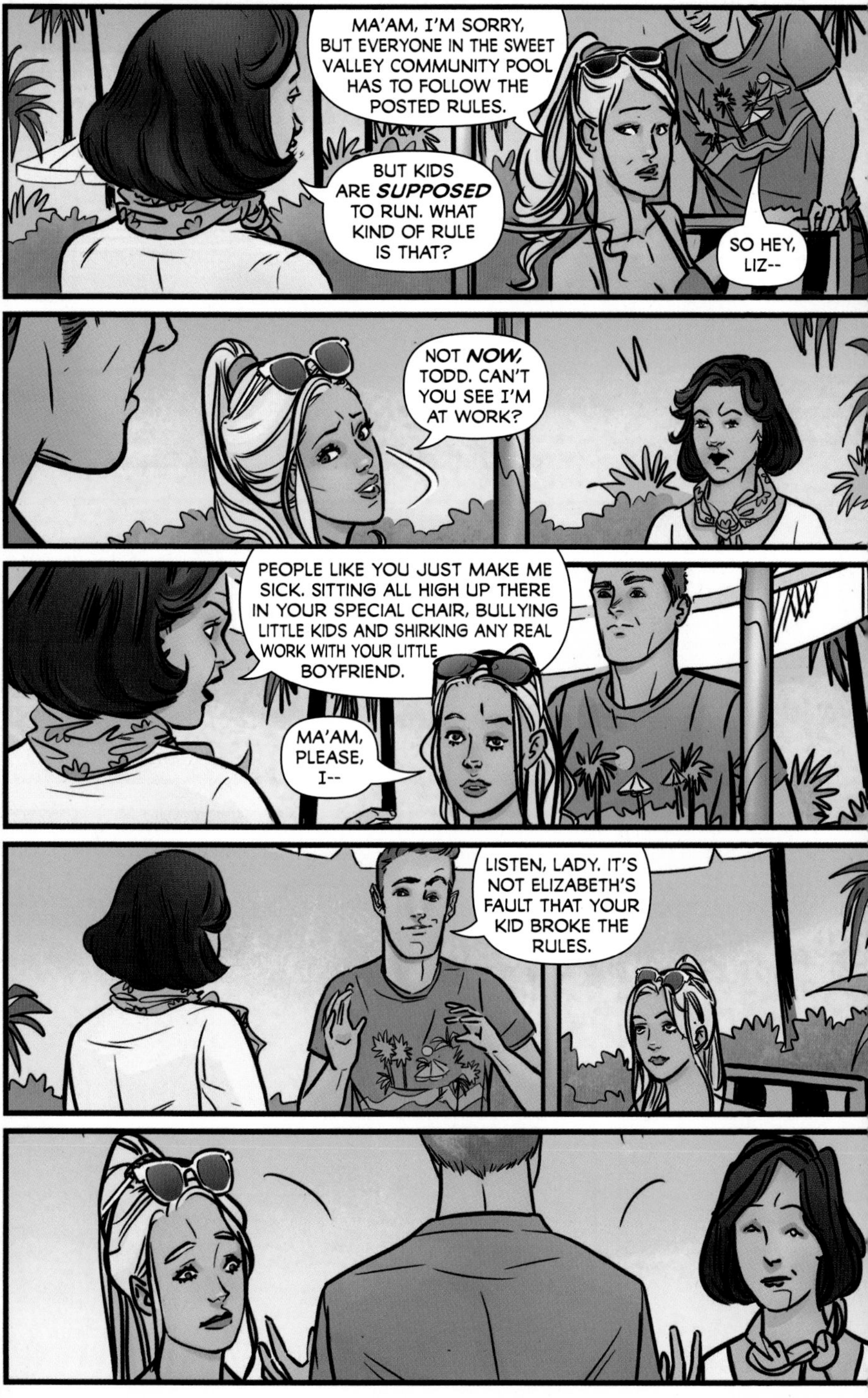
MA'AM, I'M SORRY, BUT EVERYONE IN THE SWEET VALLEY COMMUNITY POOL HAS TO FOLLOW THE POSTED RULES.
BUT KIDS ARE ***SUPPOSED*** TO RUN. WHAT KIND OF RULE IS THAT?
SO HEY, LIZ--
NOT ***NOW,*** TODD. CAN'T YOU SEE I'M AT WORK?
PEOPLE LIKE YOU JUST MAKE ME SICK. SITTING ALL HIGH UP THERE IN YOUR SPECIAL CHAIR, BULLYING LITTLE KIDS AND SHIRKING ANY REAL WORK WITH YOUR LITTLE BOYFRIEND.
MA'AM, PLEASE, I--
LISTEN, LADY. IT'S NOT ELIZABETH'S FAULT THAT YOUR KID BROKE THE RULES.

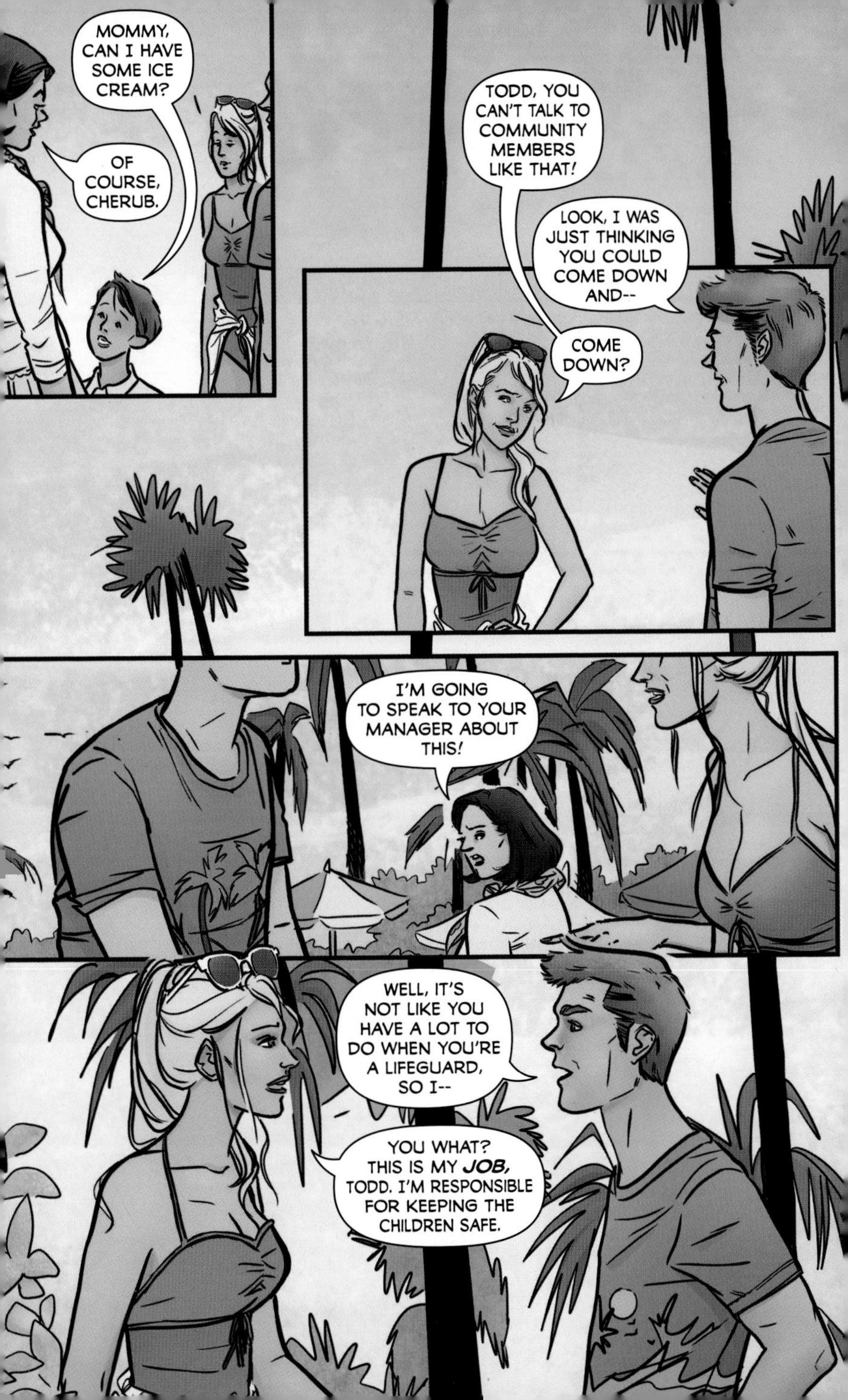
MOMMY, CAN I HAVE SOME ICE CREAM?
OF COURSE, CHERUB.
TODD, YOU CAN'T TALK TO COMMUNITY MEMBERS LIKE THAT!
LOOK, I WAS JUST THINKING YOU COULD COME DOWN AND--
COME DOWN?
I'M GOING TO SPEAK TO YOUR MANAGER ABOUT THIS!
WELL, IT'S NOT LIKE YOU HAVE A LOT TO DO WHEN YOU'RE A LIFEGUARD, SO I--
YOU WHAT? THIS IS MY *JOB,* TODD. I'M RESPONSIBLE FOR KEEPING THE CHILDREN SAFE.

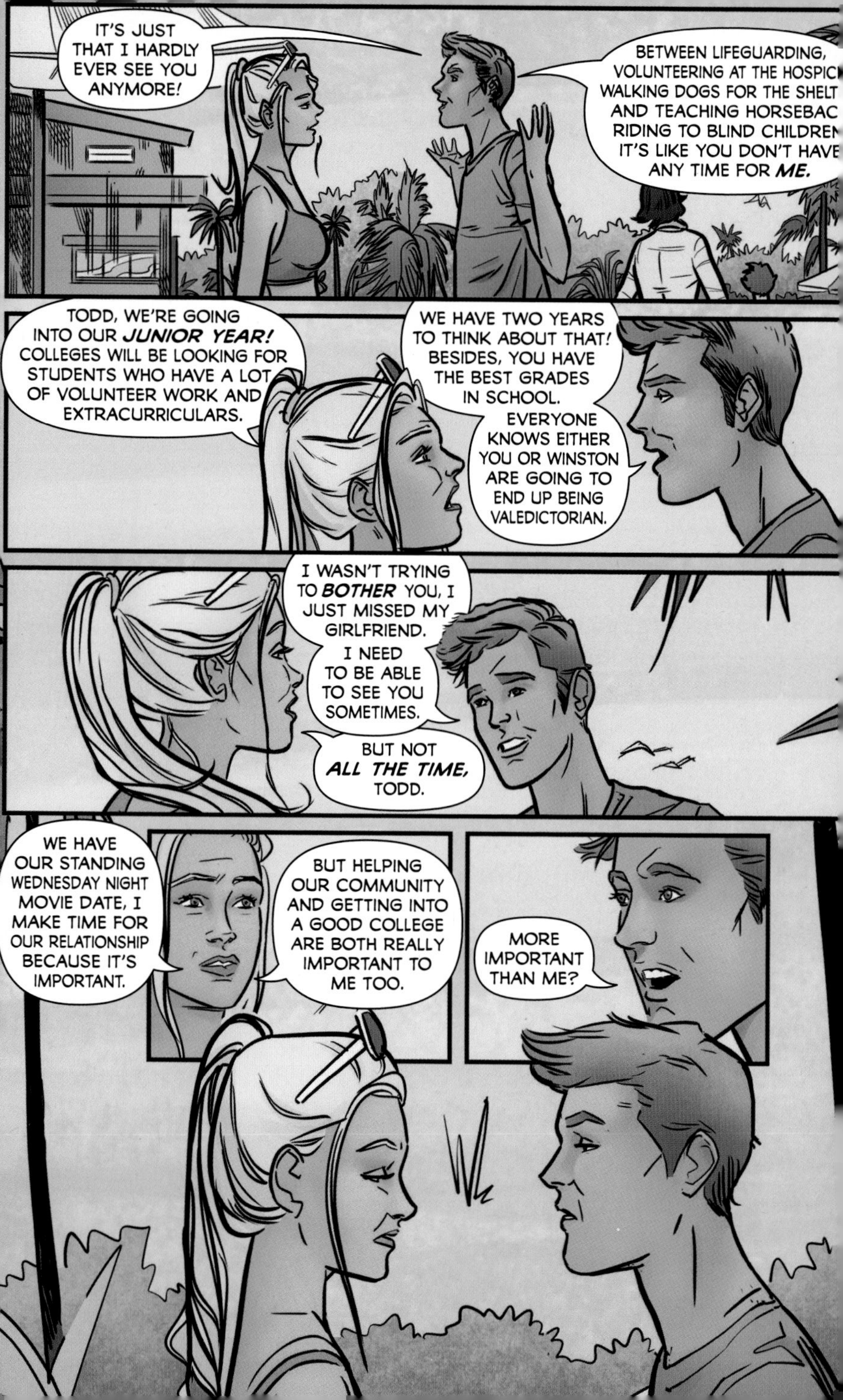
IT'S JUST THAT I HARDLY EVER SEE YOU ANYMORE!
BETWEEN LIFEGUARDING, VOLUNTEERING AT THE HOSPIC WALKING DOGS FOR THE SHELT AND TEACHING HORSEBAC RIDING TO BLIND CHILDREN IT'S LIKE YOU DON'T HAVE ANY TIME FOR *ME.*
TODD, WE'RE GOING INTO OUR *JUNIOR YEAR!* COLLEGES WILL BE LOOKING FOR STUDENTS WHO HAVE A LOT OF VOLUNTEER WORK AND EXTRACURRICULARS.
WE HAVE TWO YEARS TO THINK ABOUT THAT! BESIDES, YOU HAVE THE BEST GRADES IN SCHOOL.
EVERYONE KNOWS EITHER YOU OR WINSTON ARE GOING TO END UP BEING VALEDICTORIAN.
I WASN'T TRYING TO *BOTHER* YOU, I JUST MISSED MY GIRLFRIEND.
I NEED TO BE ABLE TO SEE YOU SOMETIMES.
BUT NOT *ALL THE TIME,* TODD.
WE HAVE OUR STANDING WEDNESDAY NIGHT MOVIE DATE, I MAKE TIME FOR OUR RELATIONSHIP BECAUSE IT'S IMPORTANT.
BUT HELPING OUR COMMUNITY AND GETTING INTO A GOOD COLLEGE ARE BOTH REALLY IMPORTANT TO ME TOO.
MORE IMPORTANT THAN ME?

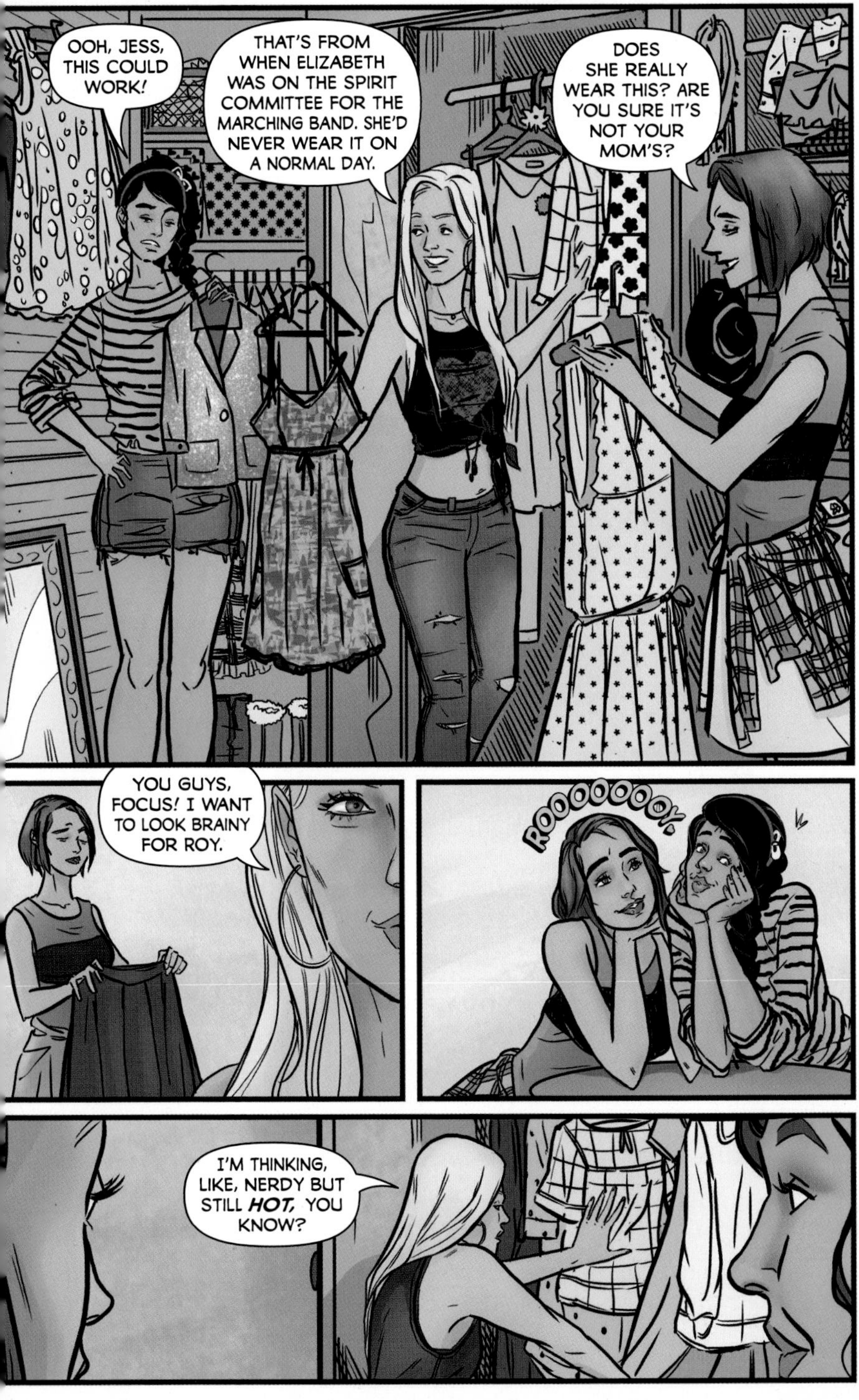
OOH, JESS, THIS COULD WORK!
THAT'S FROM WHEN ELIZABETH WAS ON THE SPIRIT COMMITTEE FOR THE MARCHING BAND. SHE'D NEVER WEAR IT ON A NORMAL DAY.
DOES SHE REALLY WEAR THIS? ARE YOU SURE IT'S NOT YOUR MOM'S?
YOU GUYS, FOCUS! I WANT TO LOOK BRAINY FOR ROY.
ROOOOOOOOY.
I'M THINKING, LIKE, NERDY BUT STILL *HOT,* YOU KNOW?

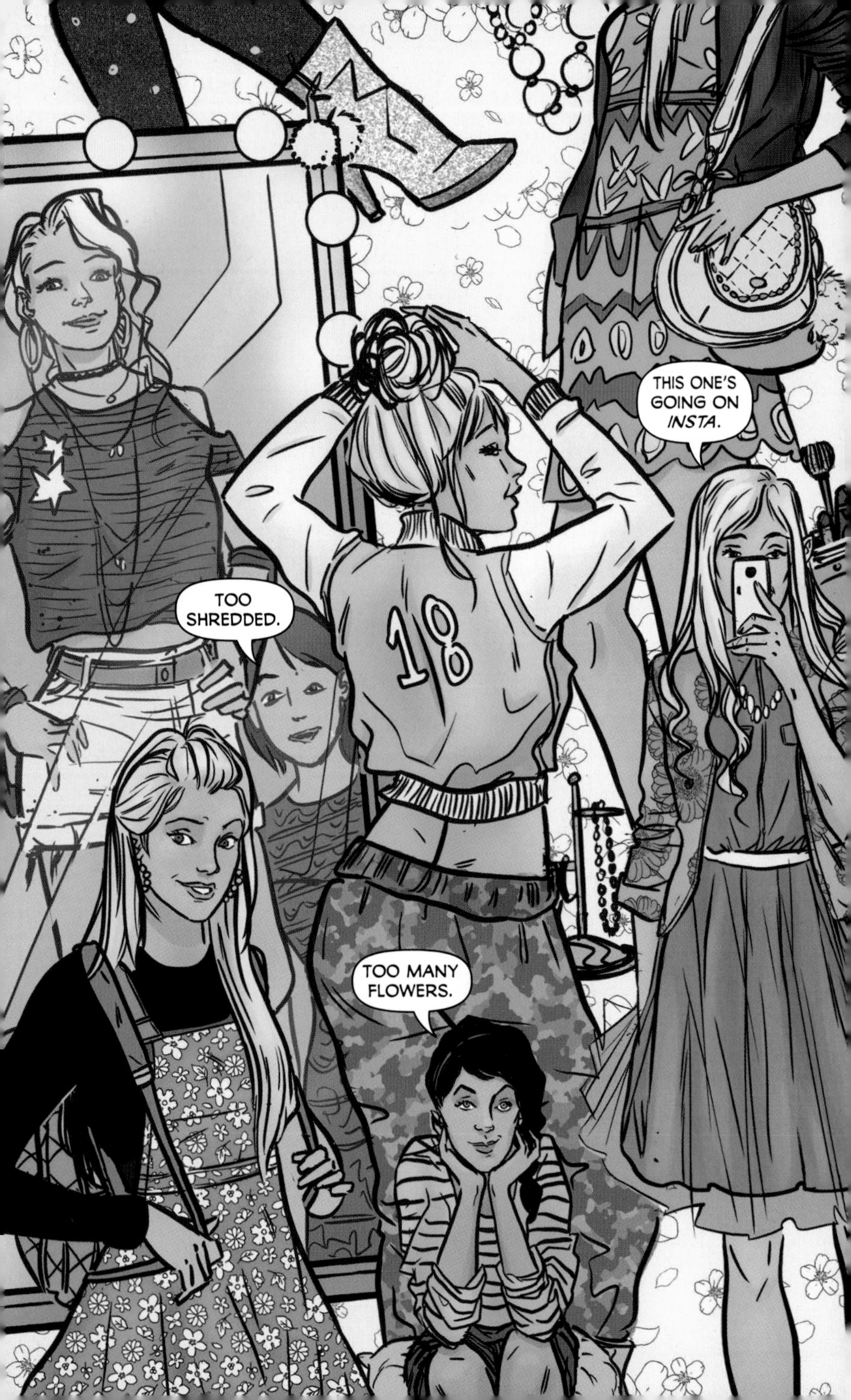
THIS ONE'S GOING ON *INSTA*.
TOO SHREDDED.
TOO MANY FLOWERS.

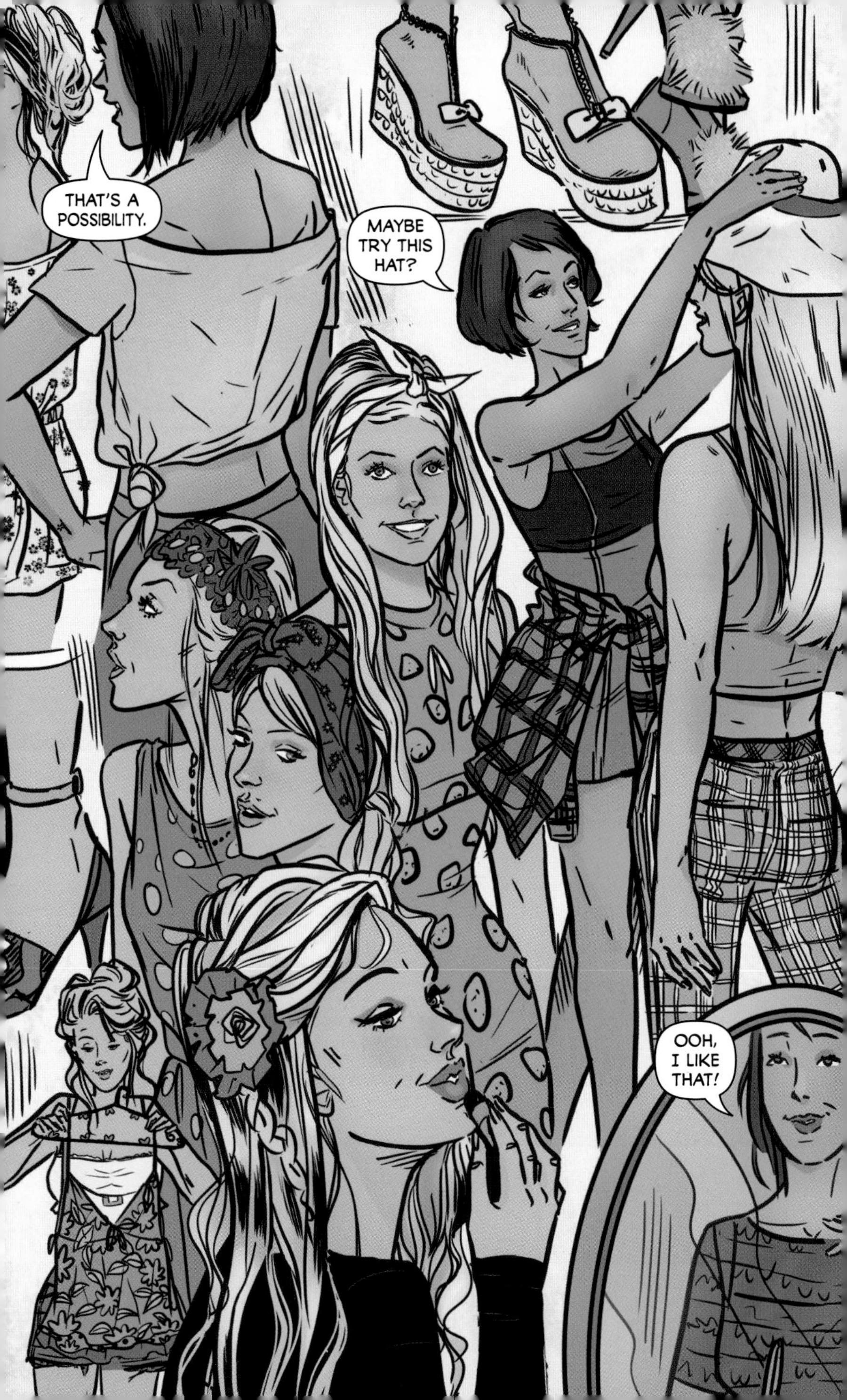
THAT'S A POSSIBILITY.
MAYBE TRY THIS HAT?
OOH, I LIKE THAT!

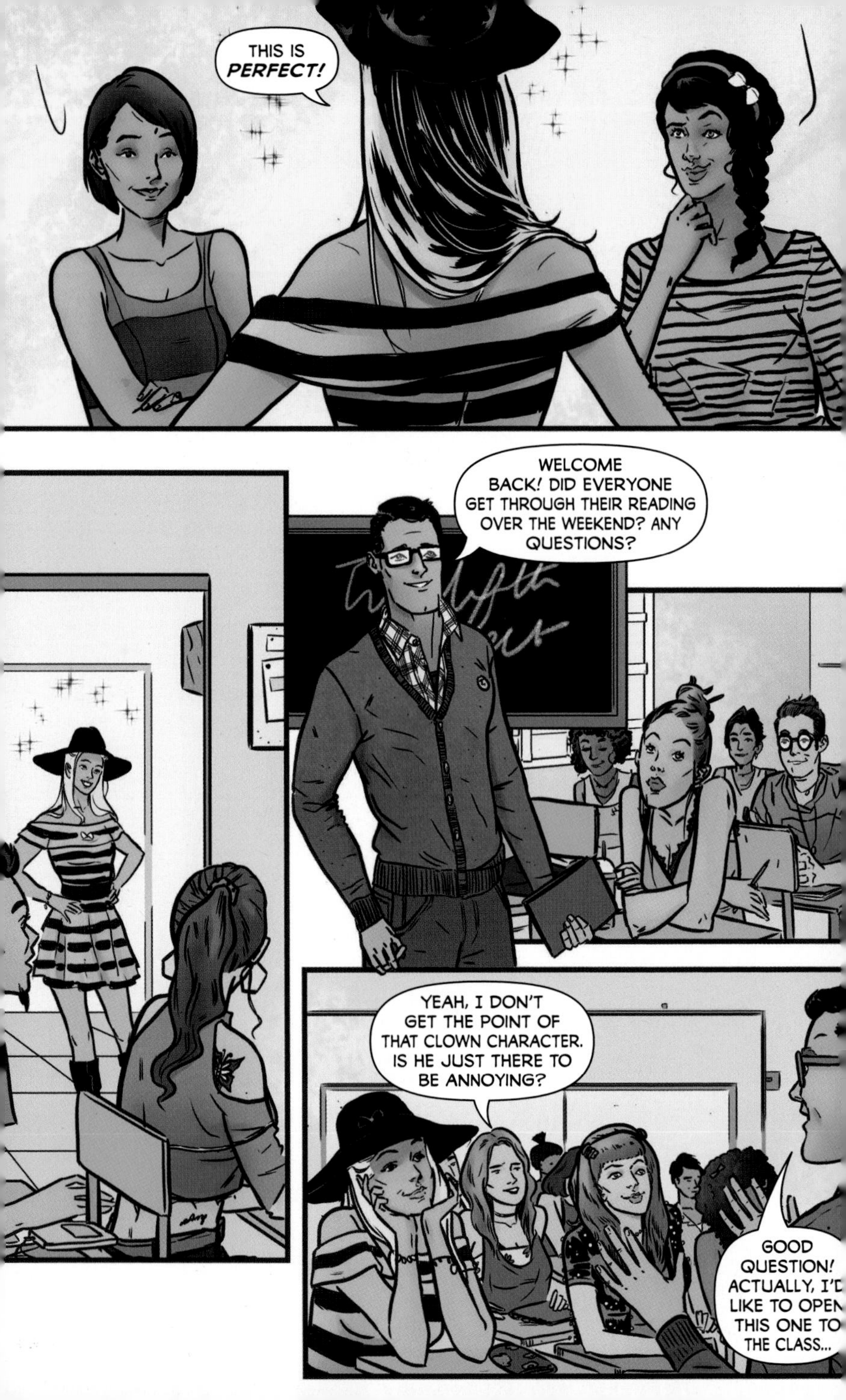
THIS IS *PERFECT!*
WELCOME BACK! DID EVERYONE GET THROUGH THEIR READING OVER THE WEEKEND? ANY QUESTIONS?
YEAH, I DON'T GET THE POINT OF THAT CLOWN CHARACTER. IS HE JUST THERE TO BE ANNOYING?
GOOD QUESTION! ACTUALLY, I'D LIKE TO OPEN THIS ONE TO THE CLASS...

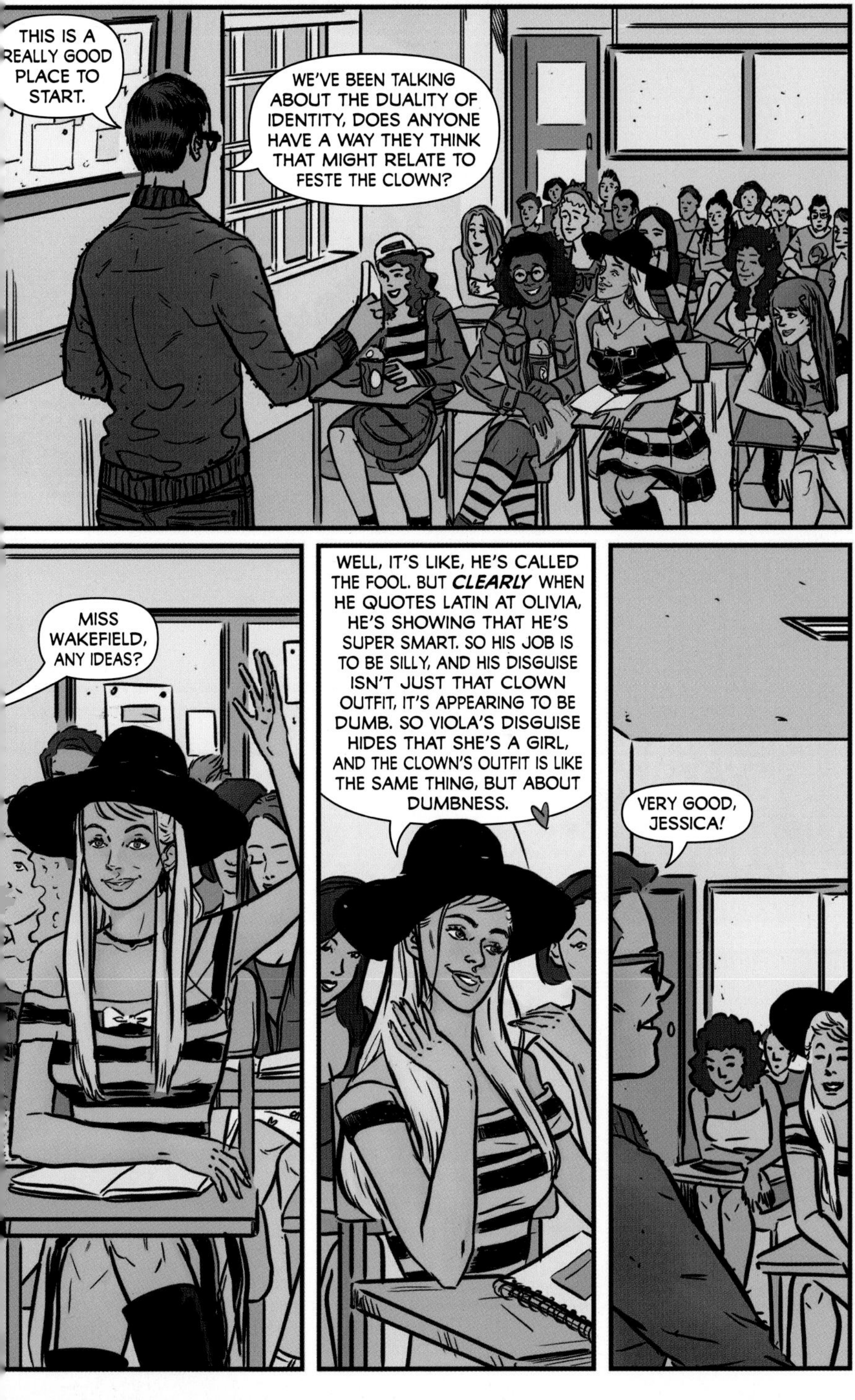
THIS IS A REALLY GOOD PLACE TO START.
WE'VE BEEN TALKING ABOUT THE DUALITY OF IDENTITY, DOES ANYONE HAVE A WAY THEY THINK THAT MIGHT RELATE TO FESTE THE CLOWN?
MISS WAKEFIELD, ANY IDEAS?
WELL, IT'S LIKE, HE'S CALLED THE FOOL. BUT *CLEARLY* WHEN HE QUOTES LATIN AT OLIVIA, HE'S SHOWING THAT HE'S SUPER SMART. SO HIS JOB IS TO BE SILLY, AND HIS DISGUISE ISN'T JUST THAT CLOWN OUTFIT, IT'S APPEARING TO BE DUMB. SO VIOLA'S DISGUISE HIDES THAT SHE'S A GIRL, AND THE CLOWN'S OUTFIT IS LIKE THE SAME THING, BUT ABOUT DUMBNESS.
VERY GOOD, JESSICA!

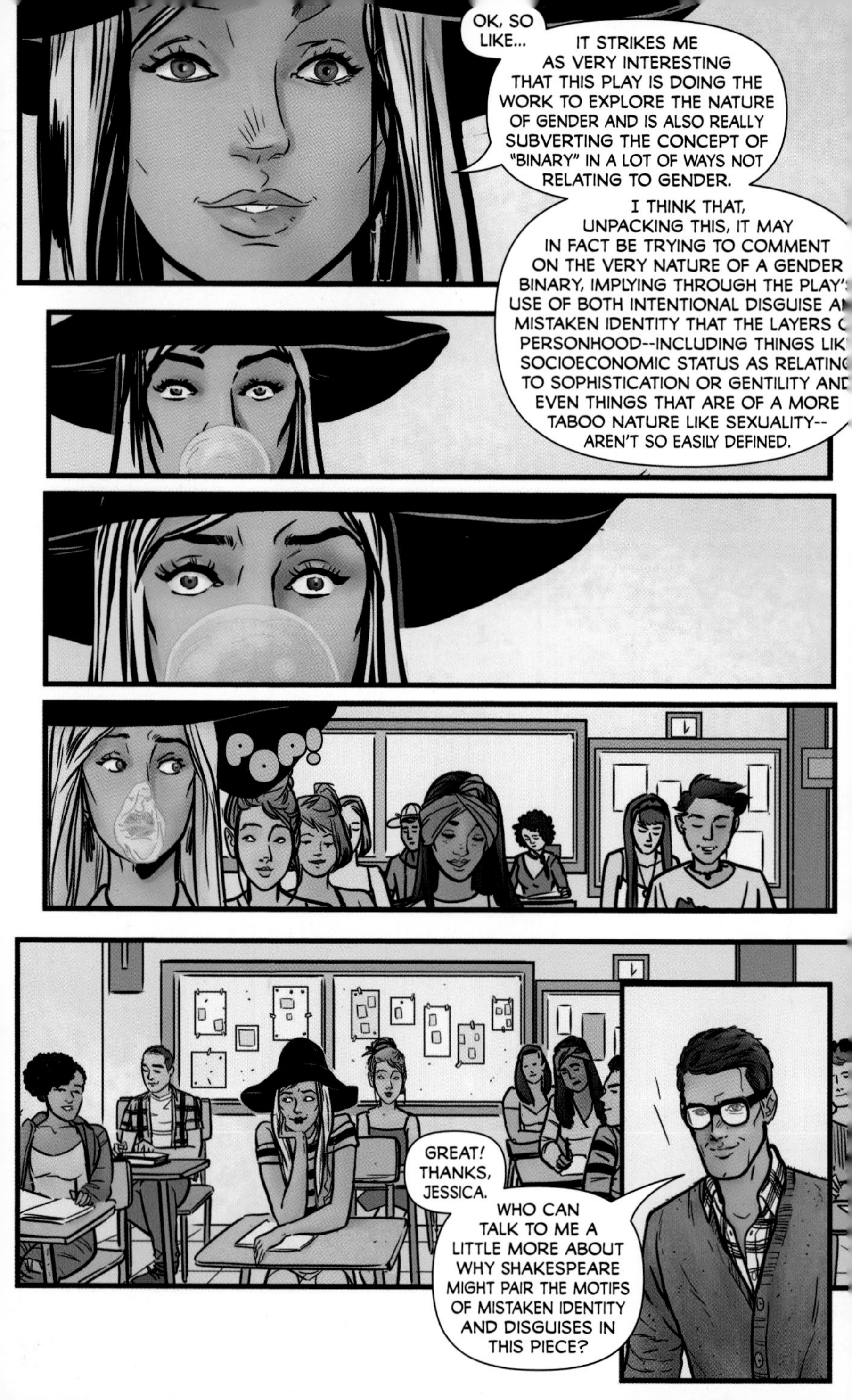
OK, SO LIKE...
IT STRIKES ME AS VERY INTERESTING THAT THIS PLAY IS DOING THE WORK TO EXPLORE THE NATURE OF GENDER AND IS ALSO REALLY SUBVERTING THE CONCEPT OF "BINARY" IN A LOT OF WAYS NOT RELATING TO GENDER.
I THINK THAT, UNPACKING THIS, IT MAY IN FACT BE TRYING TO COMMENT ON THE VERY NATURE OF A GENDER BINARY, IMPLYING THROUGH THE PLAY'S USE OF BOTH INTENTIONAL DISGUISE AND MISTAKEN IDENTITY THAT THE LAYERS OF PERSONHOOD--INCLUDING THINGS LIKE SOCIOECONOMIC STATUS AS RELATING TO SOPHISTICATION OR GENTILITY AND EVEN THINGS THAT ARE OF A MORE TABOO NATURE LIKE SEXUALITY-- AREN'T SO EASILY DEFINED.
POP!
GREAT! THANKS, JESSICA.
WHO CAN TALK TO ME A LITTLE MORE ABOUT WHY SHAKESPEARE MIGHT PAIR THE MOTIFS OF MISTAKEN IDENTITY AND DISGUISES IN THIS PIECE?

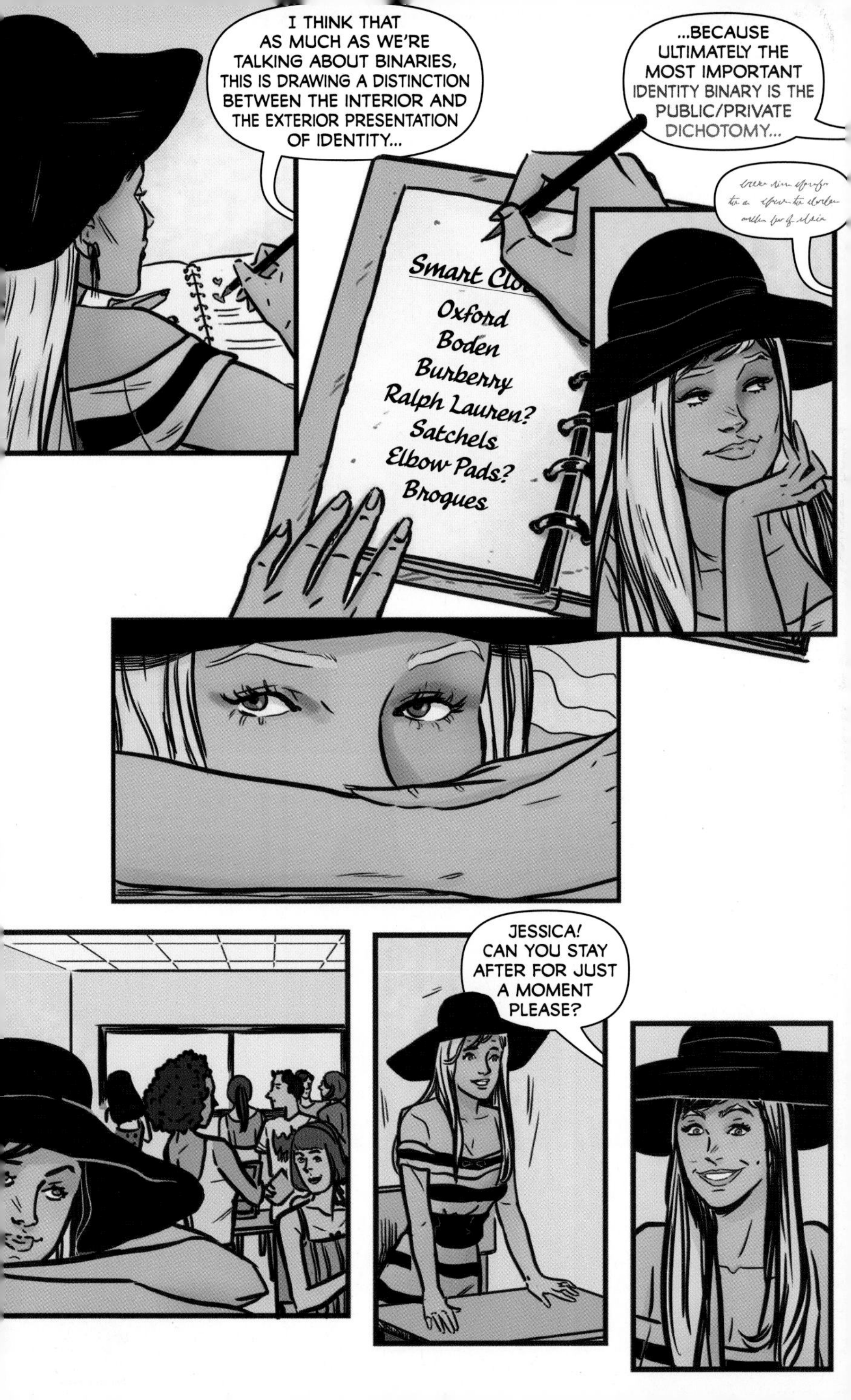
I THINK THAT AS MUCH AS WE'RE TALKING ABOUT BINARIES, THIS IS DRAWING A DISTINCTION BETWEEN THE INTERIOR AND THE EXTERIOR PRESENTATION OF IDENTITY...
...BECAUSE ULTIMATELY THE MOST IMPORTANT IDENTITY BINARY IS THE PUBLIC/PRIVATE DICHOTOMY...
Smart Clo
Oxford
Boden
Burberry
Ralph Lauren?
Satchels
Elbow Pads?
Brogues
JESSICA! CAN YOU STAY AFTER FOR JUST A MOMENT PLEASE?

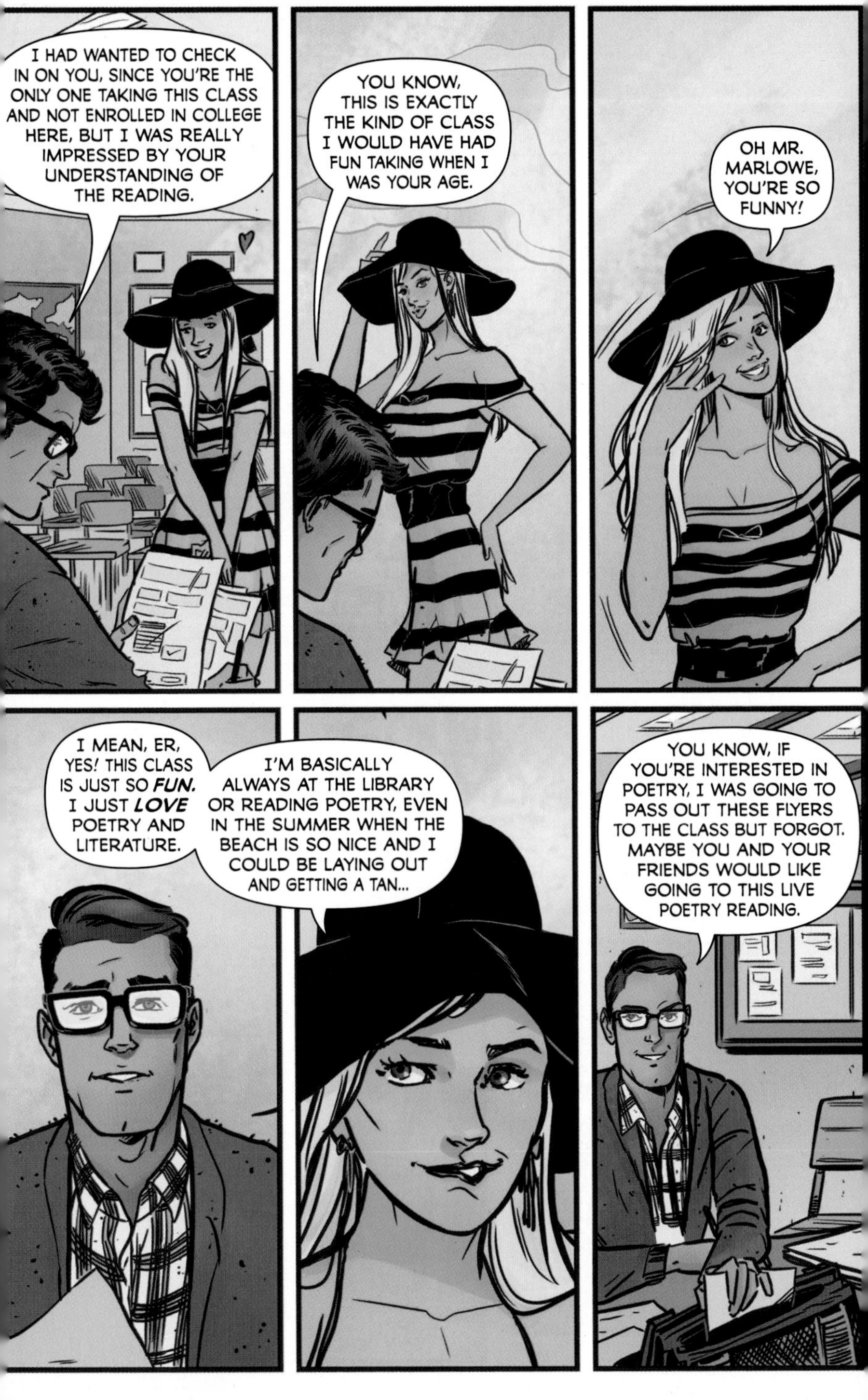
I HAD WANTED TO CHECK IN ON YOU, SINCE YOU'RE THE ONLY ONE TAKING THIS CLASS AND NOT ENROLLED IN COLLEGE HERE, BUT I WAS REALLY IMPRESSED BY YOUR UNDERSTANDING OF THE READING.
YOU KNOW, THIS IS EXACTLY THE KIND OF CLASS I WOULD HAVE HAD FUN TAKING WHEN I WAS YOUR AGE.
OH MR. MARLOWE, YOU'RE SO FUNNY!
I MEAN, ER, YES! THIS CLASS IS JUST SO FUN. I JUST LOVE POETRY AND LITERATURE.
I'M BASICALLY ALWAYS AT THE LIBRARY OR READING POETRY, EVEN IN THE SUMMER WHEN THE BEACH IS SO NICE AND I COULD BE LAYING OUT AND GETTING A TAN...
YOU KNOW, IF YOU'RE INTERESTED IN POETRY, I WAS GOING TO PASS OUT THESE FLYERS TO THE CLASS BUT FORGOT. MAYBE YOU AND YOUR FRIENDS WOULD LIKE GOING TO THIS LIVE POETRY READING.

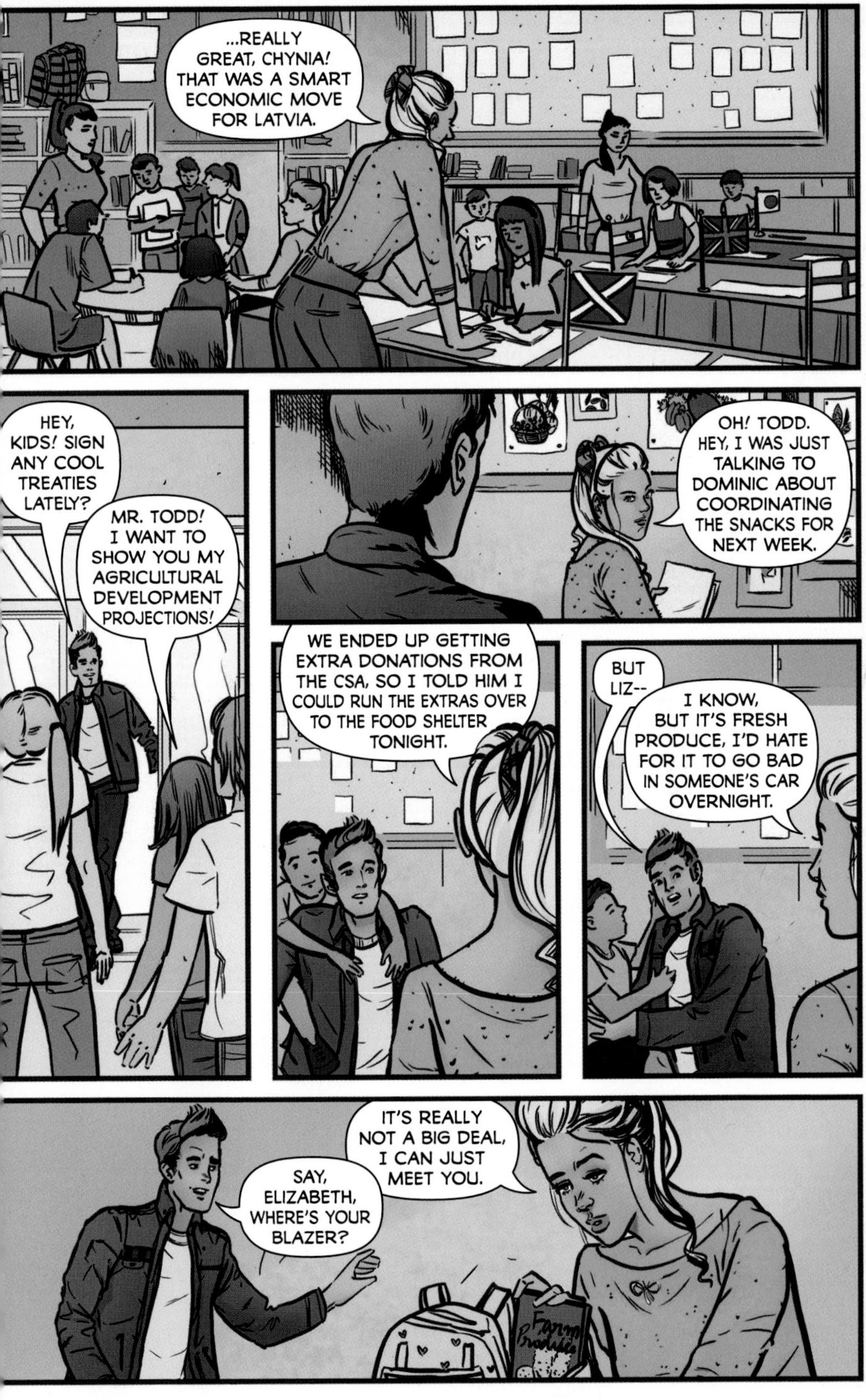
...REALLY GREAT, CHYNIA! THAT WAS A SMART ECONOMIC MOVE FOR LATVIA.
HEY, KIDS! SIGN ANY COOL TREATIES LATELY?
MR. TODD! I WANT TO SHOW YOU MY AGRICULTURAL DEVELOPMENT PROJECTIONS!
OH! TODD. HEY, I WAS JUST TALKING TO DOMINIC ABOUT COORDINATING THE SNACKS FOR NEXT WEEK.
WE ENDED UP GETTING EXTRA DONATIONS FROM THE CSA, SO I TOLD HIM I COULD RUN THE EXTRAS OVER TO THE FOOD SHELTER TONIGHT.
BUT LIZ--
I KNOW, BUT IT'S FRESH PRODUCE, I'D HATE FOR IT TO GO BAD IN SOMEONE'S CAR OVERNIGHT.
IT'S REALLY NOT A BIG DEAL, I CAN JUST MEET YOU.
SAY, ELIZABETH, WHERE'S YOUR BLAZER?

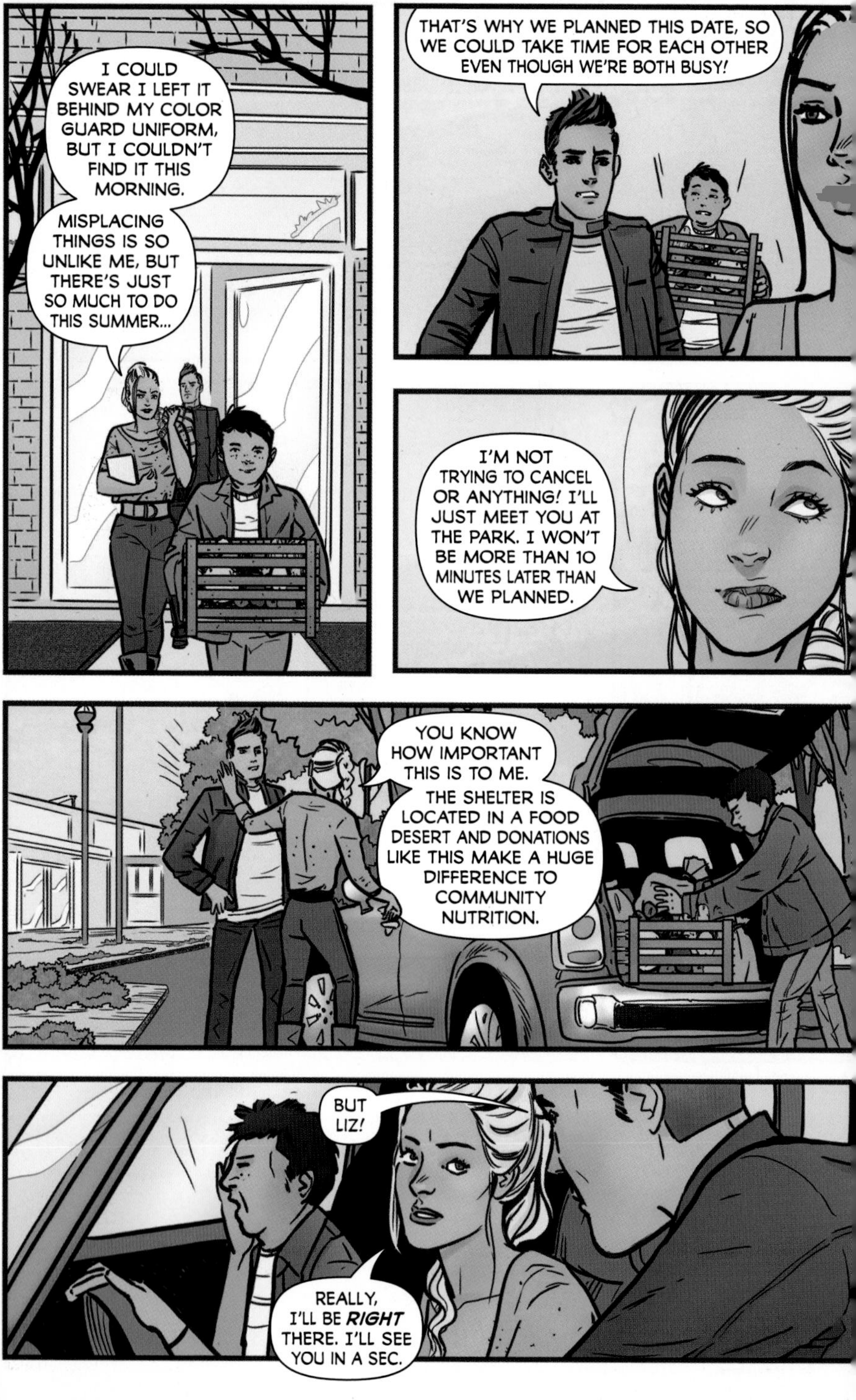
I COULD SWEAR I LEFT IT BEHIND MY COLOR GUARD UNIFORM, BUT I COULDN'T FIND IT THIS MORNING.
MISPLACING THINGS IS SO UNLIKE ME, BUT THERE'S JUST SO MUCH TO DO THIS SUMMER...
THAT'S WHY WE PLANNED THIS DATE, SO WE COULD TAKE TIME FOR EACH OTHER EVEN THOUGH WE'RE BOTH BUSY!
I'M NOT TRYING TO CANCEL OR ANYTHING! I'LL JUST MEET YOU AT THE PARK. I WON'T BE MORE THAN 10 MINUTES LATER THAN WE PLANNED.
YOU KNOW HOW IMPORTANT THIS IS TO ME.
THE SHELTER IS LOCATED IN A FOOD DESERT AND DONATIONS LIKE THIS MAKE A HUGE DIFFERENCE TO COMMUNITY NUTRITION.
BUT LIZ!
REALLY, I'LL BE ***RIGHT*** THERE. I'LL SEE YOU IN A SEC.

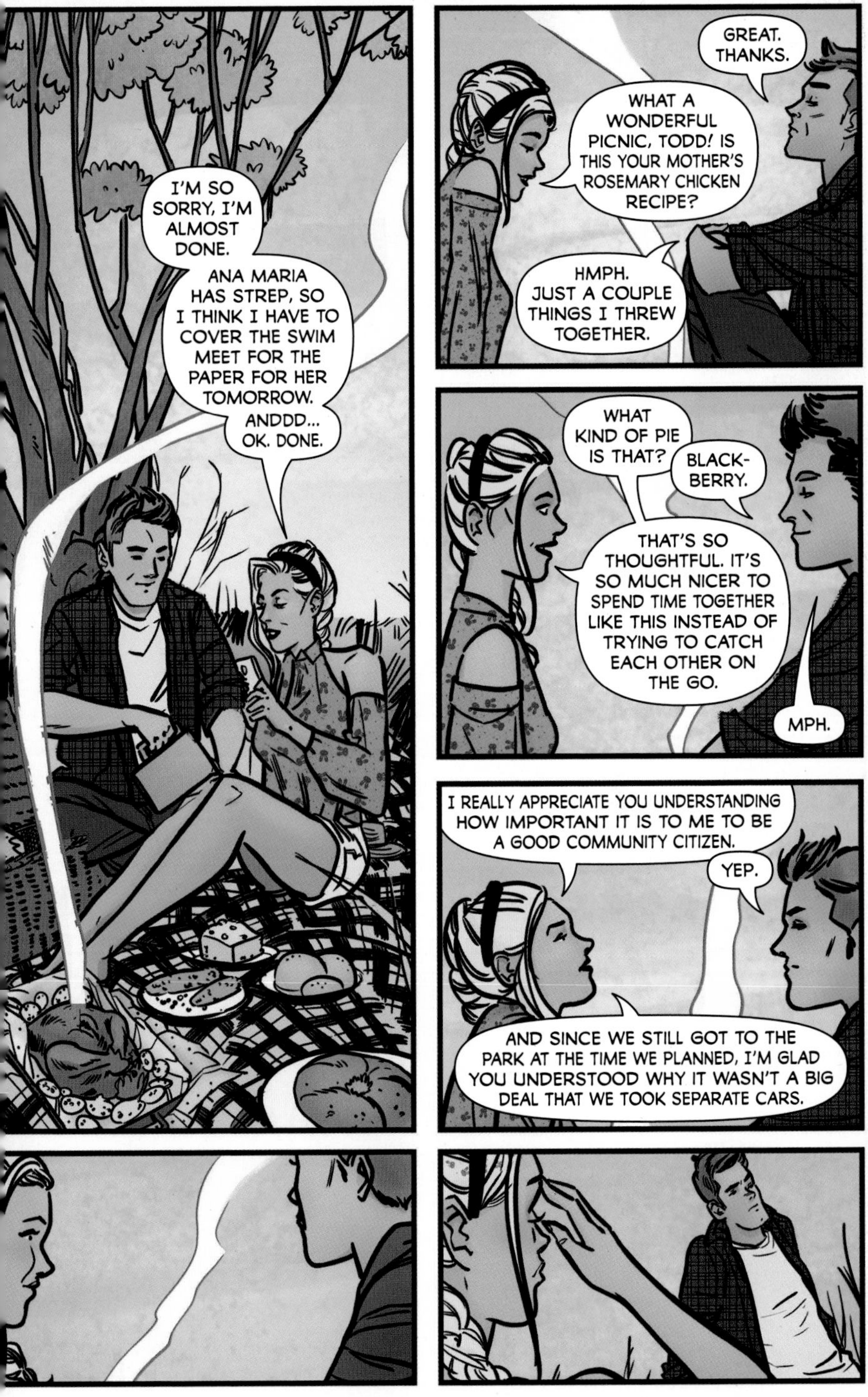
I'M SO SORRY, I'M ALMOST DONE.
ANA MARIA HAS STREP, SO I THINK I HAVE TO COVER THE SWIM MEET FOR THE PAPER FOR HER TOMORROW.
ANDDD... OK. DONE.
GREAT. THANKS.
WHAT A WONDERFUL PICNIC, TODD! IS THIS YOUR MOTHER'S ROSEMARY CHICKEN RECIPE?
HMPH. JUST A COUPLE THINGS I THREW TOGETHER.
WHAT KIND OF PIE IS THAT?
BLACK-BERRY.
THAT'S SO THOUGHTFUL. IT'S SO MUCH NICER TO SPEND TIME TOGETHER LIKE THIS INSTEAD OF TRYING TO CATCH EACH OTHER ON THE GO.
MPH.
I REALLY APPRECIATE YOU UNDERSTANDING HOW IMPORTANT IT IS TO ME TO BE A GOOD COMMUNITY CITIZEN.
YEP.
AND SINCE WE STILL GOT TO THE PARK AT THE TIME WE PLANNED, I'M GLAD YOU UNDERSTOOD WHY IT WASN'T A BIG DEAL THAT WE TOOK SEPARATE CARS.

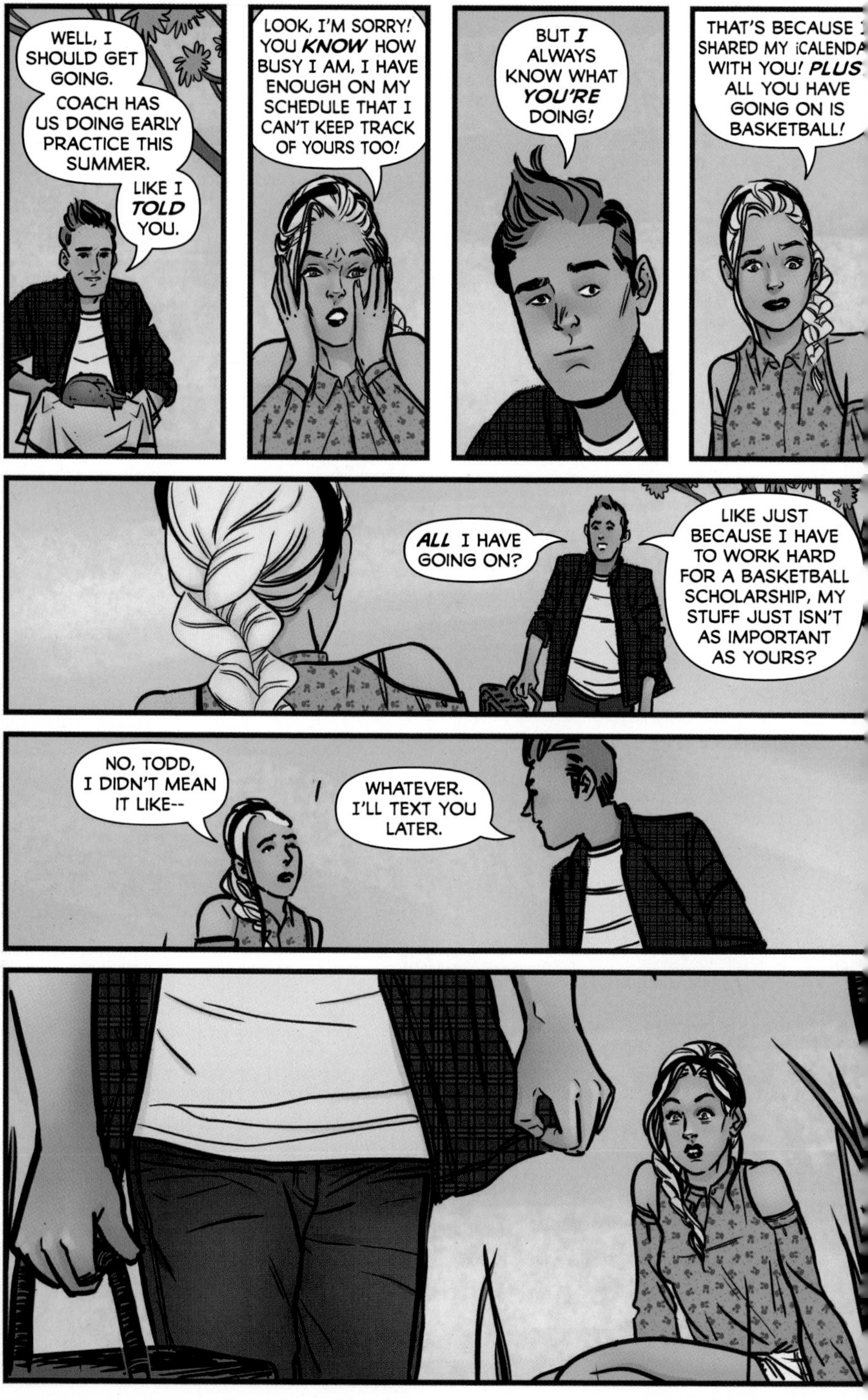
WELL, I SHOULD GET GOING.
COACH HAS US DOING EARLY PRACTICE THIS SUMMER.
LIKE I *TOLD* YOU.
LOOK, I'M SORRY! YOU *KNOW* HOW BUSY I AM, I HAVE ENOUGH ON MY SCHEDULE THAT I CAN'T KEEP TRACK OF YOURS TOO!
BUT *I* ALWAYS KNOW WHAT *YOU'RE* DOING!
THAT'S BECAUSE I SHARED MY iCALENDA WITH YOU! *PLUS* ALL YOU HAVE GOING ON IS BASKETBALL!
ALL I HAVE GOING ON?
LIKE JUST BECAUSE I HAVE TO WORK HARD FOR A BASKETBALL SCHOLARSHIP, MY STUFF JUST ISN'T AS IMPORTANT AS YOURS?
NO, TODD, I DIDN'T MEAN IT LIKE--
WHATEVER. I'LL TEXT YOU LATER.

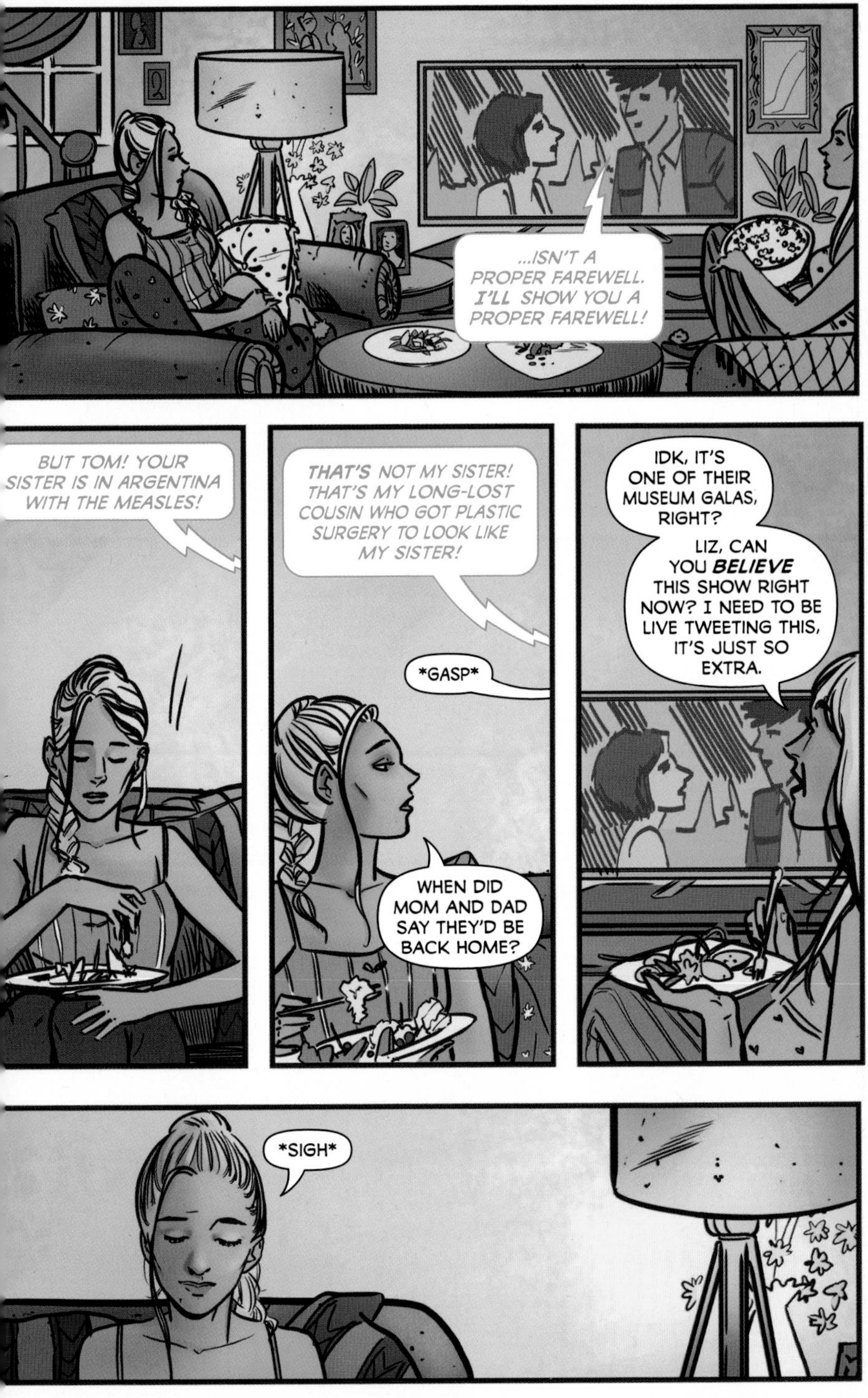
...ISN'T A PROPER FAREWELL. I'LL SHOW YOU A PROPER FAREWELL!
BUT TOM! YOUR SISTER IS IN ARGENTINA WITH THE MEASLES!
THAT'S NOT MY SISTER! THAT'S MY LONG-LOST COUSIN WHO GOT PLASTIC SURGERY TO LOOK LIKE MY SISTER!
GASP
WHEN DID MOM AND DAD SAY THEY'D BE BACK HOME?
IDK, IT'S ONE OF THEIR MUSEUM GALAS, RIGHT?
LIZ, CAN YOU BELIEVE THIS SHOW RIGHT NOW? I NEED TO BE LIVE TWEETING THIS, IT'S JUST SO EXTRA.
SIGH

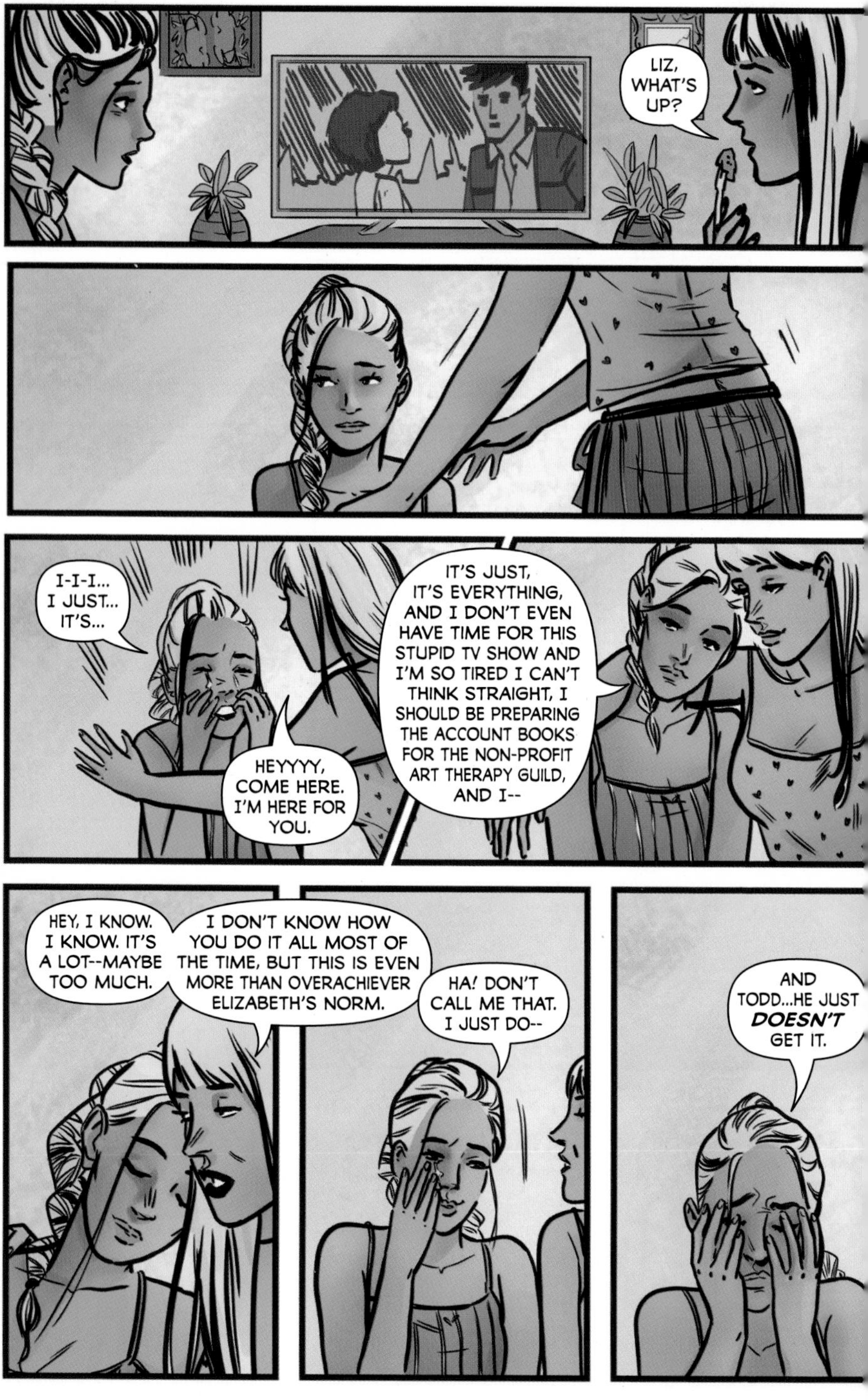

LIZ, WHAT'S UP?
I-I-I... I JUST... IT'S...
HEYYYY, COME HERE. I'M HERE FOR YOU.
IT'S JUST, IT'S EVERYTHING, AND I DON'T EVEN HAVE TIME FOR THIS STUPID TV SHOW AND I'M SO TIRED I CAN'T THINK STRAIGHT, I SHOULD BE PREPARING THE ACCOUNT BOOKS FOR THE NON-PROFIT ART THERAPY GUILD, AND I--
HEY, I KNOW. I KNOW. IT'S A LOT--MAYBE TOO MUCH.
I DON'T KNOW HOW YOU DO IT ALL MOST OF THE TIME, BUT THIS IS EVEN MORE THAN OVERACHIEVER ELIZABETH'S NORM.
HA! DON'T CALL ME THAT. I JUST DO--
AND TODD...HE JUST ***DOESN'T*** GET IT.

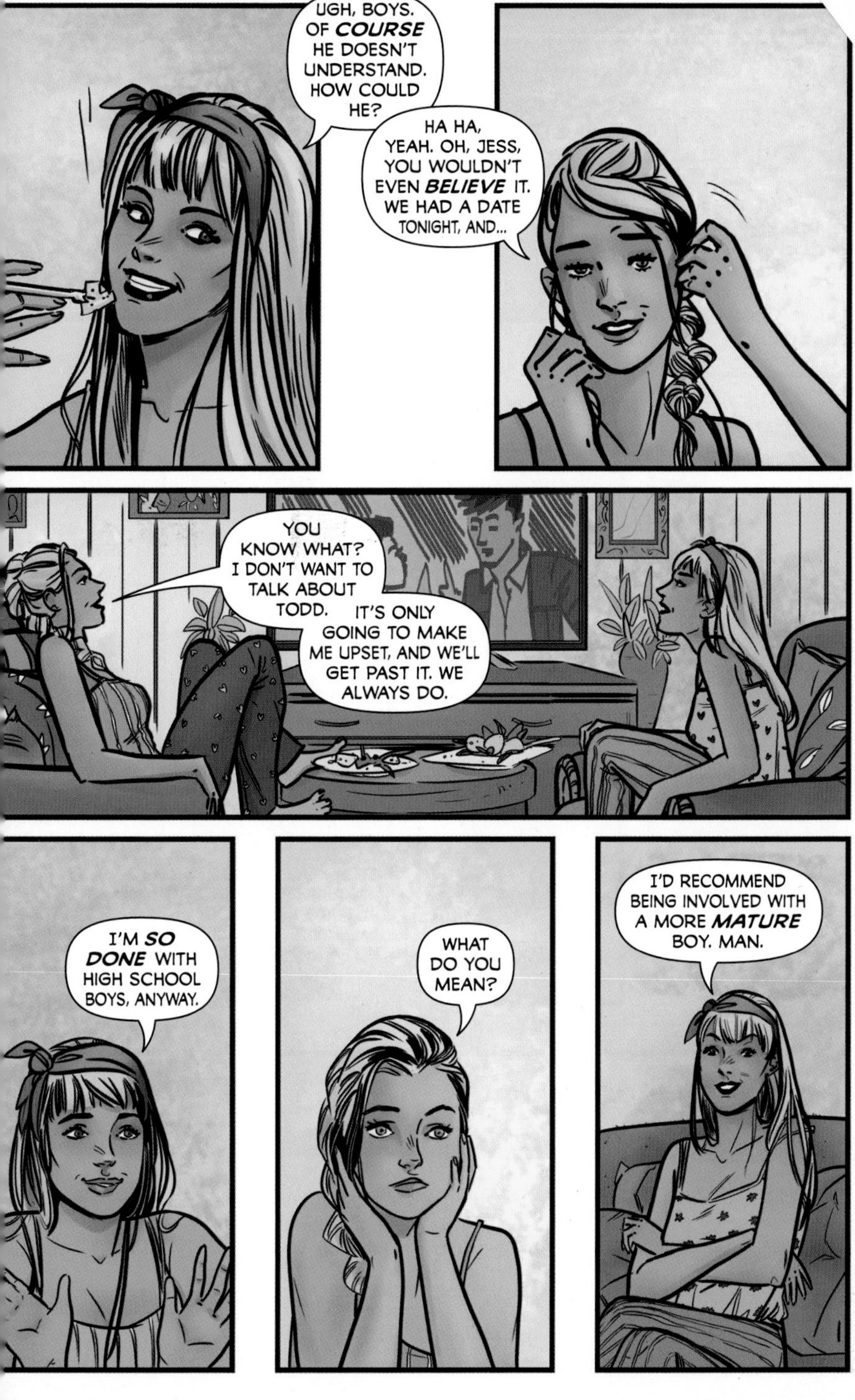
UGH, BOYS. OF COURSE HE DOESN'T UNDERSTAND. HOW COULD HE?
HA HA, YEAH. OH, JESS, YOU WOULDN'T EVEN BELIEVE IT. WE HAD A DATE TONIGHT, AND...
YOU KNOW WHAT? I DON'T WANT TO TALK ABOUT TODD.
IT'S ONLY GOING TO MAKE ME UPSET, AND WE'LL GET PAST IT. WE ALWAYS DO.
I'M SO DONE WITH HIGH SCHOOL BOYS, ANYWAY.
WHAT DO YOU MEAN?
I'D RECOMMEND BEING INVOLVED WITH A MORE MATURE BOY. MAN.

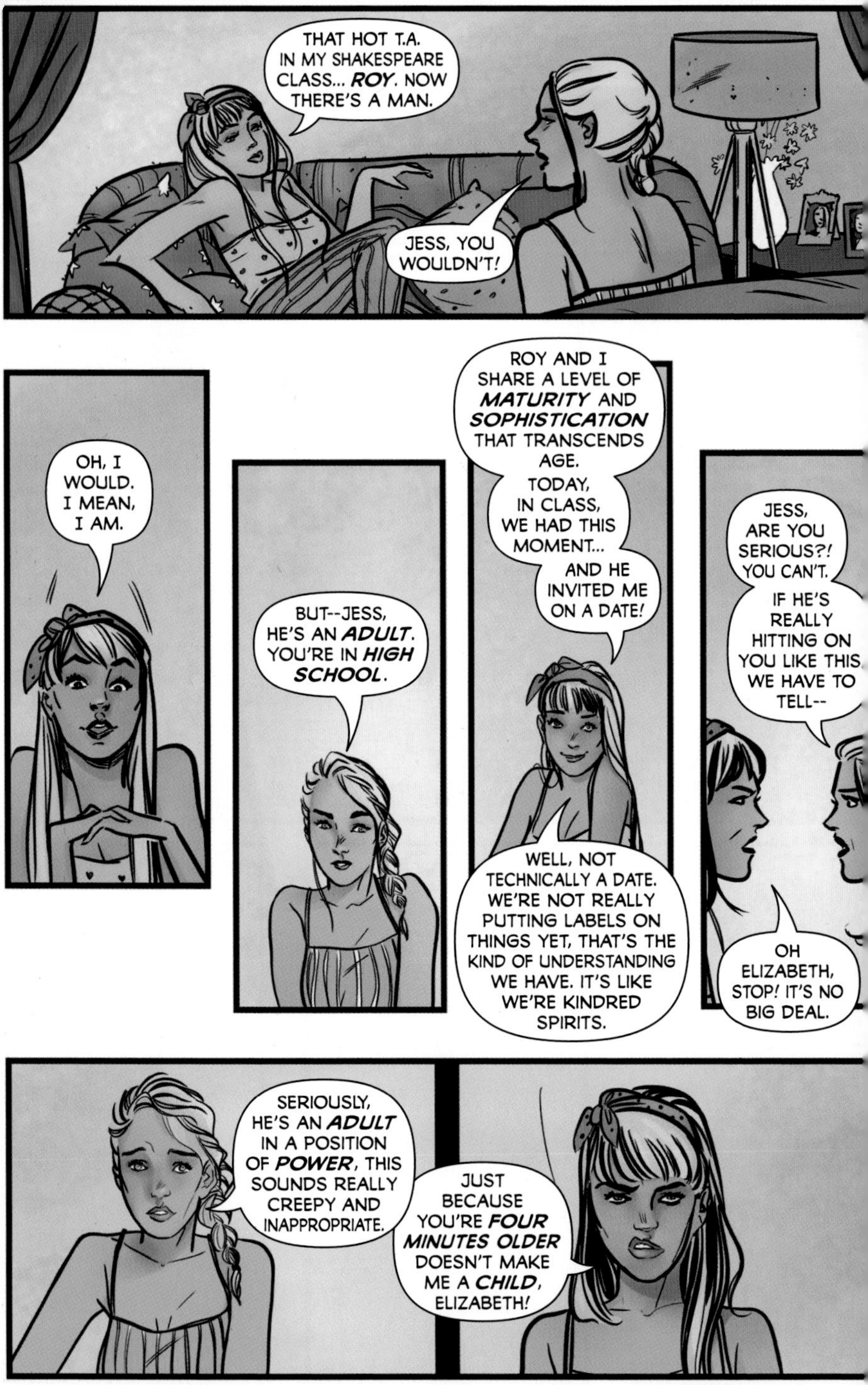

THAT HOT T.A. IN MY SHAKESPEARE CLASS... ROY. NOW THERE'S A MAN.
JESS, YOU WOULDN'T!
OH, I WOULD. I MEAN, I AM.
BUT--JESS, HE'S AN ADULT. YOU'RE IN HIGH SCHOOL.
ROY AND I SHARE A LEVEL OF MATURITY AND SOPHISTICATION THAT TRANSCENDS AGE.
TODAY, IN CLASS, WE HAD THIS MOMENT...
AND HE INVITED ME ON A DATE!
WELL, NOT TECHNICALLY A DATE. WE'RE NOT REALLY PUTTING LABELS ON THINGS YET, THAT'S THE KIND OF UNDERSTANDING WE HAVE. IT'S LIKE WE'RE KINDRED SPIRITS.
JESS, ARE YOU SERIOUS?! YOU CAN'T.
IF HE'S REALLY HITTING ON YOU LIKE THIS, WE HAVE TO TELL--
OH ELIZABETH, STOP! IT'S NO BIG DEAL.
SERIOUSLY, HE'S AN ADULT IN A POSITION OF POWER, THIS SOUNDS REALLY CREEPY AND INAPPROPRIATE.
JUST BECAUSE YOU'RE FOUR MINUTES OLDER DOESN'T MAKE ME A CHILD, ELIZABETH!

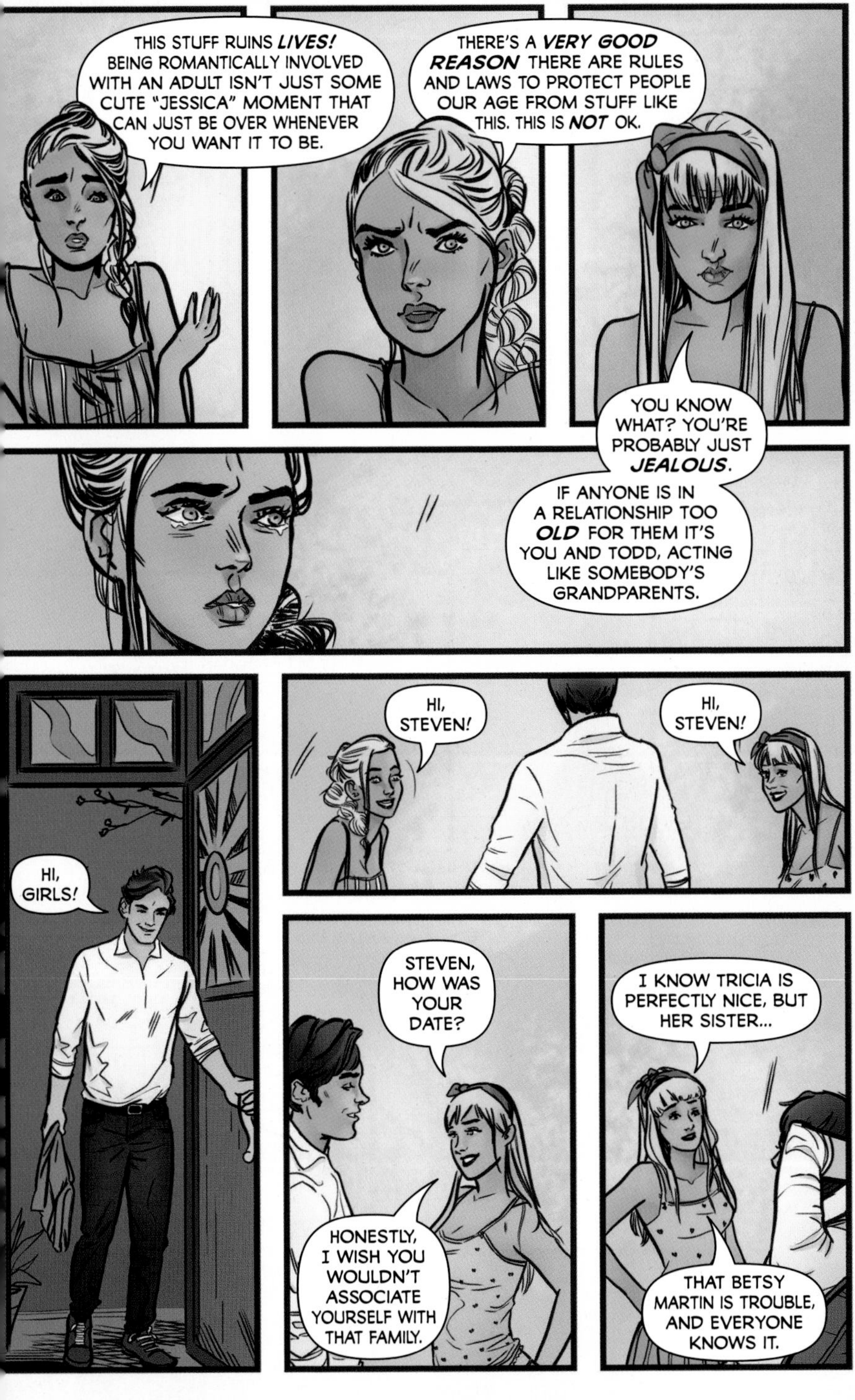

THIS STUFF RUINS LIVES! BEING ROMANTICALLY INVOLVED WITH AN ADULT ISN'T JUST SOME CUTE "JESSICA" MOMENT THAT CAN JUST BE OVER WHENEVER YOU WANT IT TO BE.
THERE'S A VERY GOOD REASON THERE ARE RULES AND LAWS TO PROTECT PEOPLE OUR AGE FROM STUFF LIKE THIS. THIS IS NOT OK.
YOU KNOW WHAT? YOU'RE PROBABLY JUST JEALOUS.
IF ANYONE IS IN A RELATIONSHIP TOO OLD FOR THEM IT'S YOU AND TODD, ACTING LIKE SOMEBODY'S GRANDPARENTS.
HI, GIRLS!
HI, STEVEN!
HI, STEVEN!
STEVEN, HOW WAS YOUR DATE?
HONESTLY, I WISH YOU WOULDN'T ASSOCIATE YOURSELF WITH THAT FAMILY.
I KNOW TRICIA IS PERFECTLY NICE, BUT HER SISTER...
THAT BETSY MARTIN IS TROUBLE, AND EVERYONE KNOWS IT.

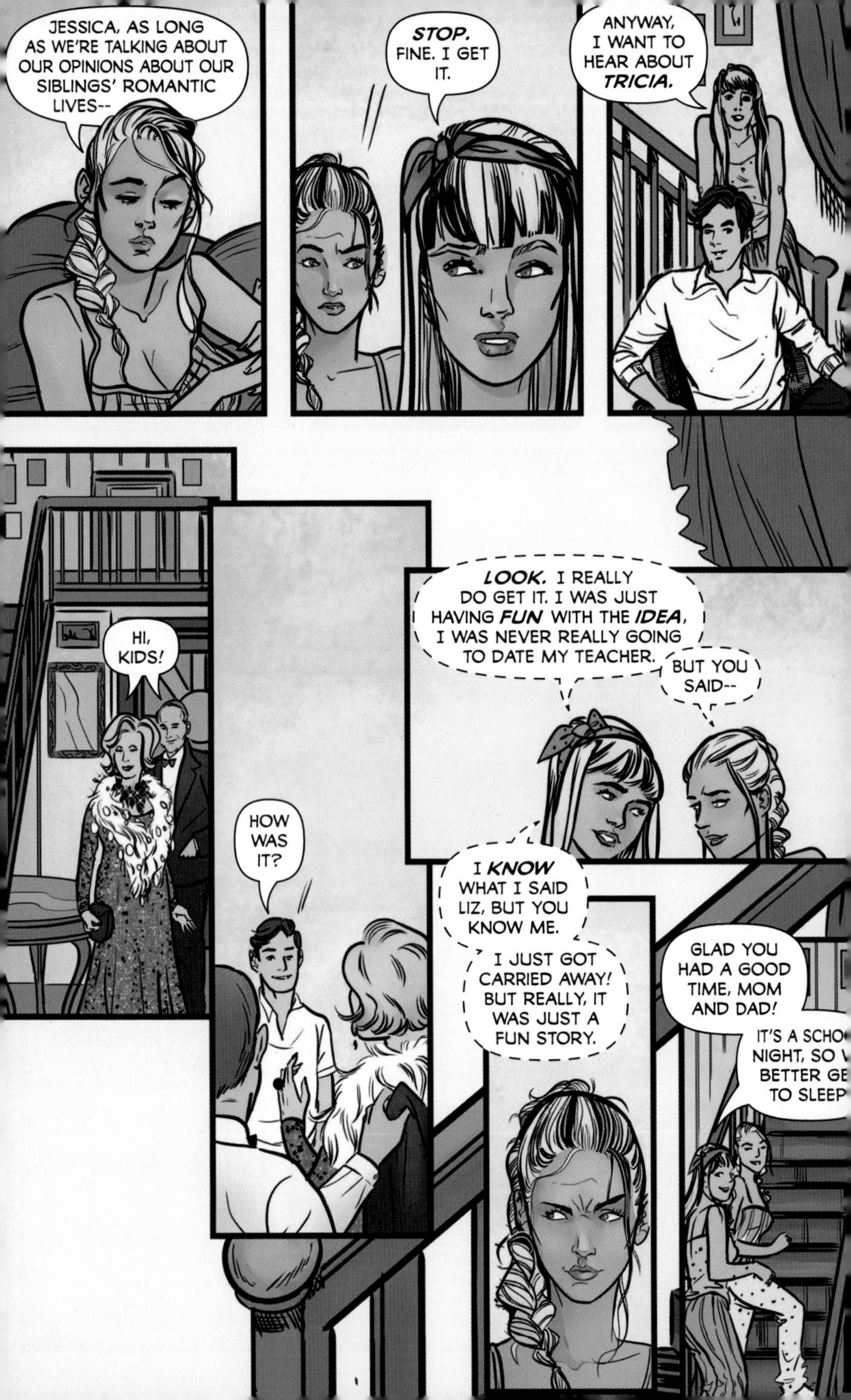
JESSICA, AS LONG AS WE'RE TALKING ABOUT OUR OPINIONS ABOUT OUR SIBLINGS' ROMANTIC LIVES--
STOP. FINE. I GET IT.
ANYWAY, I WANT TO HEAR ABOUT TRICIA.
HI, KIDS!
HOW WAS IT?
LOOK. I REALLY DO GET IT. I WAS JUST HAVING FUN WITH THE IDEA, I WAS NEVER REALLY GOING TO DATE MY TEACHER.
BUT YOU SAID--
I KNOW WHAT I SAID LIZ, BUT YOU KNOW ME.
I JUST GOT CARRIED AWAY! BUT REALLY, IT WAS JUST A FUN STORY.
GLAD YOU HAD A GOOD TIME, MOM AND DAD!

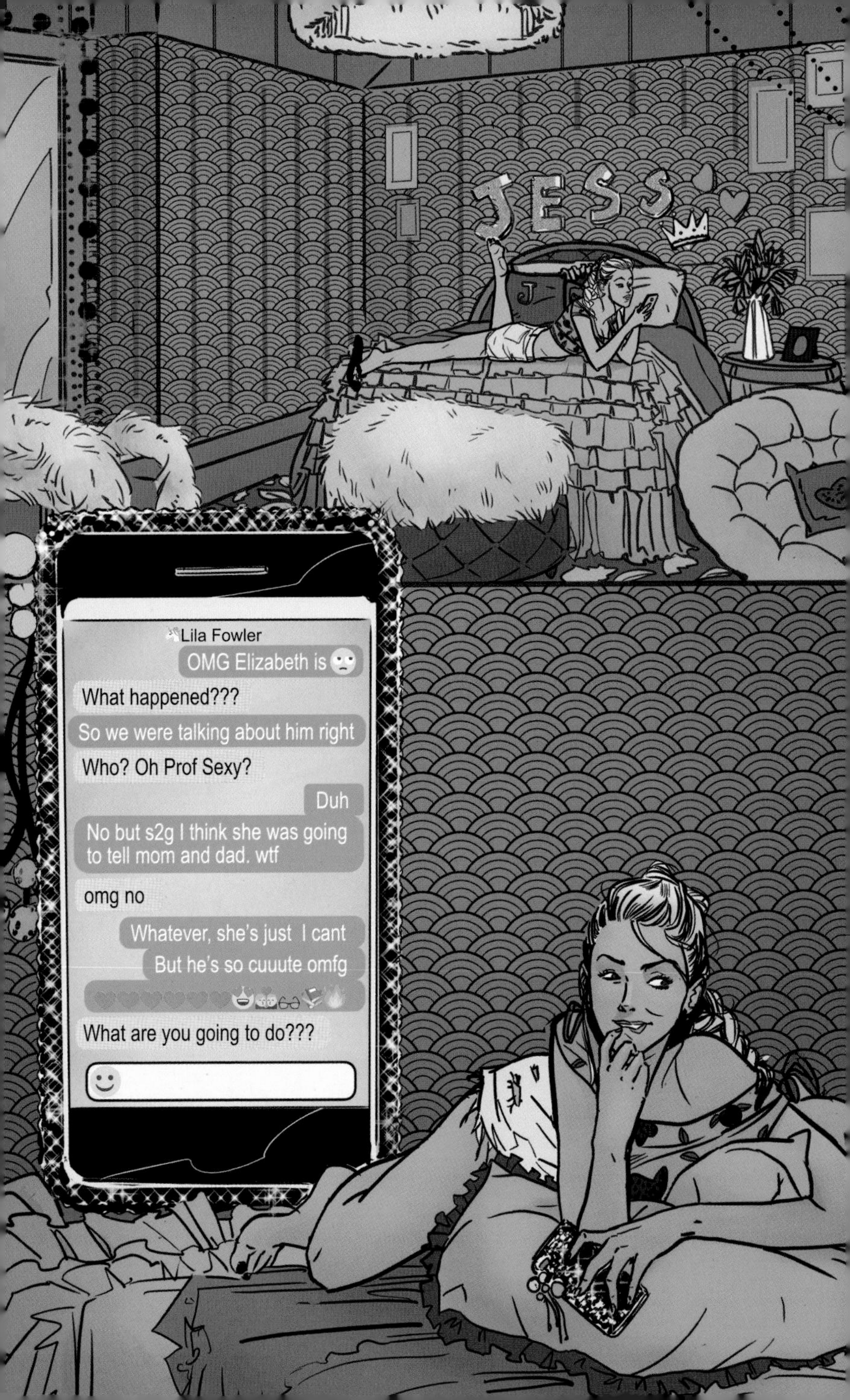
JESS
J
Lila Fowler
OMG Elizabeth is
What happened???
So we were talking about him right
Who? Oh Prof Sexy?
Duh
No but s2g I think she was going to tell mom and dad. wtf
omg no
Whatever, she's just I cant
But he's so cuuute omfg
What are you going to do???

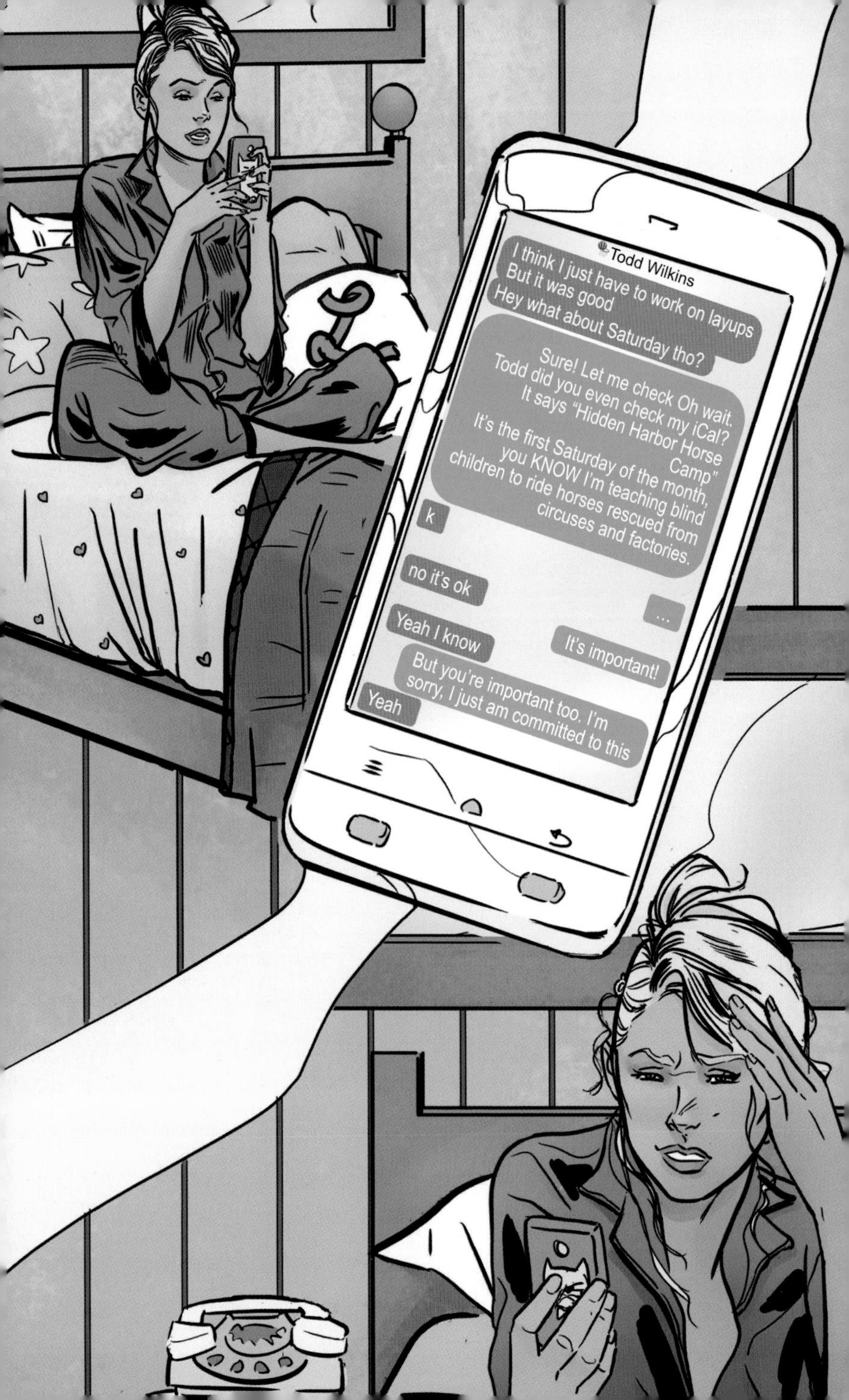
Todd Wilkins
I think I just have to work on layups
But it was good
Hey what about Saturday tho?
Sure! Let me check Oh wait.
Todd did you even check my iCal?
It says "Hidden Harbor Horse Camp"
It's the first Saturday of the month, you KNOW I'm teaching blind children to ride horses rescued from circuses and factories.
k
no it's ok
...
Yeah I know
It's important!
But you're important too. I'm sorry, I just am committed to this
Yeah

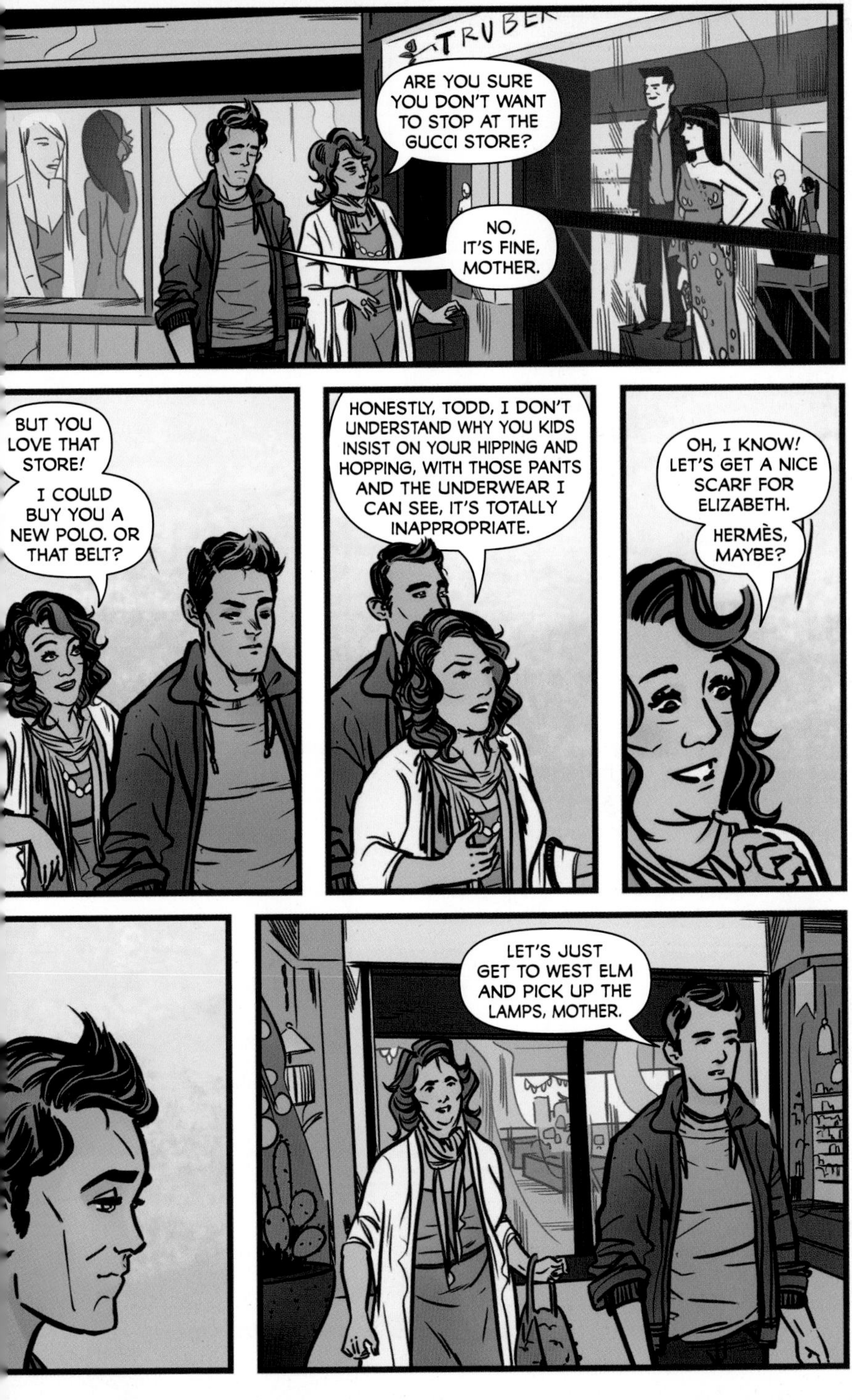
TRUBER
ARE YOU SURE YOU DON'T WANT TO STOP AT THE GUCCI STORE?
NO, IT'S FINE, MOTHER.
BUT YOU LOVE THAT STORE!
I COULD BUY YOU A NEW POLO. OR THAT BELT?
HONESTLY, TODD, I DON'T UNDERSTAND WHY YOU KIDS INSIST ON YOUR HIPPING AND HOPPING, WITH THOSE PANTS AND THE UNDERWEAR I CAN SEE, IT'S TOTALLY INAPPROPRIATE.
OH, I KNOW! LET'S GET A NICE SCARF FOR ELIZABETH.
HERMÈS, MAYBE?
LET'S JUST GET TO WEST ELM AND PICK UP THE LAMPS, MOTHER.

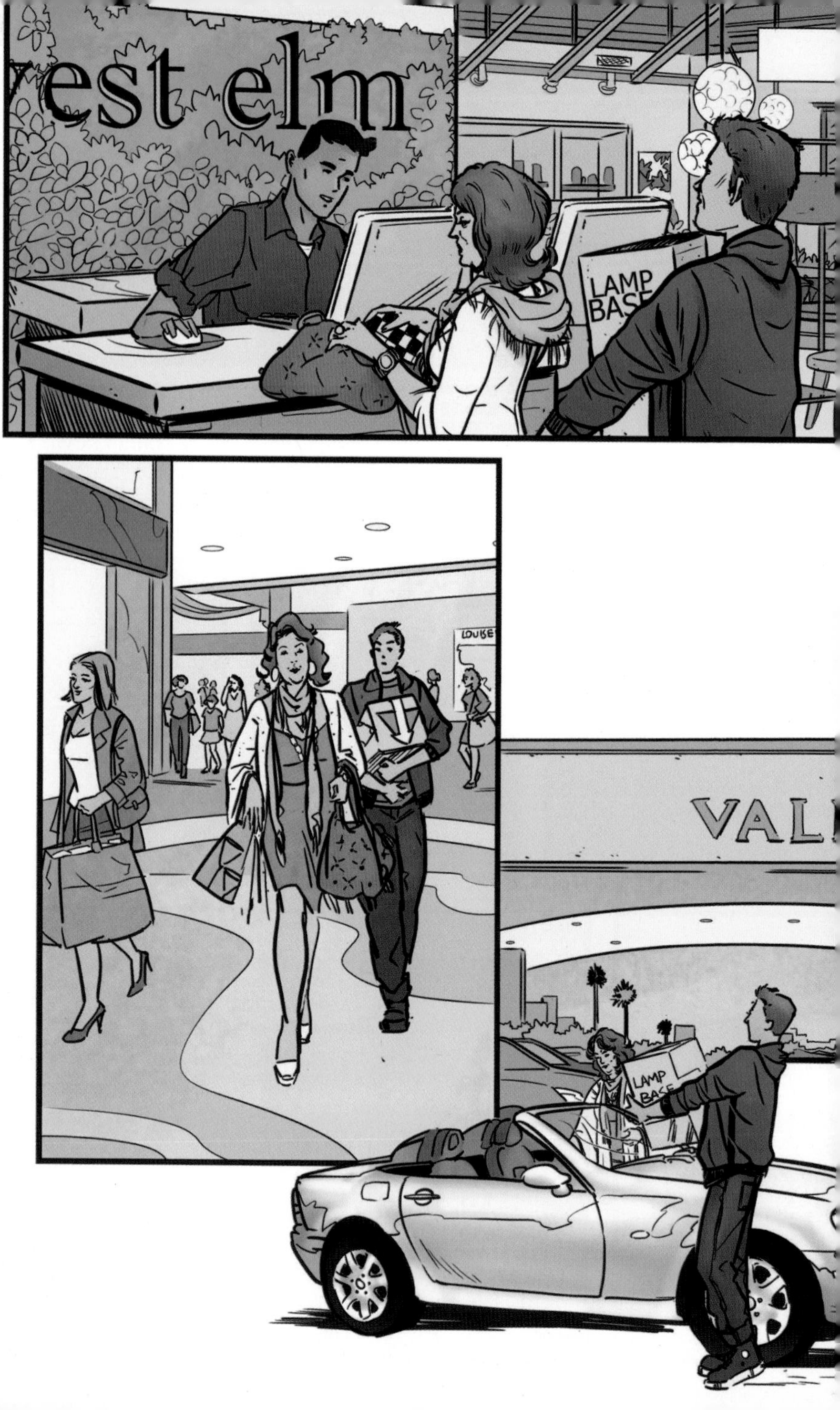
est elm
LAMP
LOUISE
VAL

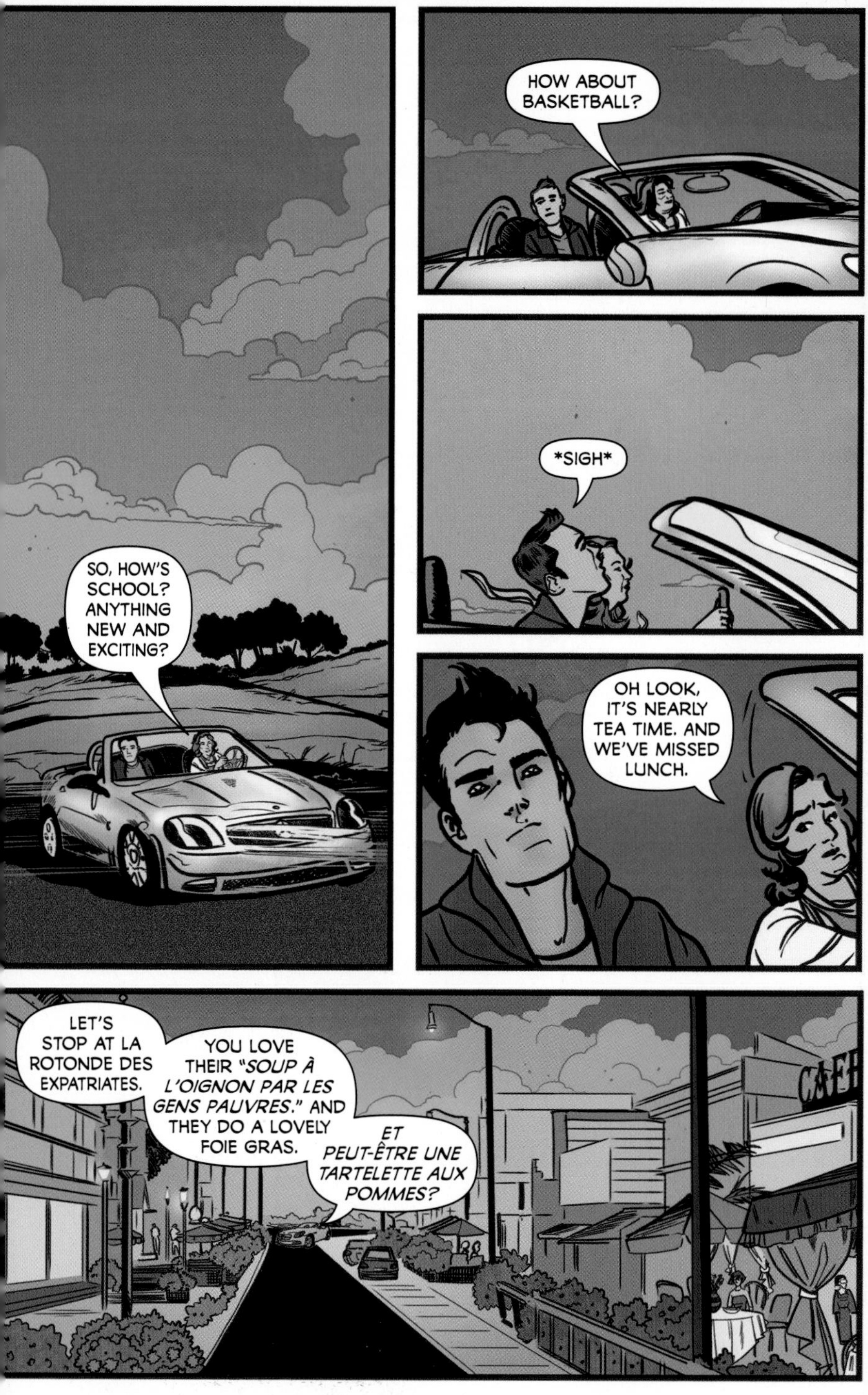
SO, HOW'S SCHOOL? ANYTHING NEW AND EXCITING?
HOW ABOUT BASKETBALL?
SIGH
OH LOOK, IT'S NEARLY TEA TIME. AND WE'VE MISSED LUNCH.
LET'S STOP AT LA ROTONDE DES EXPATRIATES.
YOU LOVE THEIR "*SOUP À L'OIGNON PAR LES GENS PAUVRES.*" AND THEY DO A LOVELY FOIE GRAS.
ET PEUT-ÊTRE UNE TARTELETTE AUX POMMES?
CAFE

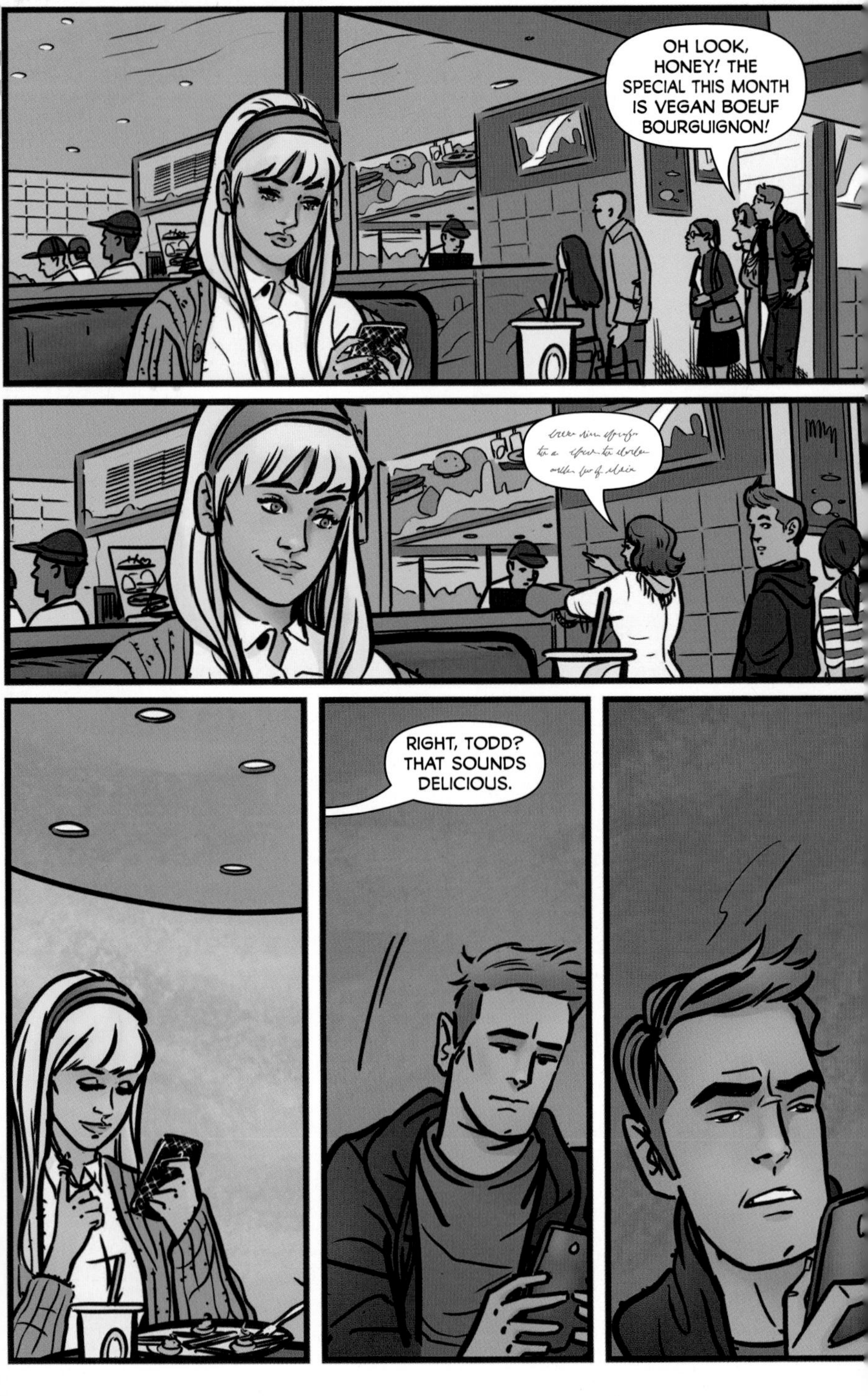
OH LOOK, HONEY! THE SPECIAL THIS MONTH IS VEGAN BOEUF BOURGUIGNON!
RIGHT, TODD? THAT SOUNDS DELICIOUS.

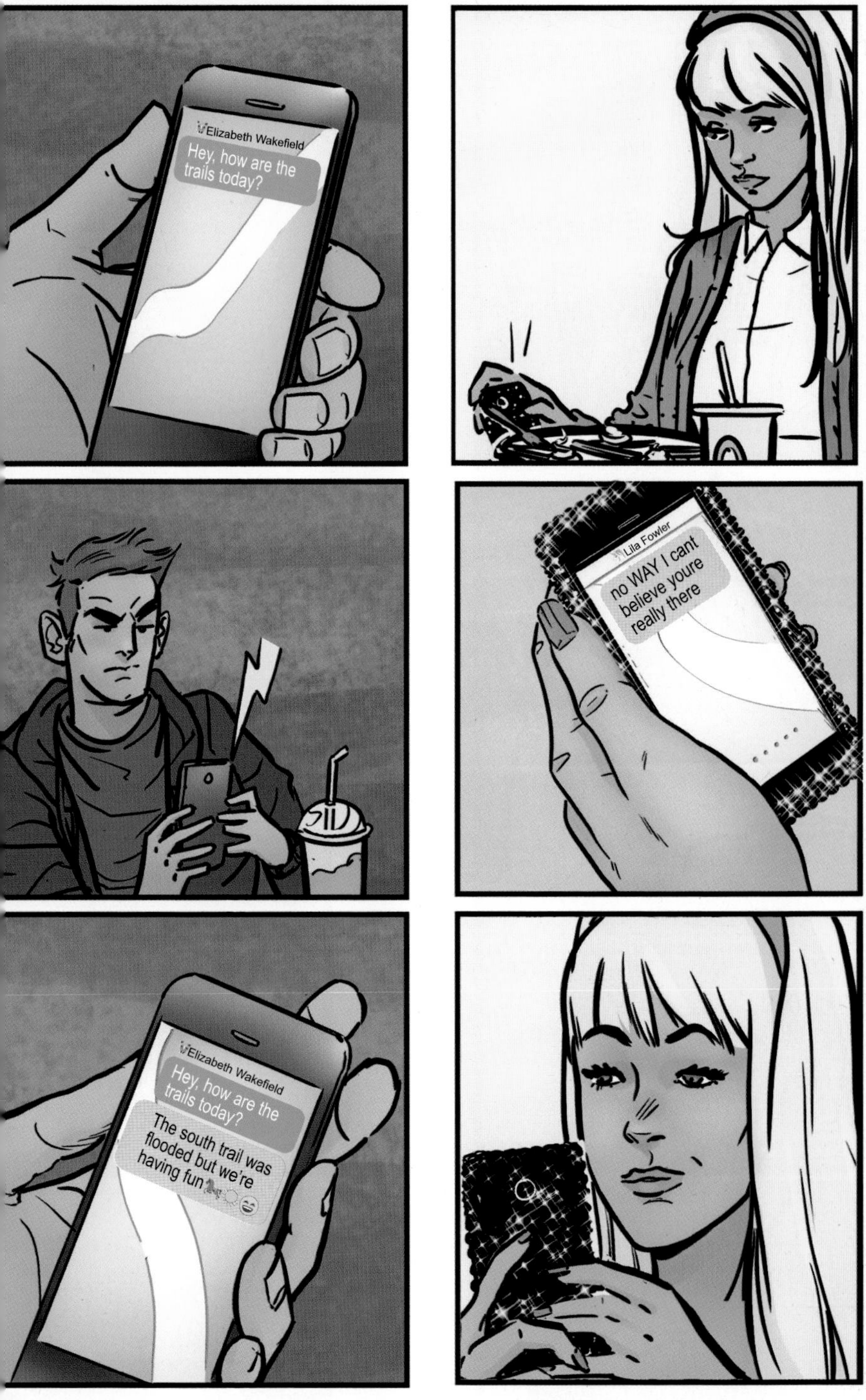
Elizabeth Wakefield
Hey, how are the trails today?
Lila Fowler
no WAY I cant believe youre really there
Elizabeth Wakefield
Hey, how are the trails today?
The south trail was flooded but we're having fun

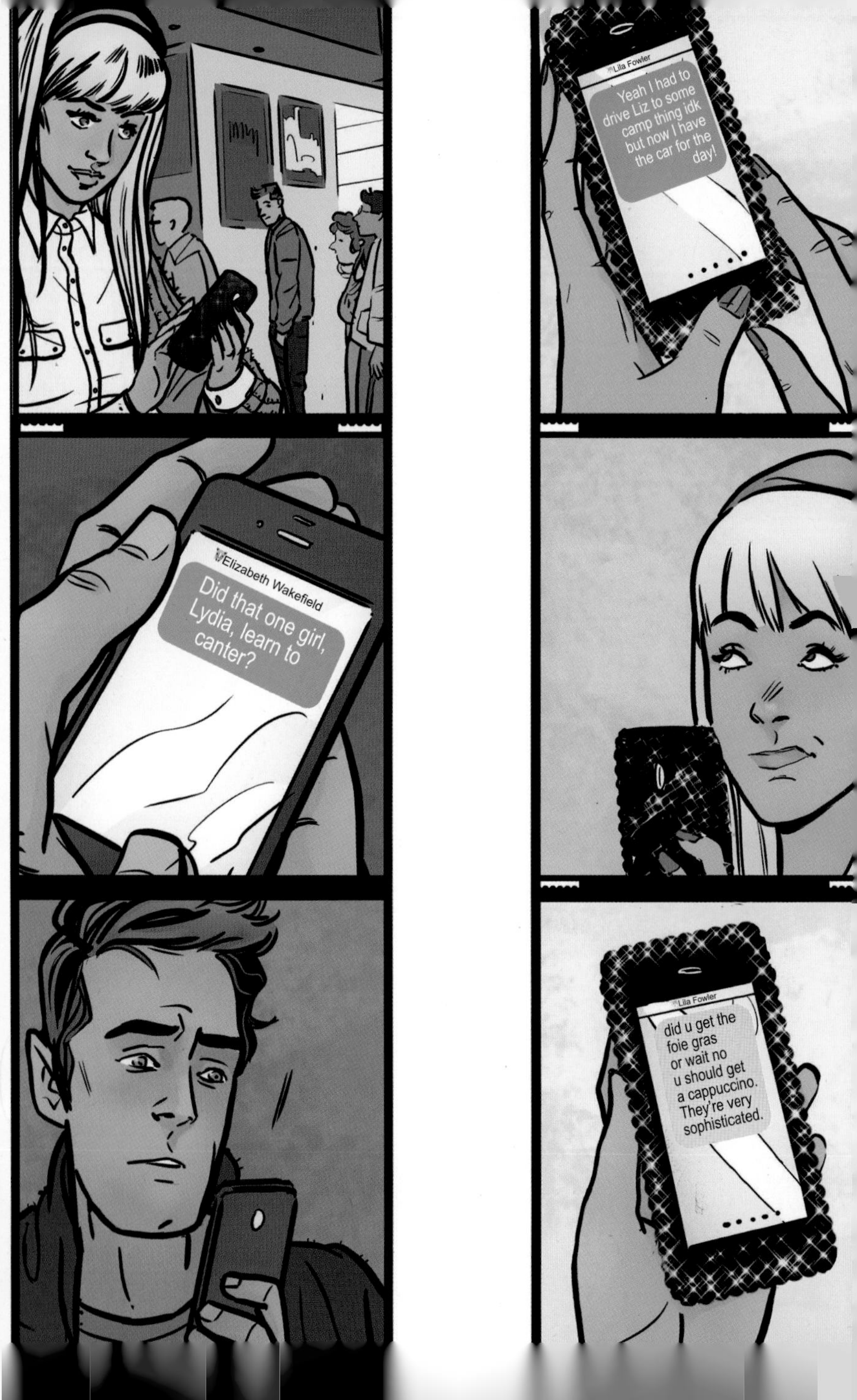
Elizabeth Wakefield
Did that one girl, Lydia, learn to canter?
Lila Fowler
Yeah I had to drive Liz to some camp thing idk but now I have the car for the day!
Lila Fowler
did u get the foie gras or wait no u should get a cappuccino. They're very sophisticated.

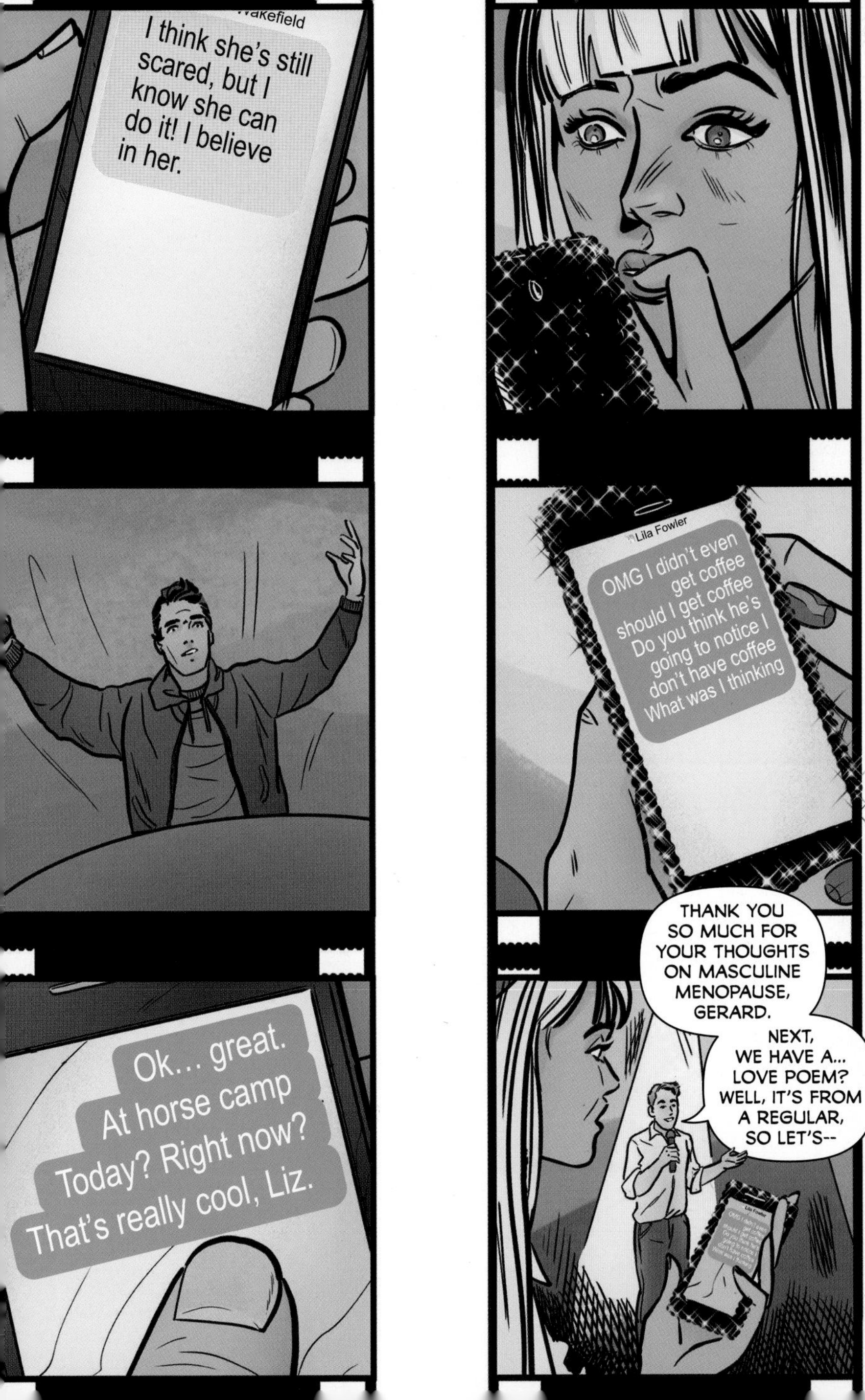
I think she's still scared, but I know she can do it! I believe in her.
Ok… great.
At horse camp
Today? Right now?
That's really cool, Liz.
Lila Fowler
OMG I didn't even get coffee
should I get coffee
Do you think he's going to notice I don't have coffee
What was I thinking
THANK YOU SO MUCH FOR YOUR THOUGHTS ON MASCULINE MENOPAUSE, GERARD.
NEXT, WE HAVE A... LOVE POEM? WELL, IT'S FROM A REGULAR, SO LET'S--

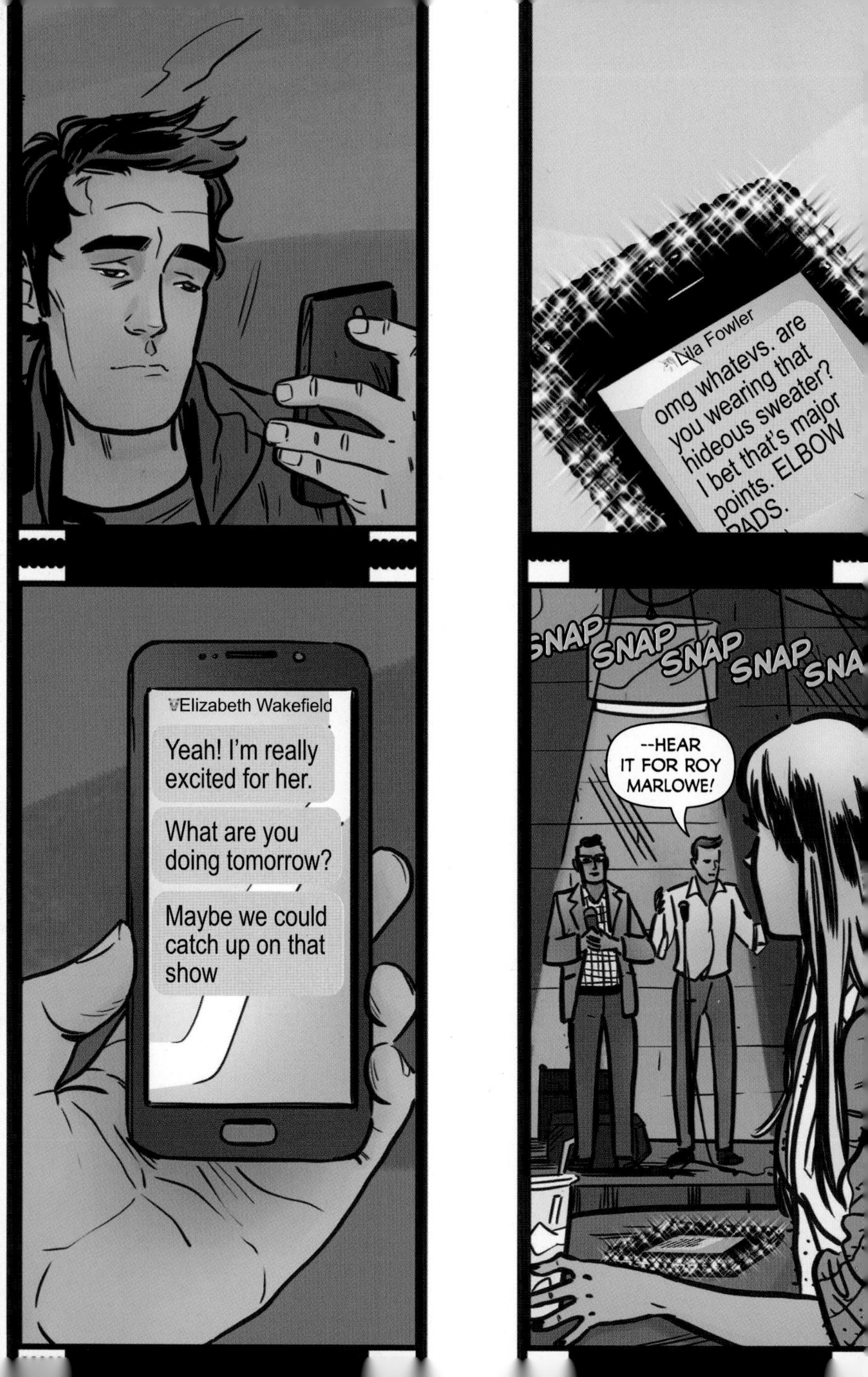
Elizabeth Wakefield
Yeah! I'm really excited for her.
What are you doing tomorrow?
Maybe we could catch up on that show
Lila Fowler
omg whatevs. are you wearing that hideous sweater? I bet that's major points. ELBOW PADS.
SNAP SNAP SNAP SNAP SNA
--HEAR IT FOR ROY MARLOWE!

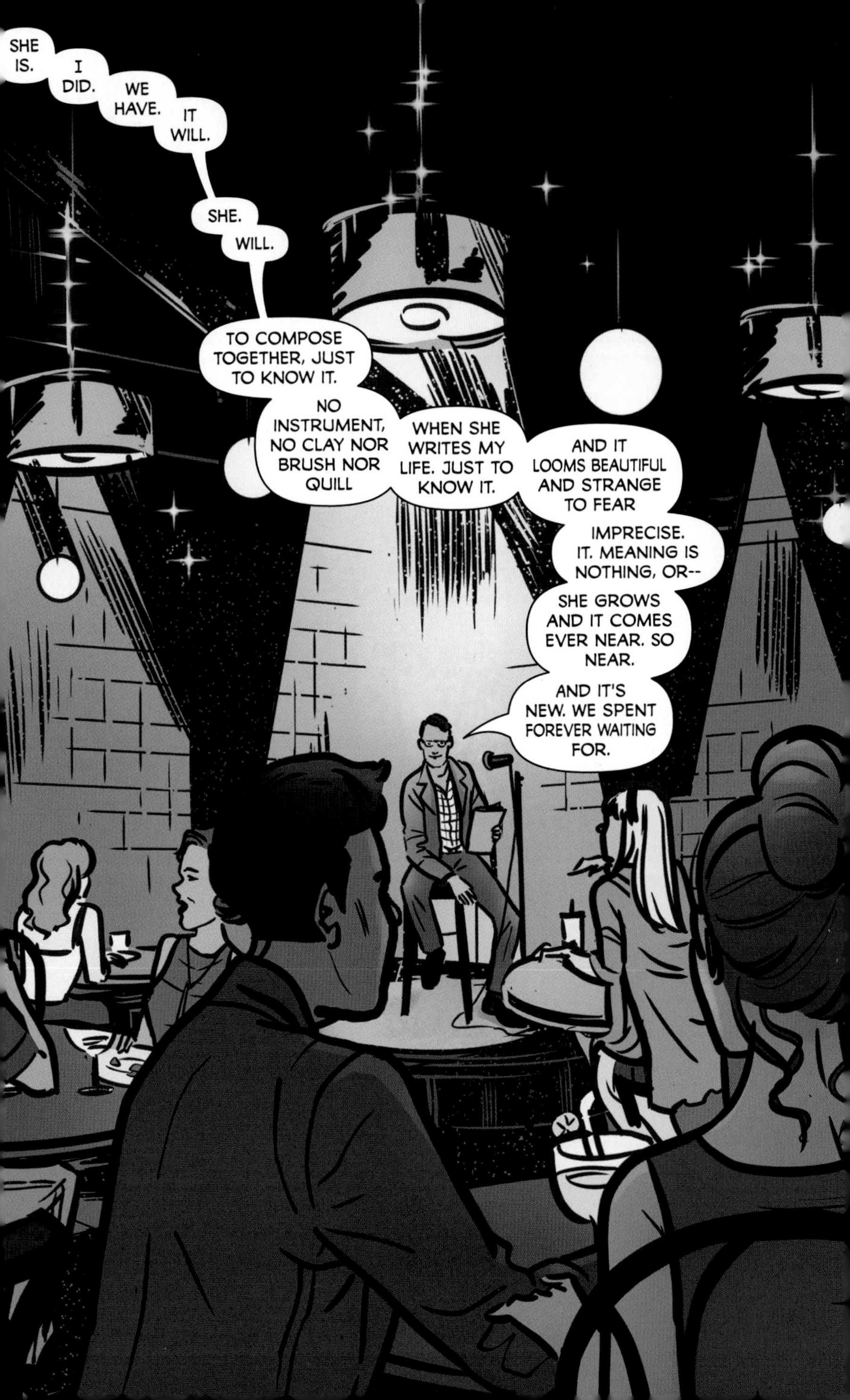
SHE IS.
I DID.
WE HAVE.
IT WILL.
SHE.
WILL.
TO COMPOSE TOGETHER, JUST TO KNOW IT.
NO INSTRUMENT, NO CLAY NOR BRUSH NOR QUILL
WHEN SHE WRITES MY LIFE. JUST TO KNOW IT.
AND IT LOOMS BEAUTIFUL AND STRANGE TO FEAR
IMPRECISE. IT. MEANING IS NOTHING, OR--
SHE GROWS AND IT COMES EVER NEAR. SO NEAR.
AND IT'S NEW. WE SPENT FOREVER WAITING FOR.

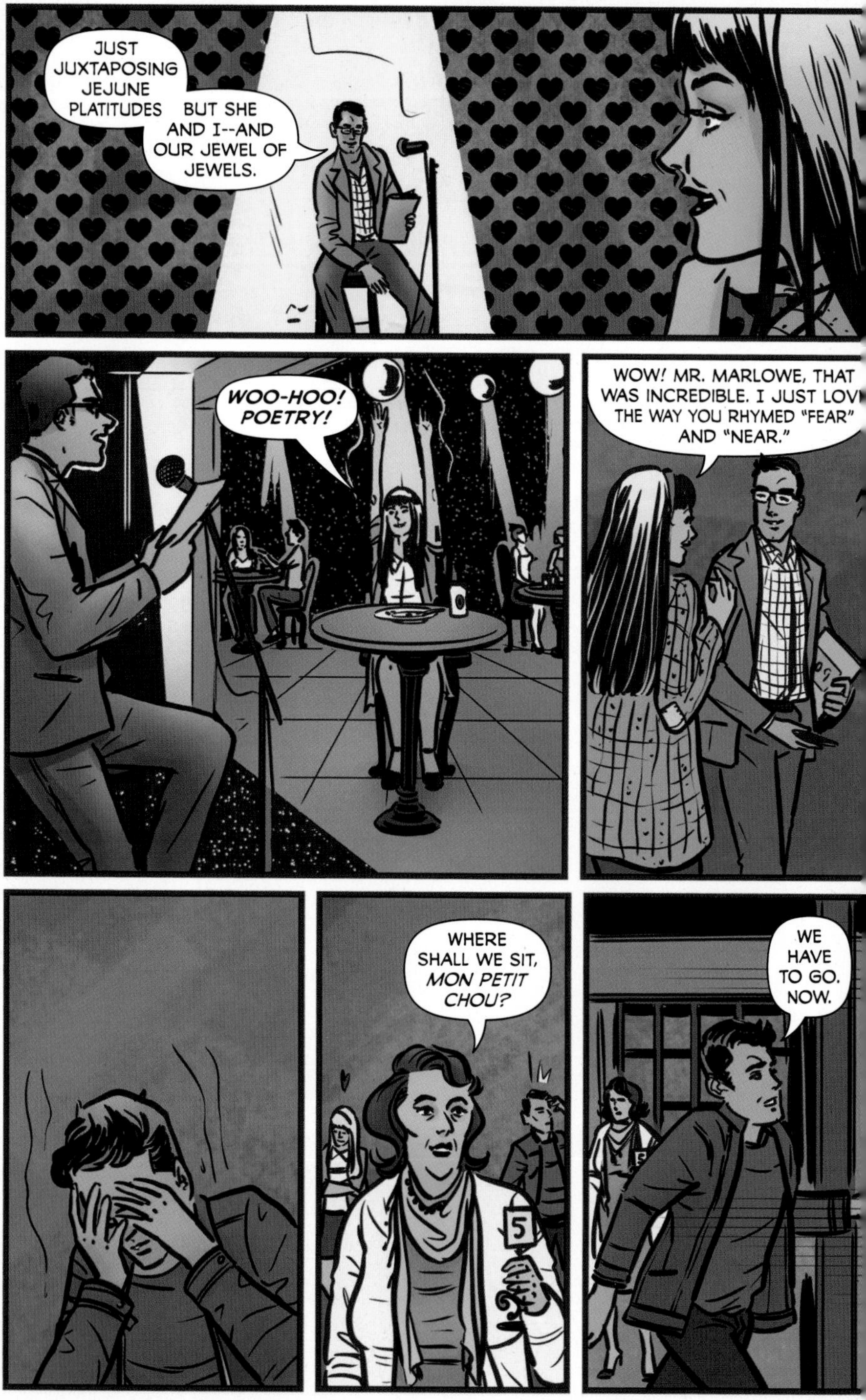
JUST JUXTAPOSING JEJUNE PLATITUDES
BUT SHE AND I--AND OUR JEWEL OF JEWELS.
WOO-HOO! POETRY!
WOW! MR. MARLOWE, THAT WAS INCREDIBLE. I JUST LOV
THE WAY YOU RHYMED "FEAR" AND "NEAR."
WHERE SHALL WE SIT, MON PETIT CHOU?
5
WE HAVE TO GO. NOW.

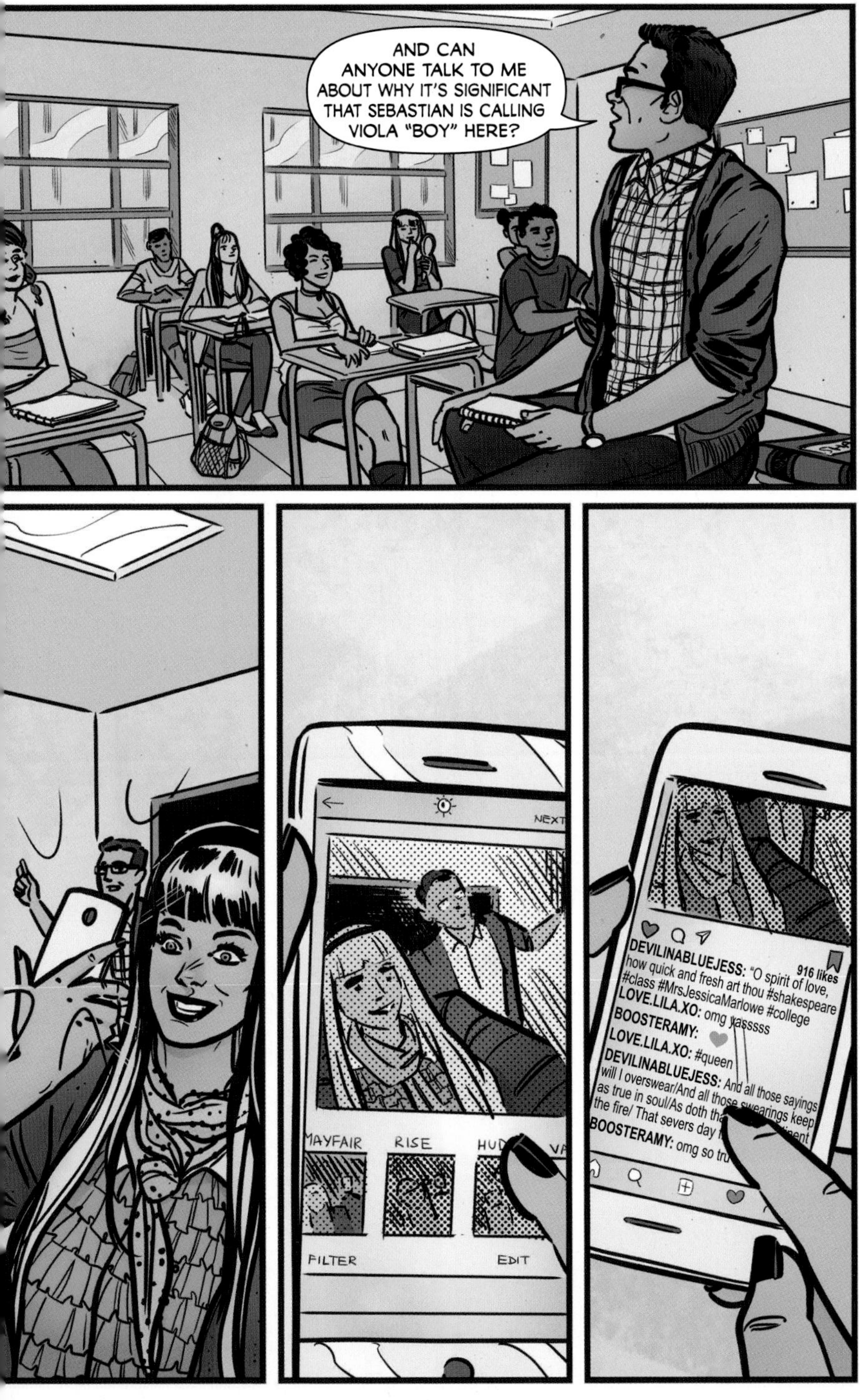
AND CAN ANYONE TALK TO ME ABOUT WHY IT'S SIGNIFICANT THAT SEBASTIAN IS CALLING VIOLA "BOY" HERE?
NEXT
MAYFAIR
RISE
FILTER
EDIT
DEVILINABLUEJESS: "O spirit of love, how quick and fresh art thou #shakespeare #class #MrsJessicaMarlowe #college
916 likes
LOVE.LILA.XO: omg yasssss
BOOSTERAMY:
LOVE.LILA.XO: #queen
DEVILINABLUEJESS: And all those sayings will I overswear/And all those swearings keep as true in soul/As doth tha
the fire/ That severs day
BOOSTERAMY: omg so tru

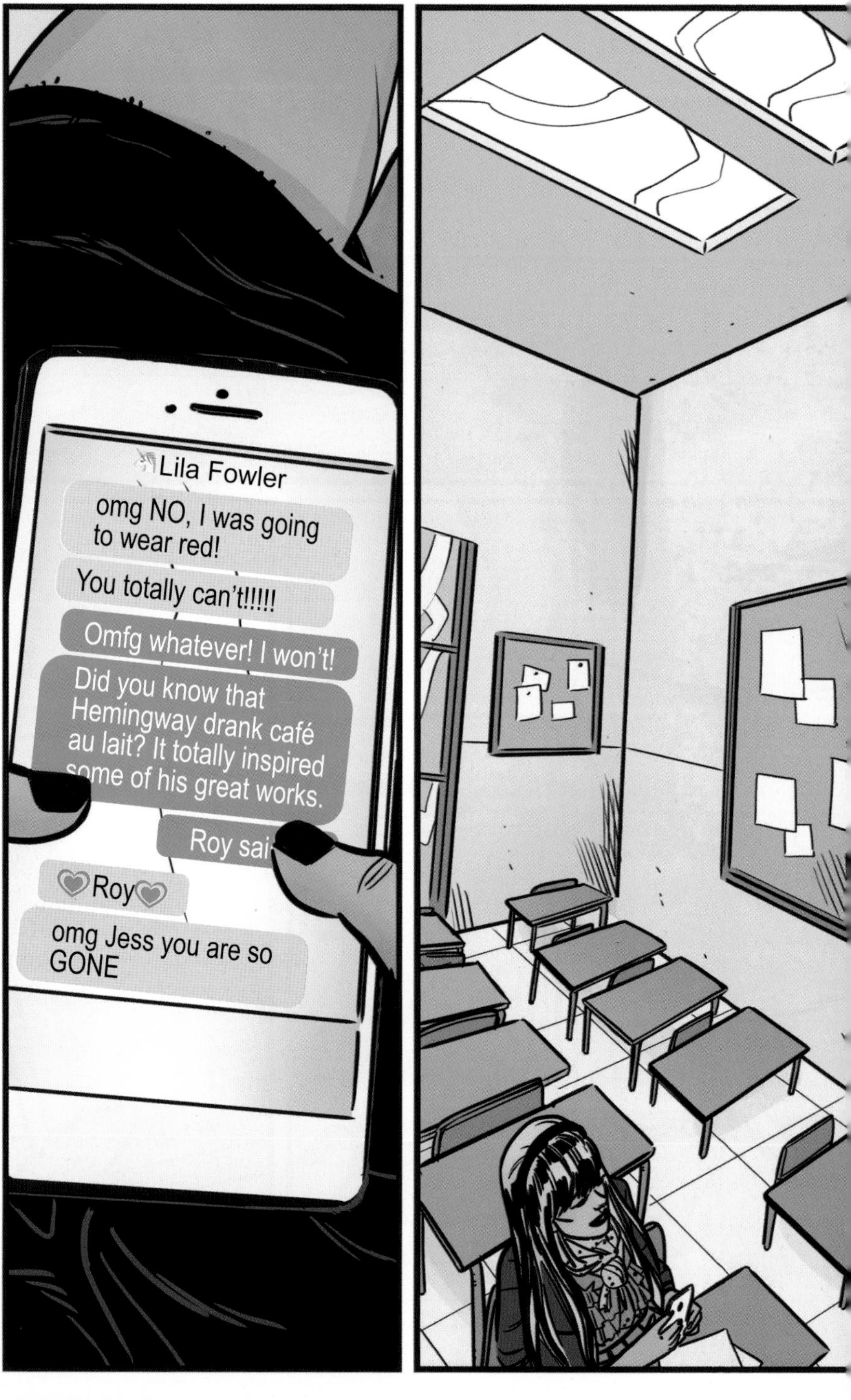
Lila Fowler
omg NO, I was going to wear red!
You totally can't!!!!!
Omfg whatever! I won't!
Did you know that Hemingway drank café au lait? It totally inspired some of his great works.
Roy sai
Roy
omg Jess you are so GONE

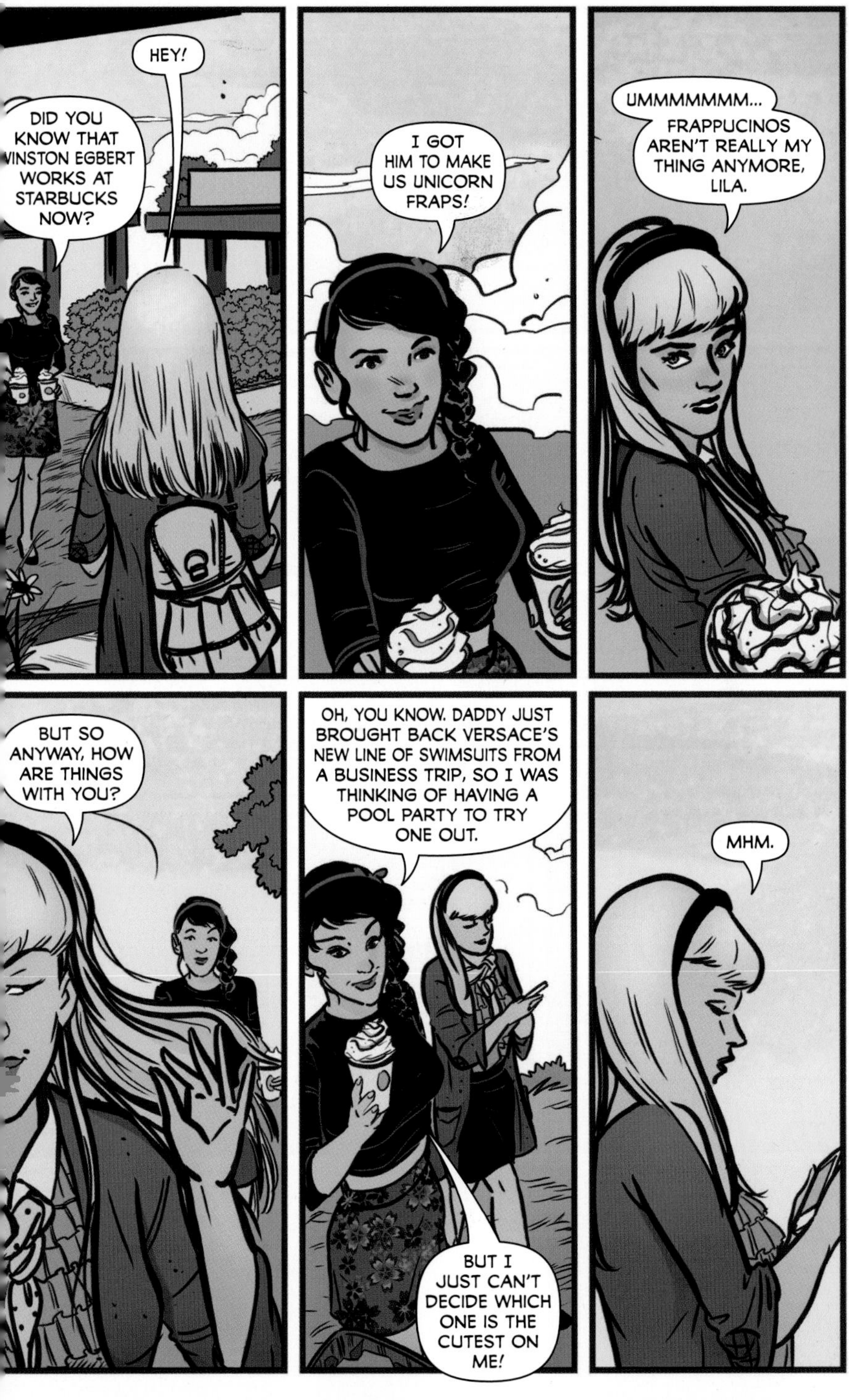
HEY!
DID YOU KNOW THAT VINSTON EGBERT WORKS AT STARBUCKS NOW?
I GOT HIM TO MAKE US UNICORN FRAPS!
UMMMMMMM...
FRAPPUCINOS AREN'T REALLY MY THING ANYMORE, LILA.
BUT SO ANYWAY, HOW ARE THINGS WITH YOU?
OH, YOU KNOW. DADDY JUST BROUGHT BACK VERSACE'S NEW LINE OF SWIMSUITS FROM A BUSINESS TRIP, SO I WAS THINKING OF HAVING A POOL PARTY TO TRY ONE OUT.
BUT I JUST CAN'T DECIDE WHICH ONE IS THE CUTEST ON ME!
MHM.

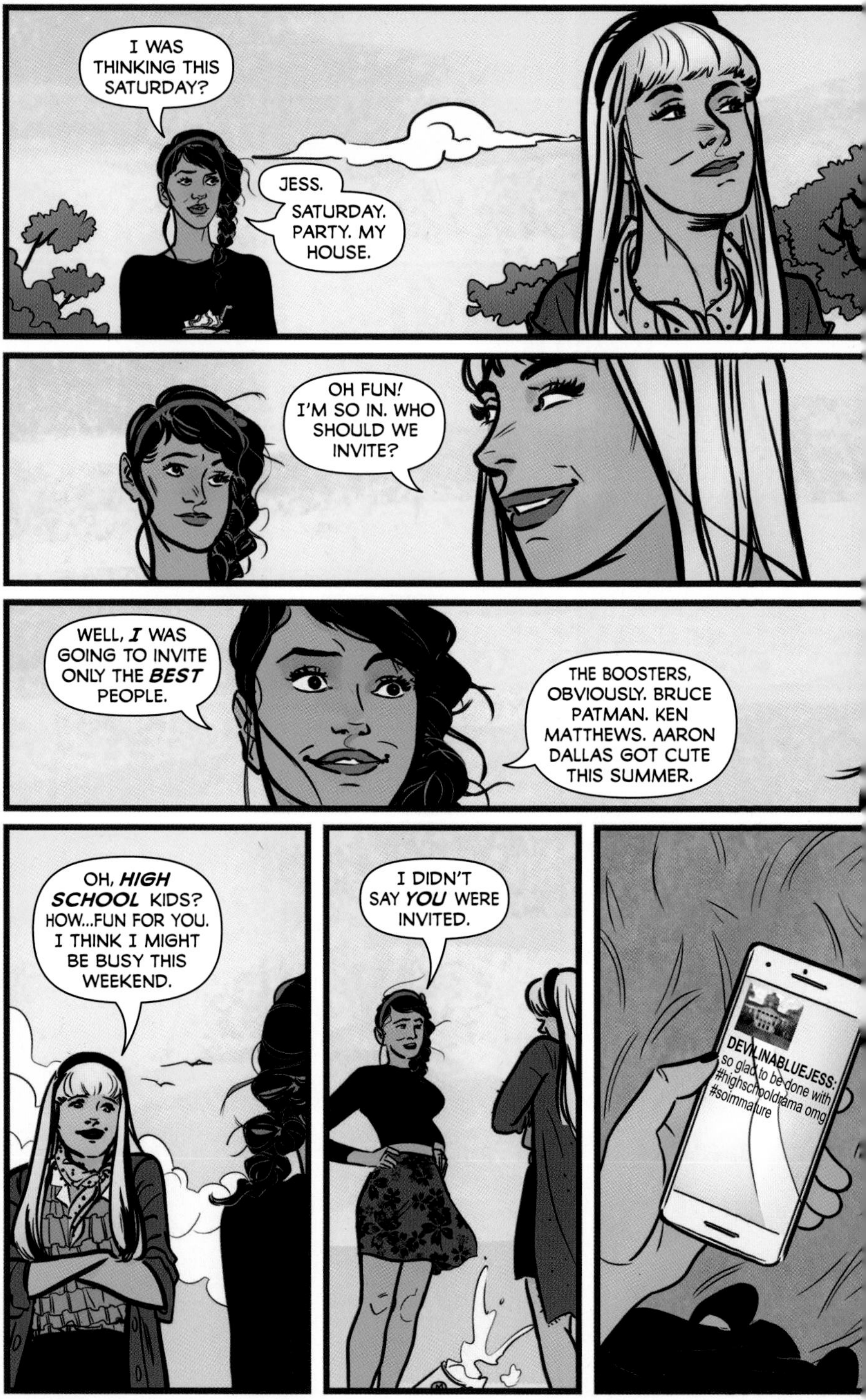
I WAS THINKING THIS SATURDAY?
JESS.
SATURDAY. PARTY. MY HOUSE.
OH FUN! I'M SO IN. WHO SHOULD WE INVITE?
WELL, *I* WAS GOING TO INVITE ONLY THE *BEST* PEOPLE.
THE BOOSTERS, OBVIOUSLY. BRUCE PATMAN. KEN MATTHEWS. AARON DALLAS GOT CUTE THIS SUMMER.
OH, *HIGH SCHOOL* KIDS? HOW...FUN FOR YOU. I THINK I MIGHT BE BUSY THIS WEEKEND.
I DIDN'T SAY *YOU* WERE INVITED.
DEVILINABLUEJESS:
so glad to be done with #highschooldrama omg #soimmature

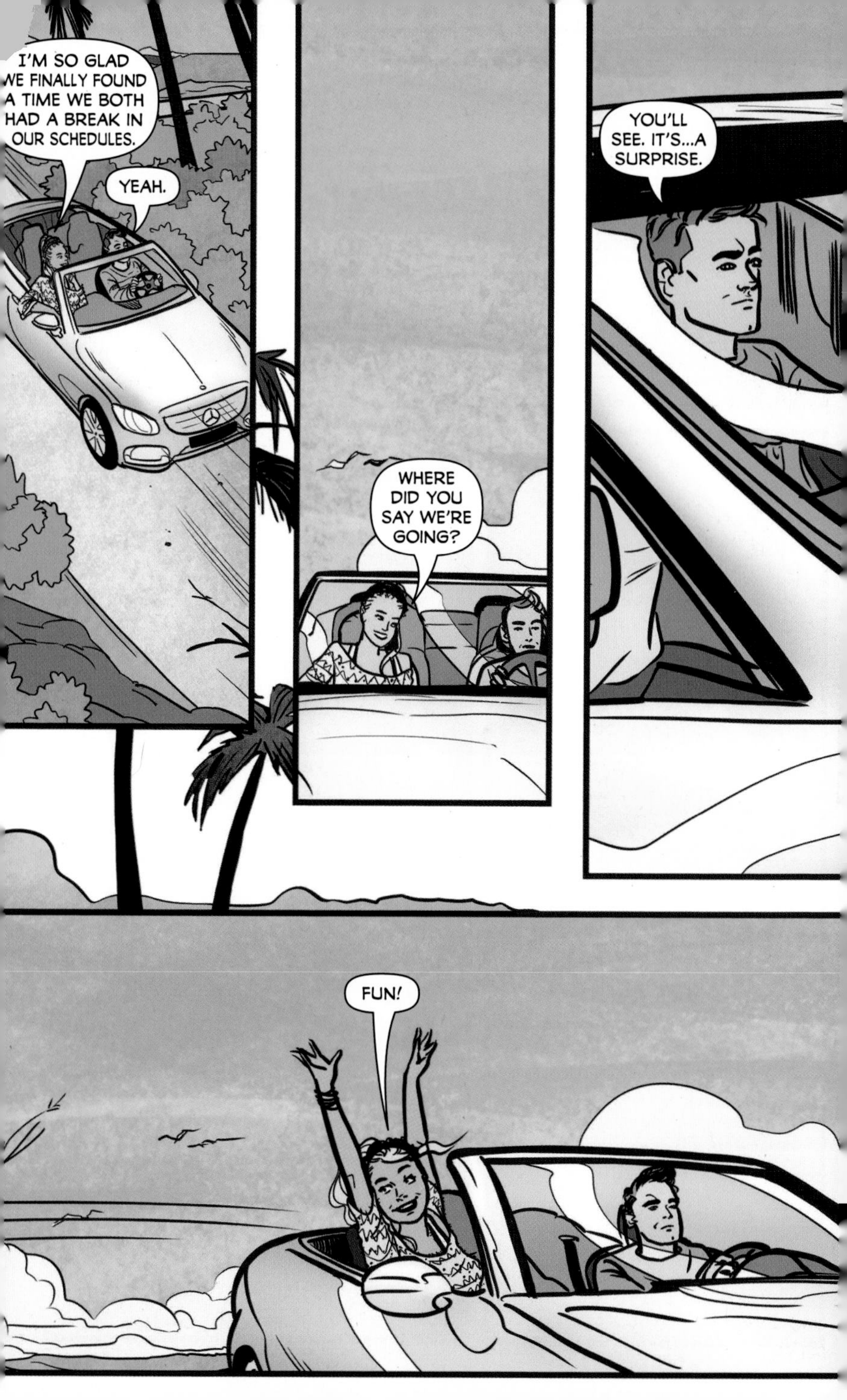
I'M SO GLAD WE FINALLY FOUND A TIME WE BOTH HAD A BREAK IN OUR SCHEDULES.
YEAH.
WHERE DID YOU SAY WE'RE GOING?
YOU'LL SEE. IT'S...A SURPRISE.
FUN!

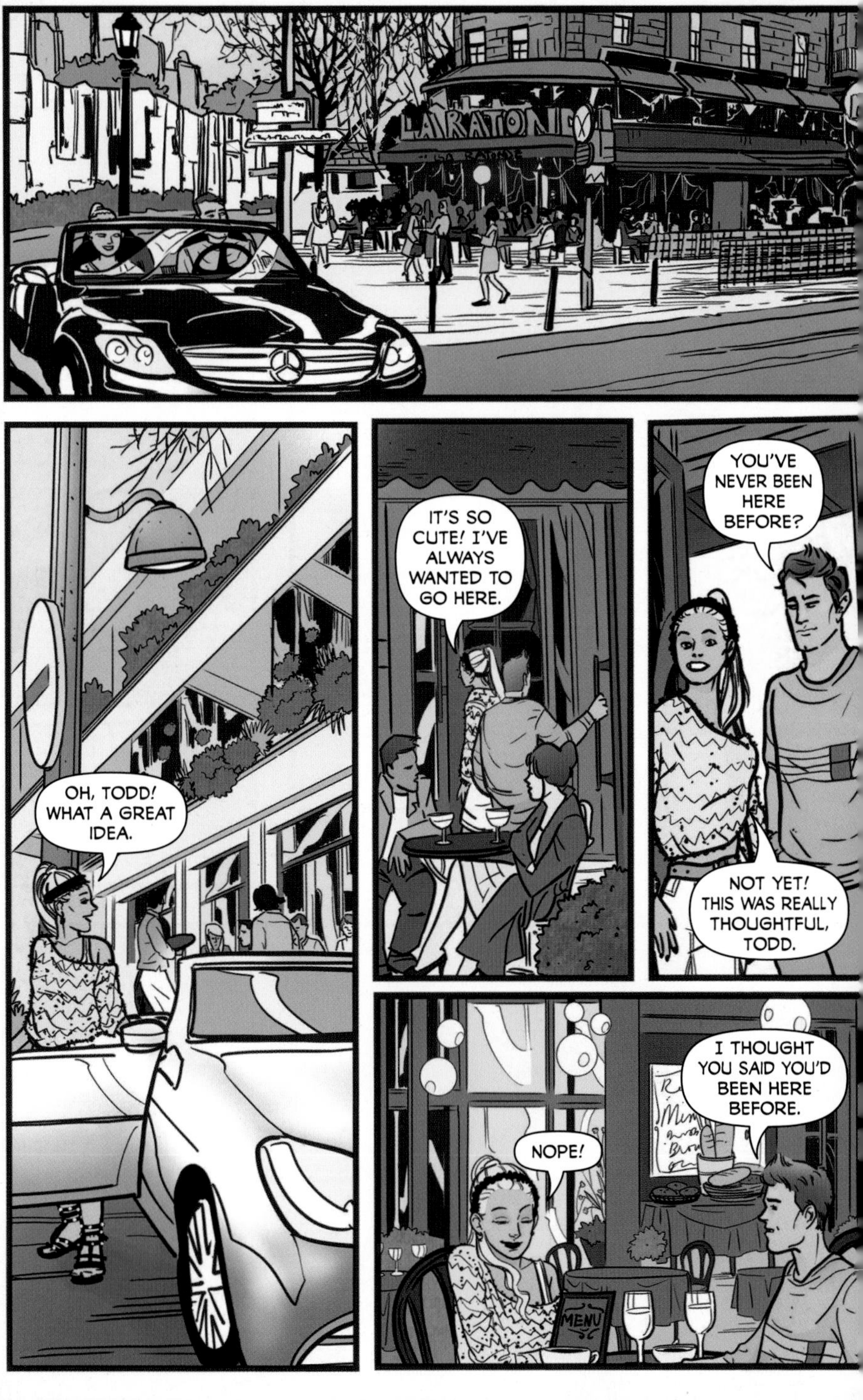
LA RATONDE
OH, TODD! WHAT A GREAT IDEA.
IT'S SO CUTE! I'VE ALWAYS WANTED TO GO HERE.
YOU'VE NEVER BEEN HERE BEFORE?
NOT YET! THIS WAS REALLY THOUGHTFUL, TODD.
I THOUGHT YOU SAID YOU'D BEEN HERE BEFORE.
NOPE!
MENU

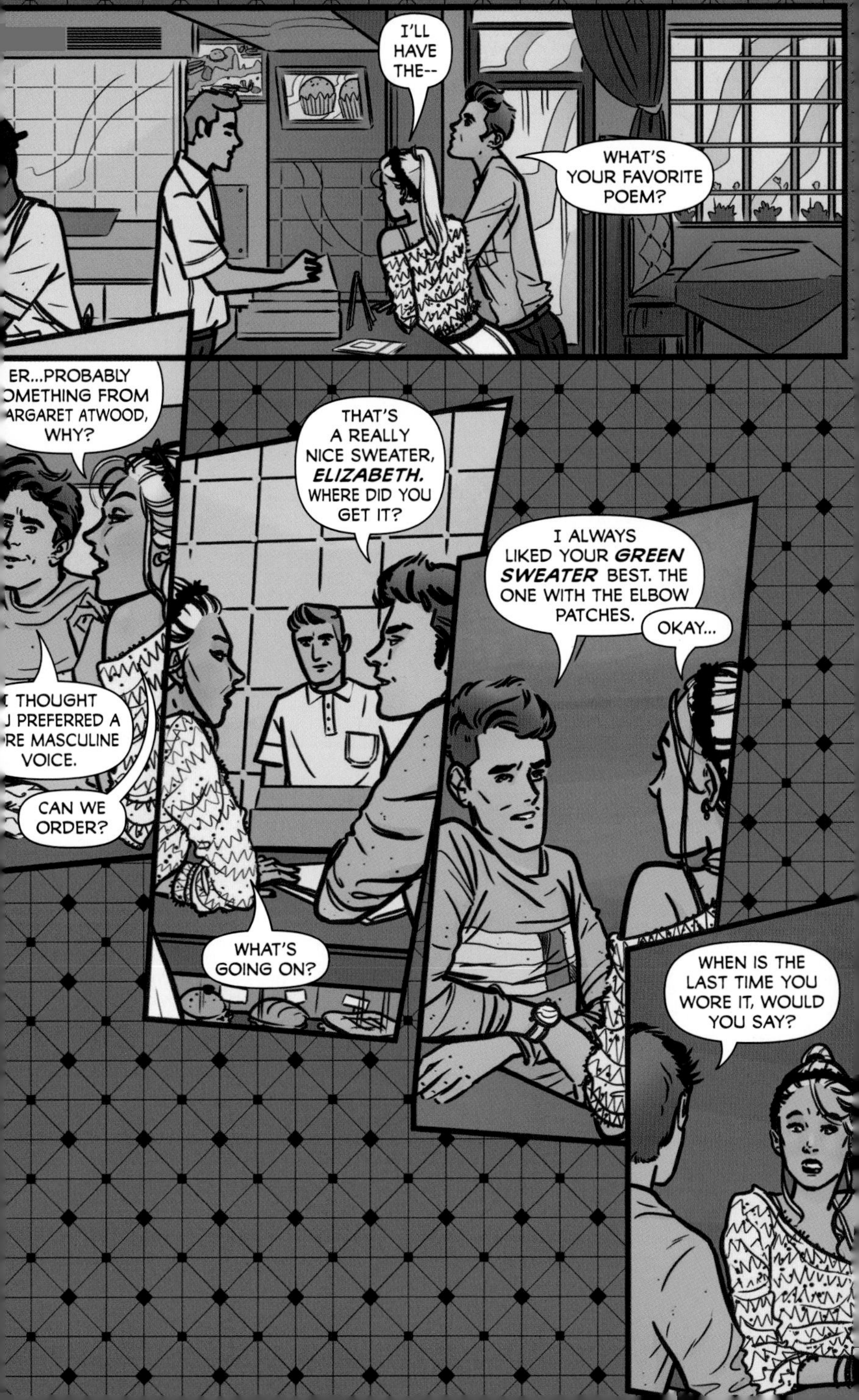
I'LL HAVE THE--
WHAT'S YOUR FAVORITE POEM?
ER...PROBABLY OMETHING FROM ARGARET ATWOOD, WHY?
THAT'S A REALLY NICE SWEATER, *ELIZABETH.* WHERE DID YOU GET IT?
I ALWAYS LIKED YOUR *GREEN SWEATER* BEST. THE ONE WITH THE ELBOW PATCHES.
OKAY...
I THOUGHT U PREFERRED A RE MASCULINE VOICE.
CAN WE ORDER?
WHAT'S GOING ON?
WHEN IS THE LAST TIME YOU WORE IT, WOULD YOU SAY?

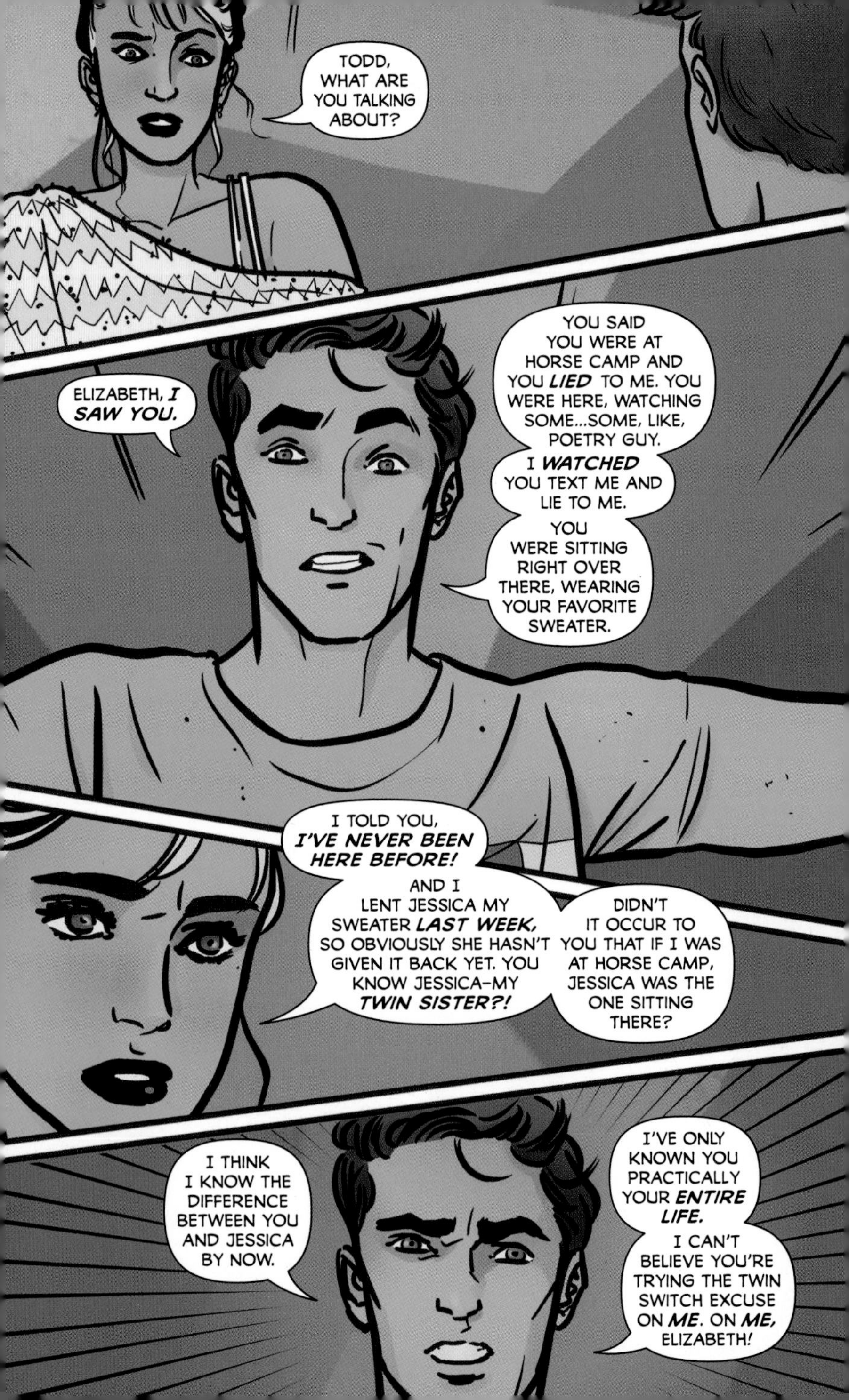
TODD, WHAT ARE YOU TALKING ABOUT?
ELIZABETH, I SAW YOU.
YOU SAID YOU WERE AT HORSE CAMP AND YOU LIED TO ME. YOU WERE HERE, WATCHING SOME...SOME, LIKE, POETRY GUY.
I WATCHED YOU TEXT ME AND LIE TO ME.
YOU WERE SITTING RIGHT OVER THERE, WEARING YOUR FAVORITE SWEATER.
I TOLD YOU, I'VE NEVER BEEN HERE BEFORE!
AND I LENT JESSICA MY SWEATER LAST WEEK, SO OBVIOUSLY SHE HASN'T GIVEN IT BACK YET. YOU KNOW JESSICA–MY TWIN SISTER?!
DIDN'T IT OCCUR TO YOU THAT IF I WAS AT HORSE CAMP, JESSICA WAS THE ONE SITTING THERE?
I THINK I KNOW THE DIFFERENCE BETWEEN YOU AND JESSICA BY NOW.
I'VE ONLY KNOWN YOU PRACTICALLY YOUR ENTIRE LIFE.
I CAN'T BELIEVE YOU'RE TRYING THE TWIN SWITCH EXCUSE ON ME. ON ME, ELIZABETH!

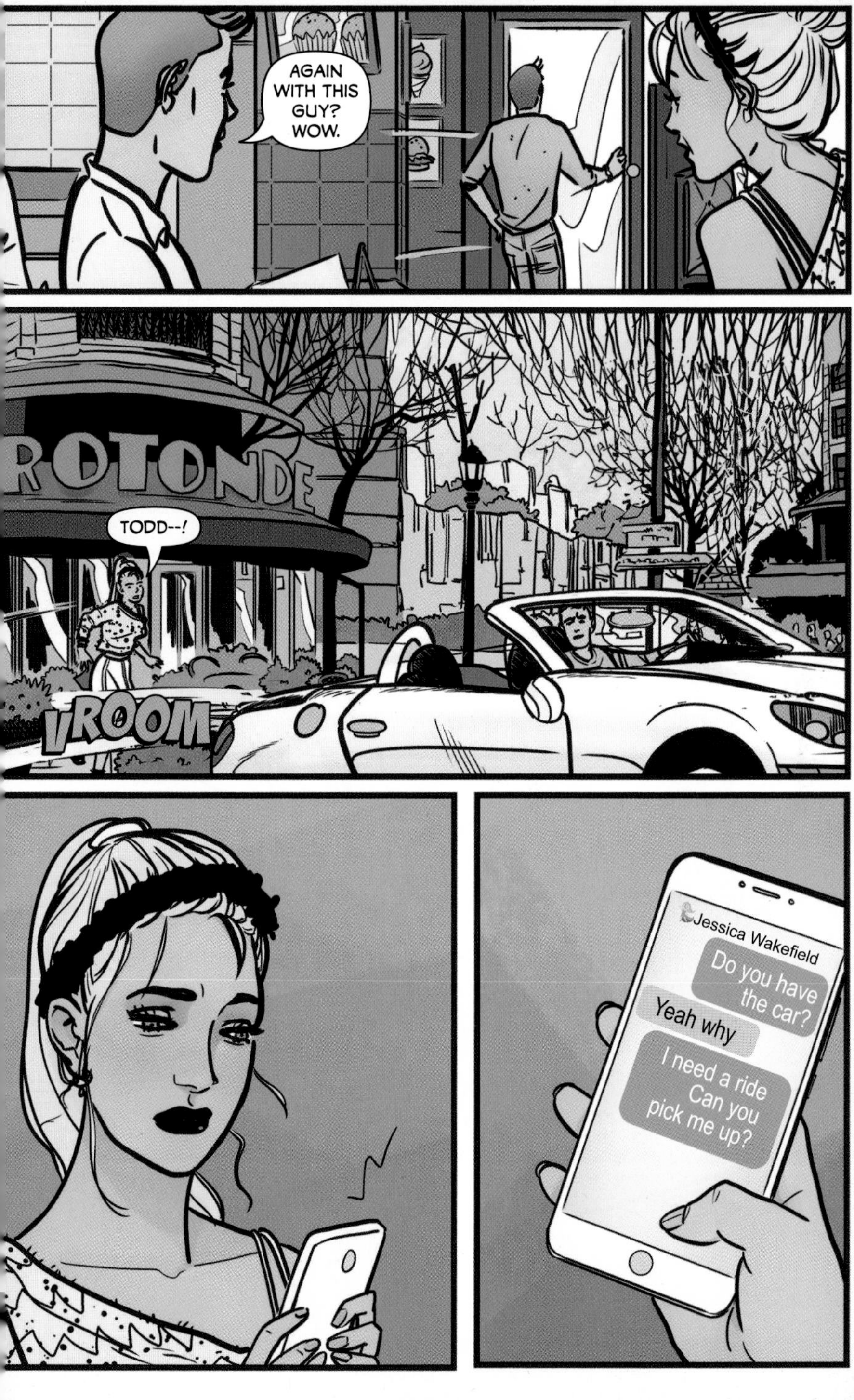
AGAIN WITH THIS GUY? WOW.
ROTONDE
TODD--!
VROOM
Jessica Wakefield
Do you have the car?
Yeah why
I need a ride Can you pick me up?

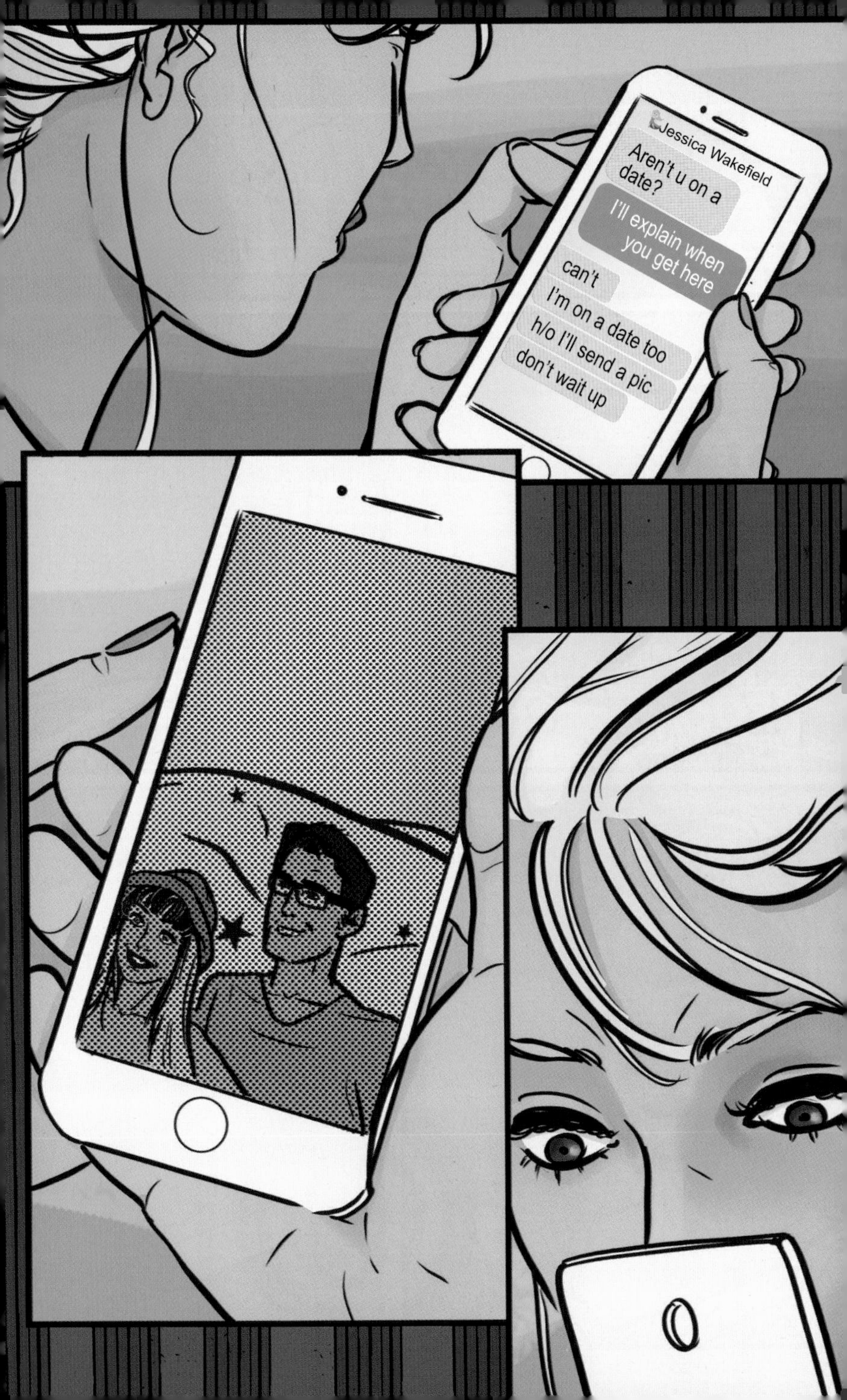

Jessica Wakefield
Aren't u on a date?
I'll explain when you get here
can't
I'm on a date too
h/o I'll send a pic
don't wait up

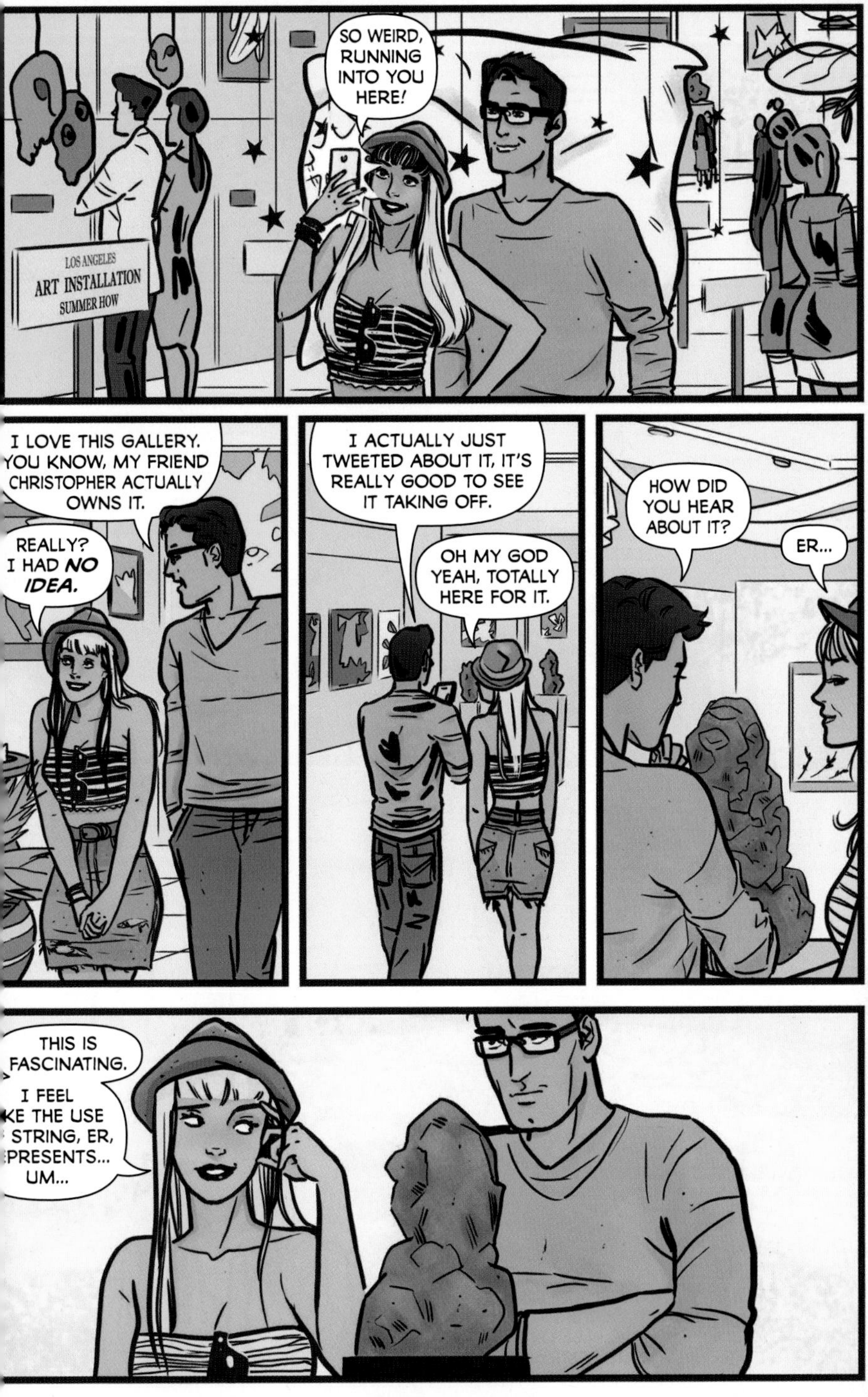
SO WEIRD, RUNNING INTO YOU HERE!
LOS ANGELES
ART INSTALLATION
SUMMER HOW
I LOVE THIS GALLERY. YOU KNOW, MY FRIEND CHRISTOPHER ACTUALLY OWNS IT.
REALLY? I HAD NO IDEA.
I ACTUALLY JUST TWEETED ABOUT IT, IT'S REALLY GOOD TO SEE IT TAKING OFF.
OH MY GOD YEAH, TOTALLY HERE FOR IT.
HOW DID YOU HEAR ABOUT IT?
ER...
THIS IS FASCINATING.
I FEEL
KE THE USE
STRING, ER,
PRESENTS...
UM...

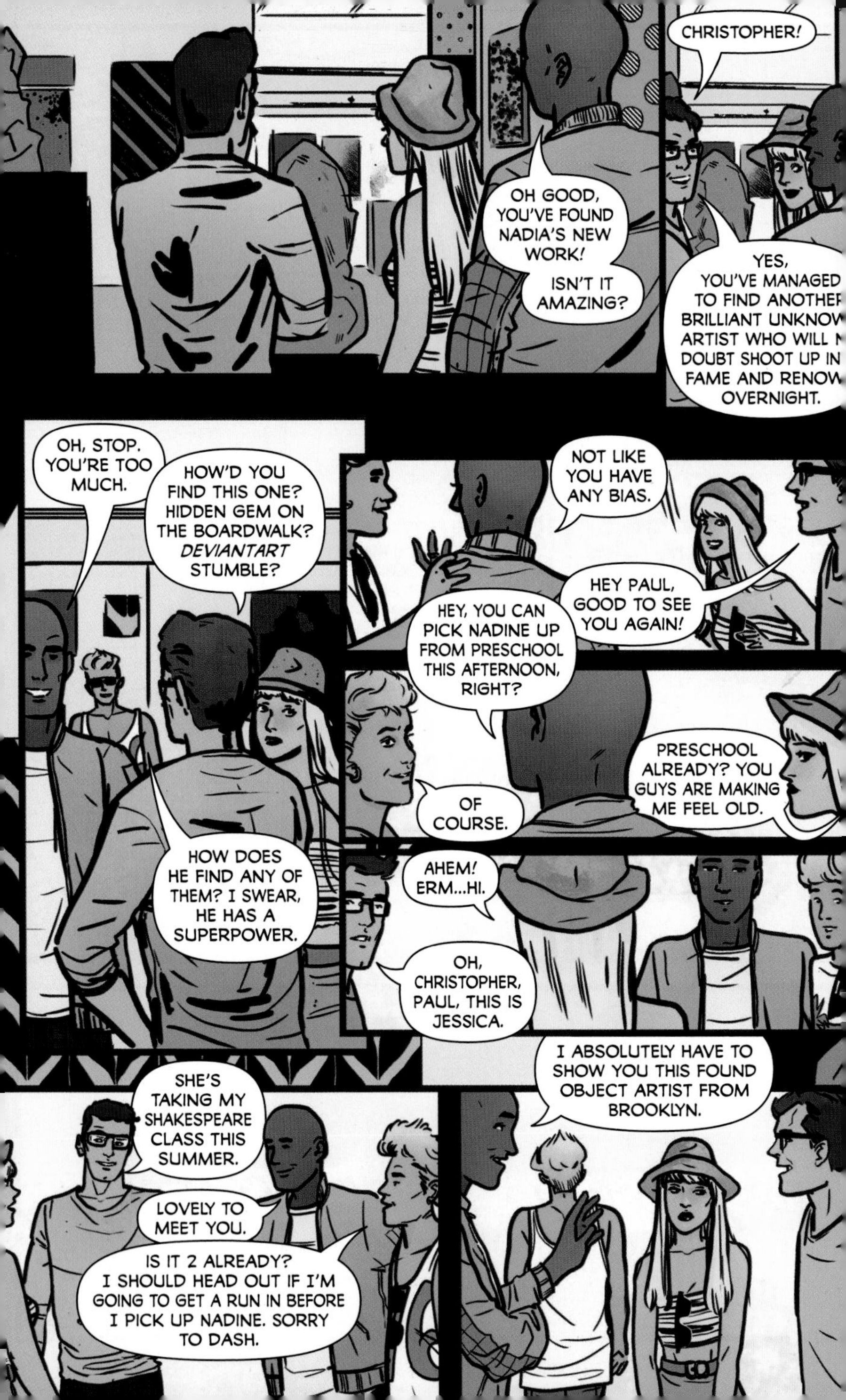
CHRISTOPHER!
OH GOOD, YOU'VE FOUND NADIA'S NEW WORK!
ISN'T IT AMAZING?
YES, YOU'VE MANAGED TO FIND ANOTHER BRILLIANT UNKNOWN ARTIST WHO WILL NO DOUBT SHOOT UP IN FAME AND RENOWN OVERNIGHT.
OH, STOP. YOU'RE TOO MUCH.
HOW'D YOU FIND THIS ONE? HIDDEN GEM ON THE BOARDWALK? *DEVIANTART* STUMBLE?
HOW DOES HE FIND ANY OF THEM? I SWEAR, HE HAS A SUPERPOWER.
NOT LIKE YOU HAVE ANY BIAS.
HEY PAUL, GOOD TO SEE YOU AGAIN!
HEY, YOU CAN PICK NADINE UP FROM PRESCHOOL THIS AFTERNOON, RIGHT?
OF COURSE.
PRESCHOOL ALREADY? YOU GUYS ARE MAKING ME FEEL OLD.
AHEM! ERM...HI.
OH, CHRISTOPHER, PAUL, THIS IS JESSICA.
SHE'S TAKING MY SHAKESPEARE CLASS THIS SUMMER.
LOVELY TO MEET YOU.
IS IT 2 ALREADY? I SHOULD HEAD OUT IF I'M GOING TO GET A RUN IN BEFORE I PICK UP NADINE. SORRY TO DASH.
I ABSOLUTELY HAVE TO SHOW YOU THIS FOUND OBJECT ARTIST FROM BROOKLYN.

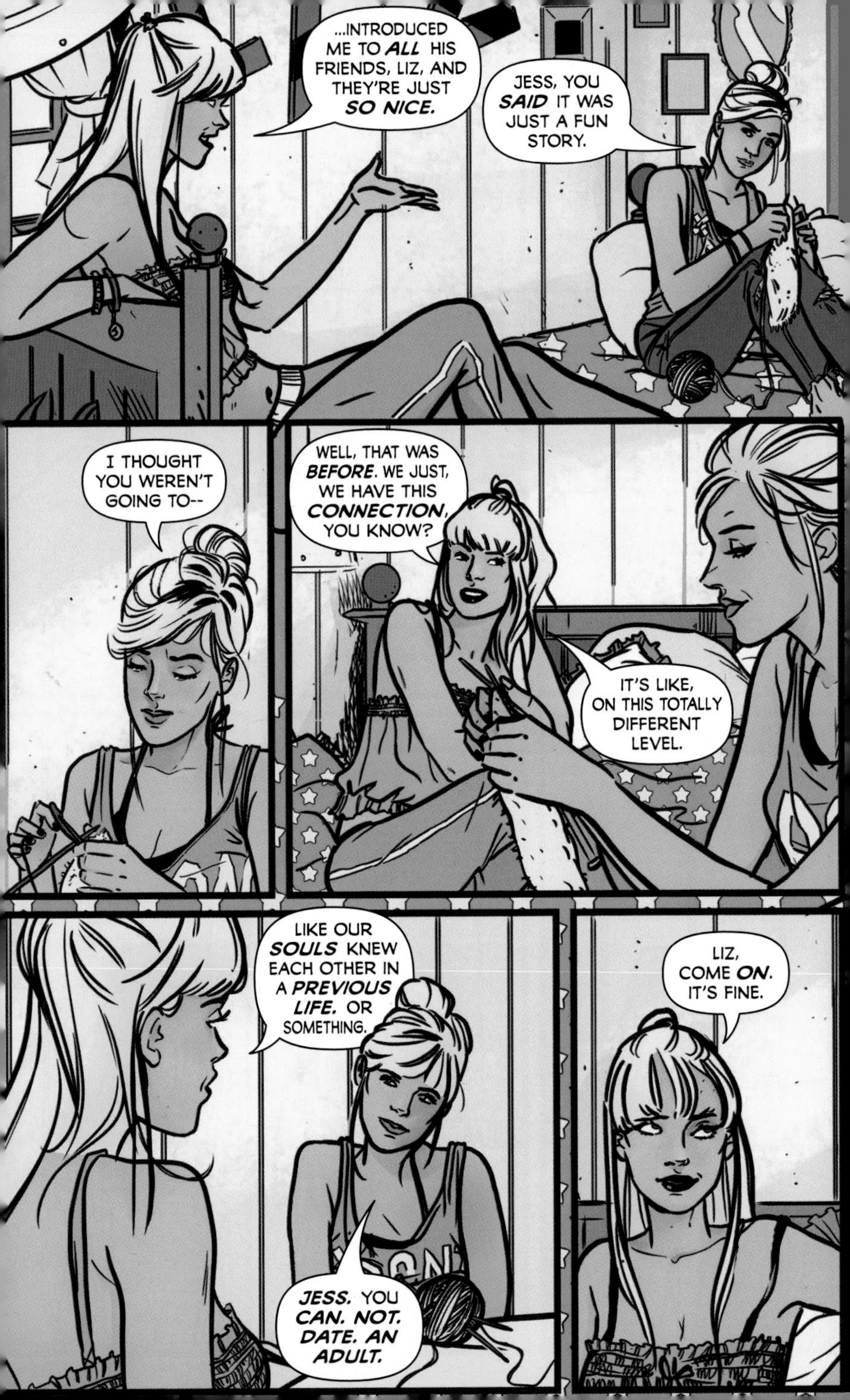
...INTRODUCED ME TO ALL HIS FRIENDS, LIZ, AND THEY'RE JUST SO NICE.
JESS, YOU SAID IT WAS JUST A FUN STORY.
I THOUGHT YOU WEREN'T GOING TO--
WELL, THAT WAS BEFORE. WE JUST, WE HAVE THIS CONNECTION, YOU KNOW?
IT'S LIKE, ON THIS TOTALLY DIFFERENT LEVEL.
LIKE OUR SOULS KNEW EACH OTHER IN A PREVIOUS LIFE. OR SOMETHING.
JESS. YOU CAN. NOT. DATE. AN ADULT.
LIZ, COME ON. IT'S FINE.

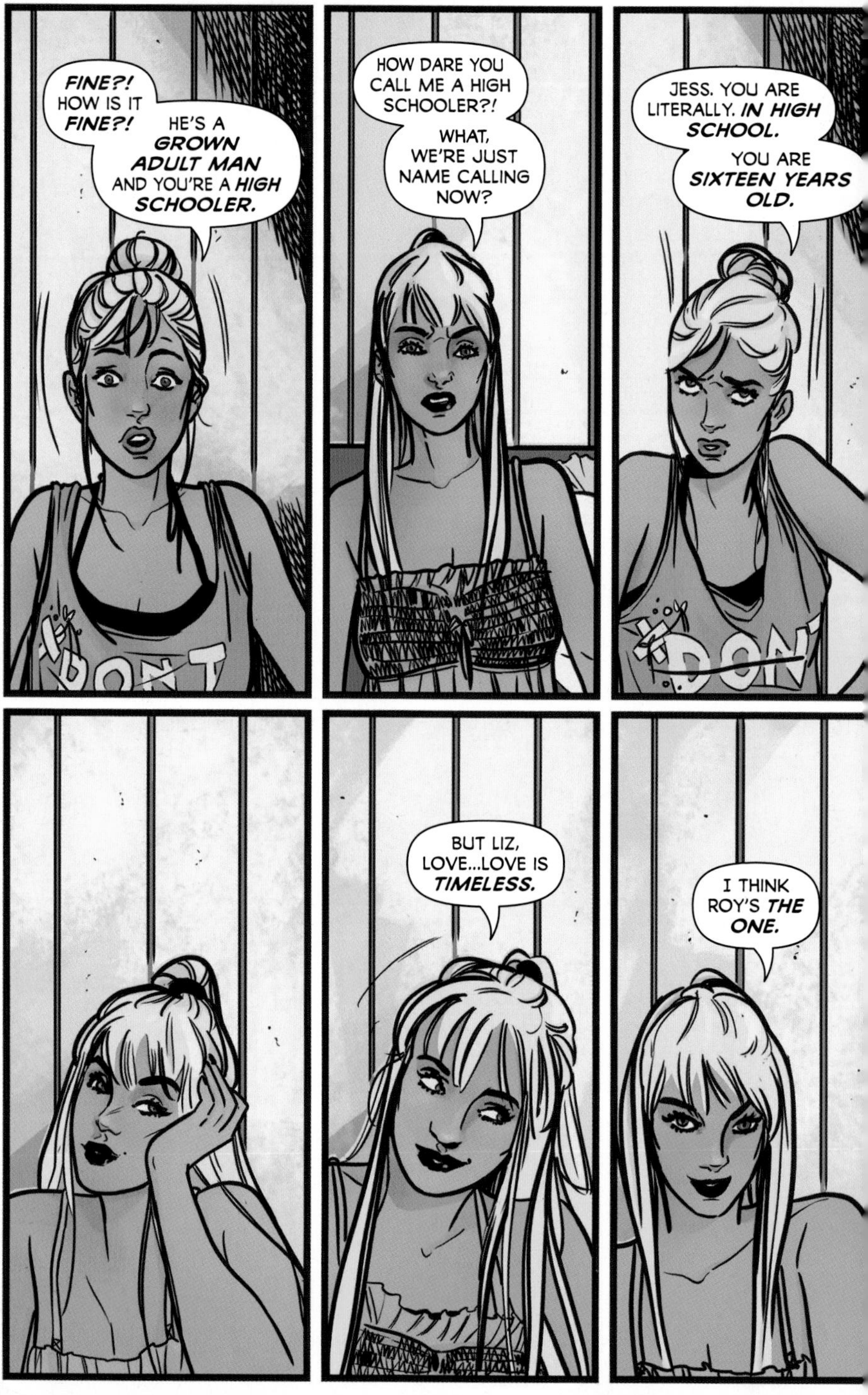
FINE?! HOW IS IT FINE?!
HE'S A GROWN ADULT MAN AND YOU'RE A HIGH SCHOOLER.
HOW DARE YOU CALL ME A HIGH SCHOOLER?!
WHAT, WE'RE JUST NAME CALLING NOW?
JESS. YOU ARE LITERALLY. IN HIGH SCHOOL.
YOU ARE SIXTEEN YEARS OLD.
DON'T
BUT LIZ, LOVE...LOVE IS TIMELESS.
I THINK ROY'S THE ONE.

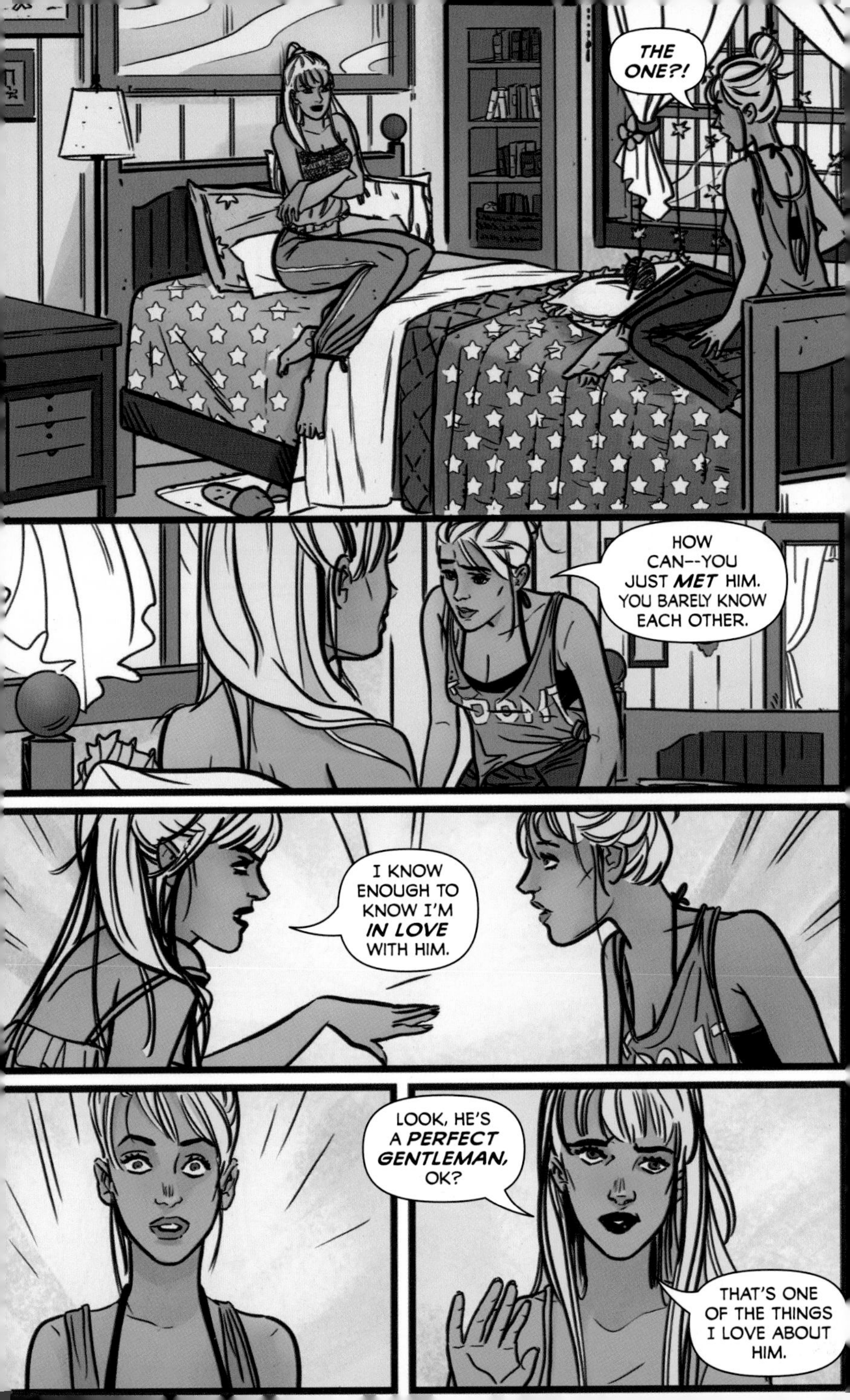
THE ONE?!
HOW CAN--YOU JUST MET HIM. YOU BARELY KNOW EACH OTHER.
I KNOW ENOUGH TO KNOW I'M IN LOVE WITH HIM.
LOOK, HE'S A PERFECT GENTLEMAN, OK?
THAT'S ONE OF THE THINGS I LOVE ABOUT HIM.

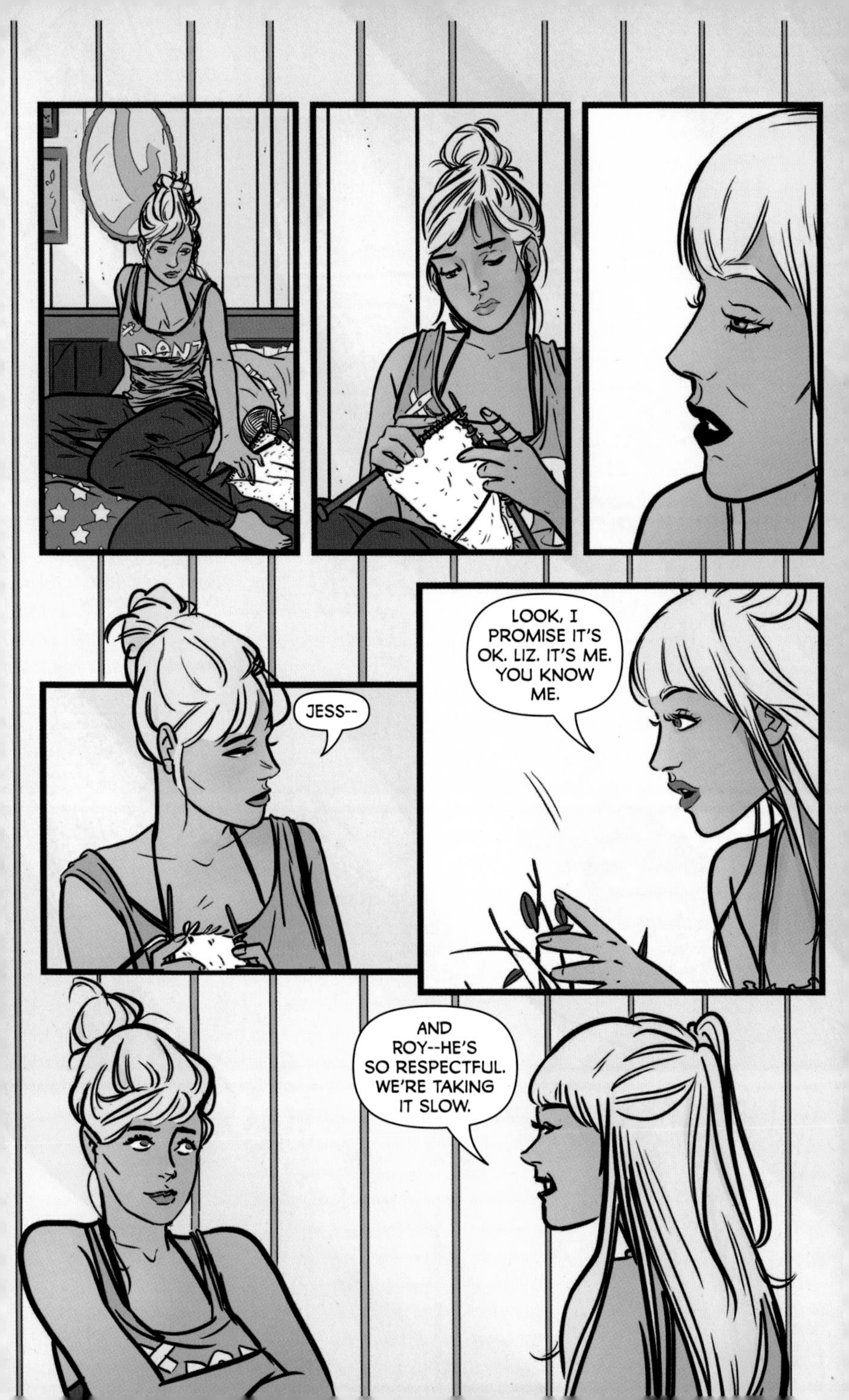
JESS--
LOOK, I PROMISE IT'S OK. LIZ. IT'S ME. YOU KNOW ME.
AND ROY--HE'S SO RESPECTFUL. WE'RE TAKING IT SLOW.

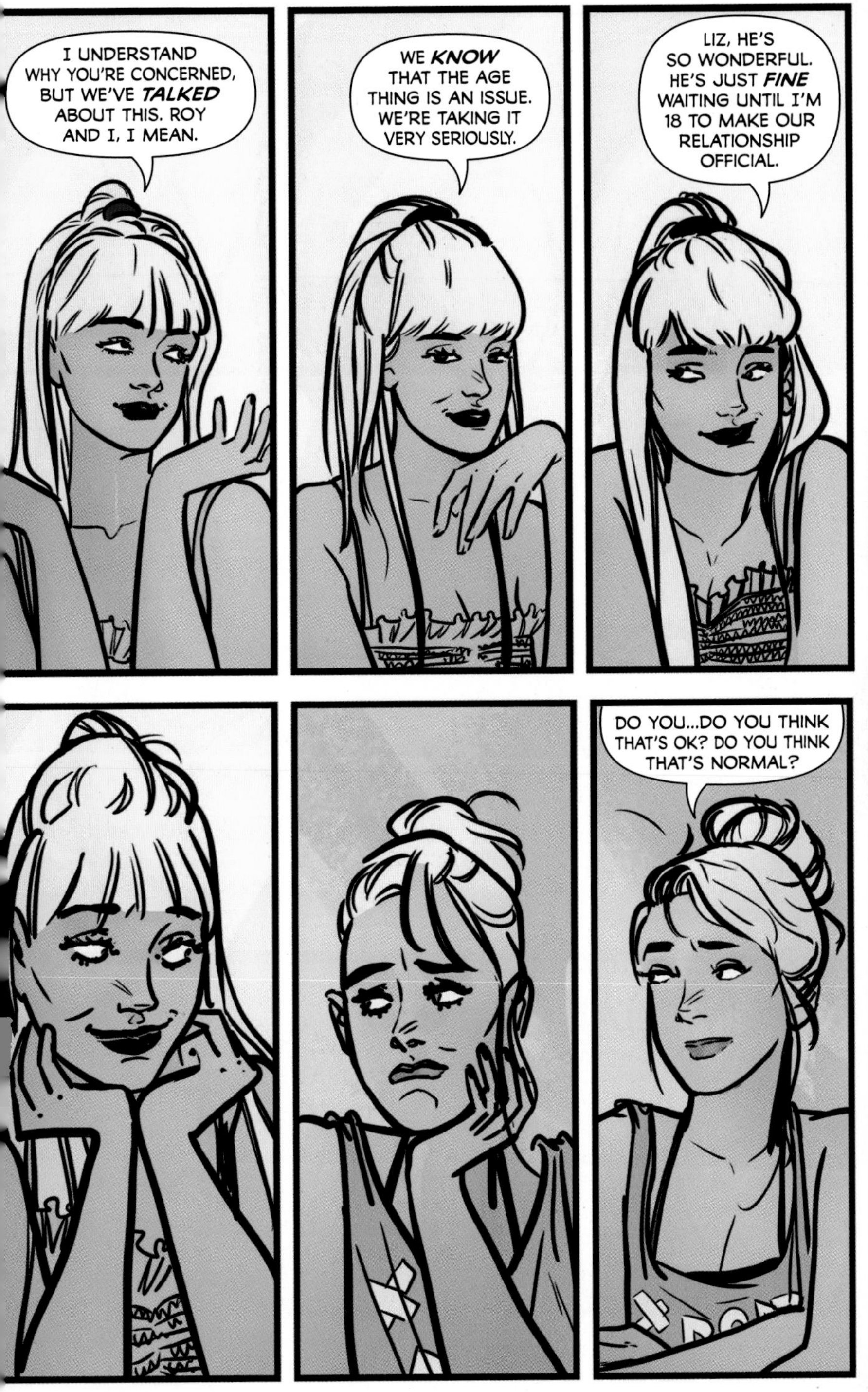
I UNDERSTAND WHY YOU'RE CONCERNED, BUT WE'VE *TALKED* ABOUT THIS. ROY AND I, I MEAN.
WE *KNOW* THAT THE AGE THING IS AN ISSUE. WE'RE TAKING IT VERY SERIOUSLY.
LIZ, HE'S SO WONDERFUL. HE'S JUST *FINE* WAITING UNTIL I'M 18 TO MAKE OUR RELATIONSHIP OFFICIAL.
DO YOU...DO YOU THINK THAT'S OK? DO YOU THINK THAT'S NORMAL?

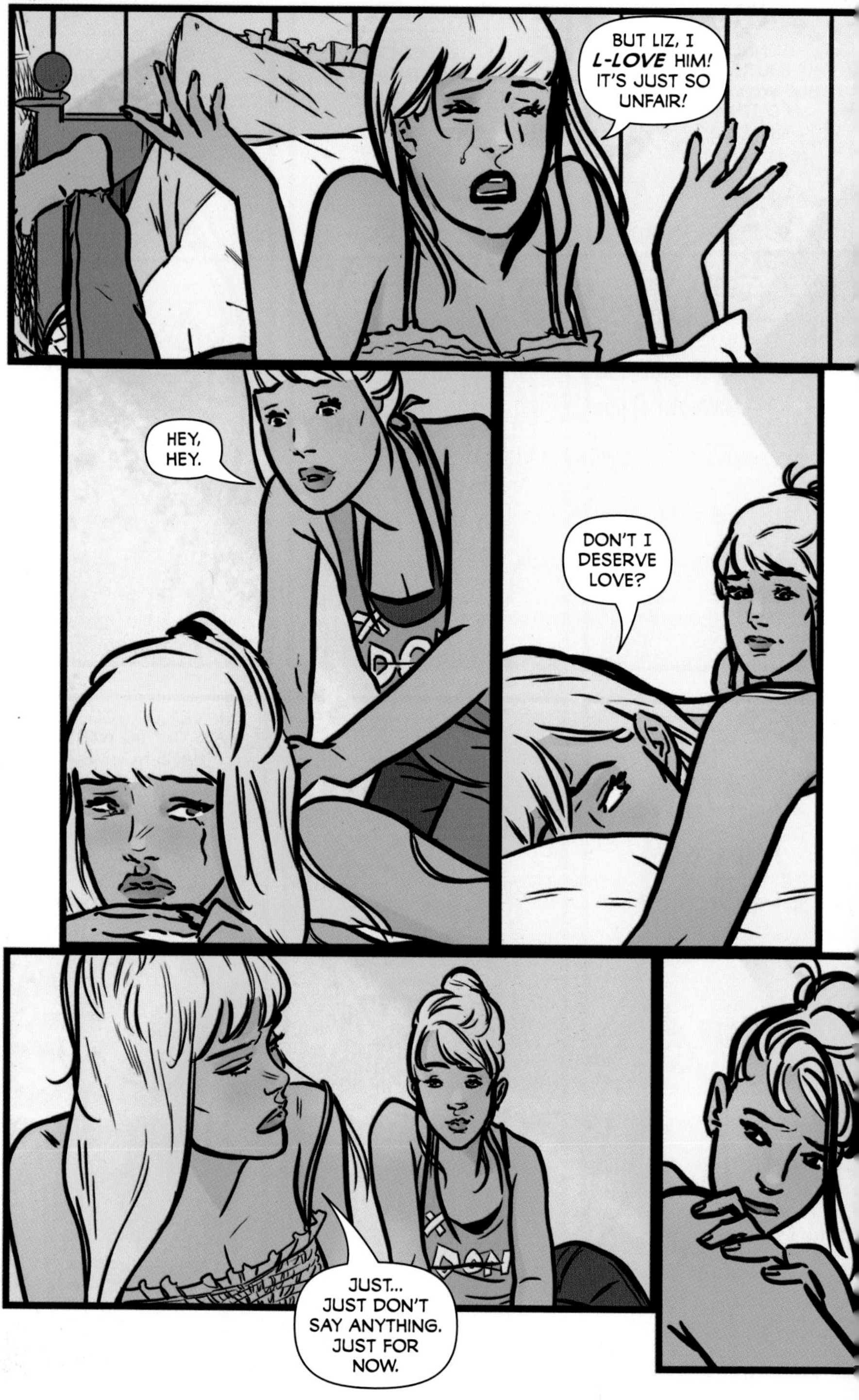
BUT LIZ, I **L-LOVE** HIM! IT'S JUST SO UNFAIR!
HEY, HEY.
DON'T I DESERVE LOVE?
JUST... JUST DON'T SAY ANYTHING. JUST FOR NOW.

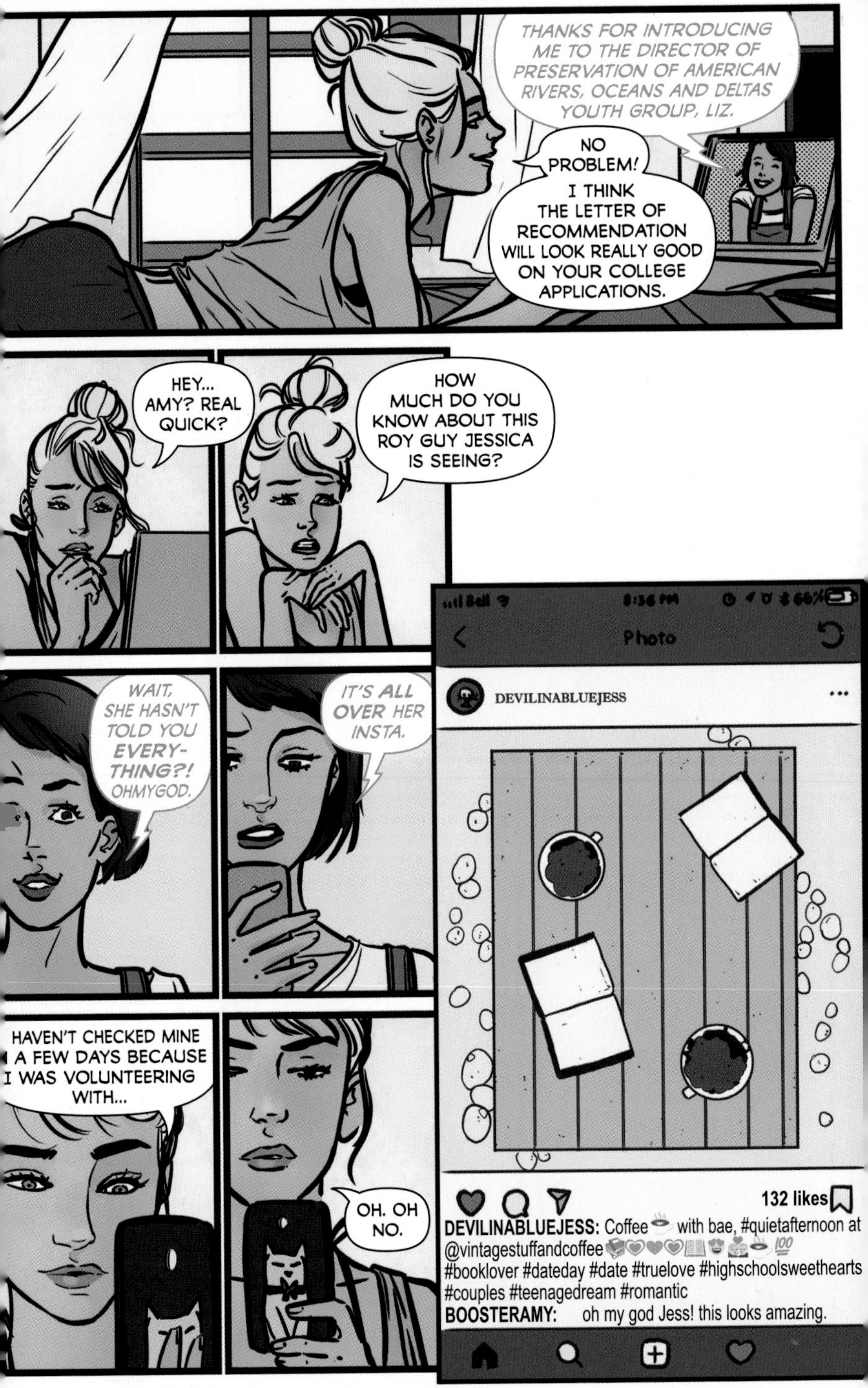
THANKS FOR INTRODUCING ME TO THE DIRECTOR OF PRESERVATION OF AMERICAN RIVERS, OCEANS AND DELTAS YOUTH GROUP, LIZ.
NO PROBLEM!
I THINK THE LETTER OF RECOMMENDATION WILL LOOK REALLY GOOD ON YOUR COLLEGE APPLICATIONS.
HEY... AMY? REAL QUICK?
HOW MUCH DO YOU KNOW ABOUT THIS ROY GUY JESSICA IS SEEING?
WAIT, SHE HASN'T TOLD YOU EVERY-THING?! OHMYGOD.
IT'S ALL OVER HER INSTA.
HAVEN'T CHECKED MINE A FEW DAYS BECAUSE I WAS VOLUNTEERING WITH...
OH. OH NO.
Photo
DEVILINABLUEJESS
132 likes
DEVILINABLUEJESS: Coffee with bae, #quietafternoon at @vintagestuffandcoffee
#booklover #dateday #date #truelove #highschoolsweethearts #couples #teenagedream #romantic
BOOSTERAMY: oh my god Jess! this looks amazing.

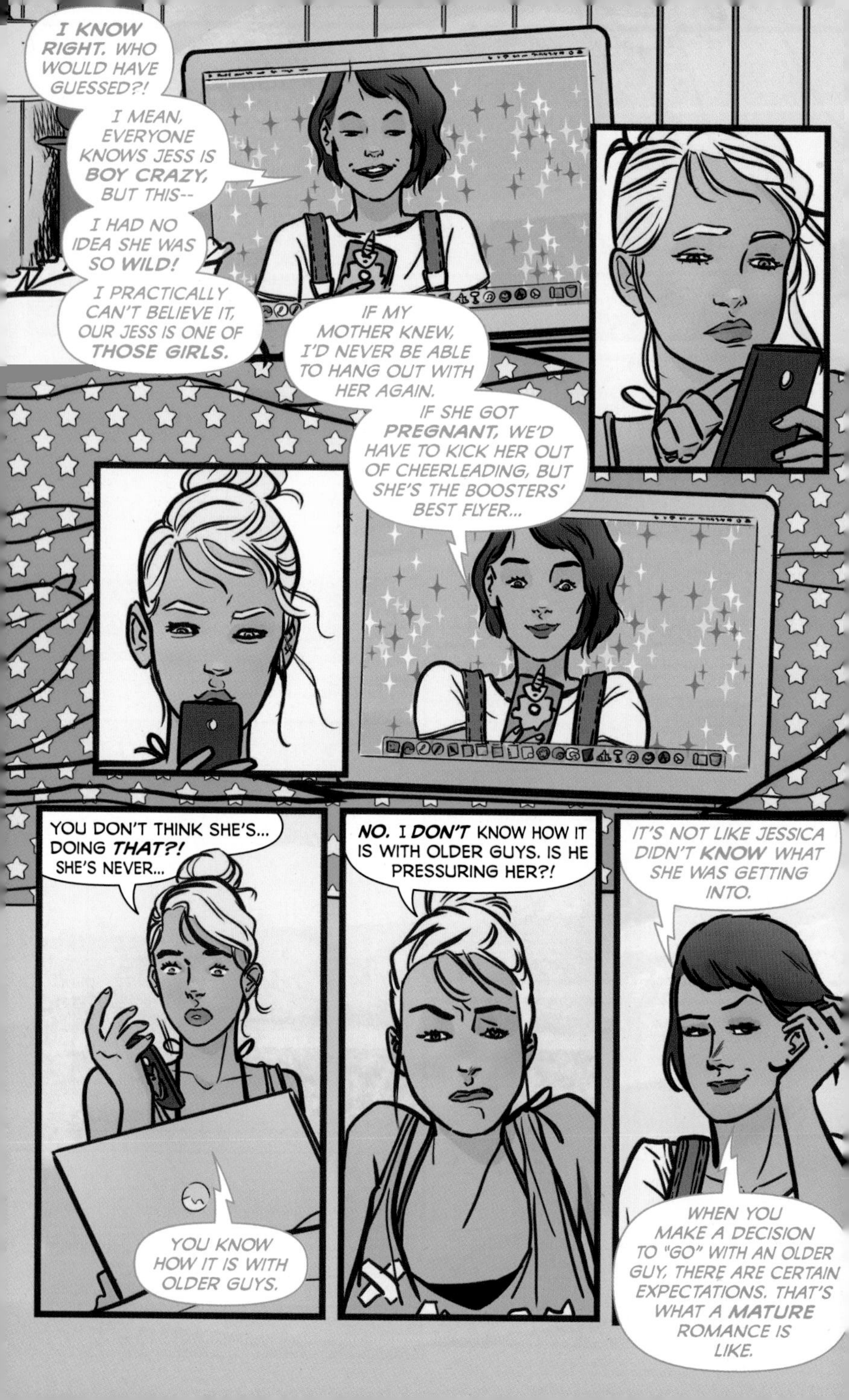
I KNOW RIGHT. WHO WOULD HAVE GUESSED?!
I MEAN, EVERYONE KNOWS JESS IS BOY CRAZY, BUT THIS--
I HAD NO IDEA SHE WAS SO WILD!
I PRACTICALLY CAN'T BELIEVE IT, OUR JESS IS ONE OF THOSE GIRLS.
IF MY MOTHER KNEW, I'D NEVER BE ABLE TO HANG OUT WITH HER AGAIN.
IF SHE GOT PREGNANT, WE'D HAVE TO KICK HER OUT OF CHEERLEADING, BUT SHE'S THE BOOSTERS' BEST FLYER...
YOU DON'T THINK SHE'S... DOING THAT?! SHE'S NEVER...
YOU KNOW HOW IT IS WITH OLDER GUYS.
NO. I DON'T KNOW HOW IT IS WITH OLDER GUYS. IS HE PRESSURING HER?!
IT'S NOT LIKE JESSICA DIDN'T KNOW WHAT SHE WAS GETTING INTO.
WHEN YOU MAKE A DECISION TO "GO" WITH AN OLDER GUY, THERE ARE CERTAIN EXPECTATIONS. THAT'S WHAT A MATURE ROMANCE IS LIKE.

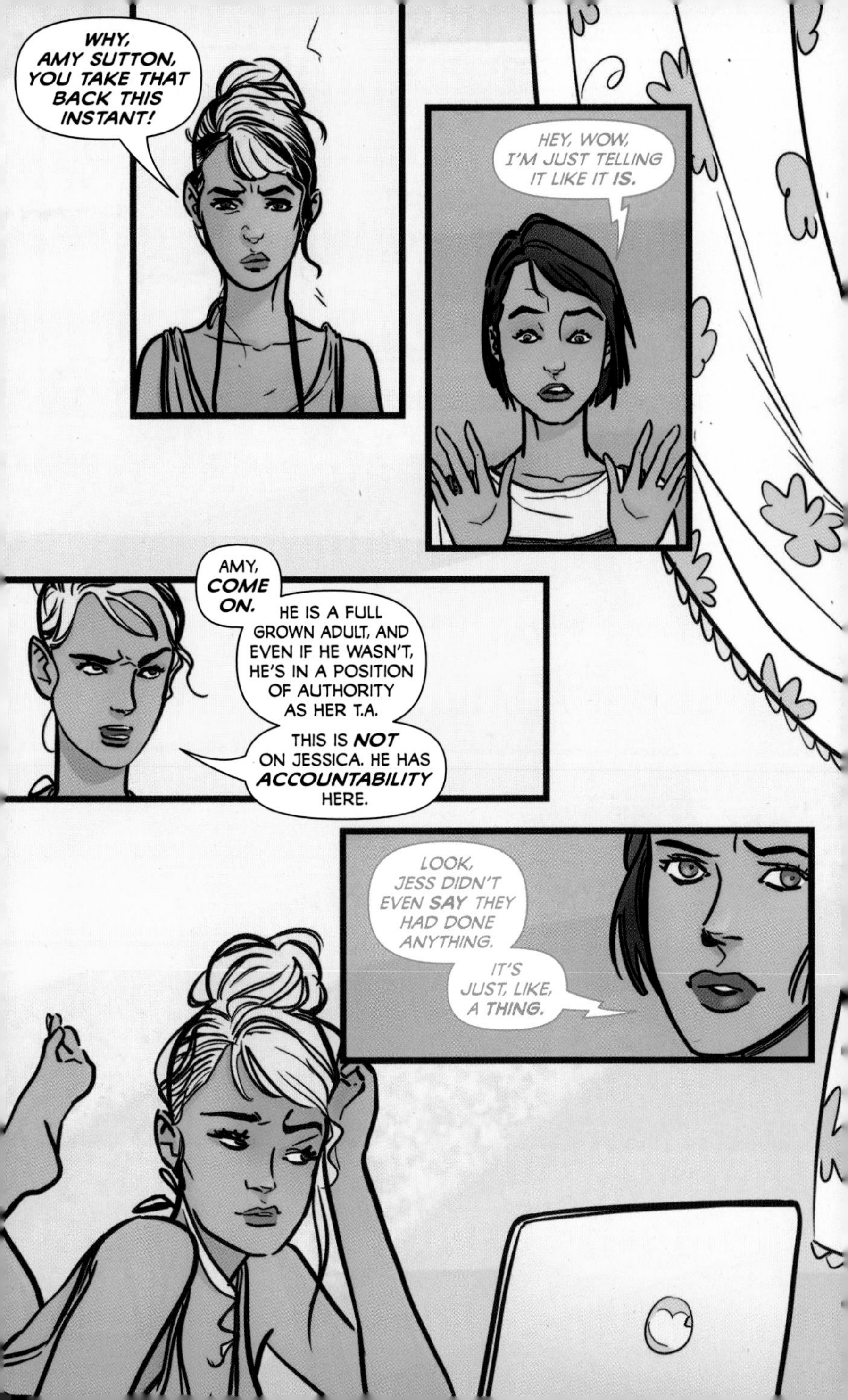
WHY, AMY SUTTON, YOU TAKE THAT BACK THIS INSTANT!
HEY, WOW, I'M JUST TELLING IT LIKE IT IS.
AMY, COME ON.
HE IS A FULL GROWN ADULT, AND EVEN IF HE WASN'T, HE'S IN A POSITION OF AUTHORITY AS HER T.A.
THIS IS NOT ON JESSICA. HE HAS ACCOUNTABILITY HERE.
LOOK, JESS DIDN'T EVEN SAY THEY HAD DONE ANYTHING.
IT'S JUST, LIKE, A THING.

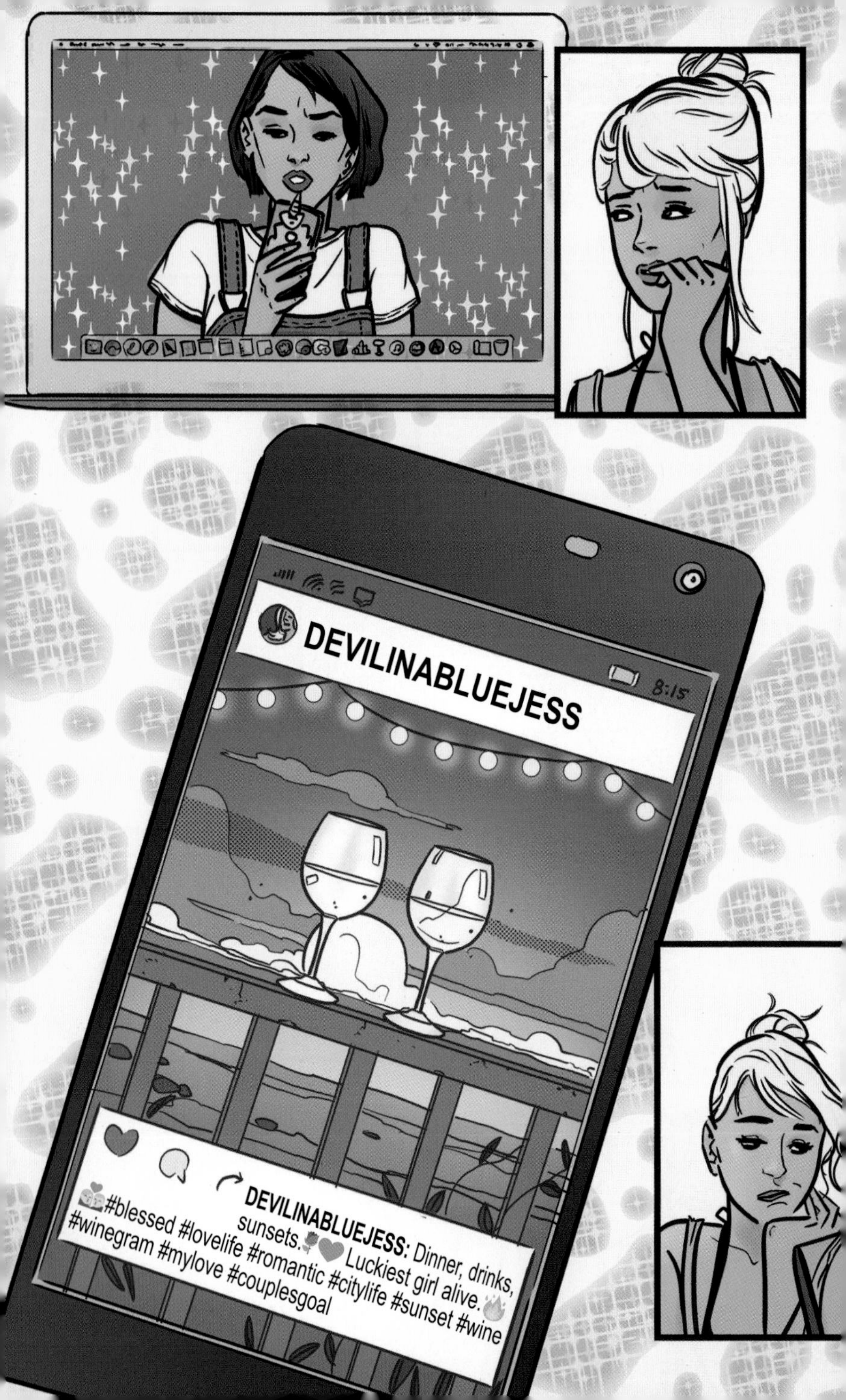
DEVILINABLUEJESS
8:15
DEVILINABLUEJESS: Dinner, drinks, sunsets. Luckiest girl alive. #blessed #lovelife #romantic #citylife #sunset #wine #winegram #mylove #couplesgoal

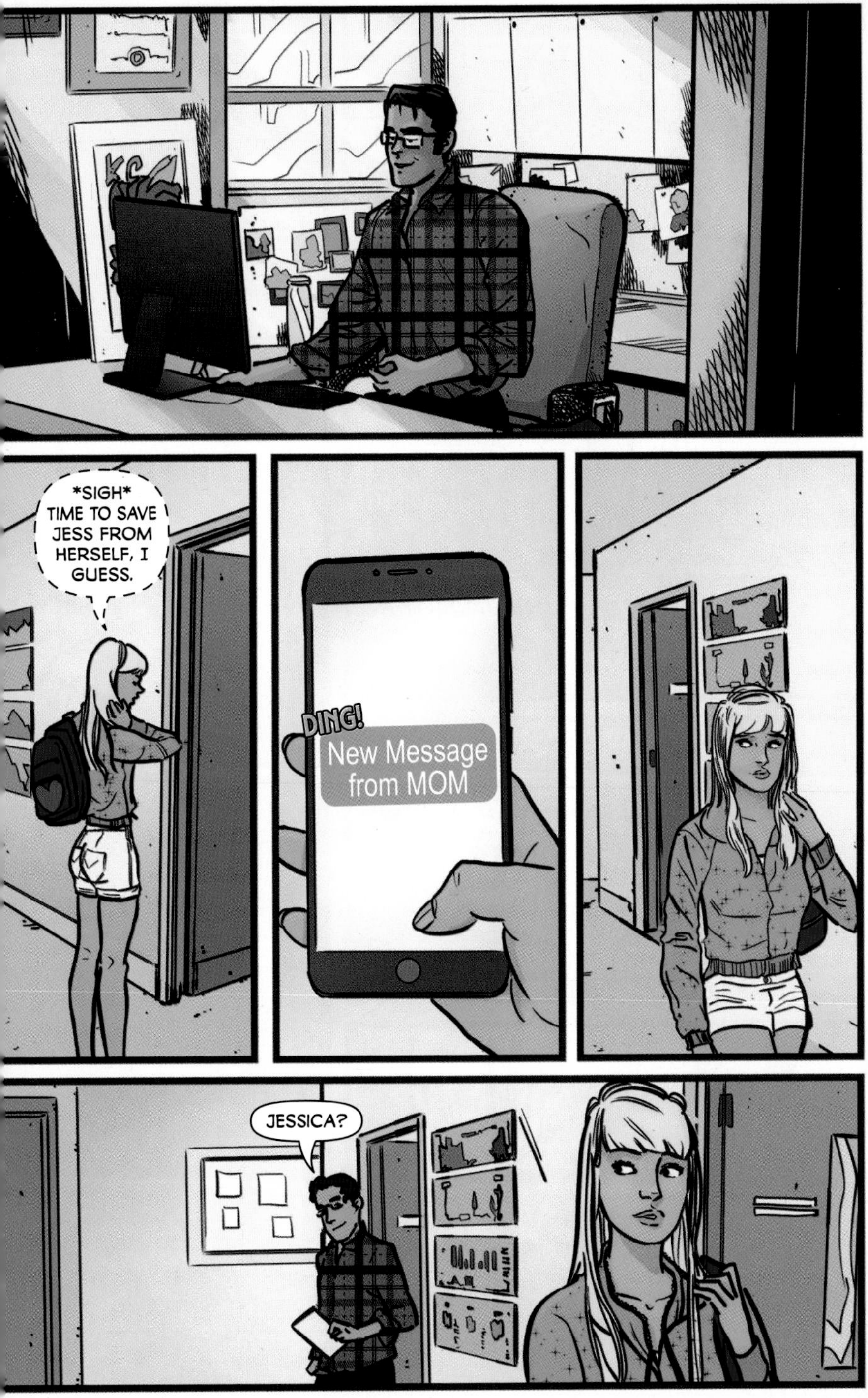
SIGH TIME TO SAVE JESS FROM HERSELF, I GUESS.
DING!
New Message from MOM
JESSICA?

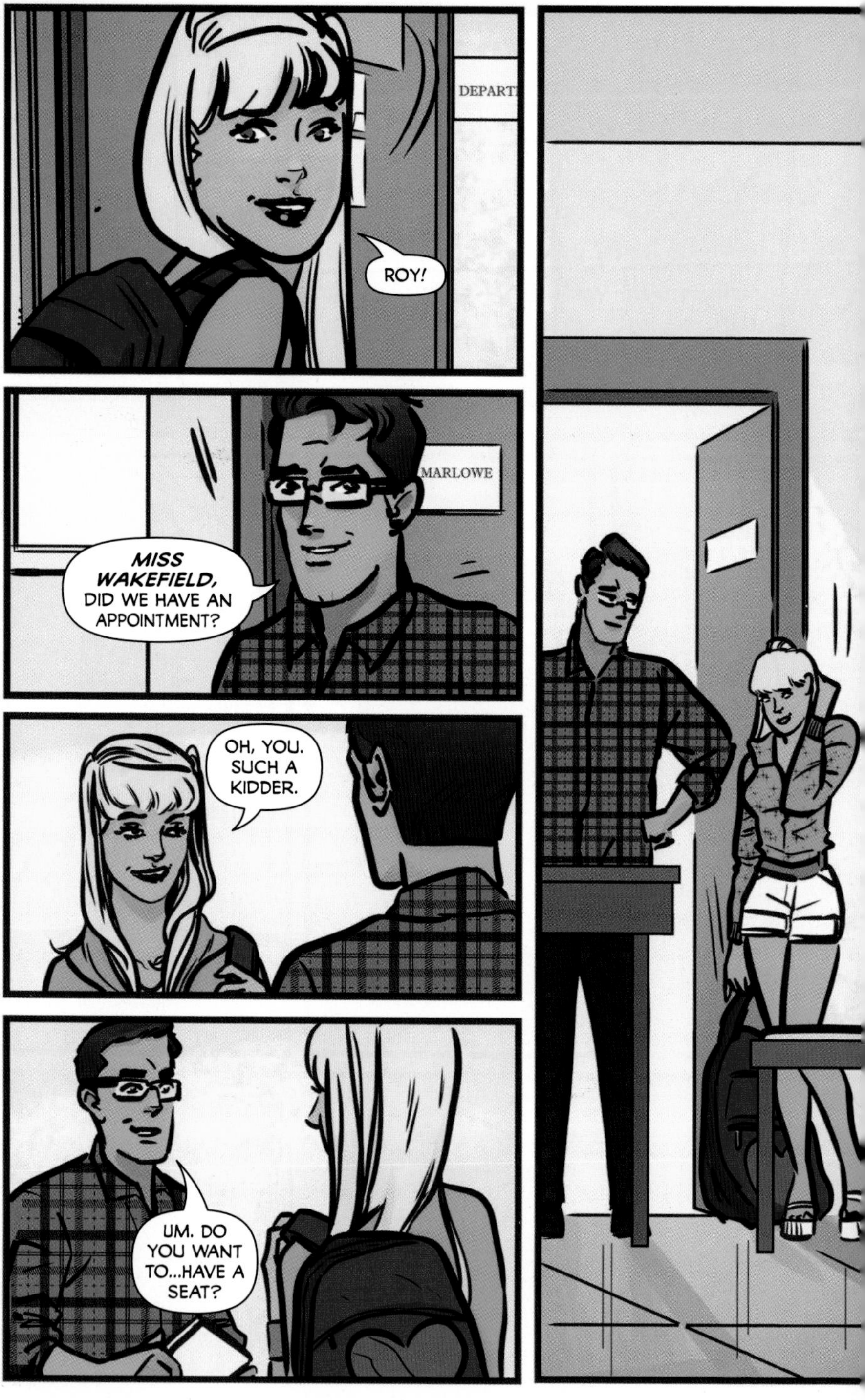
DEPART
ROY!
MARLOWE
MISS WAKEFIELD, DID WE HAVE AN APPOINTMENT?
OH, YOU. SUCH A KIDDER.
UM. DO YOU WANT TO...HAVE A SEAT?

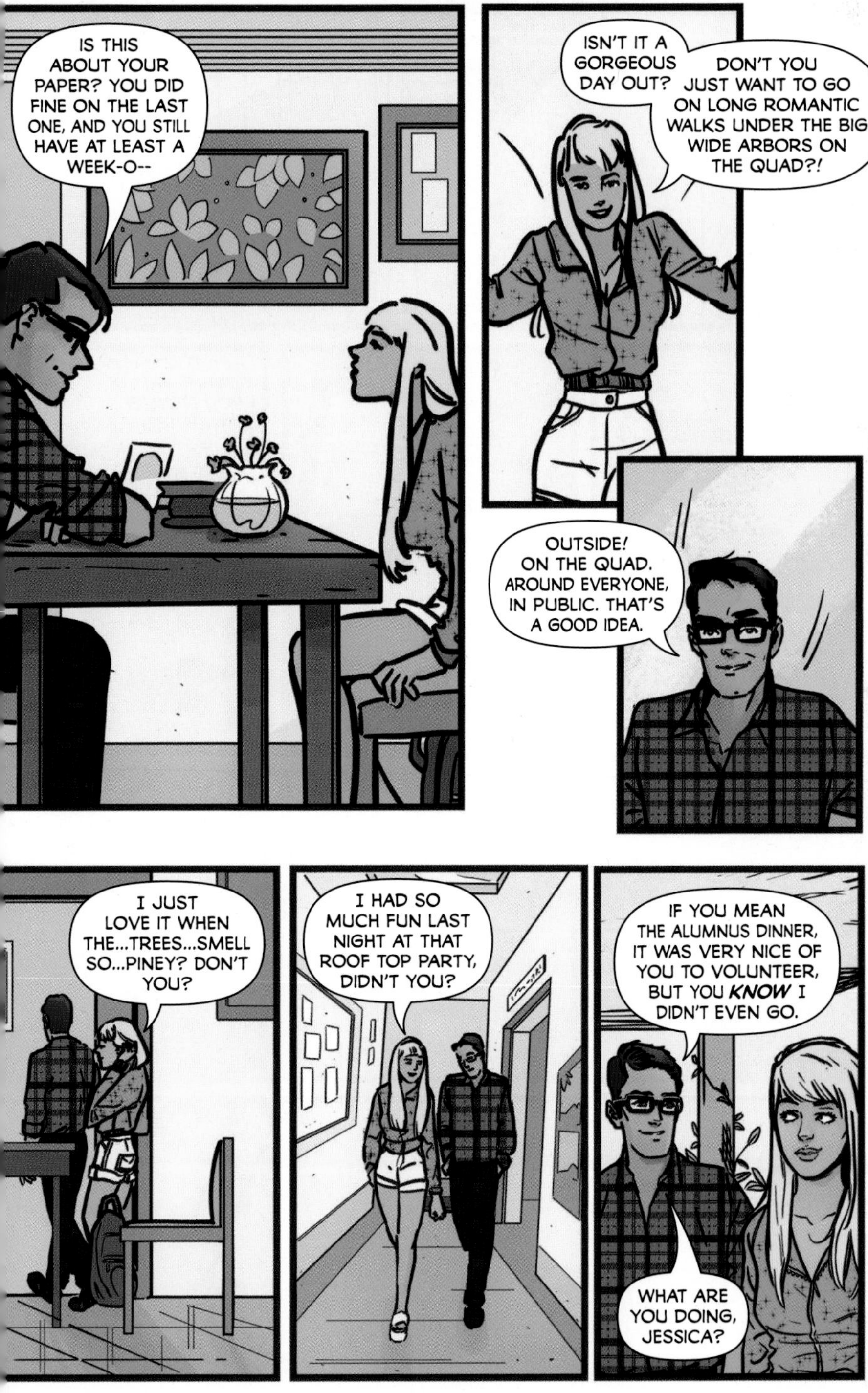
IS THIS ABOUT YOUR PAPER? YOU DID FINE ON THE LAST ONE, AND YOU STILL HAVE AT LEAST A WEEK-O--
ISN'T IT A GORGEOUS DAY OUT?
DON'T YOU JUST WANT TO GO ON LONG ROMANTIC WALKS UNDER THE BIG WIDE ARBORS ON THE QUAD?!
OUTSIDE! ON THE QUAD. AROUND EVERYONE, IN PUBLIC. THAT'S A GOOD IDEA.
I JUST LOVE IT WHEN THE...TREES...SMELL SO...PINEY? DON'T YOU?
I HAD SO MUCH FUN LAST NIGHT AT THAT ROOF TOP PARTY, DIDN'T YOU?
IF YOU MEAN THE ALUMNUS DINNER, IT WAS VERY NICE OF YOU TO VOLUNTEER, BUT YOU *KNOW* I DIDN'T EVEN GO.
WHAT ARE YOU DOING, JESSICA?

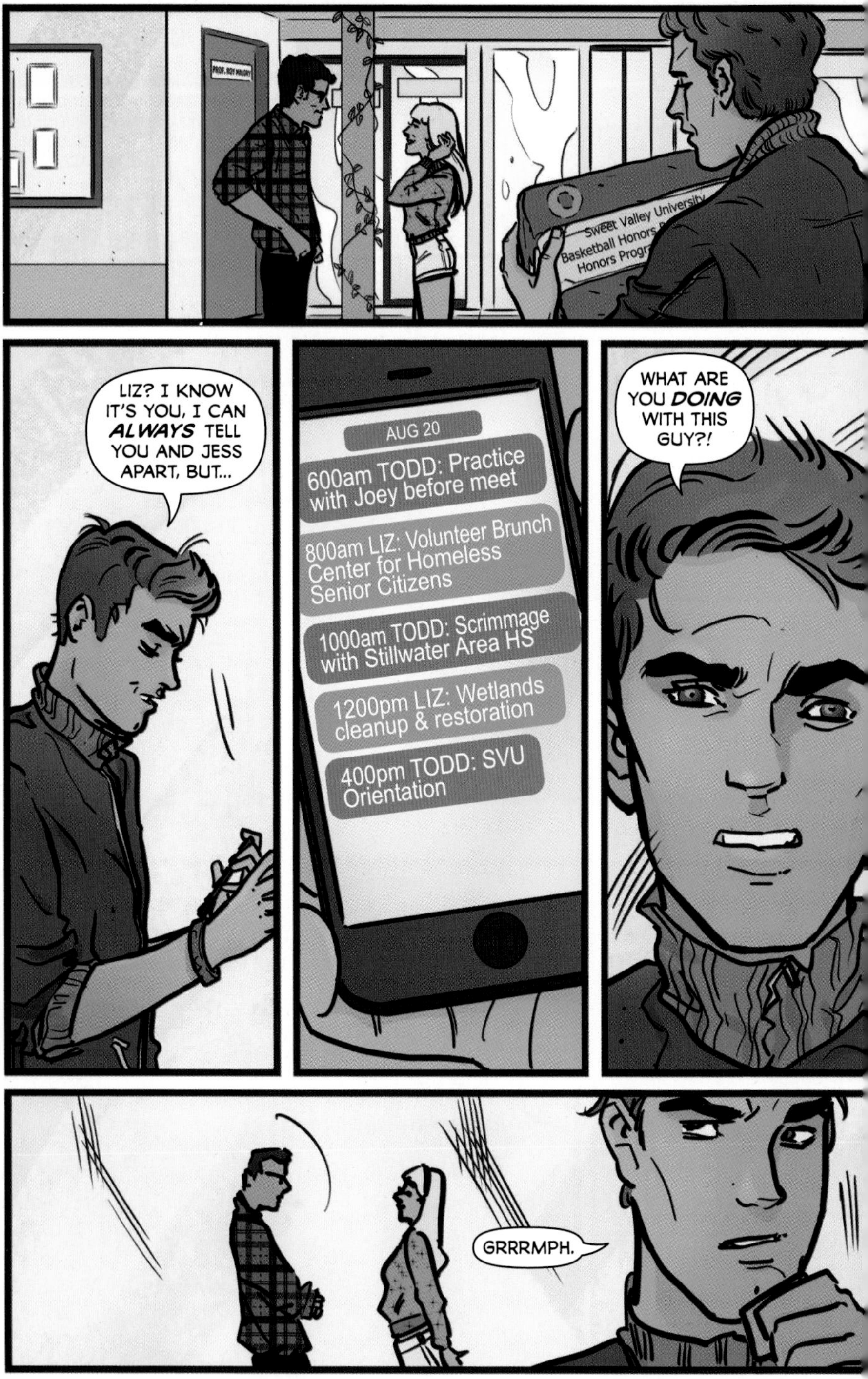
Sweet Valley University
Basketball Honors
LIZ? I KNOW IT'S YOU, I CAN *ALWAYS* TELL YOU AND JESS APART, BUT...
AUG 20
600am TODD: Practice with Joey before meet
800am LIZ: Volunteer Brunch Center for Homeless Senior Citizens
1000am TODD: Scrimmage with Stillwater Area HS
1200pm LIZ: Wetlands cleanup & restoration
400pm TODD: SVU Orientation
WHAT ARE YOU *DOING* WITH THIS GUY?!
GRRRMPH.

YOU...YOU DIDN'T?

BUT I'M GLAD *YOU* LIKED IT!

I'M ALWAYS HAPPY WHEN I CAN RECOMMEND SOMETHING AND INTRODUCE MY STUDENTS TO A WAY TO SURROUND THEMSELVES WITH FRESH PERSPECTIVES AND KNOWLEDGEABLE MINDS.

YOU KNOW?

RYAN, IN THE THIRD ROW? HE'S REALLY INTO SEQUENTIAL ART AS LITERATURE.

ANYWAY, I FOUND OUT ABOUT THIS SEMINAR, AND...

THAT'S-- YOU'RE ABSOLUTELY RIGHT, THAT'S VERY COOL.

THANK YOU, MR. MARLOWE. YOU'VE BEEN SO HELPFUL.

I SHOULD REALLY GO HOME NOW AND...DO... HOMEWORK.

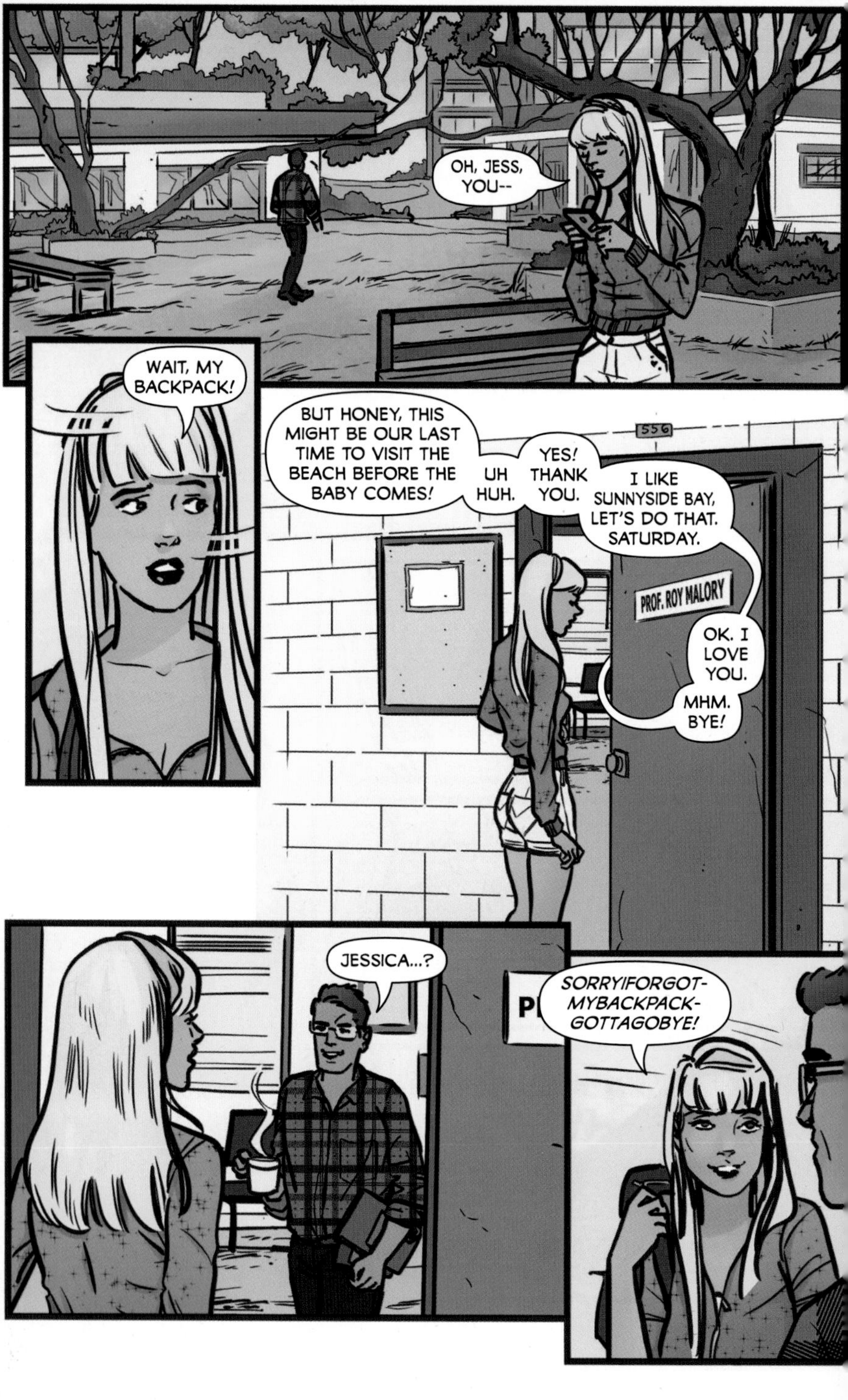
OH, JESS, YOU--
WAIT, MY BACKPACK!
BUT HONEY, THIS MIGHT BE OUR LAST TIME TO VISIT THE BEACH BEFORE THE BABY COMES!
UH HUH.
YES! THANK YOU.
I LIKE SUNNYSIDE BAY, LET'S DO THAT. SATURDAY.
556
PROF. ROY MALORY
OK. I LOVE YOU.
MHM. BYE!
JESSICA...?
SORRYIFORGOT-MYBACKPACK-GOTTAGOBYE!

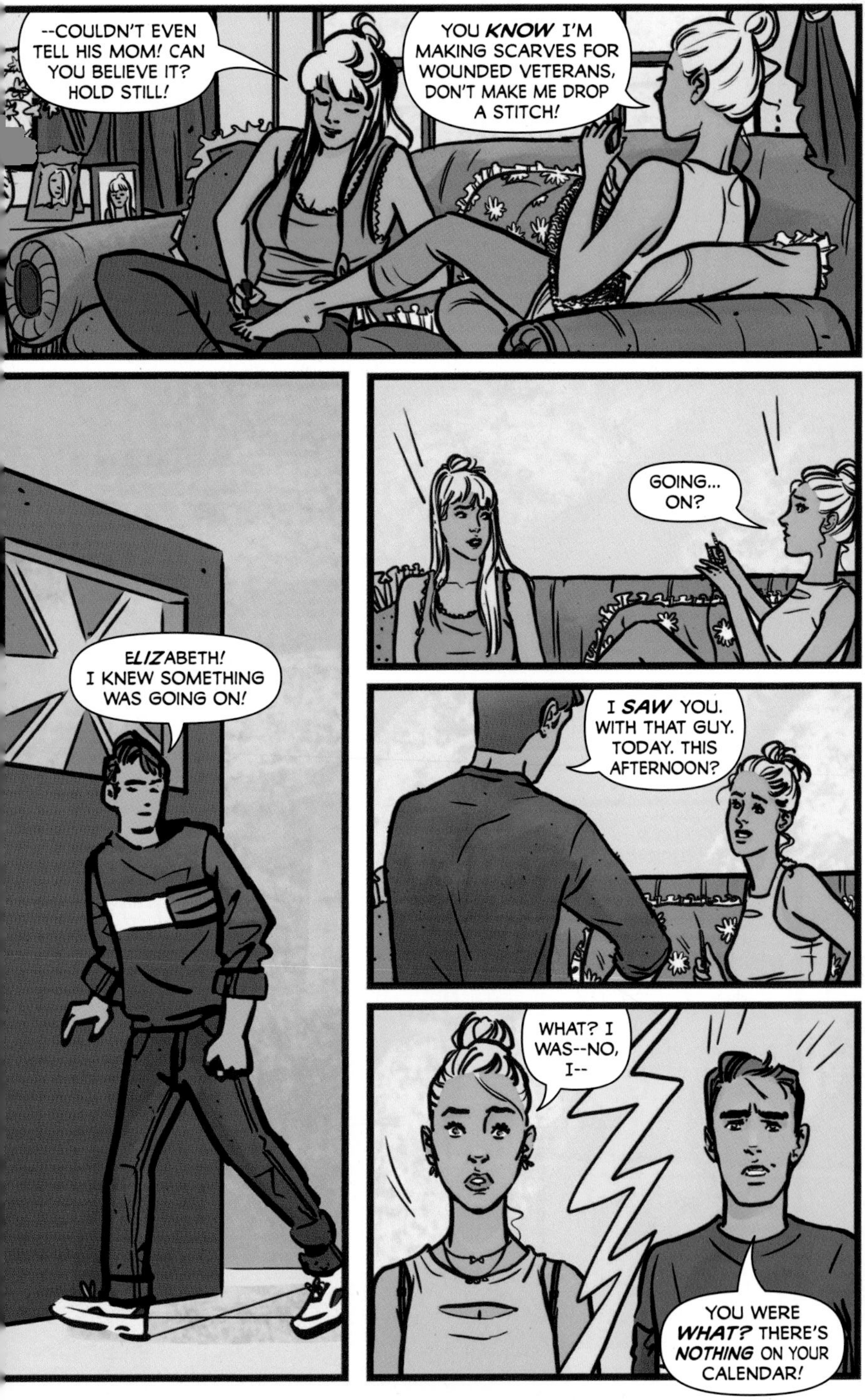
--COULDN'T EVEN TELL HIS MOM! CAN YOU BELIEVE IT? HOLD STILL!
YOU KNOW I'M MAKING SCARVES FOR WOUNDED VETERANS, DON'T MAKE ME DROP A STITCH!
ELIZABETH! I KNEW SOMETHING WAS GOING ON!
GOING... ON?
I SAW YOU. WITH THAT GUY. TODAY. THIS AFTERNOON?
WHAT? I WAS--NO, I--
YOU WERE WHAT? THERE'S NOTHING ON YOUR CALENDAR!

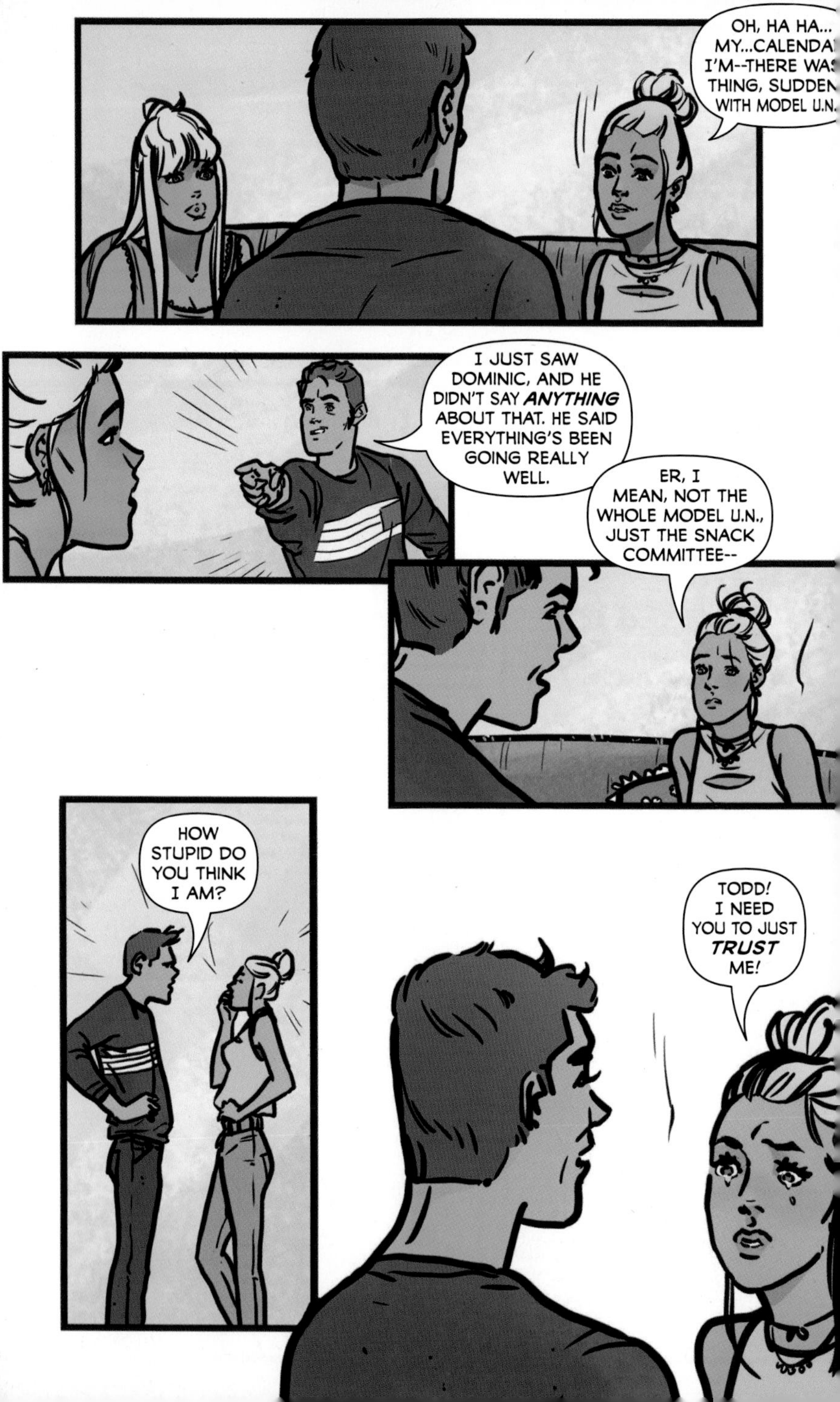

OH, HA HA... MY...CALENDA I'M--THERE WA THING, SUDDEN WITH MODEL U.N.
I JUST SAW DOMINIC, AND HE DIDN'T SAY *ANYTHING* ABOUT THAT. HE SAID EVERYTHING'S BEEN GOING REALLY WELL.
ER, I MEAN, NOT THE WHOLE MODEL U.N., JUST THE SNACK COMMITTEE--
HOW STUPID DO YOU THINK I AM?
TODD! I NEED YOU TO JUST *TRUST* ME!

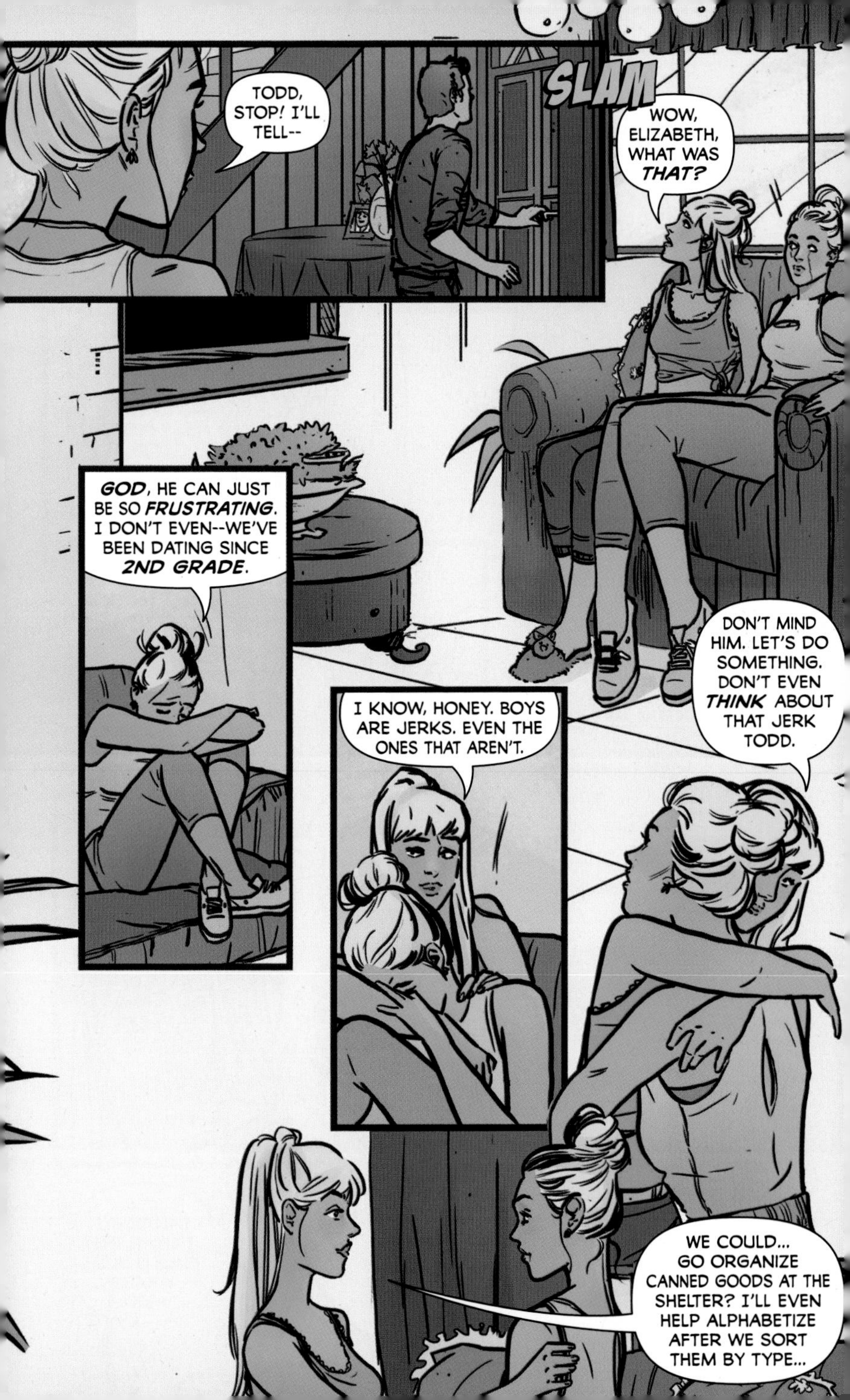
TODD, STOP! I'LL TELL--
SLAM
WOW, ELIZABETH, WHAT WAS *THAT?*
GOD, HE CAN JUST BE SO *FRUSTRATING*. I DON'T EVEN--WE'VE BEEN DATING SINCE *2ND GRADE*.
DON'T MIND HIM. LET'S DO SOMETHING. DON'T EVEN *THINK* ABOUT THAT JERK TODD.
I KNOW, HONEY. BOYS ARE JERKS. EVEN THE ONES THAT AREN'T.
WE COULD... GO ORGANIZE CANNED GOODS AT THE SHELTER? I'LL EVEN HELP ALPHABETIZE AFTER WE SORT THEM BY TYPE...

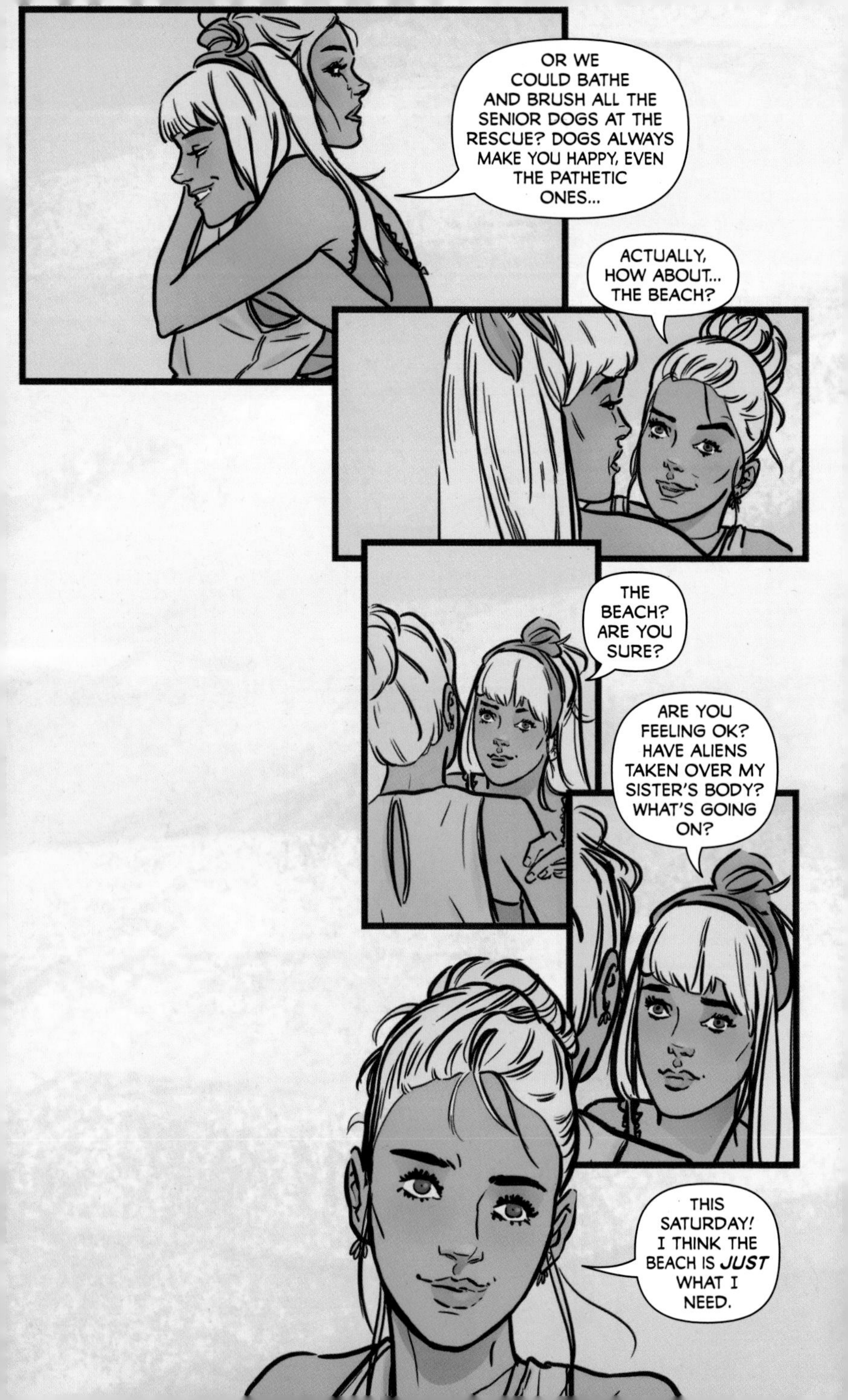
OR WE COULD BATHE AND BRUSH ALL THE SENIOR DOGS AT THE RESCUE? DOGS ALWAYS MAKE YOU HAPPY, EVEN THE PATHETIC ONES...
ACTUALLY, HOW ABOUT... THE BEACH?
THE BEACH? ARE YOU SURE?
ARE YOU FEELING OK? HAVE ALIENS TAKEN OVER MY SISTER'S BODY? WHAT'S GOING ON?
THIS SATURDAY! I THINK THE BEACH IS *JUST* WHAT I NEED.

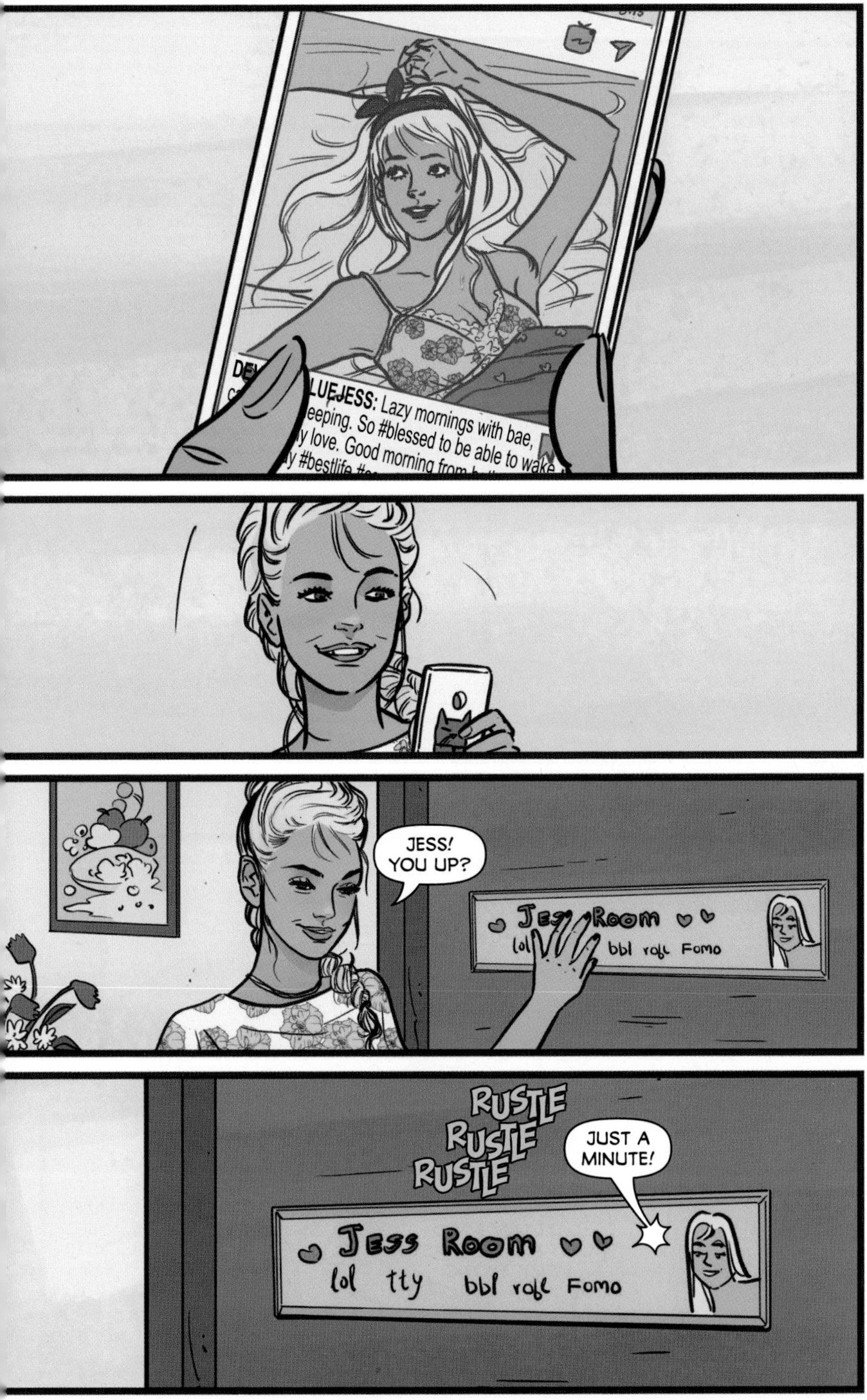
LUEJESS: Lazy mornings with bae,
eeping. So #blessed to be able to wake
y love. Good morning from
#bestlife
JESS! YOU UP?
Jess Room
lol bbl rofl Fomo
RUSTLE RUSTLE RUSTLE
JUST A MINUTE!
Jess Room
lol tty bbl rofl Fomo

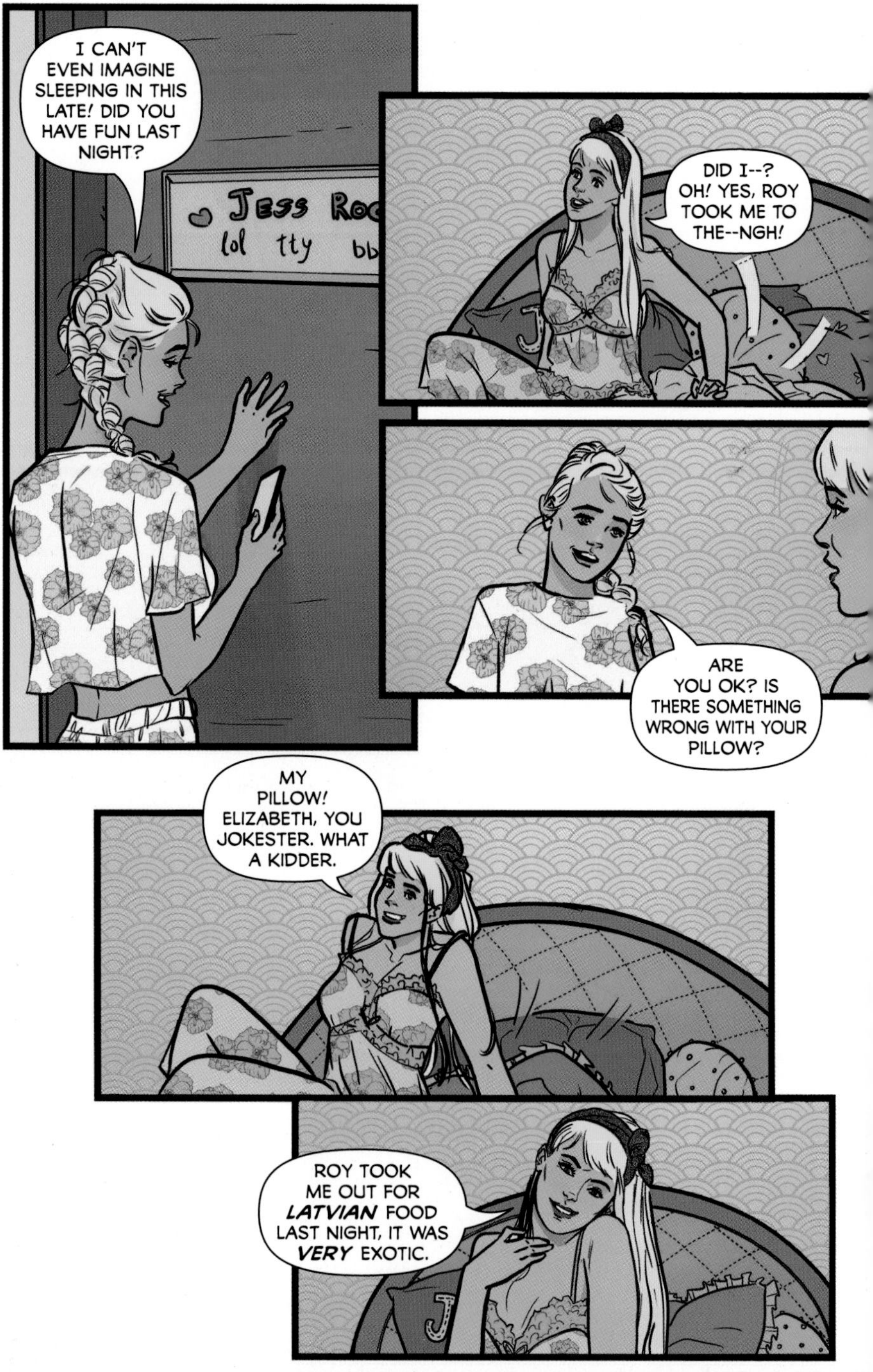
I CAN'T EVEN IMAGINE SLEEPING IN THIS LATE! DID YOU HAVE FUN LAST NIGHT?
JESS ROO
lol tty bb
DID I--? OH! YES, ROY TOOK ME TO THE--NGH!
ARE YOU OK? IS THERE SOMETHING WRONG WITH YOUR PILLOW?
MY PILLOW! ELIZABETH, YOU JOKESTER. WHAT A KIDDER.
ROY TOOK ME OUT FOR ***LATVIAN*** FOOD LAST NIGHT, IT WAS ***VERY*** EXOTIC.

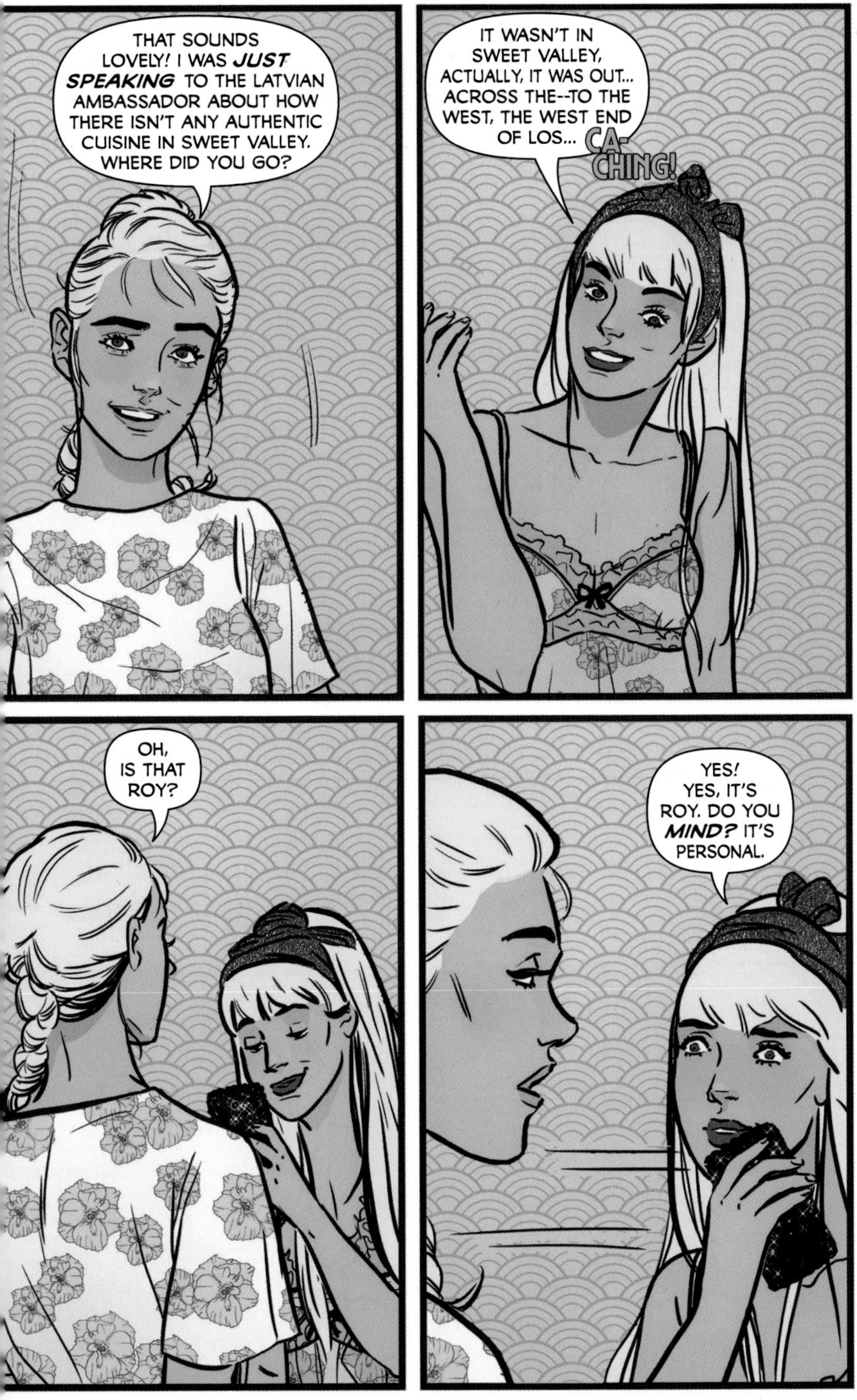
THAT SOUNDS LOVELY! I WAS JUST SPEAKING TO THE LATVIAN AMBASSADOR ABOUT HOW THERE ISN'T ANY AUTHENTIC CUISINE IN SWEET VALLEY. WHERE DID YOU GO?
IT WASN'T IN SWEET VALLEY, ACTUALLY, IT WAS OUT... ACROSS THE--TO THE WEST, THE WEST END OF LOS...
CA-CHING!
OH, IS THAT ROY?
YES! YES, IT'S ROY. DO YOU MIND? IT'S PERSONAL.

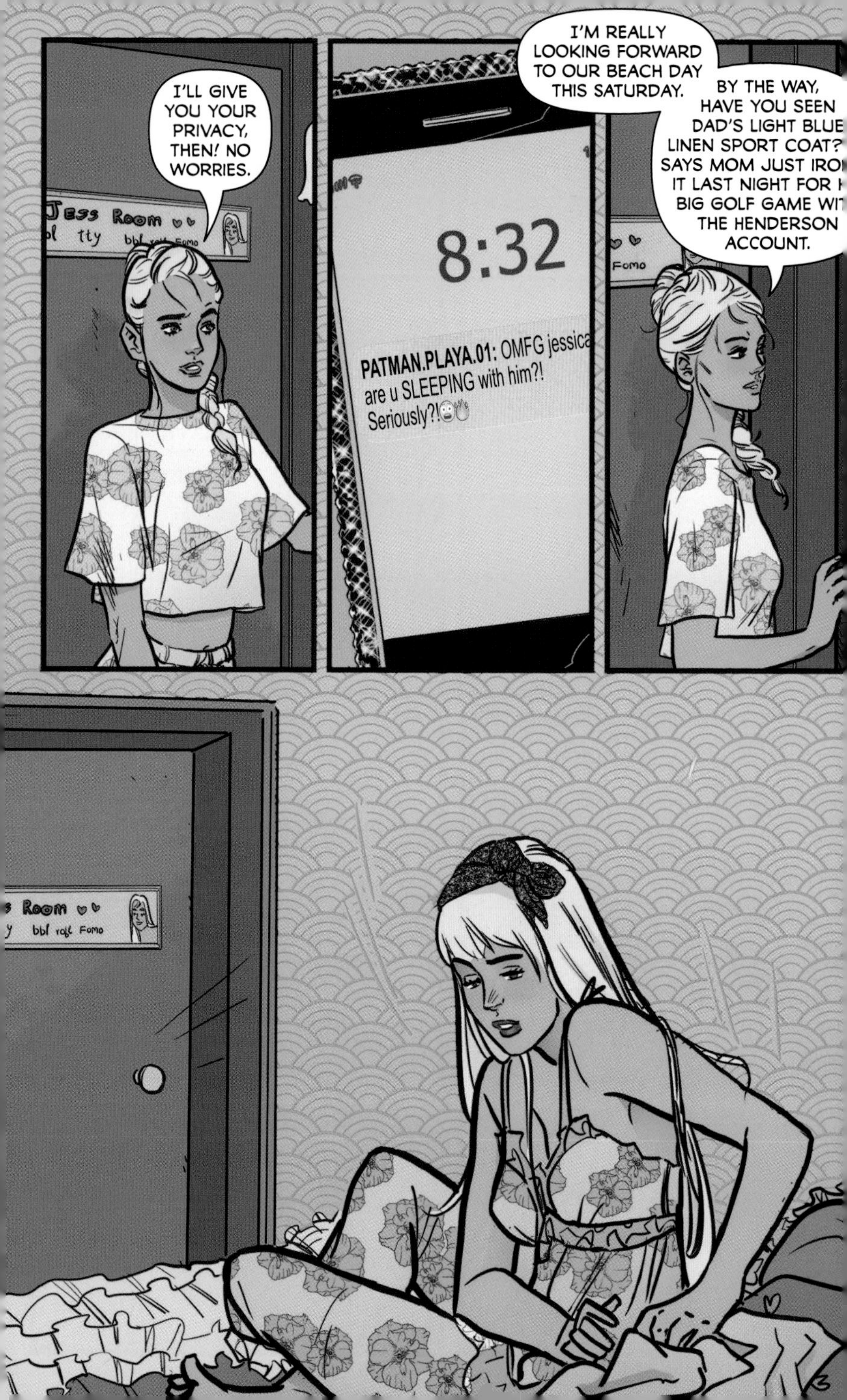
I'LL GIVE YOU YOUR PRIVACY, THEN! NO WORRIES.
Jess Room
8:32
PATMAN.PLAYA.01: OMFG jessica are u SLEEPING with him?! Seriously?!
I'M REALLY LOOKING FORWARD TO OUR BEACH DAY THIS SATURDAY.
BY THE WAY, HAVE YOU SEEN DAD'S LIGHT BLUE LINEN SPORT COAT? SAYS MOM JUST IRO IT LAST NIGHT FOR BIG GOLF GAME WI THE HENDERSON ACCOUNT.

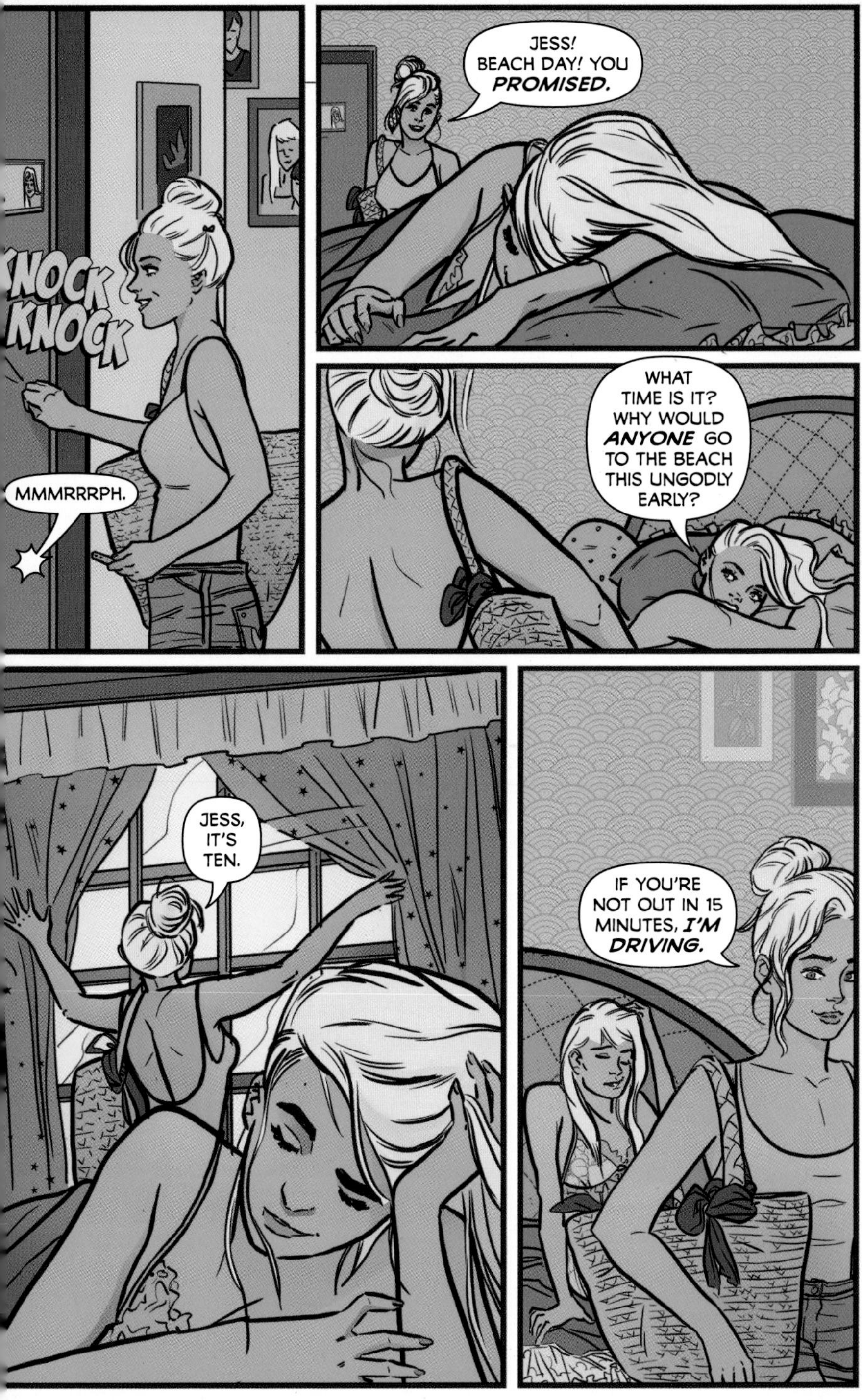
KNOCK KNOCK
MMMRRRPH.
JESS! BEACH DAY! YOU *PROMISED.*
WHAT TIME IS IT? WHY WOULD *ANYONE* GO TO THE BEACH THIS UNGODLY EARLY?
JESS, IT'S TEN.
IF YOU'RE NOT OUT IN 15 MINUTES, *I'M DRIVING.*

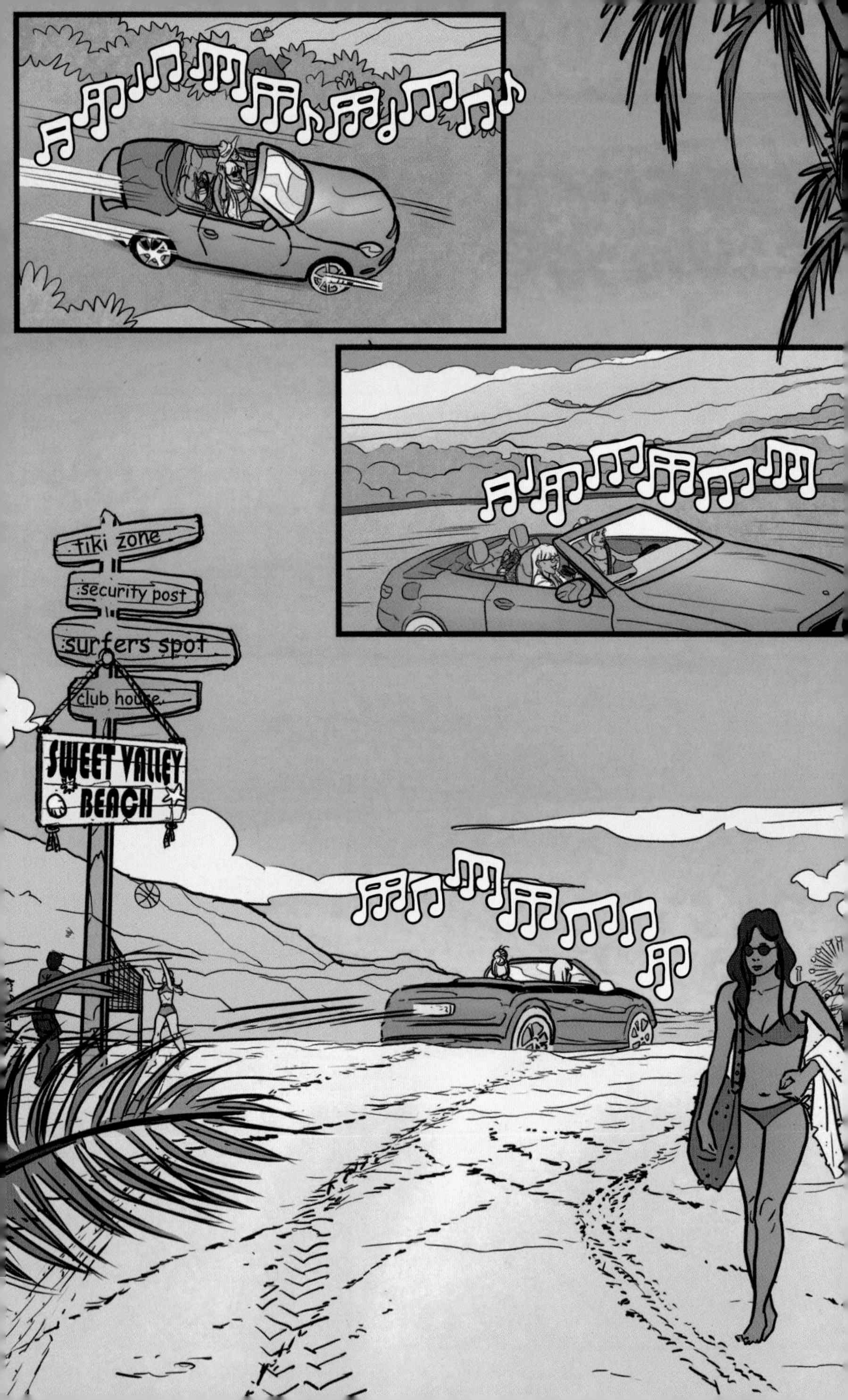
tiki zone
security post
surfers spot
club house
SWEET VALLEY BEACH

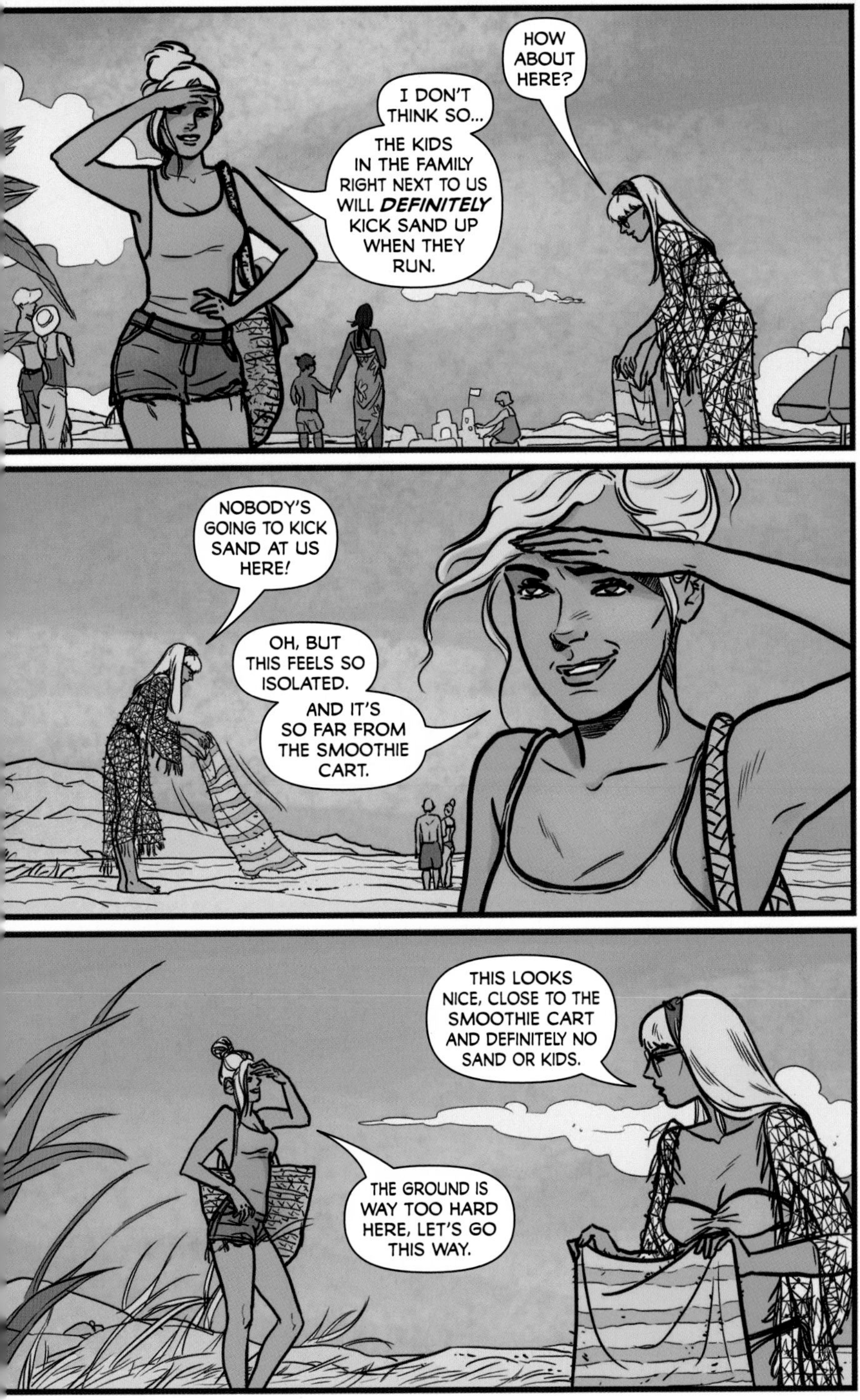
HOW ABOUT HERE?
I DON'T THINK SO...
THE KIDS IN THE FAMILY RIGHT NEXT TO US WILL *DEFINITELY* KICK SAND UP WHEN THEY RUN.
NOBODY'S GOING TO KICK SAND AT US HERE!
OH, BUT THIS FEELS SO ISOLATED.
AND IT'S SO FAR FROM THE SMOOTHIE CART.
THIS LOOKS NICE, CLOSE TO THE SMOOTHIE CART AND DEFINITELY NO SAND OR KIDS.
THE GROUND IS WAY TOO HARD HERE, LET'S GO THIS WAY.

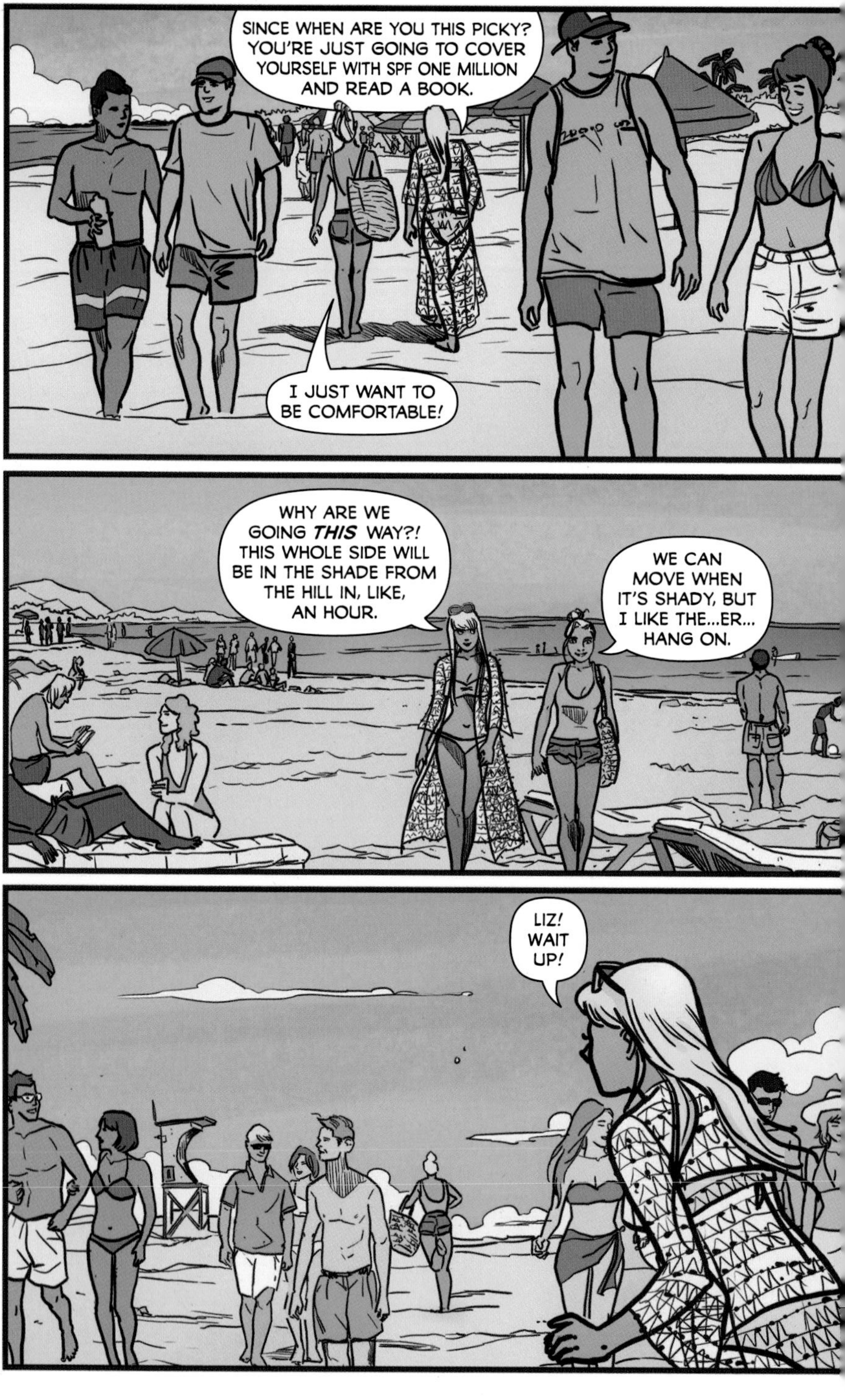
SINCE WHEN ARE YOU THIS PICKY? YOU'RE JUST GOING TO COVER YOURSELF WITH SPF ONE MILLION AND READ A BOOK.
I JUST WANT TO BE COMFORTABLE!
WHY ARE WE GOING *THIS* WAY?! THIS WHOLE SIDE WILL BE IN THE SHADE FROM THE HILL IN, LIKE, AN HOUR.
WE CAN MOVE WHEN IT'S SHADY, BUT I LIKE THE...ER... HANG ON.
LIZ! WAIT UP!

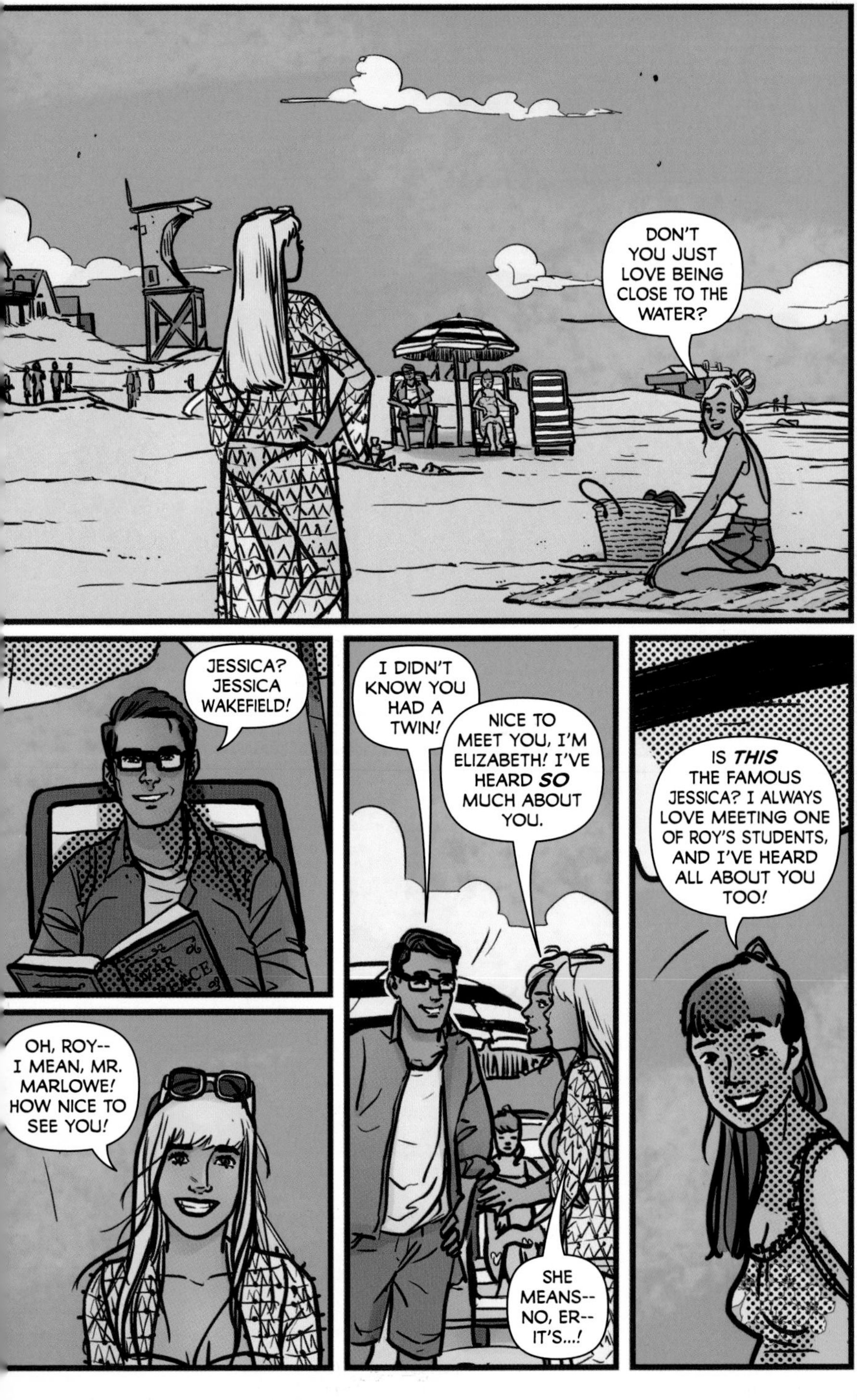
DON'T YOU JUST LOVE BEING CLOSE TO THE WATER?
JESSICA? JESSICA WAKEFIELD!
OH, ROY-- I MEAN, MR. MARLOWE! HOW NICE TO SEE YOU!
I DIDN'T KNOW YOU HAD A TWIN!
NICE TO MEET YOU, I'M ELIZABETH! I'VE HEARD *SO* MUCH ABOUT YOU.
SHE MEANS-- NO, ER-- IT'S...!
IS *THIS* THE FAMOUS JESSICA? I ALWAYS LOVE MEETING ONE OF ROY'S STUDENTS, AND I'VE HEARD ALL ABOUT YOU TOO!

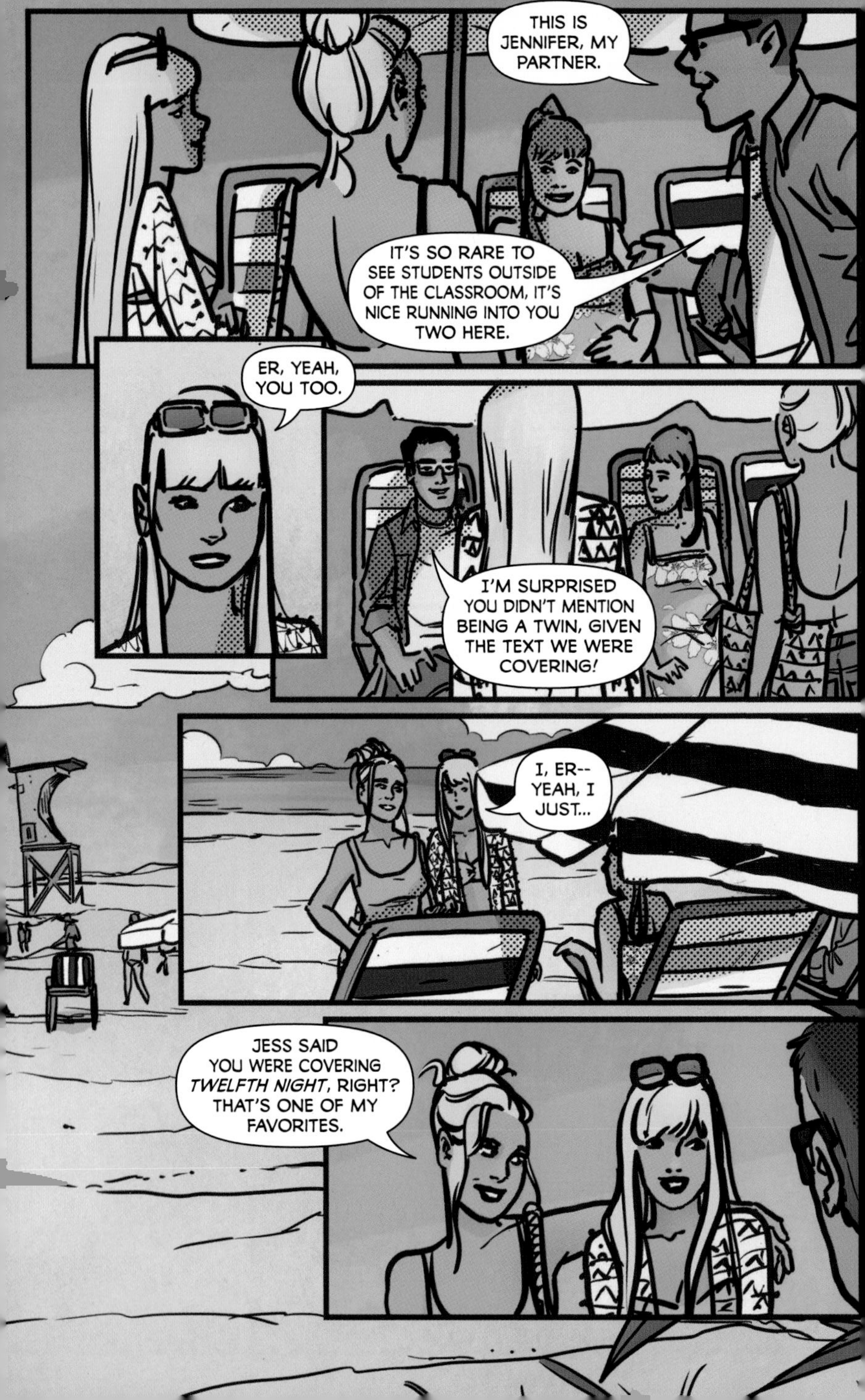
THIS IS JENNIFER, MY PARTNER.
IT'S SO RARE TO SEE STUDENTS OUTSIDE OF THE CLASSROOM, IT'S NICE RUNNING INTO YOU TWO HERE.
ER, YEAH, YOU TOO.
I'M SURPRISED YOU DIDN'T MENTION BEING A TWIN, GIVEN THE TEXT WE WERE COVERING!
I, ER-- YEAH, I JUST...
JESS SAID YOU WERE COVERING *TWELFTH NIGHT*, RIGHT? THAT'S ONE OF MY FAVORITES.

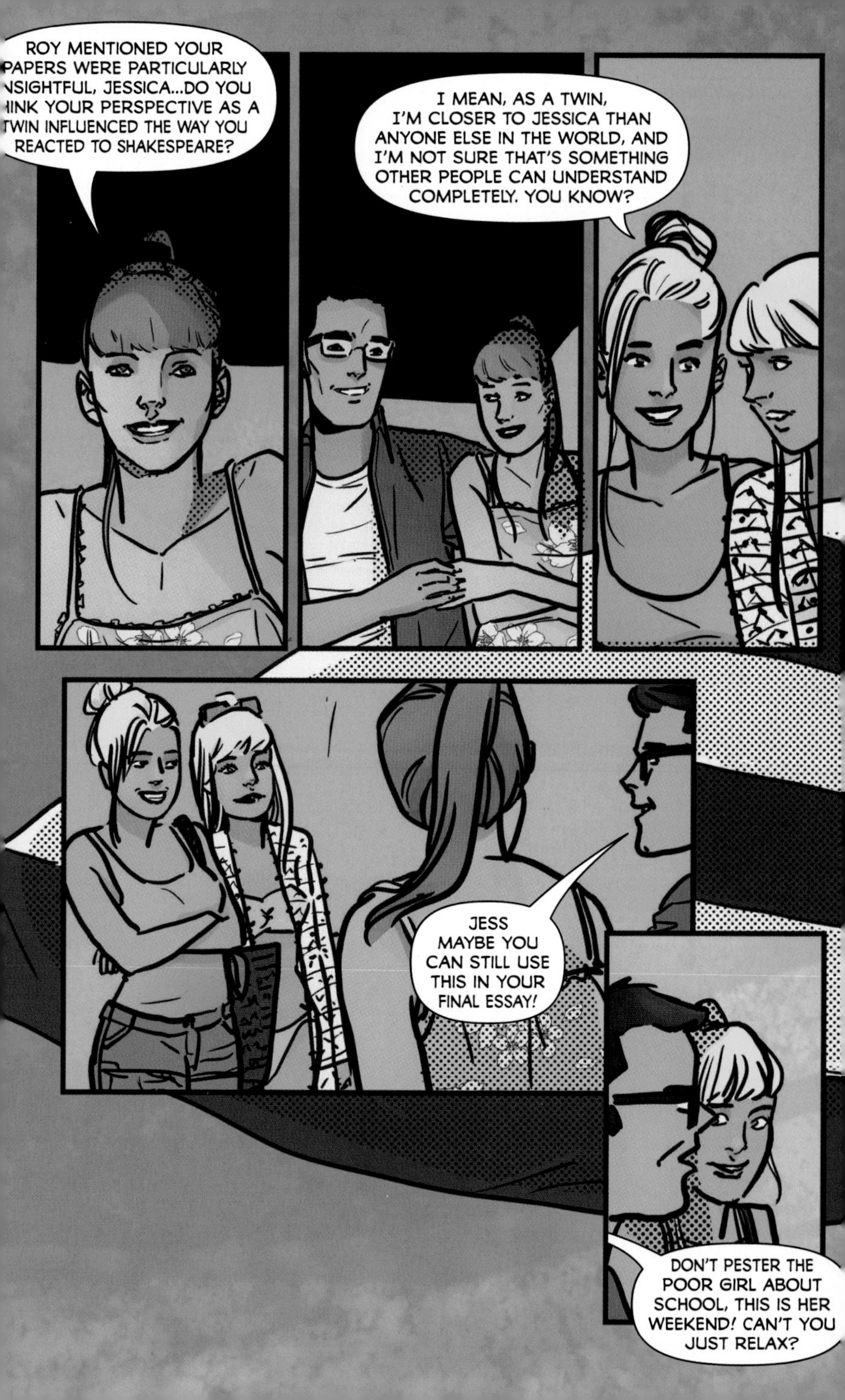
ROY MENTIONED YOUR PAPERS WERE PARTICULARLY NSIGHTFUL, JESSICA...DO YOU INK YOUR PERSPECTIVE AS A TWIN INFLUENCED THE WAY YOU REACTED TO SHAKESPEARE?
I MEAN, AS A TWIN, I'M CLOSER TO JESSICA THAN ANYONE ELSE IN THE WORLD, AND I'M NOT SURE THAT'S SOMETHING OTHER PEOPLE CAN UNDERSTAND COMPLETELY. YOU KNOW?
JESS MAYBE YOU CAN STILL USE THIS IN YOUR FINAL ESSAY!
DON'T PESTER THE POOR GIRL ABOUT SCHOOL, THIS IS HER WEEKEND! CAN'T YOU JUST RELAX?

SORRY! SORRY. AND I'M SURE YOU GUYS ARE SICK OF TWIN QUESTIONS ANYWAY, *TWELFTH NIGHT* NOTWITHSTANDING.

IT'S OK! WE'RE USED TO IT.

...YEAH.

SEE? WE'RE BORING, HONEY. WE ALWAYS KNEW WE'D GET THERE SOME DAY.

HONESTLY, DON'T WORRY ABOUT IT. WHAT A *WEIRD COINCIDENCE* TO RUN INTO JESSICA'S TEACHER AT THE BEACH, THOUGH, RIGHT?!

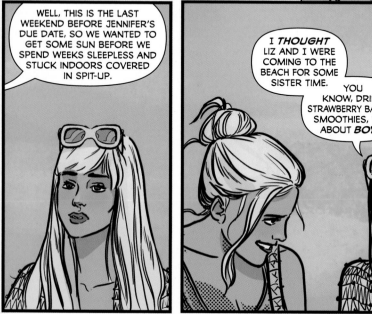

WELL, THIS IS THE LAST WEEKEND BEFORE JENNIFER'S DUE DATE, SO WE WANTED TO GET SOME SUN BEFORE WE SPEND WEEKS SLEEPLESS AND STUCK INDOORS COVERED IN SPIT-UP.

I *THOUGHT* LIZ AND I WERE COMING TO THE BEACH FOR SOME SISTER TIME. YOU KNOW, DRINK STRAWBERRY BANANA SMOOTHIES, TALK ABOUT *BOYS.*

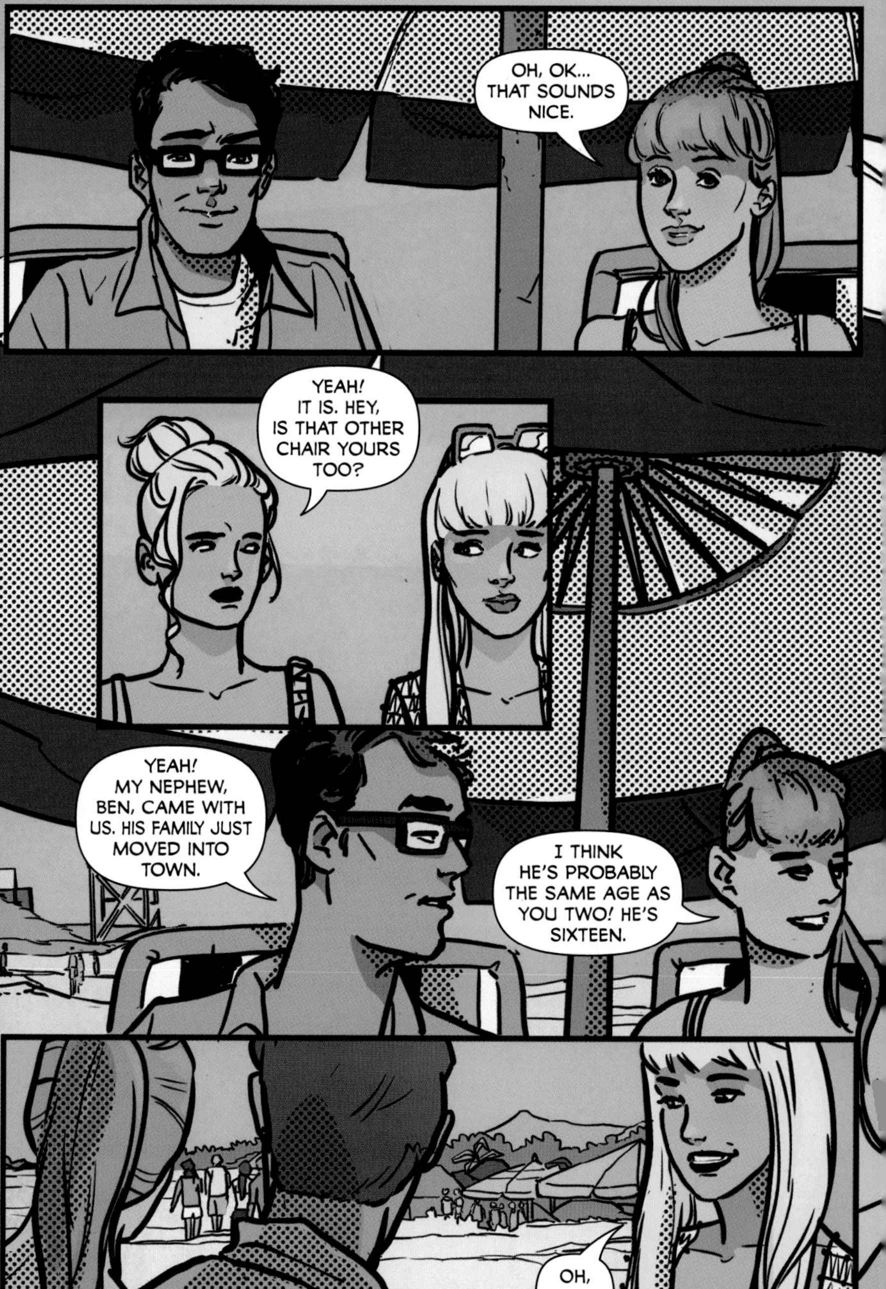
OH, OK... THAT SOUNDS NICE.
YEAH! IT IS. HEY, IS THAT OTHER CHAIR YOURS TOO?
YEAH! MY NEPHEW, BEN, CAME WITH US. HIS FAMILY JUST MOVED INTO TOWN.
I THINK HE'S PROBABLY THE SAME AGE AS YOU TWO! HE'S SIXTEEN.
OH, HOW NICE!

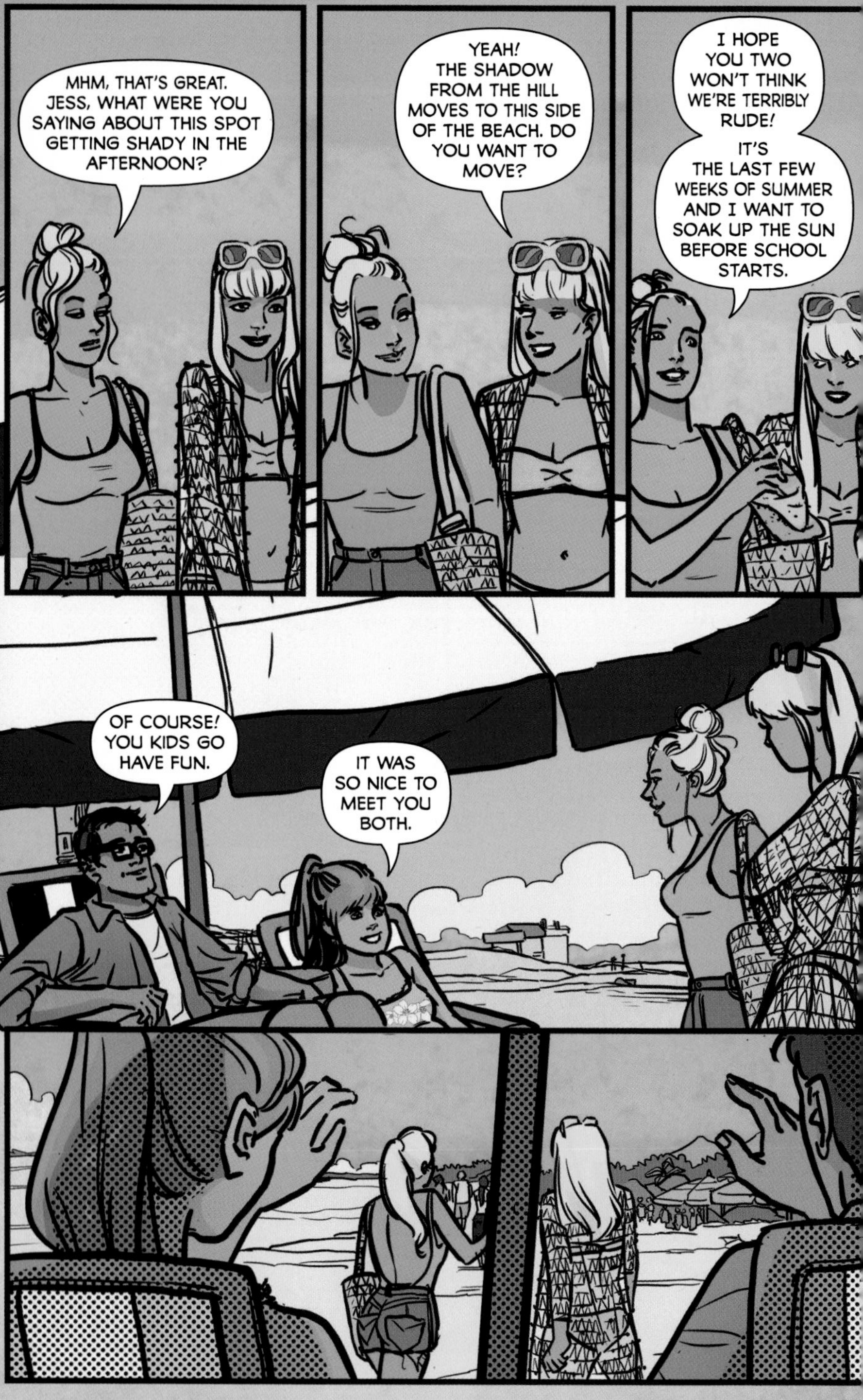
MHM, THAT'S GREAT. JESS, WHAT WERE YOU SAYING ABOUT THIS SPOT GETTING SHADY IN THE AFTERNOON?
YEAH! THE SHADOW FROM THE HILL MOVES TO THIS SIDE OF THE BEACH. DO YOU WANT TO MOVE?
I HOPE YOU TWO WON'T THINK WE'RE TERRIBLY RUDE!
IT'S THE LAST FEW WEEKS OF SUMMER AND I WANT TO SOAK UP THE SUN BEFORE SCHOOL STARTS.
OF COURSE! YOU KIDS GO HAVE FUN.
IT WAS SO NICE TO MEET YOU BOTH.

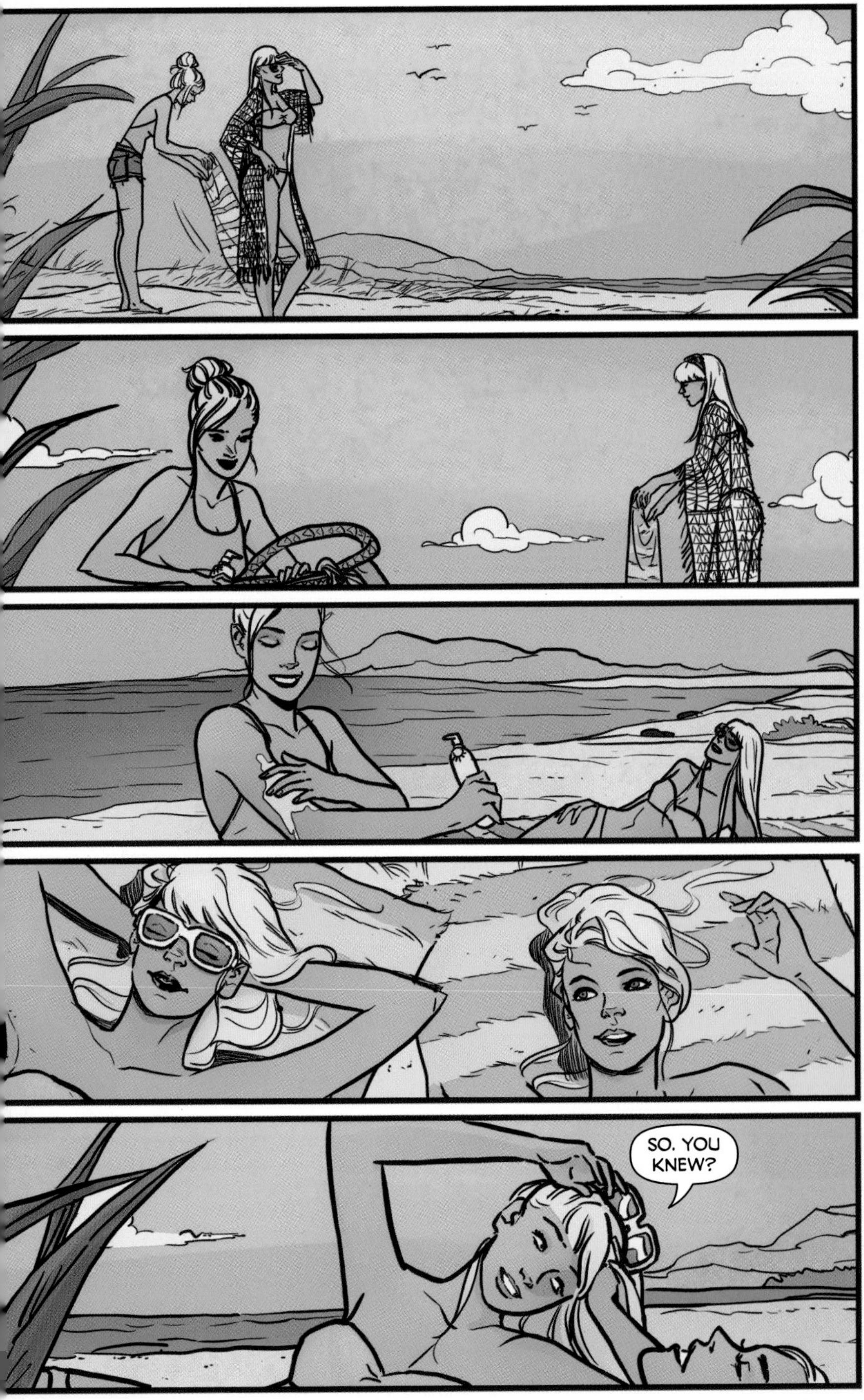
SO. YOU KNEW?

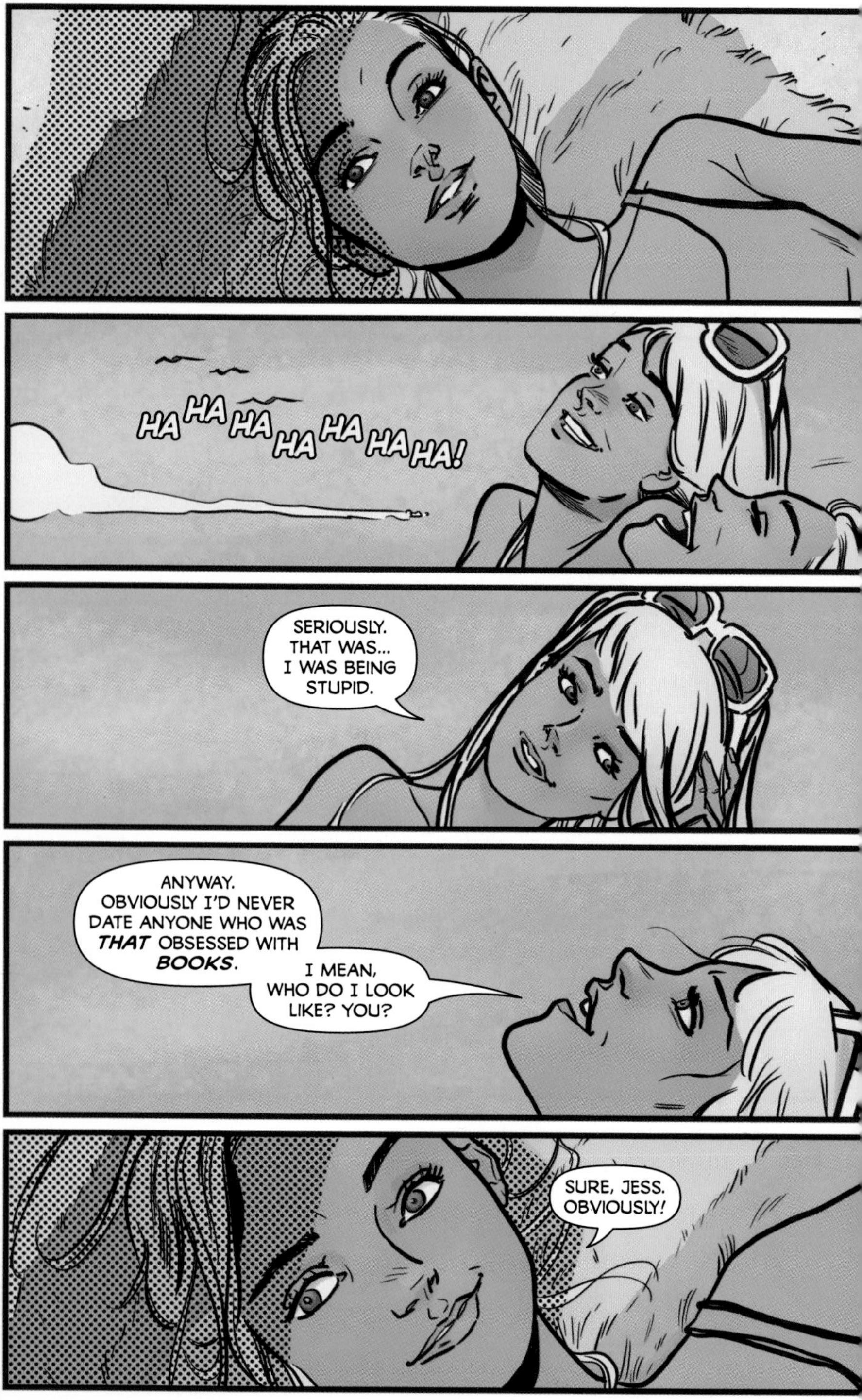
HA HA HA HA HA HA HA!
SERIOUSLY. THAT WAS... I WAS BEING STUPID.
ANYWAY. OBVIOUSLY I'D NEVER DATE ANYONE WHO WAS *THAT* OBSESSED WITH *BOOKS*.
I MEAN, WHO DO I LOOK LIKE? YOU?
SURE, JESS. OBVIOUSLY!

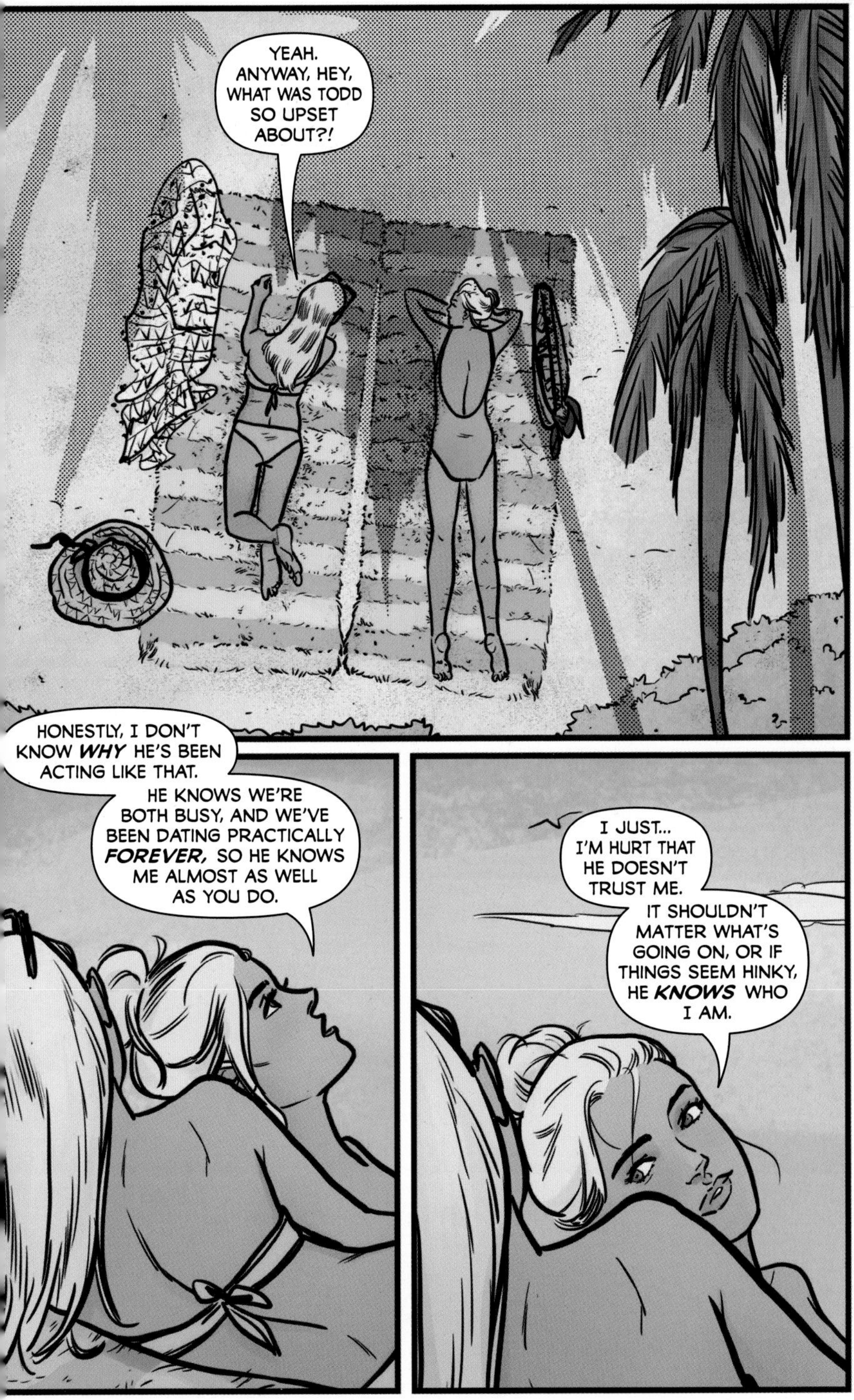
YEAH. ANYWAY, HEY, WHAT WAS TODD SO UPSET ABOUT?!
HONESTLY, I DON'T KNOW ***WHY*** HE'S BEEN ACTING LIKE THAT.
HE KNOWS WE'RE BOTH BUSY, AND WE'VE BEEN DATING PRACTICALLY ***FOREVER,*** SO HE KNOWS ME ALMOST AS WELL AS YOU DO.
I JUST... I'M HURT THAT HE DOESN'T TRUST ME.
IT SHOULDN'T MATTER WHAT'S GOING ON, OR IF THINGS SEEM HINKY, HE ***KNOWS*** WHO I AM.

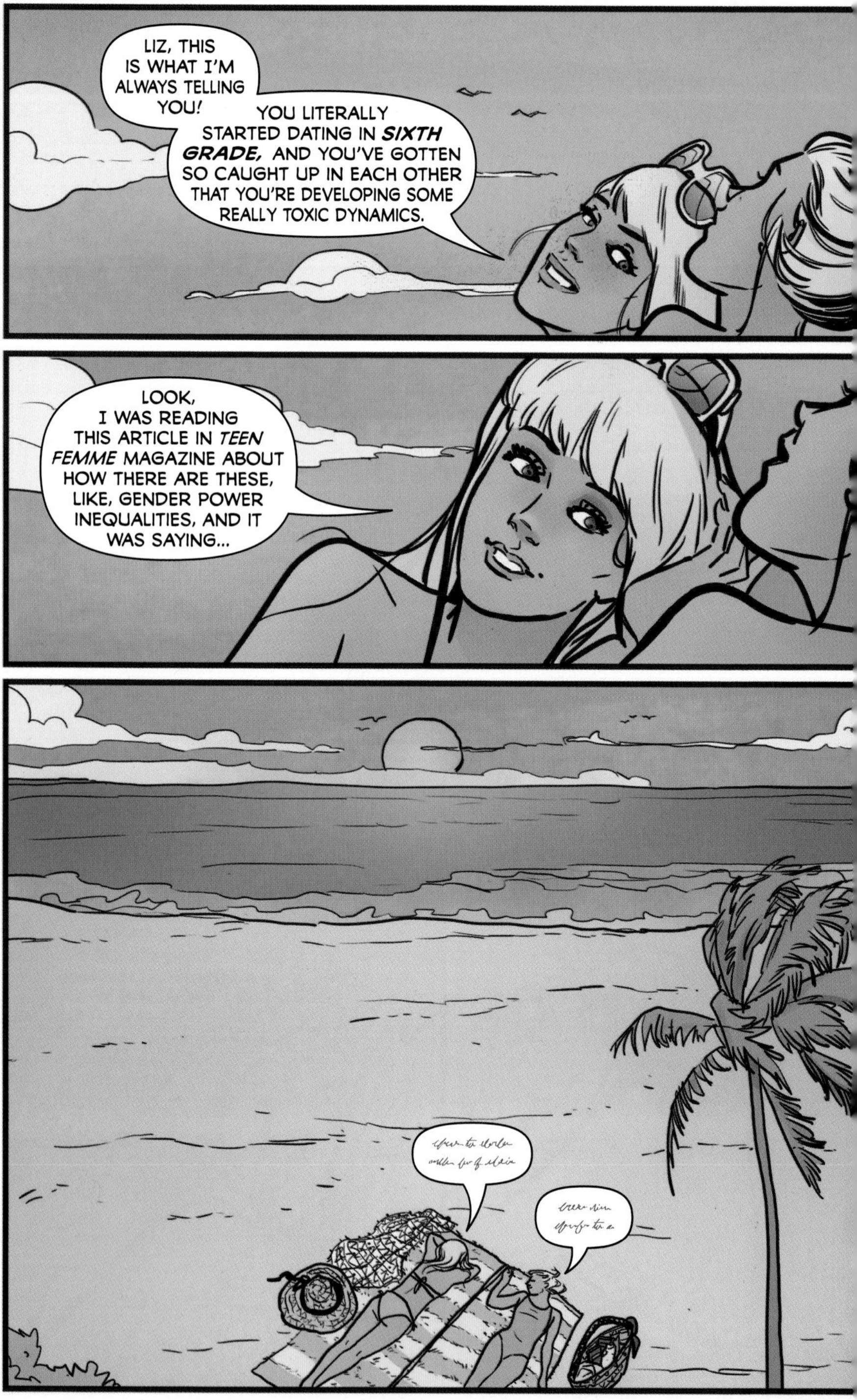
LIZ, THIS IS WHAT I'M ALWAYS TELLING YOU!
YOU LITERALLY STARTED DATING IN SIXTH GRADE, AND YOU'VE GOTTEN SO CAUGHT UP IN EACH OTHER THAT YOU'RE DEVELOPING SOME REALLY TOXIC DYNAMICS.
LOOK, I WAS READING THIS ARTICLE IN TEEN FEMME MAGAZINE ABOUT HOW THERE ARE THESE, LIKE, GENDER POWER INEQUALITIES, AND IT WAS SAYING...

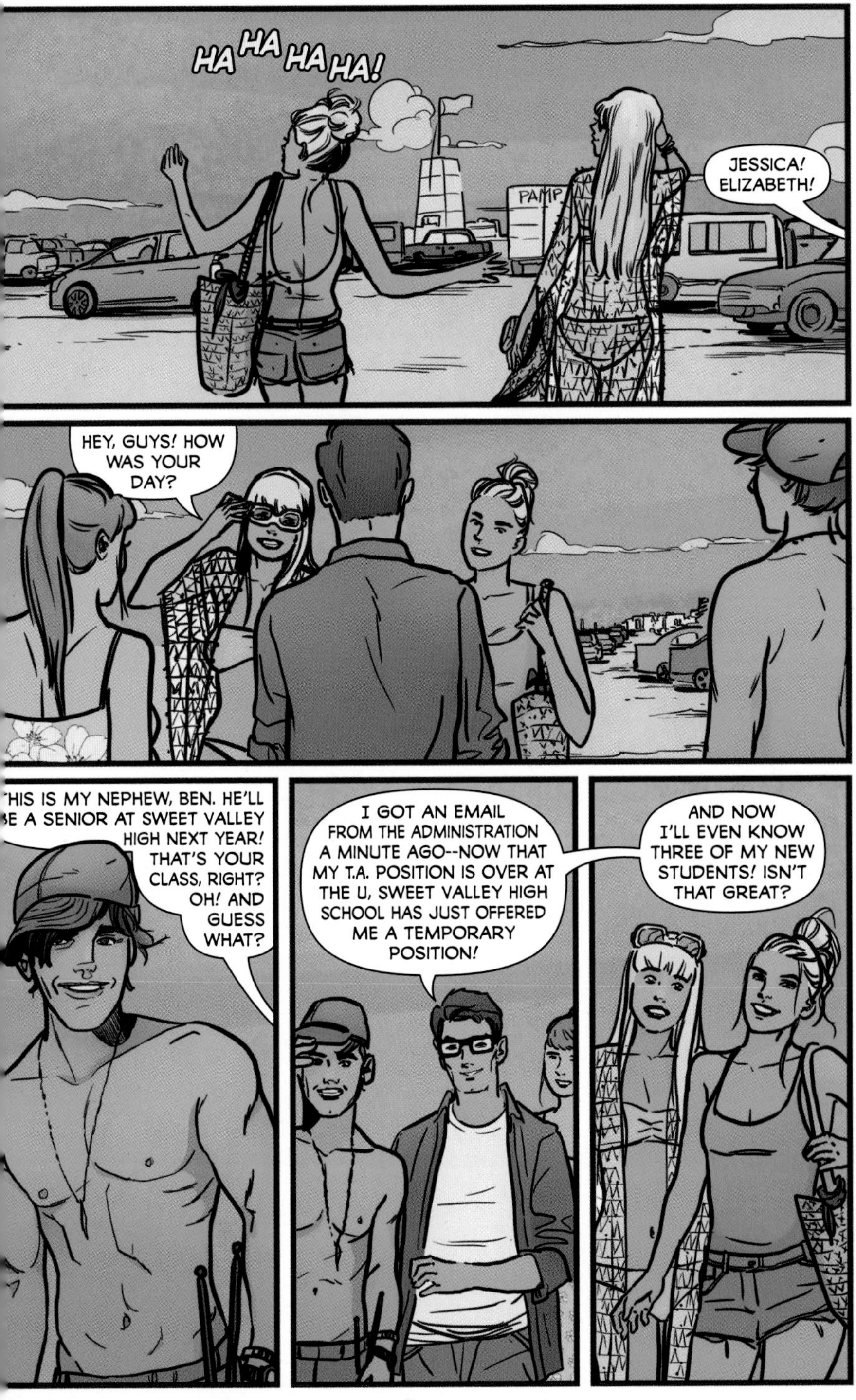
HA HA HA HA!
JESSICA! ELIZABETH!
HEY, GUYS! HOW WAS YOUR DAY?
HIS IS MY NEPHEW, BEN. HE'LL E A SENIOR AT SWEET VALLEY HIGH NEXT YEAR! THAT'S YOUR CLASS, RIGHT? OH! AND GUESS WHAT?
I GOT AN EMAIL FROM THE ADMINISTRATION A MINUTE AGO--NOW THAT MY T.A. POSITION IS OVER AT THE U, SWEET VALLEY HIGH SCHOOL HAS JUST OFFERED ME A TEMPORARY POSITION!
AND NOW I'LL EVEN KNOW THREE OF MY NEW STUDENTS! ISN'T THAT GREAT?

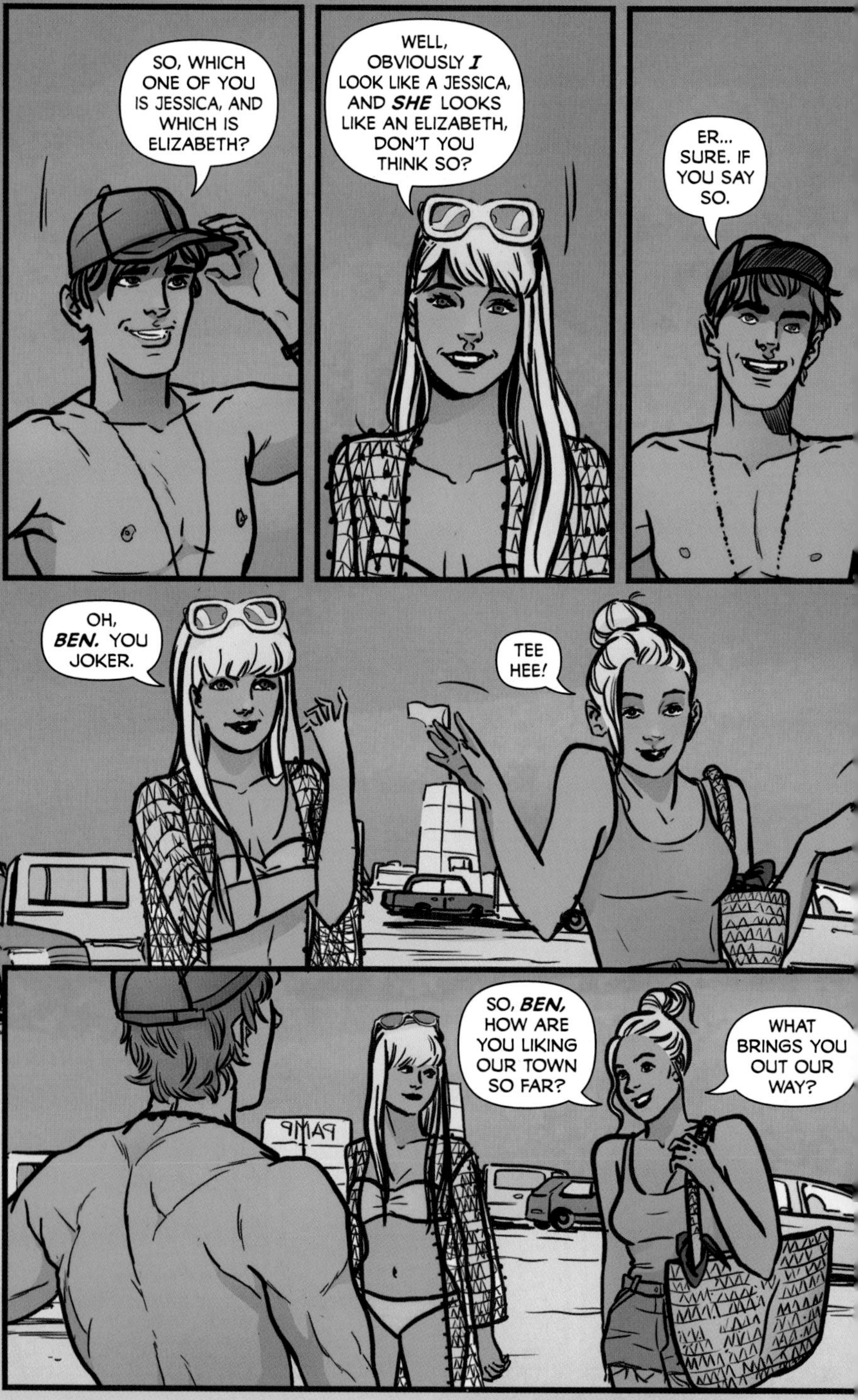
SO, WHICH ONE OF YOU IS JESSICA, AND WHICH IS ELIZABETH?
WELL, OBVIOUSLY *I* LOOK LIKE A JESSICA, AND ***SHE*** LOOKS LIKE AN ELIZABETH, DON'T YOU THINK SO?
ER... SURE. IF YOU SAY SO.
OH, ***BEN.*** YOU JOKER.
TEE HEE!
SO, ***BEN,*** HOW ARE YOU LIKING OUR TOWN SO FAR?
WHAT BRINGS YOU OUT OUR WAY?

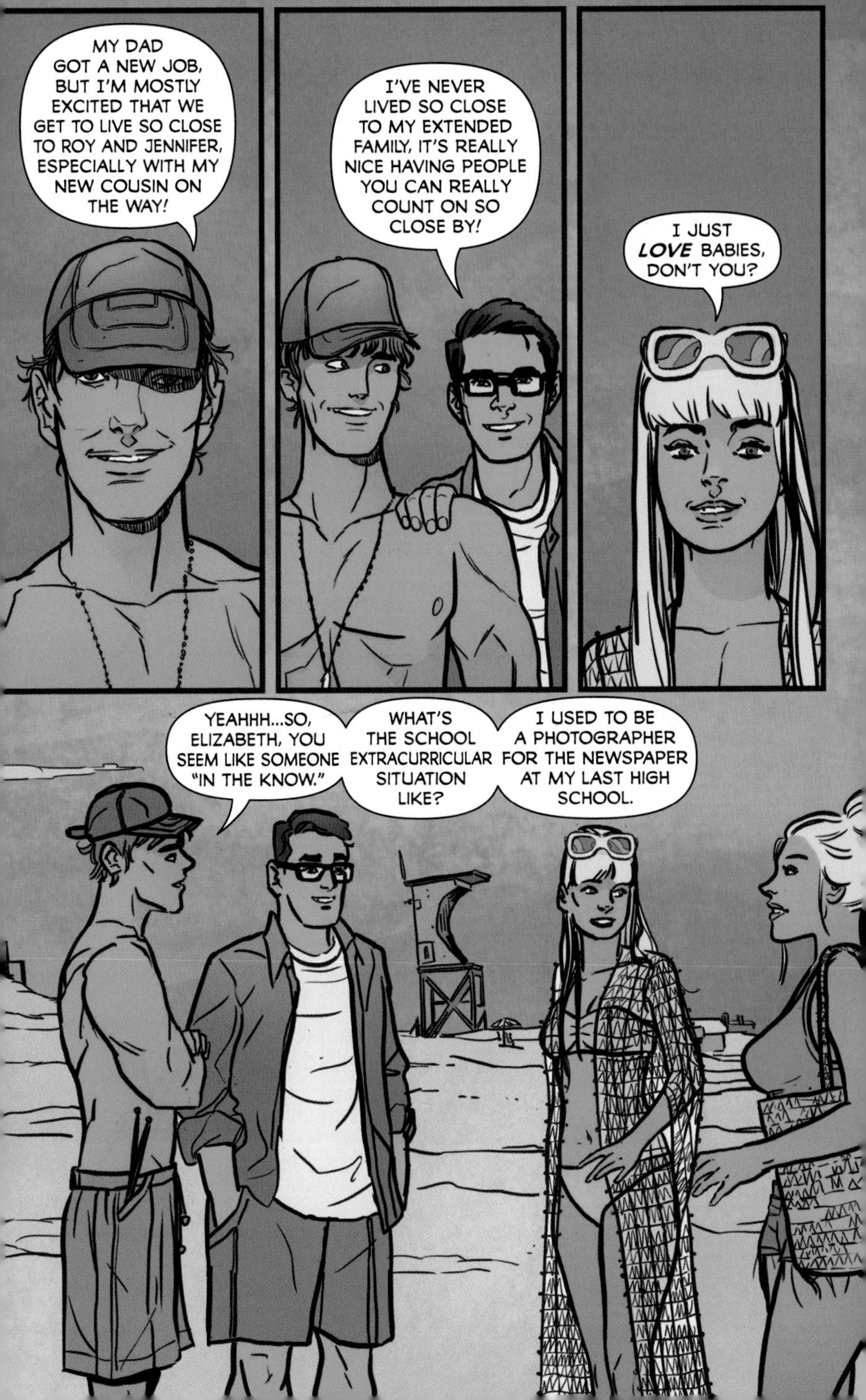
MY DAD GOT A NEW JOB, BUT I'M MOSTLY EXCITED THAT WE GET TO LIVE SO CLOSE TO ROY AND JENNIFER, ESPECIALLY WITH MY NEW COUSIN ON THE WAY!
I'VE NEVER LIVED SO CLOSE TO MY EXTENDED FAMILY, IT'S REALLY NICE HAVING PEOPLE YOU CAN REALLY COUNT ON SO CLOSE BY!
I JUST *LOVE* BABIES, DON'T YOU?
YEAHHH...SO, ELIZABETH, YOU SEEM LIKE SOMEONE "IN THE KNOW."
WHAT'S THE SCHOOL EXTRACURRICULAR SITUATION LIKE?
I USED TO BE A PHOTOGRAPHER FOR THE NEWSPAPER AT MY LAST HIGH SCHOOL.

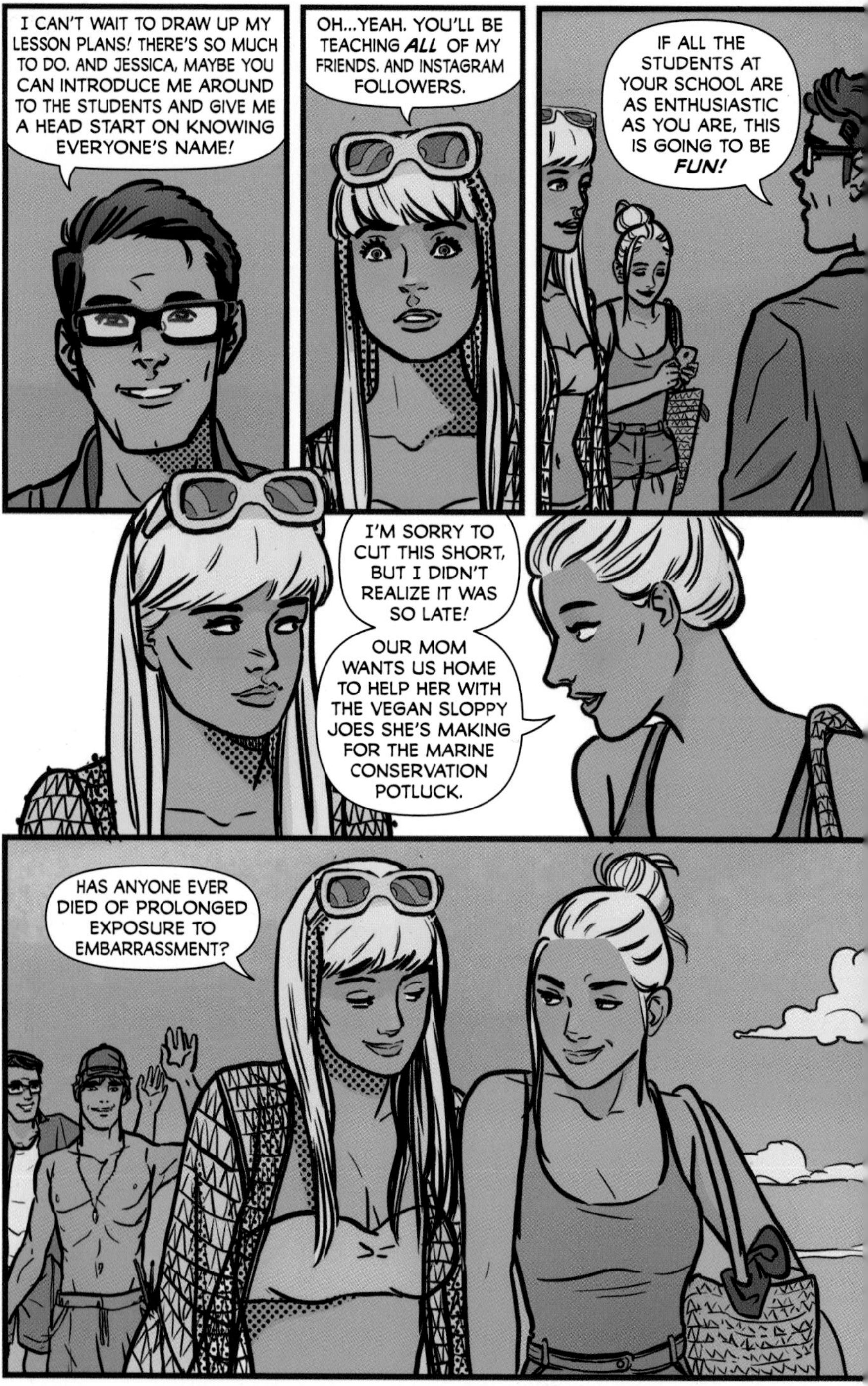
I CAN'T WAIT TO DRAW UP MY LESSON PLANS! THERE'S SO MUCH TO DO. AND JESSICA, MAYBE YOU CAN INTRODUCE ME AROUND TO THE STUDENTS AND GIVE ME A HEAD START ON KNOWING EVERYONE'S NAME!
OH...YEAH. YOU'LL BE TEACHING *ALL* OF MY FRIENDS. AND INSTAGRAM FOLLOWERS.
IF ALL THE STUDENTS AT YOUR SCHOOL ARE AS ENTHUSIASTIC AS YOU ARE, THIS IS GOING TO BE *FUN!*
I'M SORRY TO CUT THIS SHORT, BUT I DIDN'T REALIZE IT WAS SO LATE!
OUR MOM WANTS US HOME TO HELP HER WITH THE VEGAN SLOPPY JOES SHE'S MAKING FOR THE MARINE CONSERVATION POTLUCK.
HAS ANYONE EVER DIED OF PROLONGED EXPOSURE TO EMBARRASSMENT?

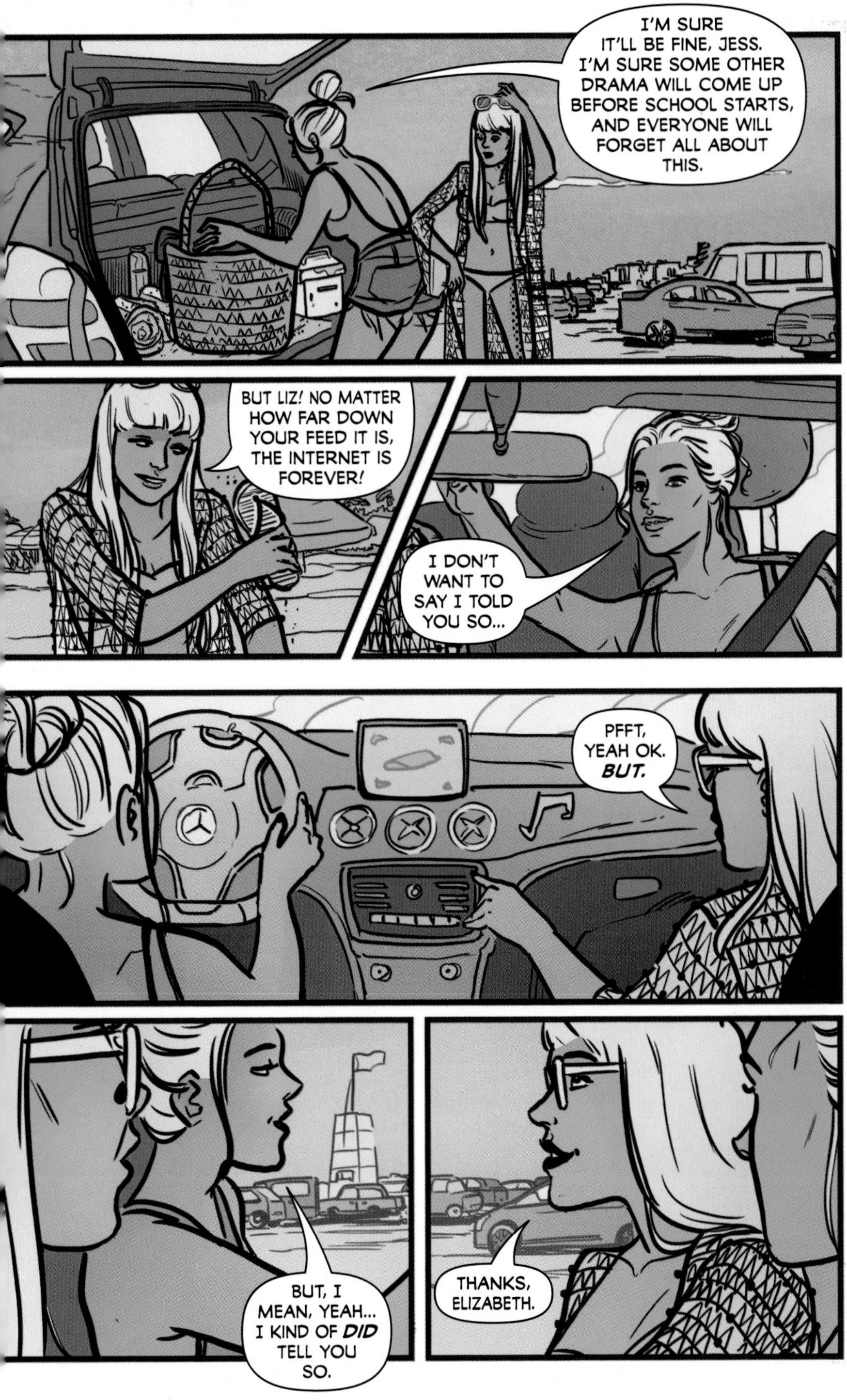
I'M SURE IT'LL BE FINE, JESS. I'M SURE SOME OTHER DRAMA WILL COME UP BEFORE SCHOOL STARTS, AND EVERYONE WILL FORGET ALL ABOUT THIS.
BUT LIZ! NO MATTER HOW FAR DOWN YOUR FEED IT IS, THE INTERNET IS FOREVER!
I DON'T WANT TO SAY I TOLD YOU SO...
PFFT, YEAH OK. ***BUT.***
BUT, I MEAN, YEAH... I KIND OF ***DID*** TELL YOU SO.
THANKS, ELIZABETH.

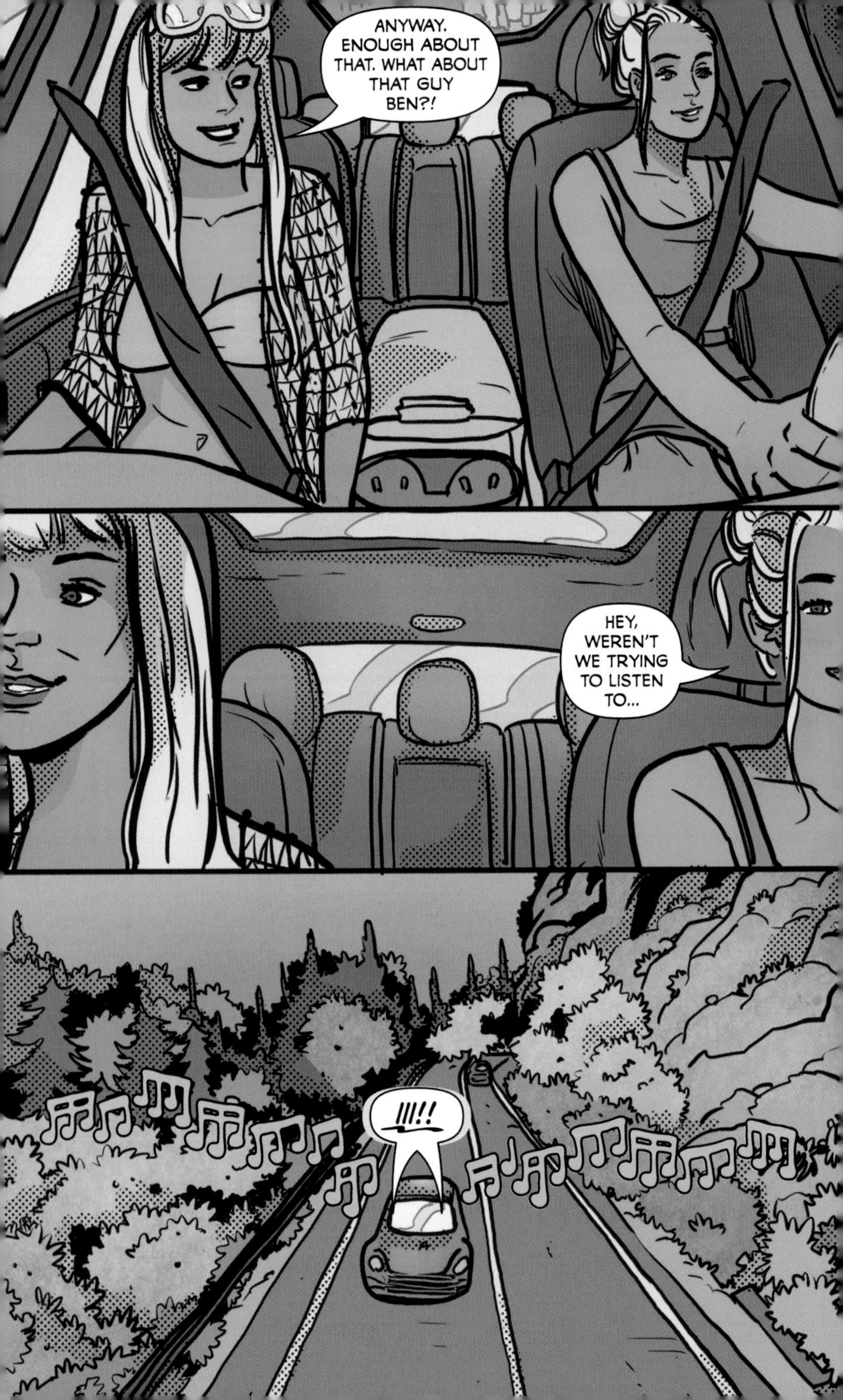
ANYWAY. ENOUGH ABOUT THAT. WHAT ABOUT THAT GUY BEN?!
HEY, WEREN'T WE TRYING TO LISTEN TO...
!!!!!

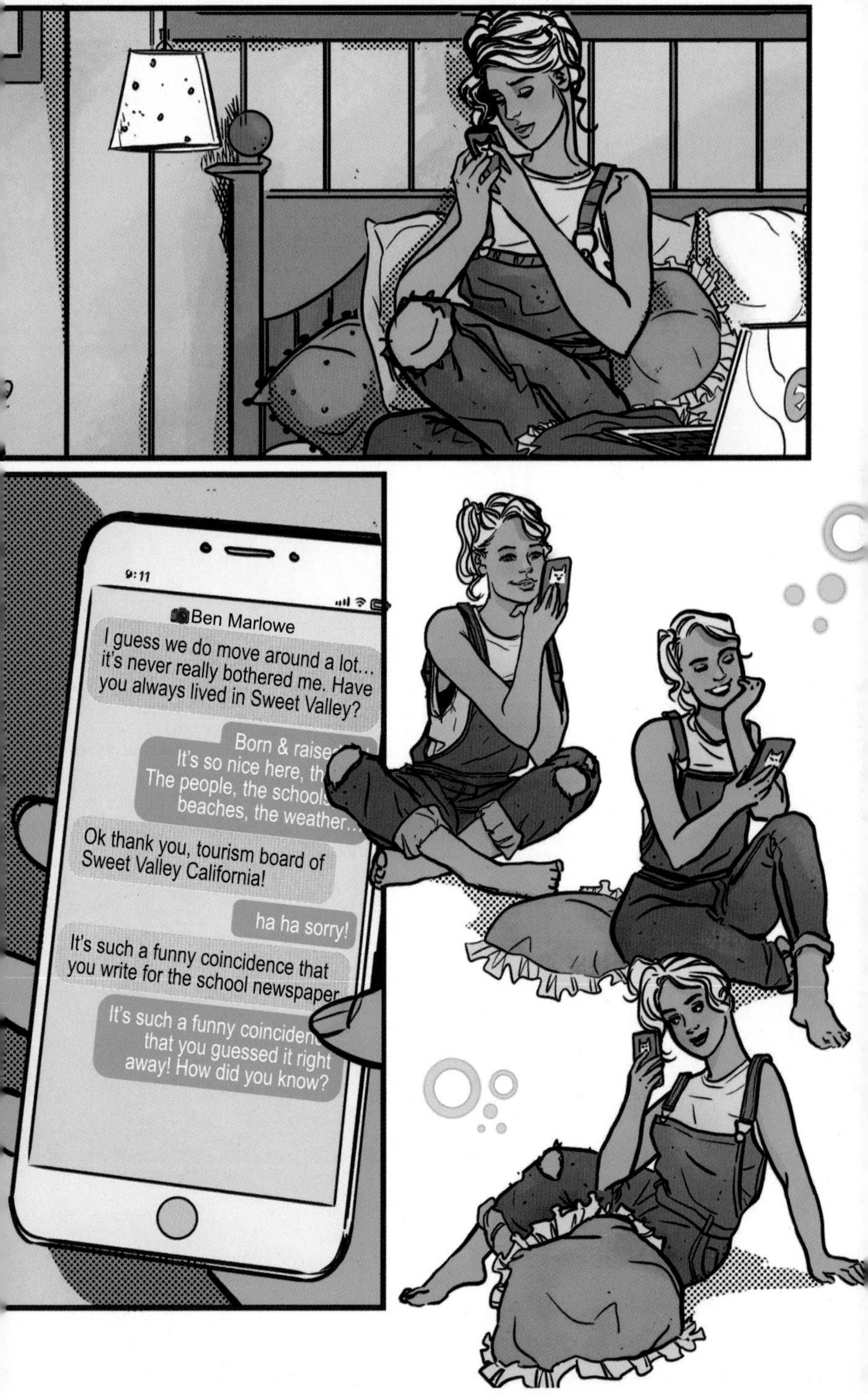
9:11
Ben Marlowe
I guess we do move around a lot... it's never really bothered me. Have you always lived in Sweet Valley?
Born & raise
It's so nice here, th
The people, the school
beaches, the weather...
Ok thank you, tourism board of Sweet Valley California!
ha ha sorry!
It's such a funny coincidence that you write for the school newspaper
It's such a funny coinciden
that you guessed it right away! How did you know?

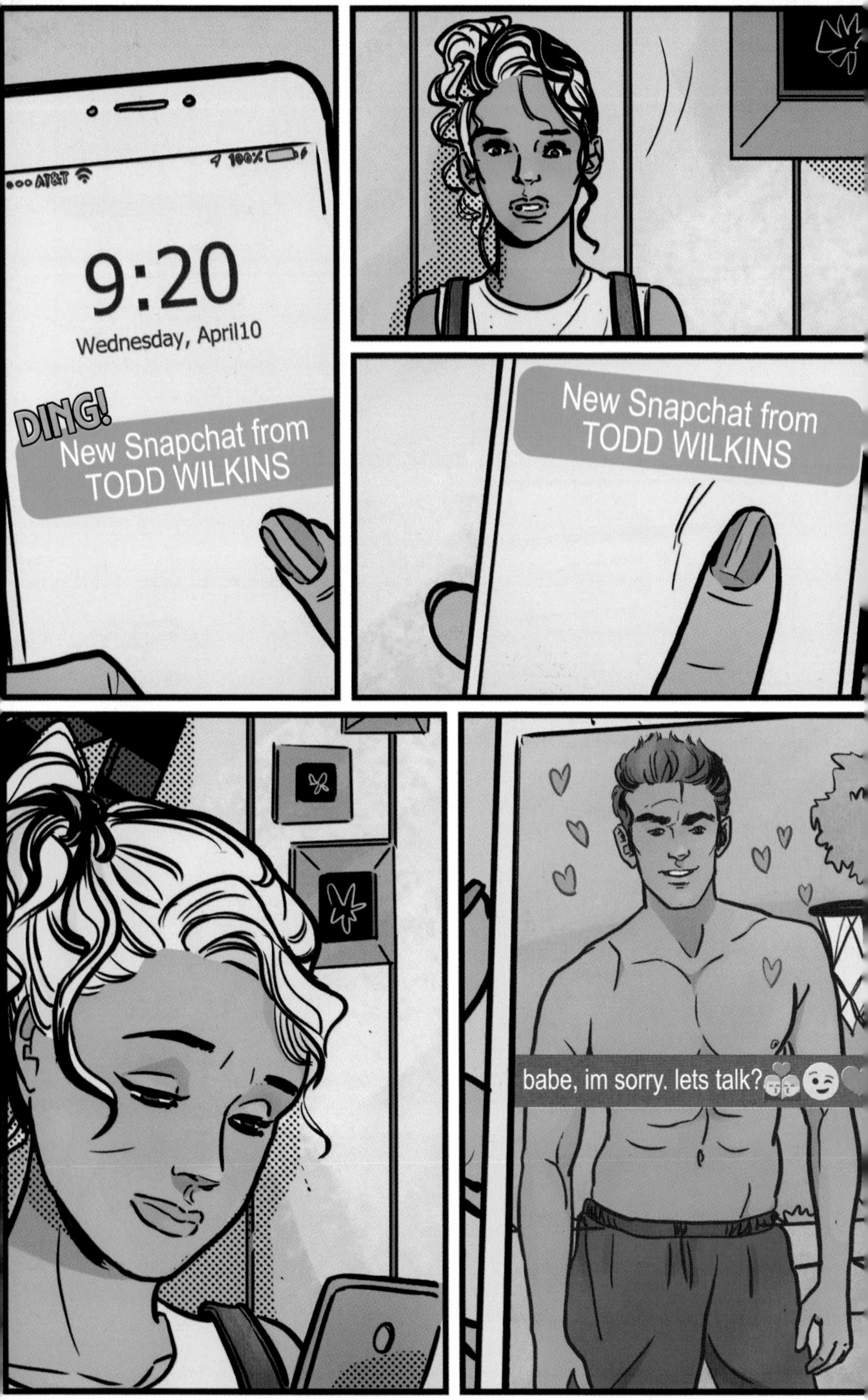
AT&T
100%
9:20
Wednesday, April10
DING!
New Snapchat from
TODD WILKINS
New Snapchat from
TODD WILKINS
babe, im sorry. lets talk?

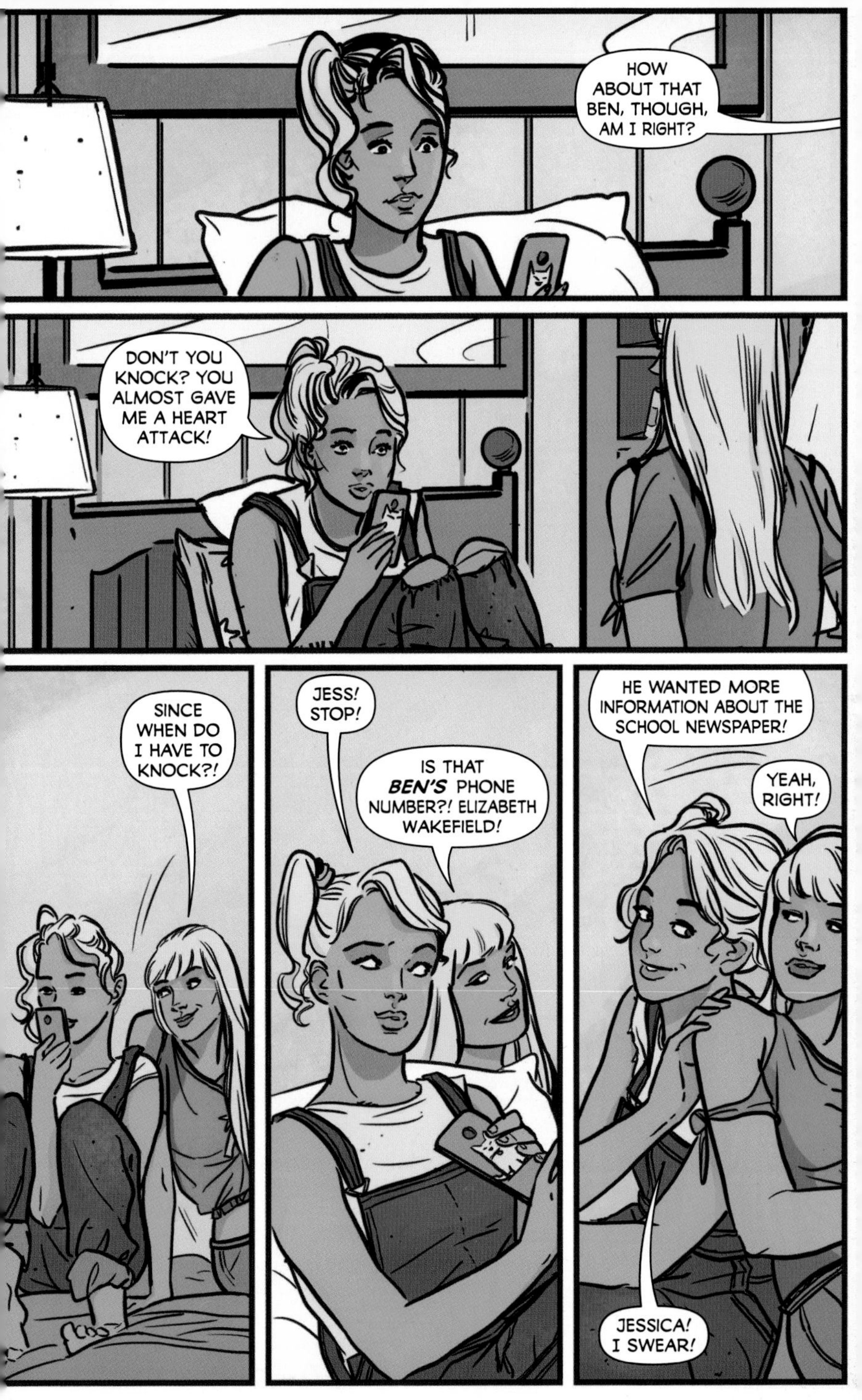
HOW ABOUT THAT BEN, THOUGH, AM I RIGHT?
DON'T YOU KNOCK? YOU ALMOST GAVE ME A HEART ATTACK!
SINCE WHEN DO I HAVE TO KNOCK?!
JESS! STOP!
IS THAT BEN'S PHONE NUMBER?! ELIZABETH WAKEFIELD!
HE WANTED MORE INFORMATION ABOUT THE SCHOOL NEWSPAPER!
YEAH, RIGHT!
JESSICA! I SWEAR!

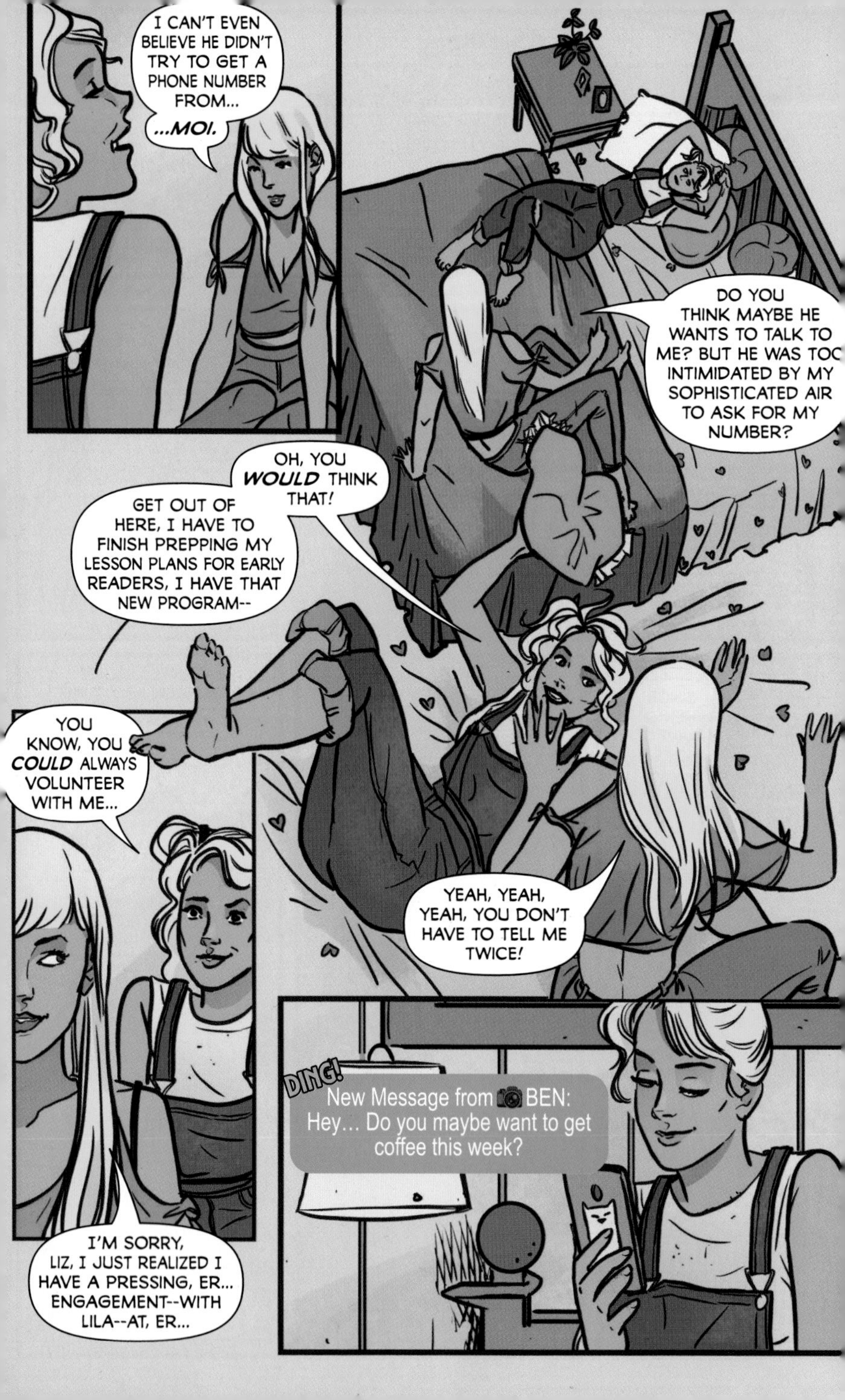
I CAN'T EVEN BELIEVE HE DIDN'T TRY TO GET A PHONE NUMBER FROM... ...MOI.
DO YOU THINK MAYBE HE WANTS TO TALK TO ME? BUT HE WAS TOO INTIMIDATED BY MY SOPHISTICATED AIR TO ASK FOR MY NUMBER?
OH, YOU WOULD THINK THAT!
GET OUT OF HERE, I HAVE TO FINISH PREPPING MY LESSON PLANS FOR EARLY READERS, I HAVE THAT NEW PROGRAM--
YEAH, YEAH, YEAH, YOU DON'T HAVE TO TELL ME TWICE!
YOU KNOW, YOU COULD ALWAYS VOLUNTEER WITH ME...
I'M SORRY, LIZ, I JUST REALIZED I HAVE A PRESSING, ER... ENGAGEMENT--WITH LILA--AT, ER...
DING!
New Message from BEN:
Hey… Do you maybe want to get coffee this week?

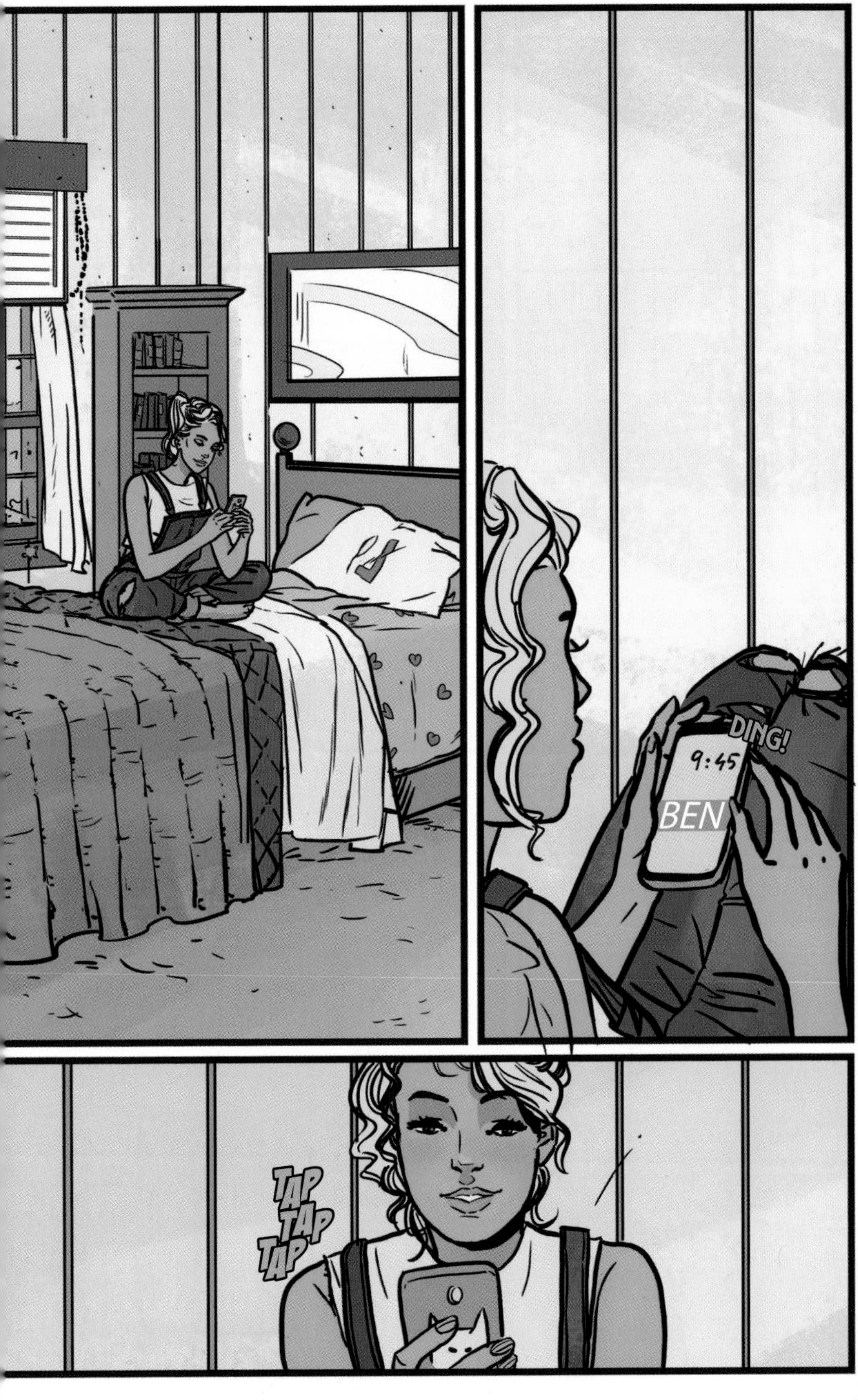
DING!
9:45
BEN
TAP
TAP
TAP

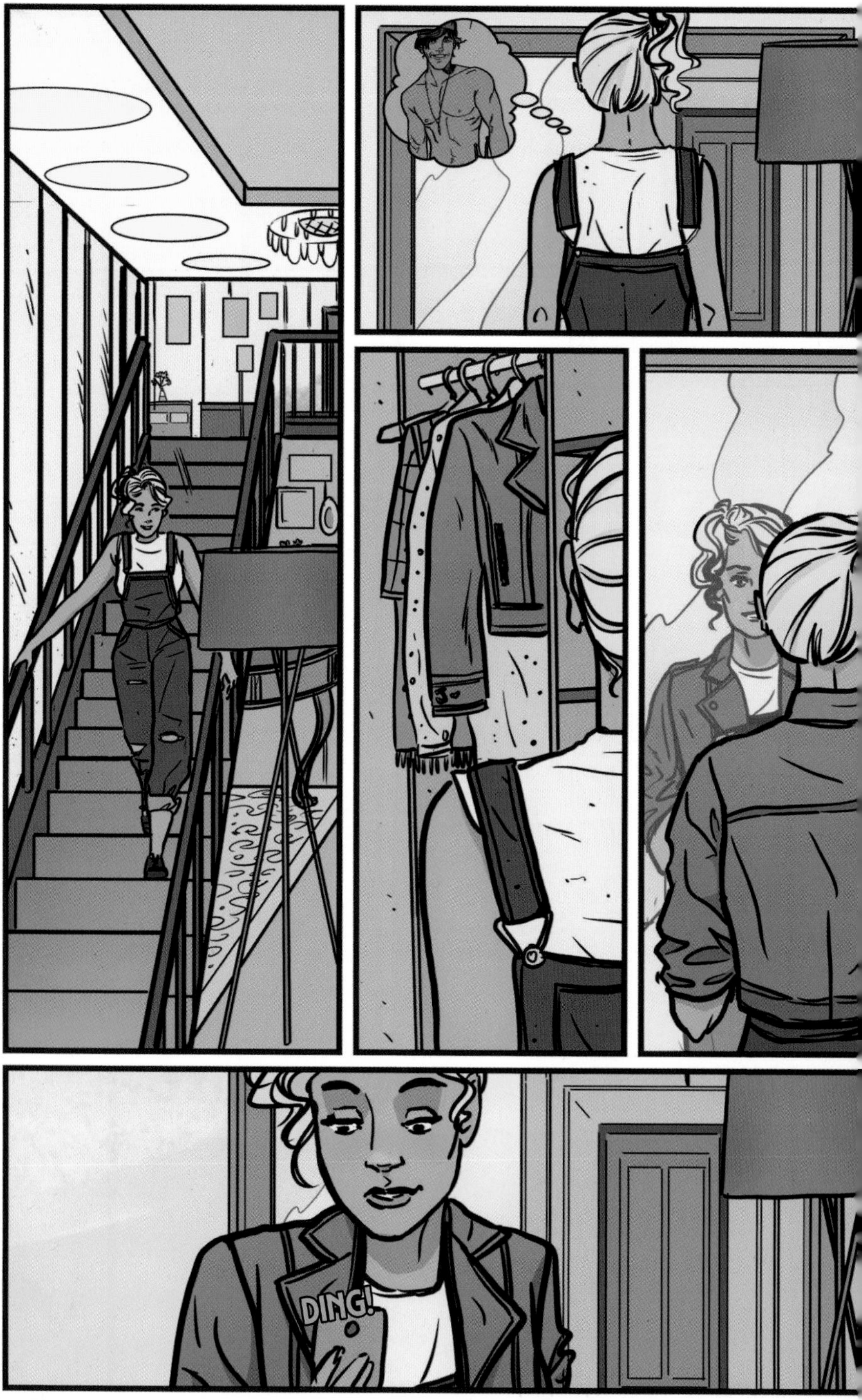
DING!

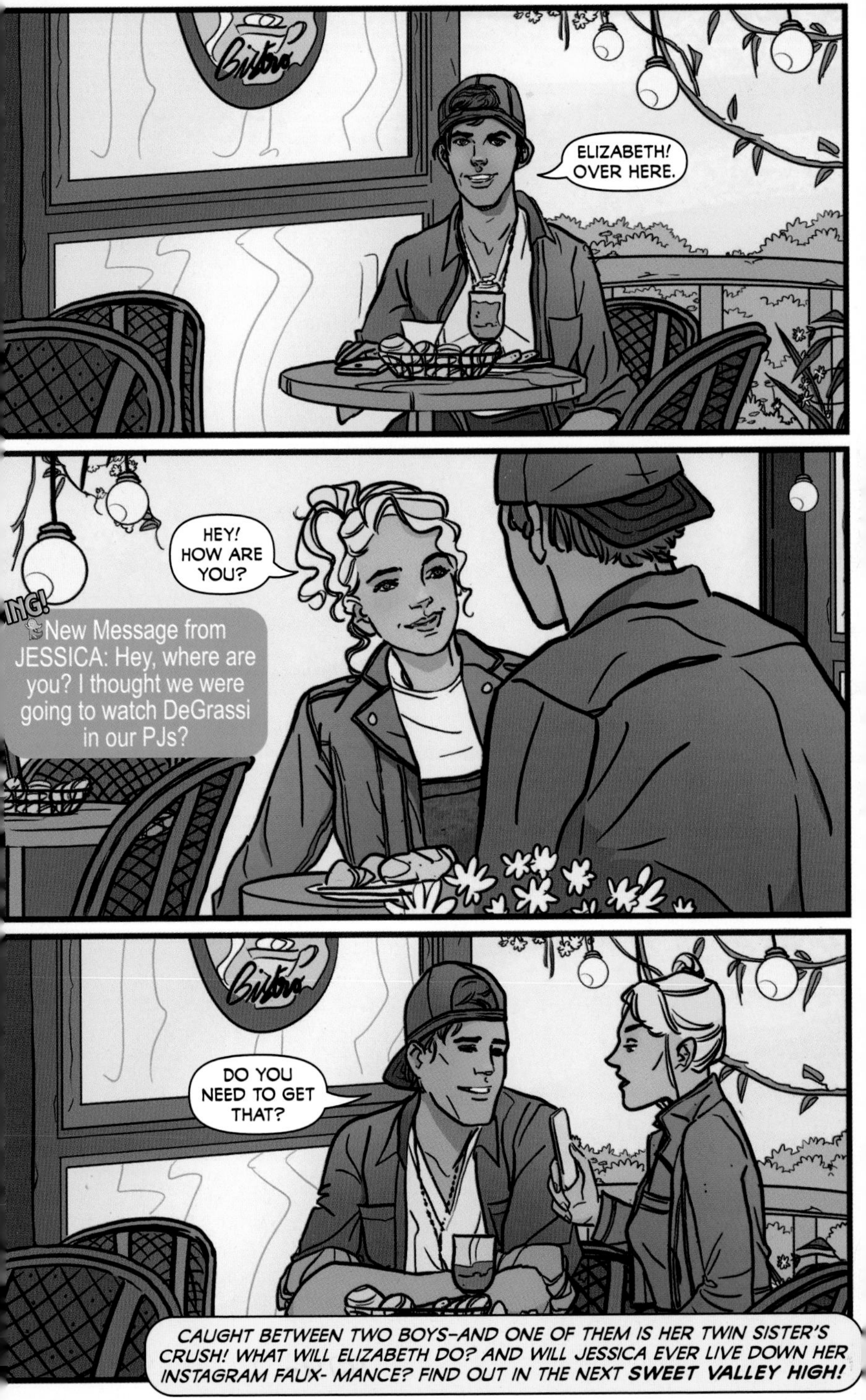

ELIZABETH! OVER HERE.
HEY! HOW ARE YOU?
ING!
New Message from JESSICA: Hey, where are you? I thought we were going to watch DeGrassi in our PJs?
DO YOU NEED TO GET THAT?
CAUGHT BETWEEN TWO BOYS–AND ONE OF THEM IS HER TWIN SISTER'S CRUSH! WHAT WILL ELIZABETH DO? AND WILL JESSICA EVER LIVE DOWN HER INSTAGRAM FAUX- MANCE? FIND OUT IN THE NEXT SWEET VALLEY HIGH!

ABOUT THE CREATORS

Francine Pascal is the creator of several bestselling series, including *Fearless* and *Sweet Valley High*, which was also made into a television series. She has written several novels, including *My First Love and Other Disasters*, *My Mother Was Never a Kid*, and *Love & Betrayal & Hold the Mayo*. She is also the author of *Sweet Valley Confidential: Ten Years Later*. She lives in New York and the South of France.

Katy Rex is a freelance writer and editor whose previous work for Dynamite included the Charmed Original Graphic Novel. She lives and works in Minnesota.

Devaki Neogi is self-taught and comic books were, as far she can recall her first passion, starting at the early age of 7 years old. Working in fashion design as well as sequential art, Devaki brings both to her work. She lives with her husband in Bangalore, India working from her home studio with her 2 cats and 2 dogs.

Pippa Mather is a comic book colourist who has worked on projects for Dynamite, 2000AD, and Image. She currently lives in Cheshire, England with her fiancé and their cat (Jess).

Cardinal Rae is a letterer for the Eisner nominated series *Crowded*, the Eisner nominated anthology *Where We Live*, and *Rose* for Image Comics.